The Jumper

Tim Parrish

Texas Review Press
Huntsville, Texas

FIRST EDITION, 2013
Requests for permission to reproduce material from this work should be sent to:

Permissions
Texas Review Press
English Department
Sam Houston State University
Huntsville, TX 77341-2146

Acknowledgements—This narrative is loosely based on the story of a man named Eldon, whom I tutored in 1988. This book is in honor of him and all the others who suffered because of the states' actions to which I allude in this novel.

Thanks to Bill Black, Patricia Bjorklund, Michael Griffith, Geoff Schmidt, David Hale Smith and Valerie Vogrin, who read drafts of this book and gave invaluable feedback and support. Thanks to Chris Bjorklund for technical advice; Mary Jane Pullen for teaching me a different way to think; Alan Michael Parker for telling me "to just get the book out there"; Big Bend and Alpine, Texas, for inspiring me; and Paul Ruffin and Eric Miles Williamson for seeing something worthwhile in the book. Also thanks to Brian Johnson, Dana Sonnenschein, Will Hochman and so many of my students for their writerly drive-bys and support at work. For financial support and time to write, my gratitude to the Southern Connecticut State Sabbatical Leave Committee, the SCSU Arts and Sciences Research Reassigned Time Committee, the Connecticut State University Research Grants Committee, Jennifer Hudson, and Dean DonnaJean Fredeen.

And most of all, my love and appreciation to Sarah, for seeing me through the final push with editing, advice, humor, patience, and caring.

Cover design by Colleen Tully

Library of Congress Cataloging-in-Publication Data

Parrish, Tim.
  The jumper / Tim Parrish.
    pages cm
  ISBN 978-1-937875-28-2 (pbk. : alk. paper)
  1. Young men--Fiction. 2. Domestic fiction. I. Title.
  PS3566.A7575J86 2013
  813'.54--dc23
                              2013013296

THE JUMPER

For Isabel, Vicki, Rich and Chris,

who let me share their amazing lives.

I jumped with great fear and great joy.

Later, we watched the dance floor from our table in the beer garden and sipped good lager and snacked on sharp Swiss cheese and spicy sausages. It took all of my self-control not to lick the froth left by the beer on the perfect little curl of Alena's upper lip.

She said, "People court danger to lose themselves or find themselves. Which one do you pursue?"

I looked at this woman I now loved and decided to always tell her the truth. "I don't know. Both, I think."

—Elise Blackwell, from *Hunger*

DAY ONE

Jimmy held the piece of paper as though it were both a gem and a bomb. *Telegram.* He knew he knew what that meant. He'd seen it in movies and on TV, heard people talk about it, but it was the brain scramble now, what his mind knew scurrying away from sense like a jackrabbit. This was what sometimes happened when things counted, when he needed the right word at work to prove he understood the bit of info that would say, "I'm smart, I'm like you, I get it." He flapped the telegram against his palm, shifted on the couch and glanced at his watch. His roommate would be home any minute, but until then . . . . Sound it out. *Tell-uh-gram. Tell-uh-phone.* Yeah, talk to the phone. Tell-uh-gram. Talk to a gram? Tell-uh-vision. Talk to what you see? That could work, but he knew it didn't. What else? He rummaged. Tell-uh-port. What did that mean? To send space people to another place. Yeah, he knew that, and he knew that lots of folks probably didn't know. So *tell* wasn't *tell* like *to* tell. It meant, what?, things going, things sent. Sounds, pictures, space people, a letter. A letter sent. So why not just let it be a letter and not a telegram?

He slapped the paper on his thigh, considered shredding it then kicked his boot backward into the couch face. The telegram was nonsense, except for his own name, which was both in the middle and the top, with what he could tell were slight differences. He stared and the letters shimmied, shifted, rose and floated from the paper, then blurred. Jimmy shook his head and shoved back into the couch.

On TV the President was speaking: "Star Wars . . . lasers . . . evil threat . . . missiles." Jimmy studied the president's face, vacant somehow, eyes glancing to words on a podium and back up where he said into the camera the words that made him president. Jimmy knew he was as smart as this man, knew he was smarter than half the people who came in the store with lists that they read from, or worse tried to hand to him, lists that carried a power Jimmy did not have. His mind worked better, his memory remembered better, then a paper with marks knocked away his clarity and confidence, making him less than a child. Anxiety ran through him like hunger shakes, his face heated. What was it he held? When the woman brought it, he'd felt poised on that familiar precipice of lashing out at someone guilty only of accidentally exposing him, or at himself. He could've asked her what it was, but she would have said again, "A telegram," beginning one of the absurd dances he was cursed to dance.

—Who sent it?

—It's right there on front.

—I mean what for?

—What for? For you.

Relax, relax. Then the step he rarely took.

—Could you read it to me?

And the look.

He popped up from the couch and snapped off the TV. The sound of Floyd's truck rattled through the thin door of the apartment, and Jimmy shifted his tightening shoulders, adjusted his expression not to show agitation and sat once more. The truck door slammed, then Floyd's aimless whistling and jingling keys filtered closer until he stepped in, his jeans dusty, his boilermaker's cap turned backwards, the Houston sun blazing behind him. "Howdy," he said.

"Hey," Jimmy said, and held up the paper. "Got me a telegram."

Floyd shut the door and took the telegram from Jimmy. He turned it to every angle as if there were a facet he might miss. "Huh. Don't think I ever seen one."

"You never got one?"

"Don't think nobody I know ever got one. Heard they used to send them when somebody was killed in a war." Floyd turned the brim of his hat forward and eased into his recliner. "Says here it's to James T. Strawhorn from J.T. Strawhorn. Didn't send it to yourself, did you?" He laughed and poked his tongue around in his mouth.

"You mind just reading it, Floyd?"

Floyd's eyebrows peaked at Jimmy's tone, and he tore open the envelope. Floyd was one of the few people Jimmy had ever asked to read to him, and it irritated Jimmy that Floyd almost never read even though he could, struck him as sad that even Jimmy knew Floyd wasn't a good reader by the way he stammered and halted. Floyd unfolded the telegram and cleared his throat.

"Here goes: 'Dear James, I am your father.'" Floyd swallowed so heavily that Jimmy saw his Adam's apple bob. He flexed the paper. "'You might be shocked. Have lots of mistakes to make up. Poor health, hard times. Want to meet you before it's too late. Have no phone. Please come to Baton Rouge. Here are directions to Baton Rouge ...' There's directions here on I-10 and such, then it ends, 'Sincerely, J.T. Strawhorn.'"

Floyd stared at the letter a while more, then lowered it to his lap. "I thought you was a orphan."

The couch quavered beneath Jimmy. An image of Pepper, good eye agleam with booze, raked through him, and he shifted in his seat. "That's what I was told."

"Then who you think this fella is?"

"Got no idea." Tremors passed through Jimmy. His head went light. "Says he's my father?"

"That's what he says. Can't figure how he'd get your address. When kids get adopted, I thought they's supposed to seal up their identity."

"I ain't adopted, just orphaned."

"Neither of them fellas Sparks nor Pepper adopted you?"

"Nope."

"Huh. Maybe you oughta call Sparks."

"Don't know what he'd have to say. Ain't spoke to him in three years."

Jimmy hoisted himself, wavered and took the telegram from Floyd. The paper buzzed against his fingertips as if a current coursed through it. Since he'd come to Houston six years ago, he knew his childhood was different, but now it struck him it might be even more different than he thought. What if this really was his father? He stared at the paper again, the word father as unintelligible as all the other words there. He locked his knees.

"What you gone do?" Floyd asked.

"Don't know." Jimmy turned and walked to his room. He shut the door and stood in the center of the small space, examined the telegram once more. *Father.* He'd barely considered the notion, never put the name to anyone, especially not Sparks, who'd mostly been thirty miles away on the main spread while Jimmy grew up. Pepper would've been more likely, but he'd died when Jimmy was thirteen, leaving Jimmy to run the smaller spread. His blood pitched. *Pepper.* Jimmy saw him as if he were written on the paper—that last night trailing whiskey and fright as he rode away on his horse. He lowered the telegram. A sizzle crossed his scalp, then he was atop a mesa, before him open sky, an expanse of land, and the urge toward them. He dropped to his seat on the bed and buttressed himself with his arms.

As if a curtain had been opened, Jimmy saw his room: a double bed, a chest-of-drawers dotted with movie-ticket stubs, his hardware-store smock stenciled with the only words he knew. He'd hopped here from west Texas with barely a thought, carrying Pepper's memory and paranoia like rocks in his car trunk. He took the job at Home Depot that Mr. Sparks had fixed up for him, the only job he'd ever had off the ranch, and there he still worked, a floor man, "The Human Inventory" his coworkers called him because he knew the store frontwards and backwards, the highest an illiterate could go. Away from work he'd stopped dating, the dread of being found out and rejected a lode stone. Twenty-four and afraid to take a chance. As mired here as he'd become in west Texas, as scared as Pepper in his last years.

Jimmy hoisted himself, staggered, caught his balance and returned to where Floyd reclined in his lounger. "You think I could get to Baton Rouge?" he asked, noticed the paper trembling and lowered it.

"You feeling okay?"

"Said you reckon I could get there?"

"Sure," Floyd said, his eyebrows dipped. "You gone check it out?"

"Just gone go." The room angled. Jimmy widened his stance.

"For good?" Jimmy nodded. "Whoa, buddy. You don't know if this fella's on the up and up."

"I don't know he ain't neither. Says he's sick, and there ain't no reason to lie. Even if he ain't who he says, least I'll be outta here."

Floyd tugged the brim of his hat. "Didn't know you was so down on here."

Jimmy wiped at the corners of his mouth and yearned for a smoke. "It ain't here. I'm just stuck. All I do is work and sit in this little hole."

"You just need to get out. I told you I knew some women."

Jimmy thought of their faces, the few women he'd dated, at the moments they realized he couldn't decipher something at a restaurant or movie theatre, thought of both the pity and revulsion, and the former was worse than the latter. Sometimes at the store he would find one flirting with him and like her, but he knew if she was smart, it wouldn't take long for her to see what he couldn't do, knew any woman who would want a man who couldn't go any farther than he could was probably a woman he didn't want. The floor rippled. He reached his hand to the wall.

Floyd stood. "You oughta take a load off. Let this mess settle."

Jimmy stared at the couch as if it were a coffin. He wiped his mouth. "What if he really is my daddy and sick, Floyd? What if I have a momma too?"

"Just check it out. You ain't got to leave everything."

He saw Pepper railing at the mesa, saw him sprawled on the plain, felt his own feet heavy in this spot and dragging him down. "If I don't go, I might never go nowhere." Jimmy's shoulder locked, but he rolled it against the tension. "I got some savings. I ain't gone leave you in the lurch."

"I figured that," Floyd said, but Jimmy barely noticed. The wall behind Floyd had gone diaphanous.

DAY THREE

Jimmy sailed over the swamp, marveling at the stilted road. He'd never seen a highway raised above an endless lake shot through with mossy cypress and abandoned platforms on telephone pole legs, but then he figured he was just beginning to see things. He took a long drag and let the smoke waft from his mouth, already on his second cigarette, his daily quota. He didn't care. Life was opening like a giant door, every cloud a promise, every interstate exit an invitation, and Jimmy was celebrating in his own small way. Twice already he had rolled his shoulders and stretched his neck against the taut cords of his muscles, then veered off the highway to some unknown truck stop in some foreign town for coffee and a doughnut or a candy bar and Coke, for a stroll through the aisles of crap he couldn't imagine anybody needing yet was himself tempted to buy, the wad of his savings urging him to pick up a belt buckle or a beer coozie or a cap he'd never wear. He was trying hard to embrace that as soon as you crossed a state line or set foot in a town you'd never been to, you were somebody new.

He took a last long inhale, let the smoke percolate in his lungs, then blew a thin stream as he stubbed the butt in his ashtray. For the umpteenth time he pictured meeting J.T. Strawhorn, *his* father, his *father,* an older man neatly dressed, frail and in need, opening the door to his modest house. Jimmy would extend his hand and say, "Pleasure to meet you, sir," and the man would invite him into a cool brightly-lit living room. Jimmy had considered calling him Father, scrolled through Daddy and Poppa, just to try them on, and had settled on Mr. Strawhorn. After all, he had no experience with this sort of event. Hell, he barely had experience with anything father-and-son-like of the sort he'd seen onscreen or heard people talk about. Yesterday, as he stored his belongings, packed and settled with Floyd, Jimmy had thought of calling Sparks to see if he knew about any of this, but that seemed like stepping backwards. Years before, Sparks had staked him five-hundred dollars and gotten him the job, but he'd never seen fit to have Jimmy schooled, never seemed much interested in him and Pepper over at the small spread, never seemed much interested after Pepper died. But then why should he have been. For a while, Jimmy had been satisfied in his life with Pepper, that is until Pepper began to slide. Once Pepper was gone, Jimmy had argued with Sparks to be left alone to run the small place, even though it was a struggle. Maybe Sparks was just being respectful.

Jimmy thumped another cigarette from his pack and lit up. In the distance a boat cut a trail through gray water. Sun glinted off the calm surface. Low in the sky where Jimmy was heading, a jet left a vapor trail. This trip wouldn't be like that trip into Houston so many years ago, the skyline rising from the plain like a threat, the interstate spreading into more lanes than a sane person could account for, the unreadable road signs crowding above him as he entered the city and tried to recall the number of the exit Mr. Sparks had told him to take. No, none of that now. Today was a fresh start.

The top of Jimmy's scalp almost levitated when he began to climb the high arching span of the Mississippi River Bridge. The brown river dropped away beneath him, the car rose at a sharp pitch, and Jimmy's head rose even higher. He locked his vision on the road.

His father waited on the other side, and he wondered what he would really find. His breath shallowed. Why hadn't he listened to Floyd, thought it through before jumping in his car and heading out? An old voice called him toward the bridge's edge. He eased to the inside lane, his palms gummy with perspiration, and fixed his eyesight on the white lines dashing past. His awareness partly broke from him, spilled outward and then down, anxiety intertwining with euphoria to tempt him toward the bridge's railing and the unfettered space beyond. He sped up, rocketing toward clear sky beyond girders, then the bridge peaked and Jimmy crested, the trees and rooftops of Baton Rouge expanding before him. His lungs let loose something between a laugh and a grunt, and his self began to unscatter as he glided downward.

The first exit number appeared, and he was thankful he'd studied a map with Floyd, matching numbers to the names on J.T.'s directions and penning them in the margin, thankful too that this interstate didn't seem as crazy as Houston's. "Baton Rouge," Jimmy sounded to himself. He'd heard people mention it, remembered it from songs, knew it was the capital of Louisiana, but that was about it. He hoped that was enough for now. The expressway banked left, carved through the center of downtown, headed toward a thicket of silver smokestacks, then curved right past an old gray mildew-streaked stadium. When the road straightened again, chemical plants and refineries lined the horizon to the left, while trees and houses appeared to the right below. Already the numbers told him he was nearing his exit, and by the time he saw number three up ahead, his palms throbbed. He ramped off the interstate, chanting the directions Floyd had read from the telegram. But the telegram only told the names of the streets and the direction to turn, not how many streets or how many lights or how far between turns, which meant that Jimmy had to do the closest thing to reading that he could: hold the directions up and try to match them with the names on street signs. He slowed at the end of the ramp and wondered if he hadn't made a huge mistake, hadn't left something safe for something stupid, felt a shadow brush him, and kept going, past deserted businesses and tiny houses. He noticed nothing but black people around him, noticed boarded-up windows and grass-sprouting parking lots, hoped he hadn't already missed his turn.

Luckily the road he was on had four lanes, so people could pass him as he crept along looking, but drivers were still honking as they passed. He hated this feeling, like trying to put a puzzle together in the dark, like pretending he couldn't read a customer's handwriting or asking leading idiot questions such as, "What exactly you want this for?" and getting answers like, "To take a bath in." He tried to work up some spit and focus on the pay-off ahead. At the next large street, he held the telegram up and studied the column of directions that Floyd had written. The street name Jimmy was looking for lay just below the number of the interstate exit, the number a good marker. He pulled to the side of the road, folded the paper and lifted it so that the street name sat just below the street sign. A match, as far as he could tell. Horns blew as he made his way from the right lane to a left-hand turn into a heavier stream of traffic. Buildings, signs, driveways, billboards and off-streets crammed the roadside. He had no clue how far until his next turn, his father's street, and the road was too busy to hold the paper up and try to match while moving. The sensible thing would be to stop and ask someone for directions—he knew the name of the street from Floyd and could say it out loud—but it seemed important that he navigate this on his own. He crawled, traffic zooming past him. He'd trained himself to mentally file so well that he knew where everything was at the store, bought a precise street map in Houston so Floyd could help him memorize specific directions, disciplined his memory to know how to get places after just one trip, yet here he was like a child again, the letters on the paper jiggling and shrinking.

A semi's horn blasted him. He banged the steering wheel, hit his turn signal and jerked between oncoming traffic into the lot of a dying strip mall. He pressed his thumb and finger against his eyes, the memory of Houston's traffic that first day coming to him as a metal river washing him along. Panic had choked him until he veered off the interstate to fight the shakes and spins.

He'd refused to call Mr. Sparks, was too uncertain to travel far from the main road and so had sat in an old service station parking lot for hours, thirsty and hungry, until he and the traffic settled enough to risk traveling once more. He'd sworn he'd never be so helpless again. And he wasn't. He wasn't sure if he had already missed his father's street or not gone far enough, but he knew he wasn't lost. His options were to backtrack and try again, keep going forward, wait until traffic slowed much later, or get out of the car and walk in order to see better. He stretched his neck to the side, the muscle popping like a whip snap against the winch of his shoulder. *Shit.* He supposed he'd ask somebody.

The mall before him was a right angle of connected stores fronted by a covered walkway. Jimmy eased into the parking lot until he reached one of the two clusters of cars, a group of three near what he could tell from the sign of a mortar and pestle was a drug store. He stepped out and strode across the burning asphalt, pushed through a glass door and into cool air. The clang of a cowbell caused him to spin. He gripped the bell, then heard a full-throated, woman's chuckle that heated his face. "It does that to everybody," she said from behind the counter and began gnawing the tip of her thumb. Jimmy blinked, the sight of her so bright and unexpected. Her hair, so blonde it was almost white, spouted in a ponytail from the side of her head and over her bare shoulder. Her blue eyes seemed illuminated in the pale skin of her face and set off by her wide, red mouth. A galaxy of green spots adorned her pink sleeveless blouse, everything large—her height, her expression, her *breasts*.

Jimmy cleared his throat. "Too much coffee," he said, pinched at his lips and sauntered over, his calm exterior the one thing he could count on.

"I had to give up caffeine," she said. "Too jittery." She jerked her thumb away from her mouth as if she'd just remembered it, then turned the paperback she'd been reading face down. "What can I do you for?"

"Pack of Marlboro Lights," he said, glanced at the cover of the book and away as if it might strike him.

"Killing yourself lightly, huh?" She smiled and took the cigarettes off the rack.

"I reckon." He laid the directions on the counter and smoothed them, pointed to what he knew was his father's address. "You know how to get to here?" Jimmy tried to cover the top of the telegram with his palm, but the woman slid the paper out and held it close to her face.

"That's just one block over, behind the mall." She lowered the paper and set the Marlboros on the counter. "You've never been in there?"

"Just come in from Texas."

"Texas. You mind if I ask why you're going there?"

"Pardon?"

"Why you're going there."

Jimmy wondered if everybody here was nosy, if coming several hundred miles could change behavior as radically as it sometimes seemed behavior was changed from west to east Texas. "Going to meet somebody."

"You don't seem like the type to meet somebody in that neighborhood."

"Come again."

"I mean, it's not my business, but there aren't many white people in there and most white people who go in there go to buy drugs. At least that's what I understand. You don't seem that type." She held him full on with her gaze, and he looked down to his cigarettes before the roundness and blueness of her eyes swallowed him.

"I'm going to meet my father." He looked back up. "I never met him before." He grabbed the pack of cigarettes and thumped it twice on the counter.

"Oh." She nodded. "That's wonderful. You must be excited."

"Ain't sure what I am. Didn't know he was alive till day before yesterday. Still don't really know for sure. You sound like this neighborhood's kinda rough."

"Don't pay any attention to me," she said. She shook her head and placed the telegram on the counter. "I'm sure it'll be fine. I just talk too much. I don't get many people my age in here to talk to." Gold flecks floated in the sky of her eyes, but her smile had left her. Her forehead was rounded to her high hairline, her lashes long and jet black. He took a half-step back.

"How much?" he asked.

She started. "Oh, nothing. They're on me. For luck,

even though I hope you'll quit." She laughed and touched her index finger to her lips, then handed him the cigarettes. "Come back and tell me how it went," she said.

"Pardon?"

"Meeting your father. How it goes."

"Sure thing."

She smiled impossibly wide, her teeth big and white and slightly crooked. He nodded and turned to leave. "Don't forget the bell," she said. "And be careful."

He entered the heat again and paused in the shade of the sidewalk's overhang, the pulse loud in his ears. The contrast between the radiant woman and the run-down mall staggered him like a collision of worlds. He wished he'd asked her name, was jarred by his old doubt and snorted. Back in his car, he circled around behind the mall, drove one street over and turned, his pulse picking up. He cruised past a row of small, identical, dilapidated houses with scruffy roofs and peeling paint. Black people sat on tiny stoops and on front steps, fanning themselves against the heat or simply staring as if paralyzed. He wondered if his father was here because he was so sick he was about to die. Or maybe he was here because he, like Jimmy, was unable to do the things you needed to do to get the really nice things. Or maybe his father was black? It seemed impossible. How could a black man produce a red-haired son? Jimmy supposed it could happen. Not that it mattered. They'd still be father and son.

Jimmy saw the number hanging sideways on a porch and pulled into the tiny yard, his legs thrumming. Someone peered through the screen door, then ducked away and shut the inner door. Jimmy checked the number again and stepped out. His muscles, tendons and scalp tingled, but his legs were as limber as if he'd sprinted from Texas. He couldn't understand why whoever was in the house had disappeared. Regret at sending for Jimmy? But, then, whoever was inside had no way of knowing Jimmy was even coming and especially not so soon. He climbed the single step onto the porch and knocked. And knocked. And knocked.

"He in there," said the woman sitting on the stoop next door. "I just seen him outside."

"Obliged," Jimmy said. He tried to peer through

the door's window but saw no movement inside. "J.T. Strawhorn?" he called out. "Mr. Strawhorn, you in there?" Silence. "I came all the way from Texas, Mr. Strawhorn."

"What do you want?" a voice came through the door.

"Is this where J.T. Strawhorn lives?"

"I asked what you want?"

Jimmy paused to consider his answer. "I'm . . . My name's Jimmy Strawhorn. Mr. J.T. Strawhorn sent me a telegram."

"Say you're Jimmy Strawhorn?"

"Yes, sir. I got this here telegram."

The wooden door cracked, then slowly swung open. The man moved up to the screen and pressed a hand to it. He was about Jimmy's height, his light hair thin and unruly, his long white face and deep-set eyes strikingly familiar, although blue and not brown like Jimmy's. He wore wrinkled khakis and a sleeveless T-shirt. His cheeks were stubbled. Jimmy figured him to be in his fifties, but he looked older.

"I'll be damned," the man said, then his mouth hung open. "I'll be goddamned." He pushed the screen toward Jimmy and extended a hand. "J.T. Strawhorn," he said.

Jimmy shook his hand, his throat tickling. "Jimmy Strawhorn. Pleasure to meet you, sir."

The edge of J.T.'s mouth lifted and his expression went goofy. He held onto Jimmy's hand even though they'd finished shaking. "Jimmy damn Strawhorn. I didn't think you'd come. Hell, I didn't think you'd even get my telegram."

"I sure did get it."

"Jimmy Strawhorn." J.T. shoved his hands in his pockets and rocked, then started as if thumped on the nose. "Come on in, boy." J.T. moved out of the way until Jimmy had entered, then glanced both ways back through the door. "You ain't got nothing valuable sitting in your car, do you?"

"Got my bag and some stuff in my trunk."

"That'll be all right. They liable to take it if you leave it where they can get at it."

"They tough customers up in here?"

"I met worse."

The small, barren room was baking. Jimmy's vision took a moment to adjust to the dimness, then he saw one straight-backed chair set in the middle of the room before a box-fan clicking at full speed. Cracks and stains decorated the walls. A narrow hall led directly to the back door. The thought that living in small places might be genetic scampered through Jimmy's mind.

"It ain't much," said J.T., rubbing his chin and studying the shotgun house as if he were a prospective buyer. "Kind of a shithole really. Only temporary, though. Been down on my luck." He gave Jimmy a desperate look, then smiled and raised his shoulders, adjusting his whole demeanor as though another person had suddenly inhabited his skin. He slapped Jimmy's shoulder. "All that's gonna change now you're here. You planning on staying or you got yourself a motel room?"

"Hadn't really thought about it."

"Why don't you stay here at least tonight so we can talk about what's gonna happen. Here, you probably need to pee. Give me your keys and I'll get your bag out the car." Jimmy nodded and dug into his pocket. The man and the room tilted off their axes. Jimmy expected it would be a while before he was set level again, but in a way that suited him fine. He handed J.T. the keys. "Jimmy Strawhorn," J.T. said. "Bathroom's just on your left." J.T. peered both ways through the door and hurried outside.

The bathroom was a steamy closet with a commode, a step-in shower, and sink with a brown-stained drain. The linoleum flooring curled at the edges and Jimmy saw several giant roaches scurry under it when he entered. He'd seen better outhouses in west Texas, half expected a scorpion to be lurking on the wall. After he finished he heard the creak of the screen and was about to step into the hall again when he eased open the rusty rectangle of a medicine cabinet above the sink. Inside were aspirin, stomach mints, a splayed toothbrush and a nearly empty tube of toothpaste, a good sign, he hoped, in that there were no medicine bottles. But then, living here, J.T. might be unable to get medicine.

"I brought this in," J.T. said, sitting in the chair with Jimmy's duffle at his feet. "I figured this was what you needed." Jimmy nodded. Questions rolled through his head at an unbelievable rate, but he was unsure where to start. J.T. sat with his legs crossed, working his foot at high speed and grinning like he was drunk. "Oh," he said, and popped to his feet, "why don't you sit down."

"No, no, I been sitting."

"You sure?"

"Yes, sir."

J.T. settled back into the chair and looked around the room, his smile fading to a frown until he focused on Jimmy and grinned once more. J.T.'s cheeks were sunken and the bones in his shoulders were visible, although Jimmy couldn't be sure if that was just age, illness, build or lack of food. He thought of offering him a cigarette, then thought how bad that would seem if J.T. suffered from a lung problem.

"You have trouble finding it?" J.T. asked.

"Naw, that lady at the drug store helped me."

"Over at that sadass mall?"

"Yep."

"I been in there." J.T. winked and recrossed his legs. He rubbed one of his ankles. "So, you must've took off work soon as you got my telegram."

"Might say that. I pulled up."

"Say what?"

"Dragged up at work and took off."

"You quit your job?" J.T. uncrossed his legs.

"Wasn't much of a job. Worked at the Home Depot."

"Hm. Well, hope you ain't expecting much here right away. I'm in sort of a tight spot."

"Don't worry about that. I had some money saved up."

J.T. nodded. "I didn't mean like I don't have anything. I only been here a few days. Lived in a real nice place, but had some, what you might call, reversals. I'm working on some things, though. I'll be right back where I was soon."

Jimmy looked at the closed windows. "Maybe we can get a little window unit to cool it off some till then."

"Oh, I'm fine," J.T. said. "Heat don't bother me. I've had lots of jobs where the heat was worse than this. Only thing is I have to dress like a bum to keep from

sweatin' on my good clothes." He tugged his shirt away
from his chest, then rubbed his palms on his knees and
smiled close-mouthed as if to prove how cool he was. He
glanced at the window, seemed to notice that the house
was sealed and popped up. "Let's open some of them
windows." J.T. tugged one open then sat again, ogling
it. Jimmy went over and raised the other two, sat on
the sill of one.

"How'd you find me, Mr. Strawhorn?" he asked.

"Call me J.T." He paused and flexed his fingers,
his gaze fixed on a spot on the floor. "How'd I find you.
Well, it wasn't easy. I tracked you. I hoped you were out
there, but I couldn't get my hands on the records. Fact
is, I wasn't even sure where to start cause I didn't know
exactly what'd happened. Your momma ran off with you
when you was little, and I just assumed she still had
you. I tried to find her, you know, I asked around and
all, but I didn't find out for years that she'd give you up
for adoption."

"How'd you come on that?"

"How'd I come on what?"

"That I'd been put up for adoption."

J.T. tapped his lower teeth with his fingertips. "I
ran into somebody I knew knew your momma and they
told me. Said your momma wasn't able to handle having
you by herself, what with all her problems. So I started
going around trying to find out from government people
where you might be, went around and around. Wasn't till
a week or so ago I finally found somebody who showed
me the records on you."

"They had my address?"

"Well, no. They, uh, gave me the number of some
slow-talking fella in Texas."

"Mr. Sparks?"

"Yeah, Mr. Sparks. I explained the situation to him
and he gave me your address. I'd have called you too, but
I thought telegramming might be better. You know, give
you a chance to think about it. Plus, I lost my phone."

"Did Mr. Sparks tell you they said I was an orphan?"

J.T. put his forearm to his forehead and looked up.
"He might've mentioned that. Last couple of weeks've
been a jumble. I can't say as I have everything lined up."

"It ain't important right now," Jimmy said. He wanted to ask about his mother, searched a moment for an image of her and thought it odd how little he'd tried to imagine her, even when she crossed his mind. Jimmy started to ask what she looked like and what her "problems" had been, ask if she might still be around, but J.T. looked worn from the few questions he'd already answered. Jimmy thought maybe he should ask him what he could help with, but it was too soon. Instead he said, "I'm obliged you tracked me, J.T."

"Me, too, son. Me too. We're gonna have a big time."

Jimmy was flying on his third beer. Perched on a bar stool next to J.T. in the Pastime Lounge, he felt both buoyant and grounded unlike ever before. Earlier, as Jimmy waited for J.T. to get ready, he had sagged with fatigue, but when J.T. emerged from his room in a flowered shirt, white pleated slacks and shiny beige shoes, his hair slicked neat as a bird's head, Jimmy's ascent had begun. His father didn't look like somebody dying but like somebody who'd hit a soggy patch and was stepping high to escape it. J.T. had offered to drive and sat proudly behind the wheel as he showed Jimmy neighborhoods with canopy oaks draping the streets, wended past a golf course and a lake, cruised through LSU's Spanish architecture, then brought him downtown and parked beneath the ramp leading onto the bridge Jimmy had crossed a few hours ago. "Best roast beef po-boys in town," J.T. had blustered, but then had entered the lounge area tentatively, scanning the several patrons seated around the square bar before notching up his shoulders and marching to a stool like he was governor. "Pitcher of Michelob for me and my son," he said, and nodded to Jimmy. "To family," J.T. toasted when their beer arrived, and Jimmy tipped his mug, washing down some of the worry over J.T.'s life and filling his gullet with something like joy.

"You know that fine neighborhood with all them beautiful trees we went through," J.T. said as he munched on a fry. "That's where I lived before."

"You lived in one of them big houses?"

"I lived in that neighborhood, in a good spot."

"Why'd you leave?"

J.T. sniffed and took a long sip from his beer, his eyebrows working. "I'd rather not get into all that right now." He set his beer down and rubbed his finger in the condensation. "Dee!"

The bartender, a wiry blonde in a GEAUX TIGERS t-shirt, sauntered over, a cigarette angled from the corner of her mouth. "Yeah, honey," she said in a raspy voice.

"I want you to meet my son, Jimmy. Dee's been here longer than the floor."

"Thanks," she said, and rolled her eyes. "Why didn't you tell me you had a son? I can see the resemblance. You in town to visit?"

"Yes, ma'am," Jimmy said.

"He's in construction in Texas," J.T. said and gave Jimmy a little wink. "We ain't seen each other in a long while."

"I ain't seen you in a while either, J.T.," she said.

"I been working on some projects. You know how it is."

"Yeah," she said, and stubbed out her smoke with a smirk. "I know how it is."

J.T. leaned over the bar. "Dee, I know this ain't your thing, but I'm feeling lucky with my boy here and all tonight. Wanta show him a good time. You know of anybody in here plays cards? Blackjack in particular. Not too high stakes, just something me and my son might enjoy."

She laughed. "I don't think so. You can see it's slow. I really don't pay much mind to that sort of thing anyway." Across the bar a man in a pink shirt with an alligator on the pocket called her. "Coming," she said, then pointed at J.T. "I wanted to tell you there was some big dude in here asking about you a couple of days ago. Wide as a trailer. Wore Coke bottle glasses." The man across the bar called again. "Hold your horses!" Dee said. "Anywho, just wanted to let you know," she said and winked. Jimmy watched her tight jeans move away, then turned to J.T., whose mouth was screwed tight.

"Why'd you say I was in construction?" Jimmy asked.

"What's the problem? Didn't it make you feel good?"

"Didn't make me feel one way or the other."

"You are in construction, ain't you? I mean, if you work in Home Depot, you handle all the things folks need to construct and you sell 'em to the constructors, right?"

"I'd say that's stretching it a might," Jimmy said.

"Stretching it is good business. Makes people feel good, makes yourself feel good." He held his glass out to Jimmy. "Here's to stretching it." He clinked his glass against Jimmy's and scanned the bar again, not with the wariness he'd had before but with something more searching. A wave of tipsiness rippled through Jimmy's head. He wasn't used to drinking and hadn't slept much the last two nights, but he still felt squarely anchored on the cushioned barstool with his father next to him.

"J.T., you got any other kids?"

J.T. raised his brow. "Why you asking?"

"Just wondering. Thought I was an orphan till day before yesterday, so I was figuring maybe I got a brother or sister."

"Not from me."

"What about maybe from my mother?"

"I wouldn't know nothing about that."

Jimmy pushed his feet against the bar railing. "You got a notion where she is?"

J.T. took a long drink from his beer and set the glass hard onto the bar. "I ain't sure this is a good time to discuss that either."

"Seems like a good time to me."

"We trying to celebrate here." J.T. cocked his head and looked sideways. "I ain't seen her in over twenty years. I don't even really know if she's alive."

"Well what about her? Anything. What was her name?"

J.T. ran his hands along the slicked sides of his hair, then grasped his beer mug with a stranglehold. "Morita. Her name was Morita."

"What did she look like?"

"Dark hair. Brown eyes. Beautiful. She was younger than me." J.T. traced the lip of his glass and stared into a corner away from Jimmy. Jimmy thought he was collecting his thoughts to tell him more, but after a while he wondered if J.T. had forgotten him.

"How'd y'all meet?" Jimmy said.

"Can I have one of your smokes there?"

"You sure that's a good idea, what with you feeling poorly?"

"It's a good idea if I want one. And what's this about me feeling poorly?" Jimmy thumped one out for J.T. and lit it. The spark in J.T.'s voice had surprised him and now J.T. pulled long on the cigarette and blew as if he was trying to put out a candle across the bar. J.T. poked the cigarette straight ahead in front of his face. "She wasn't right. Couldn't really do for herself. That ain't to say she didn't love you, but she had trouble. She was a young girl. Took to getting all irritable with me and saying we didn't have enough, even though I was working a regular job. Then one day I came home and y'all was gone." J.T. flicked his cigarette like there was a bee on the end of it. "Goodness knows I looked all over for y'all. I didn't have no idea where she'd gone with you, though, so all I could do was ask around. Went to the cops, but they said they couldn't do nothing." He shrugged. "That's about it."

"How old was I last time you seen me?"

"Hmmm. Still a tyke. Somewhere in there."

A large hand dropped like a ham onto J.T.'s back. J.T. coughed and tried to spin, but the man attached to the hand had already moved to J.T.'s side and was draping his long arm around J.T.'s shoulders so tightly that he couldn't turn. "J.T. Strawhorn," the man said, towering on the side of J.T. opposite Jimmy. "Haven't seen much of you lately. Surprised to see you out and looking so dapper."

"Moss," J.T. said, his voice shaky.

"I heard you been a little scarce lately."

"Just busy. Taking care of some business. Came out tonight to get a po-boy with my son."

"Your son? Pleased to meet you." Moss lifted his arm from J.T., reached a wide mitt toward Jimmy and squeezed as though he was trying to crush Jimmy's hand, all the while smiling. His head was a thin watermelon set on end, and he wore gray slacks with a yellow shirt and a gold chain around his neck. He reminded Jimmy of the too-tanned, brand-new snakeskin-boot-wearing sonsabitches who came into Home Depot ordering him around without ever really looking at him, asking him to tote bags of mulch or boards for their deck out to their trucks and then trying to tip him a quarter. He squeezed Moss back until the man snorted and released.

"You here taking care of business too?" Moss asked.

A tickle passed through Jimmy's chest, the sensation that he wasn't getting something he should be getting, and he almost stood and looked Moss eye to eye. "I'm in from Texas."

"Texas." Moss nodded like he knew everything about Texas. "So, J.T., I was talking to Mr. Charley the other day and he said he'd really like to get together with you. Said he'd had his assistant out checking on your whereabouts, but couldn't turn you up."

"That right. I been meaning to call him. If you talk to him again, tell him I'll be in touch real soon. Now that my boy's here I'm gonna get things all settled."

"I'll be sure and tell him." Moss slapped J.T.'s back again. "Oh, I heard you moved from your old place. Where you living now?"

"Just a couple of blocks from here. Right downtown. Landlord wasn't keeping the other place up."

"No kidding? What street would that be?"

"North. Living down on North Street. Nice little place."

"I'm happy for you, J.T. I'll tell Mr. Charley cause I know he'll be happy too." Moss slid his eyes onto Jimmy. "Good meeting you. Take care of your old man here."

J.T. sat frozen as Moss strolled around the bar, shaking more hands and howdying people like a candidate for office. J.T. leveled a look somewhere between murderer and murder victim. Jimmy had the sensation that he was watching a tornado touch down on the plain without knowing which direction it was going to track. What he did know, though, was that J.T. didn't live on North Street. Finally J.T. forced a laugh and downed the rest of his beer. "You must be tired," he said to Jimmy.

"I could stand to lay down." Jimmy motioned Dee to

tally their tab, but J.T. stayed fixed on Moss, who gave a small salute as he left the room. Jimmy said, "That fella's got a funny notion of a handshake. Who is he?"

"He ain't nobody. Used to be a cop, but even they run him off. I don't know what he does now except give people the reds slapping 'em on the neck."

"How bout Mr. Charley?"

J.T.'s nose wrinkled and he stood. "Don't you worry about him. Mr. Charley ain't your concern." He smiled. "Two shots of Jack," he said to Dee.

She plucked several bills from Jimmy's change, poured the shots, then set the remaining money and the brimming glasses on the bar. J.T. reached over, spread the cash and counted it. He picked up a penny and a one and gave them to Jimmy. "Never leave a odd tip," he said. "There's evens for some things and odds for others." He raised his glass and waited for Jimmy to respond.

"I'm gone pass," Jimmy said. He considered asking J.T. why he'd lied about where he lived, asking whether J.T.'s condition could stand whiskey, then let it lie.

J.T. shrugged, threw back the first shot, then the second. "Let's get the hell outta here," he said.

Outside, the steamy liquid air pooled in the parking lot. Traffic *zhoomed* overhead, a tugboat horn blared on the river, exotic sounds that shot a chill through Jimmy. He tugged his jeans and stretched to keep up with J.T., who scanned the parking lot. Despite J.T.'s antsiness, Jimmy let the good feeling settle in him. Whatever the shit with J.T. was didn't really matter, so long as he wasn't too sick. Jimmy had enough money to last them a while, and by the time he found a good job they'd have figured out a better place to live.

DAY FOUR

Jimmy woke up burning hot, his clothes sticking to him like sprayed glue. His neck was crimped from sleeping slumped in J.T.'s one chair. His mouth tasted like bad meat from too much beer and too many cigarettes. He'd chosen to sleep here rather than on the floor after witnessing a gang of roaches flee the light and J.T.'s subsequent dousing with a can of insecticide. J.T. apologized at length for the shabby conditions, but he didn't offer Jimmy his bed, not that Jimmy would have taken it anyway. No, sleeping in a chair had been fine.

Jimmy grunted to his feet, stretched and felt a small blossom in his chest even though the temperature was already pushing ninety. As soon as J.T. arose, they'd head somewhere for coffee and a good breakfast, spend the day tooling around town, seeing what there was to see, catching up on whatever the other needed to know. He grabbed a smoke from the pack next to his wallet on the counter, lit up and stepped outside to the tiny stoop. The morning glared absolutely still, the sky bleached by heat and humidity. He could see the roofs of the mall, could see a road he'd never woken up to before, could see . . . He coughed a cloud of smoke. Where was his car? He craned both ways down the raggedy street, as if he might have accidentally parked in front of someone else's house or someone might have moved it during the night.

"He left about an hour ago," he heard, then spotted the black woman in a chair on the stoop next door.

"Ma'am?"

"The new man lives there, he took your car about an hour ago."

Jimmy took another drag and let it settle in his lungs a while before exhaling. The need to pee burst inside him. "Scuse me a second," he said. Jimmy tromped down the hall, the pressure pushing out like a small truck in his abdomen, hurriedly unzipped and let go a stream that surprised him with its force. He peed a long time, the release clearing his head and lessening the panic that had swept him, so that by the time he was shaking the final drops, he thought it fine and reasonable that his father had borrowed the car while he slept in. When he stepped over to wash his hands, he saw the note stuck to the medicine cabinet with a weathered snippet of duct tape. Jimmy set his cigarette atop the medicine cabinet, splashed his face and toweled off, then jammed the note in his pocket. In the living room he slipped into his boots and went outside again.

The woman still sat, drinking from a blue-and-white striped cup. "Trade you some coffee for a cigarette," she said as he approached. Her skin was dark brown, her body slim but big-boned and shapely. Her dress was just above her knees, which were way too large for her legs. Jimmy guessed she was older than J.T., maybe early sixties, although she looked healthier. He crossed the dirt patch between the houses.

"Jimmy Strawhorn, ma'am," he said.

"Elma Starwood," she said, and laughed. "Sounds like we almost from the same family."

"Yes, ma'am. Did he say where he was off to?"

"He didn't say anything. Barely spoke since he moved in. He almost never comes out and when he does he looks like a hawk about to fly down and grab him. Go on in and get you some coffee. Grab that easy chair from the kitchen. Leave them cigarettes with me."

He handed her the pack and went into the little house, identical to J.T.'s except it was spotless, freshly-painted, and homey with furniture in the living room. In the kitchen, Jimmy poured himself a cup, lifted the folded lawn chair and rejoined Elma where a large magnolia tree cast shade over them. Elma leaned her head back and blew a luxurious stream of smoke.

"I quit cause of my son," she said, "so don't tell nobody." She cleared her throat and raised her skirt higher on her thighs. "You favor him. He's your daddy?"

"Yes, ma'am. Met him for the first time yesterday."

"You never saw him before yesterday?"

"No, ma'am. Drove in from Texas and me and him went out to some bar last night."

"I heard y'all come in. I listen close in this neighborhood. Last few years it got a little rough. Thought somebody might try to take your car. I guess that's what you thought happened when you poked your head out."

"Are people bad to steal cars around here?"

"They's some dopeheads living up in these old houses like mine. I been living here about ten years and these places done been condemned twice. Man puts up the signs and somebody comes take 'em down. They put 'em up again and somebody comes take 'em down again. Every time they raise the rent. They must think it improves the property to take them signs down. I just write the new name on the check and stay on." She took a deep draw off the cigarette and exhaled with a look of ecstacy. "Your daddy shoulda told you he was taking your car."

"Maybe he didn't want to roust me after I drove all day."

"He don't have air-conditioning, does he?" Jimmy shook his head. "I did one summer month here without it and almost burned up. After that my son bought me a little one for my bedroom. Can't sleep without that it gets so sticky."

Jimmy sipped the coffee, dark and rich, swallowed hard and touched his pocket where the note lay like a piece of hot metal. It seemed important to know what the note said in case J.T. asked. Eventually he'd tell J.T. that he couldn't read, just not yet. He pulled the paper from his pocket and held it out to Elma, his skin prickling. "He left this on the mirror. I didn't read it yet." Elma took the note and kept her gaze on Jimmy so steadily that he felt his brain exposed as a prune. She unfolded the paper, held it away from her and began to slowly read aloud. "'Jimmy, had to run out for things. Hope you don't mind. Shower and fix you some grits. Be back before lunch.'" Elma laid the note on Jimmy's knee. "He probly just went to fetch y'all some groceries."

"Probly. Maybe he had to get some medicine, too."

"He sick?"

"I think so."

"A man who's sick oughta have an air conditioner."

Jimmy downed the last gulp from his cup and held it in his lap. The coffee had broken sweat on him twice as hard, but the nicotine and caffeine had caused a sweet rush in his head and with it the urge to get J.T. to a better place as soon as possible.

"Thank you mightily for your hospitality, Miz Elma," Jimmy said and stood. "I'm glad J.T.'s got such a good neighbor."

"Honey, you come on back over and visit any time. My boy don't get over as often as he should. Me and you can sit in the cool later."

"Yes, ma'am."

Jimmy started off the stoop, but Elma touched his arm.

"You mind if I get a couple more smokes off you?"

Back inside J.T.'s house, Jimmy stripped off his shirt. Beneath the sink, he found a small canister of Comet and an ancient brush. He scrubbed the mossy shower floor until he was sure most of the remaining fungus-green was fossil and not living. The soap rack held a sliver of soap and no shampoo, so Jimmy retrieved a fresh bar, a tiny bottle and a towel from his duffle. He undressed in the hall rather than risk knocking a knee on the sink or a shin on the toilet, then set his pouch of money on the commode while he showered. The cold water was as warm as tea and so soft his skin became slicker the more he lathered, but it was good to get the grime of the road and the night off him. He held his forehead to the weak stream and let the rivulets trickle through his eye sockets and around his nose. It was like he'd never showered before. Somehow everything was like that, every little action and event, every second a window he'd never looked through. All his life had been a view through a dusty pane—endless flatland, endless wind, the smell of livestock and chicken manure, and a wider world he couldn't decipher. Now everything looked brand new, even J.T.'s dive. Maybe kin could make it all different, a tie unlike Pepper that nobody could cut.

He shut off the shower, toweled one foot and stepped into a boot, then did the same with the other rather than chance the grungy floor. He sponged the excess water off, knowing as soon as he was dry he'd start sweating again. He wrapped the towel around his waist and stepped into the hall. From here he could see almost the whole place, the front room where he'd slept, the tiny kitchen and the door to J.T.'s bedroom. For a moment he thought it wrong to go in there, but he needed to see, to know if he could find a clue to J.T.'s illness. He eased the door open, half expecting J.T. to be hiding. A single mattress and box spring lay flat on the floor, neatly made with only a sheet and one pillow. The bed stand was a plastic milk crate upon which sat a black comb and a hand mirror. Against the wall leaned a large suitcase. Jimmy crossed the threshold and walked to the closet. When he opened that door, the odor of must poured over him, making him sneeze and snort before he could look in again. Several short sleeve shirts and Sansabelt slacks hung there, along with two sports coats, one gray, one bright yellow. He shut the door quietly behind him as if Elma might hear him from her porch.

The old Samsonite was mangy at its edges. Jimmy carefully laid it on the worn planks, unlatched it, peeked in to make sure he wouldn't disrupt the order of the clothes, then fully raised the lid. A few pairs of underwear and sleeveless undershirts, plus a pile of socks. Jimmy opened the elastic pouch on the side, saw cufflinks and two rolled ties and a single envelope with the same name from the telegram, J.T.'s name. He picked up the envelope, looked inside, saw no medicine and replaced it. He lifted the folded underwear but found nothing there either, re-latched the suitcase and righted it on its side. He stood. Maybe J.T. carried his medicine with him. Or maybe he was so sick or the kind of sick where there was no medicine.

Jimmy gently closed the door behind him and went into the kitchen. An ancient refrigerator hummed. The stove looked even older. In the cabinet, a box of grits sat next to a pot. The refrigerator held only a jug of water. Jimmy shut it and shuffled to his chair in the front room again. The heat squeezed him. What had sent J.T. to live like this? And why had he lied last night about where he lived? A weight like stacked water pressed on him all at once.

A bang rattled the front door, and Jimmy jerked, securing the towel around his waist. A wide face appeared at the door window, slitted eyes behind large, tortoise-shell glasses.

"Hey!" it called and the man rapped on the glass.

"Hold on," Jimmy said, grabbed his jeans and retreated to the kitchen to dress. He tried to pull a pants leg over a boot, then recovered and slipped one foot at a time out of his boots and into the pants. He shoved the money pouch into his rear pocket, snatched a T-shirt out of his duffle and opened the door to the man on the porch.

"Warm one, ain't it?" the man said. His shoulders spread almost as wide as the frame. He wrinkled his nose, exposing his front teeth, then moved in close and stuck out a huge hand. "Name's Squint." Squint's hand enveloped Jimmy's as if Squint was trying to make it smaller without trying. "J.T. Strawhorn here?"

"Nuh uh."

Squint leaned to the side and adjusted his glasses to see the address. "Says fourteen right here."

"Yep. But he ain't here."

Squint released Jimmy's hand. "He lives here though."

"You mind me asking who you are?"

"Already told you. Squint. You can see why."

Jimmy could. Squint's eyeballs were barely visible through the thick glasses and the dime-thin space between his eyelids. He was amazed Squint could see at all.

"How you figure J.T. to live here?"

"Let's just say I read some old moss." Squint grinned.

"J.T.'s out for a spell," Jimmy said.

"He is, huh? You mind if I come in and wait for him?"

Jimmy didn't want Squint in the house, but he had the uneasy feeling that Squint was coming in anyway. Jimmy moved aside. Squint stepped in and scanned the place. "Y'all ain't much on home decorating, are you?" he said, and took a handkerchief from his pocket. Daintily, he dabbed at his forehead and cheeks, then shoved the cloth back in his pants.

"I don't live here."

Squint studied the floor. "That your gear there?"

"Yep."

"Where you from? Wait, don't tell me." Squint stroked his chin. "Say something else."

"Like what?"

"Tennessee, right? Don't tell me which part."

"Texas."

"Texas, Tennessee?"

"No, Texas. Texas, Texas."

"No shit. You ain't ever lived in Tennessee?"

"Nope."

"Hmph." Squint scratched his nose. "Well, you oughta watch yourself up in here. Some tough niggers living in these little shotgun shacks."

Squint seemed too big for J.T.'s house. His shoulders weren't only wide but round and sturdy as hogs' heads. His khaki pants strained to hold in his massive legs, and his gut stuck out even though he wore a loose short-sleeved dress shirt. "What's your name?" Squint asked.

"Jimmy."

"You related to J.T.?"

"He's my father."

"I thought I saw the resemblance? And you don't know when he's gonna be back?"

"Took off before I woke up."

Squint picked at the cuticle on his index finger. "You know why I'm here?" Jimmy shook his head. "Your daddy owes my boss some money. I been trying to find him, but I didn't know where he was till last night."

Jimmy's feet itched. He thought of J.T.'s circuitous route home from the Pastime and of J.T. cursing as he peered in the rearview mirror. "That fella followed us?" Squint harumphed. "You ain't got to worry. Not yet at least. Mr. Charley's pissed off about your daddy running to avoid him, but he don't like to hurt customers much. I'm mostly a bouncer. Mr. Charley fired the last fella and hired me, cause I can do what needs to be done and be a diplomat if I need to. Pays me good too. See that Lincoln out there. That's good cause you can see I need a big ride." Squint sauntered across to the far wall and tapped against it. He shook his head. "White people ought not to live like this. Hell, niggers neither."

Jimmy clicked his teeth together. "Excuse me, uh, Mr. Squint."

"Squint, just Squint, not mister. I'm not that sort."

"Squint. How much does he owe?"

Squint laughed. "Damn, you Texans sure talk slow. He owes six hundred. It'll be six fifty tomorrow. Regular interest he would've owed nine hundred, but Mr. Charley knew J.T. couldn't ever come up with that kind of money. He's supposedly known your old man a long time. Says he's always been a little partial to him cause he's a harmless kind of rascal, 'cept lately he jack-rabbitted on this money and been acting kind of an asshole. If I was Mr. Charley, I'd be treating it kind of different. You know, draw a clear line."

"He borrowed money?"

"Yep."

"And if he don't pay, what is it happens?"

"I do what it takes to get the money." He adjusted his shirt. "I mean I do what Mr. Charley says. I'm sorry I got to say it out like that, him being your daddy and all, but you asked."

Jimmy didn't think Squint had really said it out at all, but the coffee in Jimmy's stomach lurched and crested in his throat nonetheless. Six hundred dollars. It was almost half of what he had. He touched his back pocket and frowned.

"Jimmy, you not thinking of trying something, are you, cause I've had every kind of violence tried on me and it just doesn't work. I've been stabbed, I've been whacked on the head with a board, I've been punched with brass knuckles, and I've been hit from every direction in every spot on the football field. I don't feel pain like other people. Never did. So please don't try violence or you'll get hurt and nobody'll be happy cause Mr. Charley doesn't like me to do it unless I have to."

"If you don't mind me asking, how come he to borrow this money?"

"I would guess how come cause he was down in cards."

A sprout of anger touched Jimmy's lungs. He didn't want to, but he wondered if this debt was the reason J.T. had contacted him. Then he shoved down the resentment as best he could. Whatever the reason, J.T. was his father and Jimmy was determined to give him the benefit of the doubt. Pain traveled up his arm and into his shoulder from tension, but he knew what he had to do. "You wouldn't take more'n you was due, would you, Squint?"

"I ain't a thief, sir."

Jimmy pulled out the pouch and opened it. He counted six one-hundred dollar bills and held them out. Squint looked straight at him. "You sure? I mean, I know he's your daddy, but sometimes when they get a good lesson they straighten up."

"I'm sure. If this'll square it, take it."

Squint folded the money and placed it in his pants. From his shirt pocket he took a small notebook and held it inches from his face as he made an entry. "You're a good son," Squint said. "Watch yourself, though. I guarantee he'll do it again."

As he left, Squint shut the door softly behind him. Jimmy plopped into J.T.'s chair and listened to Squint crank his Lincoln and cruise away. The remaining money was a lump under Jimmy's butt cheek, but a considerably smaller lump. He ran his fingers through his hair, still damp from the shower, and tried to gauge the storm that had ripped through, leaving him dazed and considerably less wealthy. Maybe it'd been dumb to give Squint the money. Maybe J.T. hadn't owed any money at all and this was how robbers worked in Baton Rouge. After all, Moss had found out Jimmy was new in town. It was possible Moss tailed them and then planned to have Squint come by after J.T. left the house, though that didn't explain how Moss would have known Jimmy had cash enough to cover the shake down. Jimmy blew out through rubber lips like a cartoon horse. He was sure J.T. owed the money. But, then, it didn't matter if he did or not. The dumbest thing would've been to say no to a man the size of a cistern.

Jimmy heaved himself out of the chair and went into the kitchen. His stomach was chewing hard on the nothing in it, so he put some water on to boil even though the thought of eating unsettled him even more. He tugged the pouch from his pocket and took out the rest of his money. He counted it out—one, two, three, four . . . , then counted the last stack down through the ones. Seven-hundred sixty-two dollars. Still a lot. At least enough to get them started: A deposit on a new place, a month's rent, some groceries, maybe utilities hook-ups. Jimmy shuffled the stacks together again, folded them and stuffed them into the cloth sack. He licked his lips, licked them again. He'd have to start looking for work soon, and that prospect dizzied him—a swirl of incomprehensible applications, a crowd of judgmental strangers, a non-stop performance to cover what he didn't know and couldn't do.

Jimmy poured grits into the bubbling pot. He noticed something unusual, black dots, poured some grits into his palm. Bugs. Tiny bugs. The steam from the pot billowed into his nose. He slung the box across the room snowing the floor, then shook his head. Now he'd have to clean that up too.

Jimmy flinched, then reached behind him and stopped the cow bell attached to the door. He glanced around and saw the blonde woman behind the counter reading again, had a quick impulse to step back out. Then the drug store's air-conditioner breezed across him like the hint of autumn, and his stomach growled. "Howdy," he said.

"Howdy to you," she said, the sight of her so pristine he almost couldn't take her in. She wore a blood-red sundress with purple straps that exposed creamy shoulders. "I take it you found him?"

"Yes, ma'am."

"Did it go all right?" she asked, her eyebrows dropping with concern.

"Went fine. He took me out to some joint called the Pastime."

"I've been there. That's one of the couple of places I have been. Was he what you expected?"

"Didn't really know what to expect."

She touched her chin and pursed her lips. "You can come on in," she said.

Jimmy started away from the door. "Just didn't want that bell clanking. Makes me think it's milking time."

She laughed, set her book down and clapped her palms together. "What can we do you for?"

"I might just stand here and soak in this cool."

"You soak as much as you want."

The woman brushed her fingertips across the paperback's cover. A sweet aroma Jimmy couldn't begin to define wafted from her. "It get this steamy where you're from?" she asked.

"It does."

"And where's that?"

"Houston."

"Yep. I've heard it gets plenty hot and sticky in Houston." She opened her arms. "So, can I help you with something?"

Jimmy's mind blanked. "Well, ma'am—"

"Excuse me, but every time you say 'ma'am' I feel like I'm your grandmaw."

"Sorry. Just a habit."

"I understand. My habit is to laugh all the time and say too much. That bothers some people, but I can't help it. I come from a small town in north Louisiana. You got to laugh if you're from up there."

"I reckon."

"So what can I get you?"

"Guess I could use a broom. Might could stand a snack or something, too, if y'all have some."

"We can handle that." She whisked from behind

the counter and led him down an aisle. He stared at her shoulder blades, almost bumped into her when she stopped. She pulled two brooms from their slots and turned so quickly she nearly hit him.

"Pardon," he said.

"That's okay," she said, the brooms an inch from his chest. Her scent made him light-headed for a second. "You okay?" she asked. "Your blood sugar's low, isn't it?"

"No, I'm fine," he said, and took the straw bristle broom. "This'n will do."

"And a dust pan." She plucked one from its hook, replaced the nylon broom, and strode toward the front of the store again. Jimmy noticed that some of the shelves stood bare, while others were sparsely stocked. "We don't have a whole lot to eat," she said, "but let's get you something to take the edge off till you get lunch. How about some of these peanut butter crackers? They're terrible for you, but they're good." She inserted two packets into his grip. "Go ahead and eat those now. Get your sugar right before you go out in that heat again."

Jimmy found himself lost in her blue eyes. She took the crackers from him and ripped open the package. "Here, eat," she said and held it toward him. He popped one of the crackers in his mouth, the salt and peanut butter locking his jaw. The cracker grew larger with each chew, until his mouth perked up at the edge and his chest shook with laughter. "A little dry?" she said, then she was laughing too. "Let's get you a drink." At the front counter, she poured water from her thermos. Jimmy turned up the cup. The iciness spread through him, pierced his temples and forehead, but it was so good he didn't even pause. When he set the empty cup in front of her, she filled it again.

"Thank you," he said.

"Am I being too pushy?" she asked, and stopped screwing the cap on the thermos.

"Ma'— I mean, you ain't pushing me."

She tilted her head as if she didn't completely believe him. "I'm Sandra," she said.

"Jimmy. Jimmy Strawhorn. Pleased to meet you again."

She shifted the paperback on the counter. "I know

I get too blabbermouthed, but when I saw you, I thought about you meeting your father and it was exciting, because I don't really know my father either. I mean, I know his name, but I don't really know him." She shrugged. "That's neither here nor there, though." She laughed. "Working here I just don't see many people who aren't old or trying to sneak something from the shelves. I know that sounds horrible, but it's true. Most people go to the chain down the road, and I think I forget how to act." She released a long sigh. "There I go again."

"That's all right. I like to hear you talk." Sandra's cheeks blushed.

"You're sweet," she said, and touched his forearm.

He brushed at his mouth and blinked before gathering himself. "Thank you. Thank you for giving me that food and drink. I'd let myself get so hungry I couldn't think straight."

"That'll be seven dollars and thirty-six cents," she said.

Jimmy pulled out his wallet and paid, remembering J.T.'s words never to leave an odd number. When she gave him his change, he took a deep breath. He raised on his toes, teetered as he remembered the daggers of past disappointed looks, then pushed the memories away.

"Sandra, just say if you don't . . . I get that it might be too quick, but you wanta do something some time?"

She looked him over closely, smoothed strands of silky hair behind one of her ears. "Like what?"

"Nothing in particular. Whatever you wanted to do."

"I don't really know what to do around here. I've only been out a couple of times."

"That's fine, then. I'm sorry if I asked before I should have."

"I didn't say that. I said I've only been out a couple of times."

"Yeah you did. Well, we might could get a bite to eat. Mabye just walk." Sandra blinked. "I ain't trying to put you on the spot," he said. "Either way is fine."

Sandra bit at her thumbnail, then pressed the back of her thumb against her chin. "I work until five."

"This afternoon?"

"This afternoon."

* * *

Jimmy sat slumped on the porch as J.T. drove up a little after one. J.T. waved and headed toward Jimmy carrying a cylindrical paper bag and several pieces of mail. "I like the way that car drives. Hope you don't mind I borrowed it. Thought you might wanta sleep in." He stopped a few feet away.

"It ain't a problem."

"Brought us some po-boys." J.T. raised the bag, then moved past Jimmy. Jimmy followed him into the kitchen, where J.T. pointed at the grocery bags folded and stacked in the corner. "Visited that sorry Winn Dixie, huh?" He dumped the paper-wrapped sandwiches on the kitchen counter and grinned over his shoulder at Jimmy. "Hope you like fried oysters."

"A fella come by," Jimmy said.

J.T. froze. "A fella?"

"Big fella name of Squint. Said Mr. Charley sent him."

J.T. faced Jimmy, bracing himself with his behind and hands on the counter. "What did he want?"

"Six-hundred dollars. I gave it to him."

"You did what?"

"I paid what he said you owed. He said if we didn't pay, he was gone keep coming and asking for more."

"That sonofabitch." J.T. pushed his fists against him temples and shook his head. "Goddamnit, boy, he took you. He took you bad." J.T. dropped his arms. "I didn't borrow but half that." J.T. paced in front of the short counter. "Why the hell didn't you just wait? We could've doubled that."

"I thought it best just to pay and be done with it."

J.T. halted. He rubbed furiously at the back of his head as if his hair were stinging him. "He say he'd do anything if you didn't pay?"

"Didn't say he'd do anything to *me*."

J.T. forced a smile that was almost a snarl. Red blotches swelled onto his cheeks, making Jimmy wonder if J.T.'s problem might be blood pressure or a heart condition. "Excuse me." J.T. brushed by Jimmy and slammed into the bathroom. Jimmy heard the faucet on full blast, thought of asking if J.T. was all right, but instead stepped to the screen door at the rear of the house and stared at the tiny, overgrown backyard where busted cinder blocks, bike parts, tires, plastic bottles, beer cans and a rusty air-conditioner housing lay strewn and heaped as if dumped from the sky. Jimmy touched the pouch in his rear pocket. He was sure he'd done the right thing. He'd always been good with money, had always paid his bills while saving enough to have a cushion, and he felt getting rid of Squint before there was trouble was a bargain. Besides, he suspected that Squint had told the truth.

J.T. slung open the bathroom door and scowled, but his skin was less blotchy as he came over to Jimmy and slapped him hard on the arm three times. "You did the right thing," he said. "If I hadn't of took off this morning that wouldn't have happened, so that's my fault. That sonofabitch Moss's and Charley's too but that's another story. Why don't you just eat your po-boy and after that we'll go someplace where it's cool."

Jimmy itched to ask J.T. why he'd been dumb enough to borrow money from these people, to also ask why J.T. had waited until he was in debt to contact him, except knowing all that wouldn't change anything now. Intead he asked, "Why don't we go get you a AC? Think of finding you a different place to live, too."

J.T.'s tongue bulged his upper lip, then his lower lip, then circled, bulging all around his closed mouth. He took a giant breath through his nose and then snorted it out. "Why don't you just eat that sandwich then we go find some cool."

"We can do that. I just worry what with you being puny that it ain't a good idea living up in here. It's griddle hot and Elma told me how there's bad characte—"

"Elma? Who the hell's Elma?"

"That lady next door."

"That nosy, black woman? What you doing talking to her?"

"She seen me in the yard looking for the car and asked did I want some coffee. I give her a cig . . . . She told me she seen you go off."

"I left you a damn note. That ain't enough or you

got to go detectiving?" J.T. extended the fingers on both hands and wildly shook them as though hexing the kitchen. He stopped mid-shake, eyes as wide as if he saw a demon, and studied Jimmy. "It's good having you here, son, I don't want you to think it ain't, but I can take care of my own business. As for me being puny, I ain't puny, just in a jam, you understand?"

The telegram's language about not having long sparked in Jimmy, but he pushed it down.

"Yes, sir."

"And I ain't trying to say I ain't thankful for what you did this morning, and I like that woman next door just fine, even though I ain't ever really talked to her. I'm only saying I'm funny about people snooping around in my business." J.T. paused, adjusted his collar, his sleeves and the front of his slacks. "Now, let's go someplace cool before I blow a gasket."

"Yes, sir."

J.T. wiped his brow, flung the sweat off his fingers, then billowed his shirt. He didn't look good, puny or not. But he was right that getting out of this heat right now was a good idea.

Jimmy jiggled the air-conditioner in the loose window frame. There was considerable jiggling, but Jimmy figured he'd braced the unit well enough on the outside that the tiny AC wouldn't rip out. After all, he'd doubted the ancient wiring in the house could handle much pull and had bought only a 5,000 BTU, enough to cool J.T.'s room without, hopefully, setting the wires aglow and flashing off the rickety house like tinder. "Plug it in," Jimmy said to J.T., then turned the ON switch. The box rattled into action, the compressor giving a kick and spewing cool then cold air into the superheated space. Jimmy turned with a grin to J.T. J.T.'s skin radiated a color somewhere between peach and cherry. His arms dangled from stooped shoulders, as if the heat were rocks piled on his neck. His shirt adhered in sodden patches to his chest. "Lay down," Jimmy said, and J.T. obeyed like a zombie, the first time all day he hadn't rubbed some edge against Jimmy. Jimmy hustled to the bathroom, wet

J.T.'s one wash cloth, and returned to place it on J.T.'s forehead. "We should've waited till it cooled off some to do this," Jimmy said.

"When?" J.T. said. "About December?" His lips curled upward at their corners. "You did a good job."

Jimmy lifted his arms and let the AC play over his bare chest. J.T.'s words were about the first civil ones he'd spoken to Jimmy since Jimmy told him about paying Squint. While out, Jimmy had refused to take J.T. to a bar, instead took him to a Home Depot, J.T. grousing the whole time. Jimmy understood J.T.'s self-respect was wounded, but that hadn't stopped Jimmy from wanting to tell the old man to show some gratitude over Jimmy's having carved out a chunk of his savings to keep J.T.'s fingers from becoming triple-jointed, then carved out another chunk to keep him from heat stroke.

J.T. grunted beneath the square cloth draped over his forehead and eyes. "Never know where life's gonna take you. Didn't think I'd ever be living in black quarters. And I don't mean that as disrespectful to the people that live here cause I'm sure they don't like it either."

Jimmy checked his watch and sat on the edge of the bed, weakness passing through him as he remembered Sandra. He belched, tasted bile and smacked his mouth. "You mind if I smoke, J.T.?"

"Nobody usually smokes in here." He paused, lifted the rag and peeked out. "Can I bum one off you?"

Jimmy lit two and placed one between J.T.'s lips. He checked his watch again. Four-twelve. Soon he'd have to decide if he was going back to the drug store. The sweat the AC was drying dewed up fresh on him.

"Yeah," J.T. said, and blew a thin stream of smoke, the rag like a blindfold, "I figured I'd have it all by the ass by now. I had plans and they was good plans, but people are gonna screw you every chance."

Jimmy took a long drag and blew smoke against the current of the AC. Growing up, he'd worked full days in the west Texas sun, a furnace breath blowing non-stop, and rarely paused to think about the heat. It was part of who he was, like the plain and dust. Now he'd gone soft. He worried that if he had to work outside again, he'd never make it. "I need to find some work," Jimmy said.

"How's that?"

"Money I brought ain't gone last so long now."

"How much you got?"

Jimmy hesitated, studied J.T.'s scrawny chest rising and falling, his skinny arms straight at his sides, cigarette vertical from the center of his lips. "Enough to get us through for a little while."

"In a little while I oughta have us set up. I got some plans." He flipped the wash cloth and looked at Jimmy. "Don't forget I'm the father here."

Jimmy held back a skeptical look. Granted he didn't know squat about fathers, but J.T. sure wasn't what Jimmy had heard of them being. Still, J.T.'s words did hold some comfort. Maybe he did have a plan. Life had surely been strange enough these past few days to account for that.

"J.T.," Jimmy said. "J.T." J.T.'s breathing came deep and raspy. Jimmy plucked the cigarette from J.T.'s mouth and checked his watch again. Time left for a quick shower and a change of shirt.

Jimmy watched Sandra peer through the glass door, her expression flat, before she finally came out, locked the store behind her and stood almost at attention. Jimmy had placed himself off the wide sidewalk on the edge of the parking lot so as not to crowd her when she emerged. Now they faced each other for what seemed days, until Jimmy stepped up onto the walkway. "You said five. I was wondering if you might want a ride home, or try and figure something to do."

Sandra glanced down the long walk toward the main street. She pinched her lower lip, then quickly dropped her hand when she realized what she was doing. "Where's your car?" she asked.

"Round back. Wanted to make sure I didn't get lost. I mean, I know it's only a block . . . I don't really know why I parked out there. I can swing it around."

"My bus'll be here any minute."

Jimmy sniffed. He hated this ridiculous search for the correct indirect path. What he hated more was making Sandra nervous, although it stung him that she was this nervous after she'd hinted that he return. "It's okay if we call if off," he said. "I know you don't hardly know me. I just thought you wanted me to come by." Jimmy cleared his throat. She didn't move or speak. "I see you closed the store up by yourself."

"Sometimes the Rideauxs take off early. They're the older couple who own it. They've owned this store forever and they struggle with the neighborhood changing. They've been very kind to me." Sandra fanned her throat and seemed to lean in slightly to examine Jimmy. His legs thrummed with the impulse to turn and avoid the inevitable complications. Sandra tugged at her earlobe.

"It's not you," she said. "I'm out of practice with all this."

"I hear you. If you don't want a ride, it's okay." He saw her pupils contract and dilate, imagined the softness of the earlobe between her fingertips. His thoughts teetered. "Look, I ain't good at saying things like this, but I'm gone try and say it. You been real nice to me and I just thought it'd be nice back to give you a ride or walk you to the bus stop. That's it."

Sandra placed her feet together and raised her chin like she was about to sing. "You're parked in back?"

The route they took was ugly—battered neighborhoods and pot-holed roads—but with Sandra beside him, Jimmy was sailing on a cloud. For several blocks Sandra spoke only to say turn right or left, and Jimmy ballooned with things to tell her, a ballooning that made him sweat harder with fear that she wouldn't want to hear any of what he had to say, fear of what would happen if he did tell her. He wondered too why she was so quiet, this woman who had talked his head off, nearly force fed him and made an effort to tell him her name. Had she already put things together to figure out what he lacked?

"How long you been at the store?" he asked.

"Ever since I came to town. About six months."

"And you say you come from north Louisiana?"

"Yes. I didn't like it. It didn't like me. All those self-righteous hypocrites."

The car rumbled over railroad tracks.

"Man, that stinks," Jimmy said.

"You should've lived there."

Jimmy turned to tell her what he'd meant, but he saw her smirking, then her smirk disappeared. "You're not Baptist, are you?" she asked. He shook his head. Beyond her rose the barren forest of pipes, flare stacks and storage tanks, the same ones he'd seen from the expressway the day before. His whole life he hadn't been far from chemical odor, methane from oil fields, vinyl chloride from the plants on Houston Bay, now this, and still he hadn't gotten used to it. The only saving grace was it wasn't manure. "You don't have to smell this all the time, do you?" he asked.

She touched his arm with a fingertip, sending a jolt through him. "See that gray building?" He looked at the tall skyscraper with the baby-bottle tip and nodded. "That's the state capitol building, it's right by my place. Governor Huey Long built that. You heard of Huey Long?"

A test! Jimmy felt a cord stretch tight the length of his insides, yet he uh-huhed anyway. "I heard of him."

"He was governor during the Depression. The Kingfish. Great and crazy and dangerous. He came from north Louisiana. He built that building and put a statue of himself out on the front lawn where a big spotlight shines down on his grave." She touched the tip of her nose. "Or maybe they built that statue after he got killed. I don't remember that part. Anyway, somebody shot him in the hall of that building and you can still see the bullet holes."

The cord in Jimmy tightened even more from her wash of information. Did everybody know all of what she said? Should he know? He cleared his throat. "I don't know much about him," he said, surprised when he heard the words out loud. "I guess I should."

"I don't know about that. We studied him in school cause he was from up there, and when I moved so close to the capitol, I checked out some books on it. I've had a lot of time to read." He felt her eyes on him. "What do you like to read?"

The lie he'd told before came to him, the topics from Pepper's "Reading for the Blind" series, but the lie caught in his throat. He swallowed. "I guess I ain't really partial to reading."

"Oh," she said. Something dropped through his chest, but the heat stayed in his face. He looked high at the capitol again. "You can go all the way to the top," she added, her voice even more hurried. "I've been. I probably saw all the way to Texas." She chuckled and bit her thumb.

The road swung left, humping them over more train tracks. To Jimmy's right, the grassy wall of the levee appeared, but Sandra pointed left and he took that fork toward the capitol, its gray height rising above where he could see through his windshield, his balance swaying. They passed the building and traveled next to its grounds, adorned with moss-bearded oaks, cedars and magnolias. "It's beautiful here," Sandra said, but her voice had lost its energy. "I live in the neighborhood just on the other side. Every morning I try to walk over here before I catch the bus." She directed him to circle the grounds and they pulled onto her street in Spanish Town, which she told him was the original site of a Spanish settlement before the French came and named the place Baton Rouge, which meant "Red Stick" and was a translation of the Indian words for a blood-stained tree that marked the boundaries between tribes. It was another torrent of facts, but Jimmy was less swept this time. She was just as nervous as he was. "I live right there in that building." She pointed to the second floor of a pink, stucco box, crape myrtles lining the sidewalk. She exhaled. "It's not bad." She didn't move. "Thank you," she said, and held out her hand to shake.

"You hungry?" Jimmy asked. Sandra's cheeks pinkened, her eyes darting away from him. "It's okay if you ain't," he said. "You probably got things to do."

She chewed her thumbnail, then moved to her index finger and middle in quick order before jerking away from her teeth. She peered past Jimmy at her house, then picked at her skirt. "I better go, Jimmy. I'm glad you asked me, but I better just go."

"I hear you."

Sandra exited the car in a rush but jogged over to Jimmy's window. He rolled it down, and she bent to his level. "Can you come by the store tomorrow?" she asked.

"Sure."

"Okay. I'll see you there." She touched his arm, then spun and strode toward her place as if walking into a strong wind, waved before disappearing inside.

Jimmy touched the spot she had touched and felt a

feather drift down his windpipe. He rolled up his window and looked forward. Now, how exactly did he get back to J.T.'s?

DAY FIVE

From the passenger seat, J.T. put off heavy smoke. Last night Jimmy had forced himself to buy a newspaper, goaded J.T. into looking at apartment ads, then this morning almost carried him to the car to actually search. At an IHOP J.T. stalled, sipping a pot of coffee and picking at a stack of pancakes before he finally chose a couple of addresses. Then he had gotten them lost going to one and refused to slow down when passing the other. For the last ten minutes, J.T. had been directing Jimmy to cruise a downtown neighborhood where he said good apartments sometimes popped up cheap. Jimmy doubted such apartments existed. He understood the reluctance to take charity, to admit you needed help, but that didn't stop the itch to shake J.T. by the scruff of his neck and force him to accept Jimmy's help.

"Pull over here," J.T. said. Jimmy veered to the curb of the narrow road and stopped in front of a beautiful old house with a wooden sign on a post in front. J.T. tugged at his lips and smacked his mouth, then reached in his pocket and withdrew an envelope. "I want you to look at something," he said, and held a letter out. Jimmy's grip tightened on the steering wheel, his foot pulsed with the urge to press the accelerator to the floor. No way out, though. He took the letter, the paper burning his fingertips, and stared at it. It was typed. At the top of the page sat some kind of seal. He wanted both to crumple the paper and to admit he had no idea what the words said. Instead, he handed the paper to J.T. after what he figured would have been time enough to read it.

"What's this about?" Jimmy said.

"I don't know what it's about. Let's go in and ask him what it's about." J.T. nodded toward the house. Jimmy hated this maneuvering to find out what he didn't know without asking the question that would clue someone in that he didn't know. He wanted to ask who "him" was, but he supposed that would be a sure tip-off he hadn't read the letter. He glanced at the porch swing in front of the house, at the lovely white and red blossoms on the trees in the yard, wished he could floor it and escape.

"This why you been driving me around this neighborhood?" Jimmy asked.

"Hell, yeah, that's why. I didn't know how you'd take this. I got it in the mail and I thought we'd find out about it."

"What for?"

"What do you mean 'what for'?" J.T. shook the paper at him. "It might be big."

"And it might not."

J.T. tilted his head and wrinkled his nose so that his front teeth showed. "What's wrong with you, boy? You afraid to get something that's rightfully yours? This fella wants to do something for you. Maybe even give you money."

Money. The word grated coming from J.T.'s mouth, then shame joined Jimmy's irritation. How could he navigate this? Surely J.T.'s introduction would clue him to who the letter-sender was and what he wanted to do for Jimmy. Just as surely, the money was connected to J.T.'s contacting Jimmy.

"We need to find you a place."

"We *need* to talk to this lawyer. That's why I brought you over here." Jimmy felt a goat-kick to his sternum. *Over here.* J.T. didn't even know what his own words meant. Jimmy revved the engine. J.T. touched

Jimmy's forearm. "Look, I know I shouldn't of sprung this on you. I should've just told you I wanted to stop by here, but some people get funny about seeing lawyers. I can see you're one of them people."

"The lawyer can wait, J.T. We need to move you out of that shack."

J.T. slammed the paper on Jimmy's dash. "Don't talk to me like you're my daddy, you ain't the daddy. I don't need you finding me a place to live, and I don't need you paying my debts. I'm a grown man and I done just fine before you came."

"That right?"

"Yeah that's right. We wouldn't have to be worrying if you hadn't took it in your head to give that bastard six-hundred dollars." J.T. picked up the paper again, stretched out the creases, folded it and slipped it back inside the envelope. He set it on the seat between him and Jimmy. "I appreciate you thought you were doing right, but I'm telling you if you'd given *me* that money we wouldn't be worrying about no apartment, we'd be over at the Hilton or something. The least you can do is the favor of going to see this man."

Jimmy twisted his fists on the steering wheel. He pictured Squint snapping J.T.'s bones one by one, wondered if maybe that *wouldn't* have been a good lesson. It appeared easy to simply step out of the car, trudge the short sidewalk and meet this lawyer, easy also to turn to J.T. and tell him even an illiterate could read dollar signs in a man's eyes. Except that none of it was easy. And even if it was, what good was easy? He could've easily stayed on that ranch, tending chores, doing the books, alone. Could've easily stayed in Houston, grinding through work and going home to his stale apartment, could've easily tried forever to be as ignorant as maybe he was supposed to be, except if the mind didn't tell you there was more, a telegram came and told you and from there on you had to carry that.

"Where you wanta go, J.T.?"

"I wanta go in and see that lawyer."

"I ain't going in there."

"Fine. Then take me over to Mr. Charley's."

Jimmy glared at J.T. and for a terrible second

Pepper's face was there. Jimmy's hand tightened on the wheel as if he were clinging to a rock above a gorge. He turned the key and willed his eyes open again, first at J.T., who gave only the back of his head, then at the road, which seemed headed for a sharp drop.

"Turn right and loop around on Airline," J.T. said. He pointed ahead at the ribbons of intersecting highway that reminded Jimmy of Houston. Jimmy thought about not turning, about going on east toward some place where there was no Charley or Squint, some place he and J.T. could both start over. But then he wondered if that was as stupid as Pepper's drunken gallops away from the spread only to come back worse. Jimmy steered the car into the long curve and straightened them out on a congested four-lane. In the back of his mind, vultures circled.

"You gone ask Mr. Charley for the difference back?" Jimmy asked, even though he knew the question was stupid.

"What?" J.T.'s cheek twitched like a horse's flank shooing a fly.

"The difference from what I give and what you actually owed."

"Did they give you a receipt?"

Jimmy swelled with the urge to hurt J.T. He opened his mouth to breathe and tried not to see J.T. even in his periphery.

"I'm sorry about all what I said back there," J.T. said. "I ain't trying to be an ass, boy, it's just important you see that man."

Dark clouds the color of bruises drifted overhead, throwing patches of shadow. "We'll see," Jimmy said.

"I know you just trying to do right by me, but I been in the ditch before and got out. We'll get out this time if you see fit."

"You talking about that lawy—"

"Stop!" J.T. covered his ears. "I can't hear about that right now. I want you to count backwards from twenty-one. Out loud!"

"Say what?"

"I'm serious! From twenty-one. Do that for me."

Jimmy stared at J.T. On the ranch, Jimmy had encountered a drifter who turned out to be loco, having to be last through the door, taking to sleeping outside ten paces from a building, finally biting a horse that rankled him. Jimmy had told him to leave, Jimmy sixteen, and they'd fought until they were both so tired and hurt neither could move. Then the man cried and left. Could that be J.T.'s sickness? Craziness. Was that what the lawyer was about? He didn't think lawyers handled telling sons their long-lost fathers were crazy, but maybe that was it, some inheritance J.T. wasn't fit to handle or some help J.T. couldn't accept on his own. J.T. waited, his complexion crimson.

"You need to start," he said. "Twenty-one and go backwards."

Jimmy began the count, J.T. patting the dashboard at every number. When they finished, J.T. grinned. "It's erased. Now I feel lucky, real lucky. See that sign, that's Mr. Charley's."

"Where?"

"Right there."

Jimmy slid into the gravel lot and crunched to a stop. Mr. Charley's was a low, wide, ranch building with beer signs in the windows. Parked in front were seven cars, one of them Squint's Lincoln.

"You'll be glad you brought me, Jimmy. I feel it about to happen right in my chest. You ever get that feeling?" Jimmy recalled the telegram, recalled Sandra's eyes. J.T. touched his elbow. "You got any cash?"

"Do what?"

"I hate to ask. I've got some on me, but I sure could use a couple hundred if you got it to spare. You kind of owe me that three hundred as the difference anyway."

"Bullshit."

"All right, all right," J.T. said, waving his hands, "that was the wrong words. You don't owe me. Can you spot me some, though? I'll get it back to you."

"I can't believe you're asking for money to bet against the money I gave."

"For *us* to bet. I'm feeling lucky, son. With you here I can't lose."

Jimmy pushed into his seat. J.T.'s hopeful expression struck him in a way he knew only a fool could be struck, but he pulled the pouch out of his pocket,

peeled off three twenties and gave them to him anyway.
"Later we go look for a place."
"You ain't gonna regret this. Two hours from now
we're gonna have triple this."
J.T. stepped out, the heat gusting in, and came
around to the driver's side. Streams of sweat already
streaked from his hairline, his pupils shrank to black
grains of sand. Jimmy rolled down his window. "Come
watch your old man work," J.T. said. "They'll let you
in the back room if I say so." Beyond J.T., large, yellow
earthmovers crowded a warehouse lot like prehistoric
animals in a pen. "You're my good luck charm, son. Don't
let me down."
"What time you want me to fetch you?"
J.T. scratched his scalp. His nose and mouth danced
in different directions. "I'll get a taxi. Then I'm gonna
take you to supper."
J.T. put out his hand, and Jimmy shook it, he didn't
know why. When the bar door closed behind J.T., another
gust kicked up the dust in the parking lot and lifted the
letter from the seat. Jimmy considered following him in
to make sure there wasn't some post-payment treatment
that Squint would need to inflict. He imagined the stale
beer and cigarette stink, and put the car in reverse.
"Hey!" Jimmy heard. Squint was loping toward the
car. He filled the window as he leaned down, his thick
glasses magnifying his slits. "That your old man?"
"Yep."
"Mr. Charley said his name when we was passing
at the door. How much you give him?"
Jimmy wondered how Squint had read his mind.
"Sixty."
Squint turned his head into the wind, stepped back
and stood straight. "You're fuckin' up, but I understand."
He turned back to Jimmy. "My old man wasn't a loser,
but he was a mean fucker. Made me cut the whole front
yard with a pair of scissors once. Wanted to teach me
discipline. At the dinner table he taped tacks on the arms
of the chair to make me keep my arms off 'em and hit me
if I ate the portions out of order. I still went to see him
on the weekend before he died." Squint dug a finger to its
knuckle into his ear, his eyes strangely opening while he

did it. Then he slapped the car, startling Jimmy. "Gotta go. I'm sure I'll be seeing you."

As Squint's huge back moved away, Jimmy thought of going back inside and pulling J.T. out. That last night, he'd watched Pepper go and had done nothing. Uneasiness skittered through him like a tarantula. Surely something harsh would come of his not stopping J.T., but what could he do? If he stopped him, wouldn't the old man just hail a cab and be back within an hour?

Jimmy shivered, rolled up his window and merged into the traffic heading where he'd come from, knowing that he'd eventually stumble onto the expressway. A hard chill shook through Jimmy despite the day's heat, then his muscles tensed. He swept the envelope onto the floor of the passenger side, then lit a cigarette and scanned the horizon where gray clouds sped across the sky like the bottoms of battleships. A blast of wind shook the car and sent a sail of dust unfurling across the road. A thin stream of smoke rose to his nostrils.

He thought of Pepper again, the closest thing he'd ever had to a father. Jimmy had been thirteen the day he found Pepper's body a quarter mile from the house. He had shooed the buzzards, then covered Pepper's head with his own shirt while he galloped back to call Mr. Sparks. "Broke his neck, looks like," Jimmy said, when Sparks finally got to the phone. He felt as heavy as if he'd thrown Pepper's body across his shoulders. "I'll be damned," Sparks said. "We'll be over directly." Jimmy took Pepper's rifle and rode out to him again, not looking at the mesa that had haunted Pepper and now seeped into him. He sat ten yards from the body at the base of the mesa and fired into the air when the vultures circled too low. The desire to both yell at Pepper and to try and shake him back to life shook through him like a virus. Had Pepper tried to ride up the steep side and tumbled off? Jimmy's mind scrolled back to the previous night and what he should have done. But there had been so many nights. Maybe Pepper's body had simply caught up to the death it had been chasing. Still, Jimmy didn't look up at the mesa, certain it wanted to claim him too, then spat at the ridiculousness of it.

An hour later a plume of dust signaled the arrival

of Sparks and his foreman in a pick-up. Jimmy stood, fired into the air and waved the rifle. The two men stepped from the truck and sauntered over to Pepper, while Jimmy stayed back. "Yep," Mr. Sparks said, "neck's broke. He trying to ride up this slope drunk?" he said to Jimmy, who nodded but couldn't stop the thought that maybe drinking had nothing to do with Pepper's fall. In all his years, he'd never seen Pepper even close to thrown. The men wrapped Pepper in a blanket and put him in the bed of the truck. Sparks offered Jimmy a spot in the cab between them, but Jimmy sat in back.

That evening at the main ranch, Mr. Sparks said Pepper had been a good hand and a tough son of a bitch, then told a story of a trip to Boystown he and Pepper had taken years ago, Pepper winning a tequila-shooting contest and dancing on a bar clad only in boots and Stetson, before slapping a woman and being thrown into the street. The foreman read a Bible verse, and the older hands shoveled dirt onto Pepper's casket. It seemed like Sparks could have done more, talked to Jimmy, but Jimmy didn't know what more could have been done. Pepper was dead. The work had to go on. Jimmy asked to go home and Sparks sent another hand to stay and help out, but when they arrived, Jimmy told the man to leave, then goaded him to fight until the man got back in the truck and drove off.

All that night, Jimmy had stared at the nearby mesa, outlined in the moonlight against the black distance behind it, its huge flat top, parallel sides and rounded edges making it seem man-made and dropped from the sky. Jimmy had once thought Pepper silly to worry so much over a whittled-down mountain, but the dread had infected him. He trembled. At sunrise, he saddled his horse and rode out, the mesa rising as if it might tip toward him. He leaned into the rhythm of the gallop on the rocky ground. Prickly pear, yucca and scraggly shrubs snagged at the horse's legs until Jimmy eased to a trot. A dry wind pushed against them, but they kept on, the mesa's striations of rock coming clearer, layers Pepper had deciphered for him when Jimmy was young, then eventually never mentioned. The ground remained rough but flat, the mesa's odd symmetry jutting without reason or connection to anything around it. The long slopes at its ends extended like ramps, but Jimmy could see with every yard the craggy bluffs of compressed stone he would have to climb. When he neared the mesa, he quivered and hunched his shoulders, even though the day was blazing.

He checked for rattlers at the mesa's foot, then swung off the horse. He dizzied without even looking to the peak, kicked at rocks, cursed Pepper and himself. He felt the mesa towering, felt frightened, then ashamed. It was nothing but a hill, but it had somehow killed Pepper. He wondered if he had helped kill him. He didn't know, and that made him sick. He looped the reins around a bush and started up.

The climb was steep and spiny with cactus, each step a search for a foothold in the loose rock and baked dirt. His boots slipped every few yards. Before he was halfway up, his arches ached and his legs shook. The slope steepened even more, but the mesa wasn't as high as he'd thought. He wondered if things would have been different if he'd forced Pepper to climb it, then saw Pepper's stubborn, bitter face and ropy muscles. The back of his neck heated as if someone had lain a hot skillet there.

The wind expanded in Jimmy's ears. The sky lost more and more of its color. The peak's distance became uncertain, at once closer and farther away. He picked his way through a path to the top and looked out. The world spread forever. Plains forever and also other mesas far beyond the tiny cluster of buildings below. So much, so far. Too much for Pepper. For Jimmy too? His heart thumped. He staggered and knelt to keep from toppling backward. The mesa quaked beneath him, a quake Jimmy knew was in his own knees, but yet struck him as laughter, as scorn at being frozen to help Pepper. A tiny twister spun up inside him. He dropped his head, but the twister uncoiled, ferocious and defiant. Grief raked through him. What did he have? Pepper was dead, he himself barely able to balance on solid ground. The drop from here could cure it all.

He stood, bullied his eyes up and out, vertigo wavering him, then met the sky. Let it pour in and swirl.

He raised his arms and knew that he could fly out and all this swirling would be gone, but Pepper's bent neck came to him, and the nothing of dark night too, and he didn't want that. He dropped his arms and looked to the tilting horizon, endless and calling with what he didn't know.

WHEN J.T. RECEIVED THE LETTER

J.T. barely noticed it among the stack. He tossed the mail onto his kitchen table, then sat and skimmed the rental ads for the tenth time. He had two-hundred fourteen dollars and no car. Even the smallest garage apartment in this neighborhood started at one-fifty a month and that didn't include deposit or utilities. Plus, he'd been in this spot for two years and it was beyond sweet for the price. His only hope to pay off Mr. Charley and stay here not too far from the college was a blackjack game tonight, actually a pretty good hope since blackjack was his game. After all, he was up almost two hundred for the year—if you didn't count losing his car and it was a shitty old car anyway—just badly down the past month. His luck was due for another change upward. Still, he didn't like going in without confidence or at least a good feeling and the only real feeling he had was a slither and coil like a boa constrictor wrapping around his windpipe.

J.T. shoved the newspaper aside and glared at the stack of envelopes. Surely more bad news. He shuffled, BILL PAST DUE, shuffled, BILL PAST DUE, shuffled, SALE, shuffled, Ray Bourgeouis, Attorney at Law. He wrinkled his nose. Shit, not a lawsuit too. He glanced at the cabinets he knew were empty. Oh, well, he had nothing to lose. He slipped his finger under the flap and ripped, removed the letter and unfolded it.

"Dear Mr. James Thomas Strawhorn,
We are seeking James Thomas Strawhorn born August 25th, 1959, as a possible plaintiff in a class-action suit against the state of Louisiana. If you are he, or if you know his whereabouts, please contact our office at the above number. This matter is of utmost urgency."

J.T. let the letter slip from his grasp and scratched his chin. James Thomas Strawhorn, August 25th, 1959. He reread the letter, numbness building in his fingers. So long ago that he sometimes barely remembered he had a son. No, that wasn't exactly true. Sometimes he remembered, mostly in unexpected flashes—a young dark-skinned woman with that certain manic charge about her; a baby that scared the shit out of him—late at night when the money was low and no luck in sight. Years ago he'd even thought of searching for him, but that thought only led to impossible questions: How to start? What to ask? And why track him at all? What would J.T. say if he found him? That his father had been scraping by all these years after he'd split from baby Jimmy and his mother, that there was still nothing he could give, not even clear details of what had actually happened. He doubted if he even knew the real details, was reminded by a sharp poke inside his gut that he most likely did, but doubted it would do any good to plumb for them. His ears burned worse.

He picked up the letter. "Plaintiff against the state of Louisiana." That had a lucrative ring to it. How much could a good lawyer shake out of a state, especially a state as flimsy and corrupt as this one? More importantly, how much would an abandoned son be willing to share? Who knew. All he knew was he had to come up with serious cash or get the hell out of here before Charley sent that blind gorilla out to collect. That was something J.T. definitely wasn't up for. Spending a little time contacting this lawyer didn't seem like a bad bet.

J.T. lifted his phone and smiled. Still in service. He dialed the number on the letter, thinking how everybody

in life received one big break. Granted for some people,
suckers and losers, that big break might just be being
born, or dying, but for anybody with savvy and initiative
that break offered something major, something large,
something to line your cage.

"Good morning, law office of Ray Bourgeouis,
Janet speaking."

"Good morning, Janet. This is James Thomas
Strawhorn. I just received a letter in the mail about
a class-action suit, and I'm calling in to see what the
deal is."

"Yes, Mr. Strawhorn. Are you the person named
in the letter?"

"Yes, ma'am, I'm James Thomas Strawhorn."

"And were you born on the date given in the
letter?"

"Not exactly. The person you're talking about is
my son."

"I see. Are you in contact with him, or do you know
where he is?"

"I don't. To tell the truth, I haven't seen him since
he was a baby and his mother lit out with him. That's
why I was calling, to see if y'all knew where he was."

"Mr. Strawhorn, would you hold please?"

J.T. tugged at his lower lip as the On Hold music
tinkled through the receiver. He was sure he'd screwed
up since he was pretty sure there was some law that
kept parents who'd left their kids from getting their
grown addresses, like the state had the right to that
business. He should've just gone to the office, looked
somebody in the eye and worked it that way.

"Mr. Strawhorn," came a man's voice.

"Yes, sir. James Thomas Strawhorn."

"I'm Ray Bourgeouis. I'm handling the class-action
suit which I believe your son could be a litigant in. You
say you don't know where he is?"

"No, sir, I don't. But I'd like to. I ain't, uh, haven't
seen him since he was just a baby and his mother ran off
with him. She had, how do you call it, mental problems,
and it wasn't till today when I got y'all's letter that I'd
had any word on him. I thought maybe my son was
dead or something."

J.T. strained during the pause, believing he could hear a pencil tapping on a desk top.

"Well, Mr. Strawhorn, I hope the letter didn't give you a shock. I wish you the best in sorting all this out, but we're disallowed by law from giving you information on your son, even if we had it to give. We were actually hoping that you might be your son. We're mailing out to any similar names we can find through the phone book or parish records."

J.T. cleared his throat at the thought of being so easily trackable. "So you're saying you don't even really know if my son's alive?"

"I can't divulge that information. We're just trying all opportunities to find people who might benefit from this suit and since your name is the same as your son's, you received this letter. I'm terribly sorry."

"Hold on, hold on, it's all right. I just want to ask you if you could tell him about me if you do find him? Could you do just that?"

"To tell the truth, right now I don't know if we will find him. Most of the plaintiffs in this case have already come forward, and the case is actually very far along, so the people in this latest mailing are the ones we've had a great deal of trouble locating."

"Does that mean you won't tell him?"

"That's just not part of our function. We would be in very tricky territory there."

A thin coat of heat scurried over J.T. He shifted the receiver to his other ear. "*You'd* be. I got a son I ain't seen since his mother snuck off with him and you're in tricky territory. Let me tell—"

"I'm terribly sorry, Mr. Strawhorn. I'm sending you back to Janet now."

The click was a pencil stab to J.T.'s ear drum. Typical. Some hot shot double-talker sluffing him off. He should've gone down there. Still could . . . "Mr. Strawhorn?"

"Yes, ma'am?"

"Is there anything else we can do for you?"

J.T. worked his fingertips on the stationary's letterhead, as if some secret message might be revealed. "I guess not, Janet. You've been mighty kind. You can imagine this all comes as pretty much of a shock, finding out like this that James Junior might still be alive and not knowing how to find him."

"I'm very sorry."

"It ain't your fault, yours nor Mr. . . . uh, Mr. Bourgeouis'. I just wish there was some way to let him know I'm still around if you do contact him."

"We can't really—"

"I know. The law. I understand. I wouldn't want y'all breaking the law, especially since y'all're just trying to help my son, I understand that." Silence. "Janet, thanks so much. Good luck and thank you for listening."

J.T. hung up, a hollowness in his sternum he didn't expect. He breathed deeply and blew out hard, shook his arms. No time for slowing down. He glanced at his watch. 2:27. Charley used to be flexible, but that had changed some. If you paid him within a week, the interest rate was only fifteen percent. The second week it bumped up to thirty-five percent. The third, a hundred percent and the threats began. Or so J.T. had been told. He'd never gotten in this much of a jam before. Tomorrow was the start of the third week and he'd heard stories that Charley's new man meant bad business.

He opened the phone book to the yellow pages— "Rentals"—and skimmed until he found "Vacancy Smashers." He didn't like the sound of that, but he had to be out of this place by tomorrow night. Still, he thought he'd detected a note of pain and sympathy in Janet's voice and that was at least a crack in the wall. He picked up the phone, paused, peeked at his watch again, and dialed for a taxi.

Luckily, across the street from the law office was a bus stop bench beneath an oak tree's canopy and J.T. took up his spot there. The office was an old renovated house downtown, its porch adorned with ornate railing, shutters painted peach in contrast to the forest green of the house itself, and a large crape myrtle in pink bloom in the small yard. A house like J.T. would never have. Most likely. Unless. He picked at his cuticles, hoping that the lawyer would leave first, hoping that he could pick Janet out and talk to her before she reached her car. From her voice, he guessed her to be in her forties or so, a mother herself if he was lucky, but no matter what age and experience he felt good about his odds. J.T. spread his arms on the back of the bench and stretched his legs. A gust of wind kicked up and the sun disappeared as thunderstorm clouds scudded over. Rain would be a definite inconvenience, but being a little drenched might also help him in the pity department. Nonetheless, he would rather stay dry. This was his best of two suits and he didn't want to worry about it being ruined during the next couple of days when things would be moving fast. He'd found a cheap crummy apartment pretty quickly over the phone while waiting for the taxi, and now all he had to do was pay the kid with the pick-up two houses down twenty bucks to cart his bed and clothes to the new place, which he knew was a ghetto, but still probably the safest place for him. It was a risk to let even the kid know where he was going, but he didn't see any other way to take some of his few belongings with him.

J.T. breathed in deeply, the heaviness of magnolia blossoms nicely sweet for a moment, then nearly sickening. There had been a brief time when he'd had a place with a magnolia in front, down on 12th Street he seemed to remember, although now he couldn't be exactly sure of when or where. So many jobs, so many moves, so much history thrown like puzzle pieces and no time or inclination to fit them together. It was a chore to clearly remember Morita, much less their son, remember her thick black hair, her intense dark eyes, her glowing mocha skin . . . He veered sharply away, shaking his head. No need to go to that unpleasantness. Enough was enough for one day. Nonetheless, the memory of her brushed through him again with harsh wings, and he stared straight ahead at a fire hydrant, its strange contours blurring yellow.

A gust shook the tree. A burst of rain opened at an angle, and J.T. hopped up and hid on the side of the tree trunk away from the wind. The haze he'd briefly encountered cleared some. He shook his arms, stomped his feet and pressed the center of his forehead as if restoring circulation. He wondered for a moment what his son would look like, then shook that off. It was more important what he would tell a grown son should he meet him, the sketchy story he feared was lurking in him or a story that made everyone feel better? Not that it mattered yet. The whole thing was a long shot. Jimmy and Morita had been a brief, bizarre invasion, and it was better to leave it like that for now. For all he knew his son was dead or at least unreachable. The main concern was to find out what he could.

The thunderstorm sped through, the last plump drops falling when J.T. saw a Mercedes heading out of the lawyer's driveway. A twinge of panic shot through him as he realized his miscalcuation. Janet was probably parked in back, would go to her car there rather than leave through the front, and that would make things trickier, make it more threatening if J.T. showed up in the rear of the house. The Mercedes was most likely the lawyer's car, which meant Janet might be inside alone, wrapping up the day, getting ready to leave through the back, or already in the parking lot. J.T. brushed the rain from the shoulders of his sports coat and hustled across the street and up the steps. On the door a sign read "Come In," but he still knocked lightly before turning the knob and entering, a sigh of relief leaving him at finding the office still open. The receptionist's desk had no one behind it. Its top was neatly ordered. A radio whispered music. J.T. considered stepping over to the desk, quickly checking what he might, but he decided to stay where he was and call out, "Hello, anybody here?"

A woman in a green dress strode into the room, smoothing her skirt. "You surprised me," she said. "I thought I'd locked that door. I was just getting ready to leave." She moved behind her desk but did not sit. She looked to be in her early fifties, a good-looking woman whose waist had thickened and whose face had lined.

"Are you Janet? I'm sorry to bother you. We talked on the phone earlier. I'm J.T. Strawhorn."

She looked puzzled. "*You're* Mr. Strawhorn?" She seemed to think a moment, then her mouth tightened. "I don't quite see how that can be your son," she said.

"That's his birth date. My boy's."

She gave a look as though she smelled something

bad, glanced down at her desk and shuffled a couple of papers. "Mr. Strawhorn, like I said on the phone—"

"Yes, ma'am, I know, and I'm not gonna push this, but I just want to ask you one question. Do you have children?"

Janet touched her auburn hair above her brow, then put her fingers to her chin. "Yes, I do, but I still don't see how he could be yours."

"I don't know why you to say that. He is and I only have the one and I've never seen him since he was a baby."

"I'm terribly sorry—"

"My wife just wasn't right, Janet. I tried hard to take care of them, but she had spells when she wouldn't trust nobody, she was sick, and one day I came home from work and her and my son were gone, just gone. I waited and waited for her to come home, I tried to get the police to help me, I asked all around and kept asking for years, even kept going to the police and they wouldn't help me and nobody at the state would help me and now after all these years . . . " Janet didn't speak or move and neither did J.T. He could see his words working their way through her, her face contracting then softening. He held his arms out in a plea. "Janet, I know your boss has to serve the law and do what he does, I know that. And I know you have to protect your job, but this is my only chance to find my son who I ain't seen in twenty-some years. I swear, if you help me, you won't ever hear of me again unless my son one day tells you the happy story about finally getting together with his dad. I'm begging you."

She breathed in for what seemed an hour. Parts of her face twitched in calculations J.T. could only guess at. "After we talked I double checked," she said. "Your son's been incredibly hard to locate, but we do have another possible address for him from years back, in Texas. We sent a letter off to that address too, but we never received an answer."

"Did y'all call there?"

Janet's shoulders rose. "We have hundreds of plaintiffs. We can't call them all."

"I could call." Janet exhaled heavily and turned

to a filing cabinet behind her. She removed a file, set it on her desk top and motioned him over. She turned the file toward J.T., placed a pen and paper in front of him. He didn't move. He stared at the words on the page, his name, his son's birthday, his son's address. He picked up the pen, but she covered his hand with hers. "I've worked here fifteen years," she said. "I can't lose this job." J.T. nodded, then scribbled down the address in Texas, a stranger's name, Sparks' Ranch, a route number and a zip code.

"Who's this?" he asked.

"I can't tell you that, and you have to promise not to tell him how you got this address. Do you promise?"

"I promise." J.T. finished writing and looked up. "You don't have a phone number, do you?"

Janet lifted the folder from in front of him, slightly squinted and turned to replace the file in the cabinet. "That's all we have." She examined the paper as if she suddenly wanted to snatch it from him. He folded it and placed it in his pocket, wondering if the tone of his voice had shifted to tell her something, thinking of how he'd never been good at poker.

"I don't know why I'm helping you," she said. "What did you expect, doing what you did?"

J.T.'s mind careened to an image of him handing the baby to a stranger at a hospital, something Janet couldn't possibly know, then he recognized the tone of voice, thought of Morita's dark skin and Jimmy's birth certificate. "You don't know what I did, and you don't know why."

"Hold on right here," J.T. said, and the cab driver pulled up short. In front of his apartment sat a gold Lincoln Continental, a car he recognized from Charley's. "Cruise on down the street and drop me around the corner." The cab bucked into motion with J.T. slumped in the back seat, peering out the side window. As they passed the house to the rear of which he lived, J.T. looked down the driveway and saw a large man with his face against the window of J.T.'s place. "Shit," J.T. muttered. He hadn't expected Charley's new man to show up early,

even though it figured that the harder-assed Charley
might send this messenger to spook him, figured that
something would be working to derail the streak that
getting his son's address had started. J.T. peeled off a
five for the cabbie, then crept to the corner and peeked
from behind a tree. He had seen this gorilla around for
a month but had only met him once, a seemingly good-
natured ex-LSU defensive tackle who could barely see
and had paws the size of skillets. J.T. knew for a fact,
though, that this new boy wasn't good-natured when it
came to business and that's exactly why Charley had
hired him. That pissed J.T. off.

J.T. scurried through two yards and ducked behind
an azalea bush at the exact moment the huge man
appeared, strolling toward his car. J.T. crouched and
peered through the leaves. The man paused, lifted his
chin as if to sniff the breeze, then gazed in the direction
of J.T.'s hiding spot. J.T. swallowed and stayed still. As
big as the man was it still seemed unlikely J.T. could
outrun him, but then he thought how unlikely it was the
goon would grab him on the street. And fuck Charley.
J.T. had never owed this much or been this late before
or avoided letting Charley know the deal, but still, why
was that asshole hounding him like J.T. wasn't going to
pay? He waited for the goon to move to his car door, then
J.T. scooted from behind the bush and onto the sidewalk,
where he sauntered toward him, whistling and jauntily
swinging his arms. The man paused and craned toward
J.T., and J.T. fought the dryness of his mouth to keep
on blowing a tune. "Howdy," J.T. said as he moved along
the opposite side of the car.

"J.T. Strawhorn?" the man asked.

"Pardon?"

"You're J.T. Strawhorn, ain't you?"

"No, uh uh. Name's Don. Don Bourgeouis."

"Don Bourgeouis," the man said, looking sideways
through his thick glasses. "Well, Don, you wouldn't
happen to know the fella that lives back there in that
little apartment?"

"What's his name?"

"You figure it out." The size of the man was even
greater than J.T. recalled. Standing here on the street

in the wide world made him larger rather than smaller, a dumpster set on end. J.T. thought maybe he had made a mistake leaving his hiding place, but he couldn't help giving a jab to Charley's boy that Charley would surely eventually understand was a jab at him. "Don't know the person who lives there," J.T. said. "I live a couple blocks over."

The gorilla leaned on the top of the Lincoln. His eyes looked like gelatinous disks. "I was told he's a red-headed fella like you. Told he was about your height and might be a smart-aleck. And I recall seeing you at the bar. You still don't know him?"

"No, sir. I'm just out for a walk."

The gorilla smiled. "Well it's a pretty nice afternoon for a walk. Especially for those that can walk."

"I'm lucky my legs are in fine shape."

"Uh huh." The gorilla stood straight and tugged his shirt collar. "Do me a favor. If you do happen to run into this fella, you tell him I'll be coming back real soon to settle with him. And tell him that the special rate for a smart aleck is a little extra thrown in for free."

"I don't suppose I'll meet him, but I'm sure he'd like to hear about all that friendly attention."

The gorilla bonged the roof of his car once like a kettle drum, then ducked inside, cranked it and crawled off. J.T. watched until the Lincoln was out of sight, trying to work spit into his mouth and to decide if he should wait a while before entering his apartment. He didn't have time to wait, though, so he headed up the driveway, wondering whether he'd miscalculated by antagonizing Charley's man yet still glad that he had. Charley always held the high cards. This time J.T. was going to show him.

It took J.T. a while with an operator before he could find the area code and number for the man whose name Janet had given him. He was relieved that the phone was still connected but had begun to worry on the seventh ring that the line might be cut before the call went through. Then the phone picked up, and eventually a deep slow country voice answered.

"Yeah, hello," J.T. said, suddenly unsure of how to proceed. "This is J.T. Strawhorn, James Thomas

Strawhorn Junior's father. Somebody told me that I could reach him at this number."

"Say your name is Strawhorn?"

"Yes, sir. Are you Mr. Sparks?"

"Yeah, I'm Sparks. What'd you say your business was?" Sparks was the slowest talker J.T. had ever heard. Between each word J.T. supposed he could count to one-thousand one, and he found himself slowing down to match the pace.

"It's a long story, Mr. Sparks. Let's just say that my son was taken from me when he was a baby, and I've found out that he might be at this number working or something."

"How'd you come on my number?"

"A lawyer gave it to me. He's trying to find my son because he stands to make some money from a law suit." The silence stretched out. He pictured Sparks as John-Wayne like, not exactly John Wayne, but John Wayne-sized and with Winchester rifles racked on the walls near a mounted head of a longhorn steer.

"Jimmy Strawhorn growed up on my land. I brought him in as a foster child over twenty year ago. You say you his father?"

J.T.'s throat tightened. A quiver traveled through his entire body. He'd found him. "I know this is cockeyed, Mr. Sparks. See, I've been trying to find out where he went for years and today I got this paper in the mail thinking I was him and it put me onto your number. You say you call him Jimmy?"

"That's right."

"He lives there?" J.T. waited for an answer. He knew he should have planned this better, but even if he didn't get an answer, he knew he could find this place somewhere out in Texas, thought maybe he should just go there, find his son and tell him . . . tell him what? He swallowed.

"Mister," said Sparks, "I don't know how a man sposed to been dead long as you come to call me on the phone. I ain't sure you ain't some government man trying to find something you ain't got a right to neither. I got a letter that I throwed out." There was another long pause, so long J.T. wondered if the man had left the phone, except that he could still hear breathing. "What color hair you got, Mr. Strawhorn?"

"Red hair. And blue eyes. I don't know if that's what my son would have now, but that's what he had as a baby. The hair I mean. His mother had dark hair and dark eyes."

"Uh huh. Look, I'm gone tell you what. I don't know what to make of all this business, so I'm gone just give you Jimmy's phone number and you can take it up with him."

"I'd appreciate that, sir. I'd really like to get his address, too, if I could though. I might like to write him before I talk to him, make sure he wants to talk to me."

"Writing might could be a problem." Sparks gave a long exhale. "Reckon I could do that anyhow though. Hold your horses a minute." Sparks left the phone for what seemed like five minutes. J.T. peeked through the curtains to make sure Charley's man hadn't sneaked back down the drive. He began to drum his fingers. He didn't have many belongings, but he doubted he could risk packing them all. He would take the essentials and return later if the opportunity came. If not, it wouldn't be the first time he'd shed and run, a thought that made him belch.

"Mr. Strawhorn," came Sparks' voice, startling J.T. "I wanta tell you something, and I want you to listen. I best not find out you tricked me into giving you these here numbers and you ain't who you say you are. I don't take kindly to folks playing crooked with me. You hear?"

"Yes, sir, I hear. I guarantee I am who I say I am."

DAY FIVE, AFTERNOON

"I've never been here," Sandra said as they strolled along the sidewalk of the campus parade ground. Above them the crape myrtles dripped rain and tiny flowers. Nearby, the university clock tower chimed three. "I'd heard it was pretty, but I didn't really have anybody to go with."

"It is pretty," he said, but his fingertips dented the can of Coke he carried. He regretted agreeing to go across campus. Everyone carried books. Everyone looked like they were going to read a book. Inside every building lurked books. His brain screamed nakedness. His tongue threatened to burst from his mouth and confess his ignorance, just end it now before it went too far and she cut him loose. But he kept walking beside her, between beige stone buildings with arched walkways and red-tiled roofs, the soupy air sweet but not so much that Sandra's aroma didn't reach him. He almost found solace in her presence, but when they passed the glass front of the library, he remembered himself slinking toward a library in Houston where he'd seen on TV they taught reading, imagined his expression that day as drawn and pale as if he were about to be slaughtered. He'd stopped on the fourth step, the heat of judging eyes already on him, even though a breeze had blown November cool and the inside of the library was twenty feet away. He'd turned and long-stepped to his car, thrown up beside it before heading home. The desire, now, to shatter this library's windows flitted through him. "I lived on a campus for a while," she said. Jimmy snapped to, worried that Sandra had sensed his emotions, but she was scanning her surroundings, her arms hugging her own waist. He felt translucent, but the sight of her made him inflate a little with happiness, something he didn't expect or trust. "Not a college campus, a sort of high school campus in California. My momma sent me."

"Your momma sent you?"

Sandra nodded, her lips pressing together, tilted her long neck toward Jimmy and brushed damp strands of hair from her forehead. "She was into all kinds of stuff at one time or another. Macro-biotics, zen, Shiatsu. When I was real young, she didn't like where we lived, right in the middle of the Bible Belt where she thought people disapproved of us because she was different. I don't know why we didn't move, except she had a steady little job with a lawyer and she didn't know much about anywhere else." She smiled. "It made us like sisters, though, us against the world. We could talk about anything, I could dress like I wanted to, kind of do what I wanted to, and she just told me to ignore the girls at school who went on about how we didn't go to church and how my momma had me without being married or how if you got me started talking I had a hard time stopping." Sandra hugged herself and watched the ground as she kept walking.

"So you went to that school," Jimmy said.

"Oh, sorry. I get off the point. It's just I haven't talked much to anybody except the Rideauxs and customers at the drug store, I mean not talked to anybody about anything that counts . . . . Does my talking bother you?"

"I like it."

"You say that." She searched him for a second as if he might be trying to steal something. "Anyway, yeah, she sent me. Something terrible happened to her when I was fourteen. I guess she got tired and lonely and horribly depressed living in that claustrophobic place. She used to once in a while bring home these sweet, strange, odd men—not keep them around long but just see them a while—and then that stopped all of a sudden, and she got sad and depressed. I thought I was going to lose her. It was like something took her over for months. Then almost out of the blue, she married this furniture salesman and it was like she started seeing me through his eyes, the same eyes as all the people she'd always said thought we were strange. Whatever it was, they packed me up and sent me off to this school in California."

Jimmy rubbed his palms together. He felt as though a pile of rocks had come loose from a hillside and were tumbling over him. So much information, and yet he liked that she was opening up. He remembered exactly the last time someone had done that, thirteen months before, a woman he went out with for a couple of months, a sweet woman, even when she decided without explanation they couldn't see each other anymore. He figured he knew the reason. He cleared his throat, worried for a moment that his thoughts had broadcast to Sandra. What to say?

"I've never been to California."

"Well you wouldn't have wanted to go where I went. It was supposed to be enlightened, the brochures said it was, but it ended up being as strict as a fundamentalist or military school, except with a hodge-podge of Eastern religions as cover. Every morning they got us up at four a.m. to chant, and they had us chant again at lunch and before bed, and they walked around like drill sergeants making sure you didn't skimp on your chanting. If they thought you weren't serious, they kept you there chanting until they thought it was right and it didn't matter if you were sick or what. Then at night they had curfews, so we couldn't go off-campus except with designated groups and chaperones, and we couldn't listen to music either, except this plinky sitar music. They said they wanted us to focus all our energies on our upper chakras and if we listened to rock n roll, all our energies would get trapped down in our lower chakras. I finally snuck out every chance I got and went into town, even though it wasn't much of a town. One night the head watchdog caught me sneaking back in late from seeing a boy and they kicked me out." Her mouth grinned, but her eyes didn't. "I was so happy they did. I hadn't really told my momma on the phone what was going on, wasn't really talking to her that much, but I thought when I got back to Louisiana she'd be changed back the way she used to be and understand because she was glad to see me. I was so stupid." Sandra rested her palm on the base of her throat and raised her face to the damp wind. Jimmy's eyes traced the smooth cords of her neck, the creamy ridge of her windpipe, saw himself leaning to place his lips there. She glanced at him with watery eyes and snapped to attention. "I'm sorry," she said. "You don't need to hear all that."

"You ain't got to keep saying you're sorry. I wanted to hear."

"You're sweet," she said, but he wasn't sure her face said it. "It's just so nice being out of that store I get carried away."

"I'm glad you told me."

"You really are?"

"I am. I like to know what's going on." He pinched at his lower lip. "You mind telling me what your momma did when you got home?"

"She barely did anything. She hardly noticed me. Her husband made some remarks that came down to I was a slut and he wouldn't put up with it under his roof, but they both just mostly ignored me. I got out of there as soon as I finished high school."

They were still walking, but Jimmy's feet seemed wrongly jointed to his legs. He wanted to put his arm around Sandra and tell her it was all right, but his thoughts shorted at the thought of how he barely knew her, at her possible reaction and at so much he didn't comprehend—zen, shiatsu, chakras. "You want a sip of Coke?" he asked. She took the can from him, tilted it and handed it back. Jimmy stared at the place her lips had been, a slight lipstick smudge left behind.

"Oh," she said, "I should've wiped that." She reached for the can, but Jimmy moved it from her. "It's all right," he said, and raised the drink to his mouth, her taste sluicing through him like cool water. She touched his forearm.

"Did it bother you, me mentioning I was seeing boys?"

"I didn't consider it."

She nodded. "Hey," she said, pointed and tugged his wrist toward two small green hills between a road and the cluster of buildings they had just left. "I've read about those." She brought them to a plaque and began to read. Jimmy turned sideways and pretended to scan the campus, heat creeping up his throat. He'd usually say something like *What exactly you think they're getting at*, but he didn't want to say those words, felt that he *couldn't* say those words to her.

"This is interesting," she said. "Indian burial mounds. You should read it." He nodded. She touched her chin and sucked in her lips for a second. "You sure you don't want to look?"

"I'm fine." She rubbed the ends of her hair.

"You ever seen a tiger?" she asked. The football stadium's gray rim stood above the other buildings, and they headed down a slope toward it until they came to a cage where a tiger sprawled on the concrete. Jimmy wanted to bolt and run, felt acid rising into his chest and throat, but he forced himself to walk as if this were the most leisurely stroll of his life. When the cage came into sight, Sandra skipped up and wrapped her hands around the bars. The tiger's side rose and fell, his white underbelly and orange stripes radiant, his torso as long as a man's whole body. Jimmy had never seen a tiger in person, but he'd watched about them on TV, heard about them on the tapes Floyd had helped him order. Jimmy pictured the cat striding after an antelope, then imagined him chasing a rider across the Texas plain. He smiled.

"He's beautiful," Sandra said. "It's sad to see him in there all by himself."

"I hear they like to be off to themselves." She looked at him. "Maybe we oughta let him aloose, though. I could take him to J.T.'s. They could set a spell together."

Sandra squinted. "J.T. That's your father, right? I've been going on and on, and I should have asked you about him. What's he like? If you don't mind saying."

Jimmy tried to place what J.T. was like. His arms tingled and itched. "I reckon he's all right."

"All right?"

Jimmy fiddled with his cigarette pack, then dropped his hand. "Well, he borrows money and gambles it away."

"That's not good." Sandra picked at her thumbnail with her other thumbnail, then bit at it before snatching it down. She extended her fingers, displaying nails painted navy blue, all of them gnawed short. "I guess at least getting to know him is something."

"I reckon. So you don't carry your daddy's name?"

"No."

"And here I am carrying J.T.'s and didn't even know he was alive."

"How'd that happen?"

"I don't rightly know." Jimmy bent and peeled a wet leaf from the concrete. He tore it along the veins, balled the pieces and tossed them one at a time. "I was taken in by a man name of Sparks when I was just a tyke and he told me I was an orphan. Then all of a sudden I get a telegram from a man claiming he's my real father."

"Do you know where he's been?"

"Said my momma run off with me and he couldn't track me down until recently."

"And Sparks didn't adopt you?"

The tiger stood and sauntered into the darkness of his den. Jimmy scraped his boots on the cement. "Nope."

"Did you ever ask why?"

He shook his head and inadvertently sucked air through his teeth. Why hadn't he asked? He coughed and felt his cheeks warm. "Spose I should have, shouldn't I. Never much thought about it. He was over to the main ranch and I was out on a smaller spread with Pepper, the man that mostly raised me, till he died. After that I pretty much run the small spread on my own."

"How old were you?"

"Thirteen, just about fourteen. Rough age for both of us, seems like. Sparks sent hands over to help when I needed 'em, and I had a truck for when I needed to go to town, so I was all right."

"That's an odd story, Jimmy."

"Maybe so. J.T. reckons my momma gave me up for adoption, and Louisiana mixed it all up and called me an orphan."

"So Sparks took you in in Louisiana?"

"Texas."

"So maybe your mother took you to Texas. I guess that *would* be hard to track."

Jimmy's vision spun a quarter rotation. "You want to take a spot on that bench?" he asked, and they walked over, Jimmy's eyes hard on the ground. The concrete of the bench was damp, and Sandra smiled and shrugged when they sat. A young man and woman with book sacks strolled past them and over near the bars. They wore white T-shirts and khaki shorts that set off their deep tans. The young man put his fingers to his mouth and whistled loudly, called to Mike to get out here so they could take a look, then laughed. Jimmy could tell they weren't much younger than he was, but it seemed he was much older, seemed too they radiated a power and ease he could only imagine. They had the look of money, had the posture that made him doubt they even saw him, or saw him at most as simply a drone to do something for them like so many of the people who ordered him here and there at the Home Depot. He didn't have any reason to judge them like this, didn't even know why he noticed unless it was being on this campus where he didn't belong. "Ain't many folks out for such a big place," he said.

"Summer school. Might even be between sessions."

Jimmy sneaked a look at Sandra to see if he'd committed some sort of giveaway, and she straightened and turned fully to him. "You didn't say what school was like for you."

He scrolled through misdirections he'd told before, then looked just past her at the creamy gray backdrop of clouds, feeling regret already. "I didn't go to regular school. Pepper taught me."

"You never went to school at all?"

Jimmy's neck flushed. He held the edge of the bench. "I reckon I learned what I needed."

"Yeah, of course. I didn't mean to say you didn't."

They sat silently for a while, Jimmy's mind anticipating the words she would eventually say to signal that they wouldn't be spending any more time together. He sipped his Coke again, the taste of her lipstick surprising him. He looked to her, figured if he had nothing to lose then he might as well find out more.

"How you'd come to be here, Sandra?"

"In Baton Rouge? I just had to get away."

"How come you to land here?"

"Because it was the first bus out of town." She picked up the Coke, took a long drink and clunked it down on the bench. "If I tell you now you won't like me, and you won't like me later anyway if I don't."

"You don't have to te—"

"It's screwed up. I'm screwed up." She pressed her palm to her forehead. "I may as well get it out of the way." She fixed on him as if she'd been challenged. "I had to leave. I was with somebody and he left and I had to get away."

"Had to?"

"I felt like I had to. He just stopped wanting me. I was stupid to hook up with him anyway." She pumped her feet as if working organ pedals. "It was like when I moved out from my momma's and Buddy's, I thought I might go to college or something, but I ended up just working in restaurants and bars and partying, I don't know, just to show her I guess or I don't know why. It was fun. I got caught up in it. Then a couple of years went by and I was kind of sick of it, not being with anybody more than, you know, a little while. Less than a little while. I just felt by myself." She exhaled through her nose, leaned forward and put her elbows on her knees.

"So I met this guy—Hilly was his name, a funny name—not from around there, from out west, and I really liked him because he was sweet and he listened and he didn't get impatient with me going on and on and we," she glanced at Jimmy and shrugged, "we had good chemistry. I guess I thought that if I stuck with him things might be different, but they didn't stay different for long. He moved in with me and it was good for a couple of months and then he started getting impatient and he got jealous about men I'd been with before and started telling me I was weird and I oughta just make up my mind about things and do them. Then one day I came home and his stuff was gone and he was gone." She shot to her feet and turned away. "See, it's stupid. We should go, I need to get home." Jimmy watched her back, wondered if she was crying and almost laid his hand on the small of her waist. She spun to him as if she'd read his mind. "What are you going to do?" she asked. He nearly fell backwards off the bench.

"Nothing."

"Are you going to stay around here or head back to Texas?"

Spots swam before Jimmy. He rubbed his neck. "I spose I might stay here. I got to get J.T. settled and all, maybe try to find out something about my momma."

"Well, I hope you do stay," she said, almost as if cursing. She kissed Jimmy lightly on the mouth, then strode away in the direction they had come.

As Jimmy turned onto J.T.'s street, Sandra's kiss lingered, despite her odd behavior. Walking back from the tiger cage, she had fallen silent, had stayed silent all the way to her house, and Jimmy hadn't spoken to break the quiet. He had sensed things, distance and sadness mostly, but he had no idea if his senses were right. In front of her apartment he asked her if she was working tomorrow (she was), asked her if she would mind his dropping in (she wouldn't), told her that he'd had a great time (so had she) and then she was gone without another touch, without even a solid look. She was as strange as he felt. Up ahead, on the side of the road, three young black men stood on J.T.'s shoulder where Jimmy had parked before. Two wore sunglasses, but Jimmy could tell they had fixed on him even before he angled toward them and slowed. They didn't move. Jimmy considered tooting his horn, thought better of it, stopped and rolled down his window. "Y'all mind easing over so I can pull in there?" he asked. The trio stared on. One wore on his head a red bandanna with tiny knots tied at the corners, one a backwards baseball cap, while the third had a high flat top with razor lines cut at a diagonal. Jimmy's pulse kicked up. Finally, the three inched into the yard and almost onto the porch. Jimmy's throat constricted. He worried that they had broken into the house and done something to J.T., or that they were at least considering it. He knew he was jumping to conclusions, but Elma had told him about bad actors in the neighborhood. He turned off the car and stepped out, aware of the lump of remaining money in his pocket. Chemical burnoff from the plants burned his nose. The three men, who, he could now see, were teenagers, eyed him like meat.

"Y'all live around here?" Jimmy said.

"What's it to you?" the flat top asked.

"Just asking. I'm staying up in there with my daddy."

"*You* staying up in here?" asked the baseball cap. He and the bandanna laughed. "Didn't know no white folks living in these shacks. Times must be real hard cross town." The teenagers slapped hands, but the flat top kept a level gaze. Jimmy would have to go through or squeeze around them to reach the stoop, but he wasn't even sure J.T. was home and if not he had no way inside. Flat top raised his chin. "Thought you was wanting something coming in like that," he said.

"I ain't wanting nothing. Just coming to see if my daddy's home. Y'all mind if I go on in."

No one moved, so Jimmy took a couple of tentative steps toward them, turning his shoulder, until flat top and bandanna parted enough to let him slide through sideways. He climbed the two steps, found the door locked, knocked hard, waited, banged, turned toward the trio and shrugged.

"You sure he in there?" baseball cap asked. "Maybe he took off when you was gone."

"Ain't sure he come home," Jimmy said. "Y'all seen a taxi?"

Baseball cap shook his head. Bandanna spat and scratched his chin. "Where you from?" he asked.

"Texas."

Bandanna tugged at his ear lobe and looked at the others. "Cracker," he said. The three of them burst into laughter. Flat top nudged baseball cap and the trio slowly pivoted and strolled away, talking loudly. Jimmy almost pounded the flimsy plywood again, then he hopped off the stoop and waded through the tall grass on the side of the house to the air-conditioner rattling in J.T.'s window. He rapped on the glass and the curtain parted to reveal J.T.'s startled face. He motioned to the front.

"Come on in the cool," J.T. said, beer in hand, the

sour smell of a bar wafting off him as he let Jimmy in. The odor of bug spray saturated the superheated living room. J.T. locked the door behind Jimmy and strode past him toward his bedroom. "You saved my life with that air-conditioner, son," he said, and held the bedroom door open as Jimmy entered. "Pull up a piece of bed and grab a beer." On the floor lay two crumpled cans. J.T. broke a fresh one from its plastic circle, gave it to Jimmy and motioned for him to sit. "Where you been?" he asked Jimmy. "I left the game early to come see you."

"Been out with that woman works over at the drugstore. Sandra."

"Oh, yeah? That's fine, mighty fine." J.T. grinned. "Got something for you." He pulled bills from his pocket and counted out sixty on the bed. "That's what I borrowed." He laid down seventeen more in fives and ones. "And here's some toward what you paid."

J.T.'s hair stood straight up in the rear where he had been lying on it. His rheumy eyes glistened as he grinned. Jimmy thought of the three men outside. "We got to get you moved."

J.T. scowled. "Yeah, yeah, we'll do that. Right now I want you to pick up that money. Tonight I'm taking you out to celebrate with a steak, on me."

"How's it you taking me out when I paid six-hundred dollars to keep you from getting busted up?"

J.T. sipped from his beer. Jimmy wished he hadn't said what he said, but he had said it and he'd meant it and he wasn't taking it back. J.T. sniffed, sat cross-legged on the bed and pointed at the money. "That there's for you. And I'll repay you your money even though I didn't ask you to pay it in the first place. I don't squelch."

Squelch? Jimmy thought. He picked up the money, took the pouch from his pocket and folded the new bills in with the old. "Why won't you help me get you out of here?"

"Why won't you see that lawyer?" Jimmy turned from J.T. and rested his butt on the edge of the mattress. "That's what I thought," J.T. said. He fiddled with a button on his shirt, then seemed to count the buttons, tugged at one as if he was considering how firmly it was stitched on. "Look, I'm on a roll again because of you. I took myself out of a winning streak to come here and tell you. Let's drink these beers and celebrate. All the shit'll still be here tomorrow."

Jimmy tasted the tepid beer, metallic and bitter, and set it down. He fixed J.T. with a look that made J.T.'s cheek twitch. "Why'd you search me out now?" he asked.

"What're you getting at?"

"Why not five years ago, or ten, or twenty? Is it something to do with that letter?"

J.T.'s lips pooched to a point. He scratched the tip of his nose. "What is it with you, boy? Can't you have a good time? I track you down and here you are giving me the third degree. I didn't have to go find all them records at the government office and bribe that woman to tell me stuff she wasn't supposed to. I just decided it was time."

"So there ain't no reason."

"No reason but what I said."

"Meaning you ain't sick like you said in the telegram?"

J.T. chugged his beer, swallowed wrong and broke into coughing. When he caught his breath, he cleared his throat several times with a sound like a bullfrog. In a strained voice he said, "How was I sposed to bring you here? I had to say something."

"You could of just said you were my father."

"I said that. Goddamnit, what bug flew up your ass. You the one left me across town."

"Don't do me like that," Jimmy said.

J.T. slumped and turned from Jimmy. Jimmy took out his cigarettes. "You want one?" he asked.

"Are you charging me?"

Jimmy snorted, lit two and gave one to J.T. Jimmy took a long drag, and suddenly Sandra's kiss was filtering through him again. He exhaled and poked his tongue against his teeth. He wished he could know what she was thinking. But then she'd seemed to talk straight to him, and what woman had done that in a while? What person? He focused on J.T. again, thought of asking about his mother, thought how maybe he understood why she'd pack up and leave this man, then decided he'd had enough frustration for the moment. "You ever been

to Texas, J.T.?" he asked. J.T. was examining close-up
the burning tip of his cigarette.

"What?"

"Texas. You ever been?"

"Worked a shitty job in Beaumont once."

"When I think of Texas, I think of chickens about
half the time. Dumb, stinky chickens. Raised cattle and
hogs a slew more years, but chickens are what I think
of most often."

"There's shitty jobs everywhere. And chumps to
take 'em. We bust our asses and the rich man takes the
money. I'm done busting my ass for a rich man."

"I don't think I'll ever eat chicken again. I still eat
beef, but I know I won't eat chickens. It ain't only to do
with how dirty and stupid they are, it's to do with how
pitiful. Ain't that something, born a bird and can't even
fly more'n a few feet."

J.T. spewed smoke, then killed his beer. "Chickens
are chumps," he said.

"I reckon," Jimmy said.

J.T. dropped the cigarette into his beer can with a
hollow hiss. He swung off the bed, pulled a comb from
his pocket and flattened the hair the pillow had raised.
"I'm taking you out, so if you need to wash up, get on
it." He slipped his feet into his loafers, opened his wallet
and thumbed through it, then gave Jimmy a look that
glinted. J.T.'s clothes hung on him even though they
were skinny clothes to begin with. J.T. *needed* to eat a
steak, needed to eat the whole world, and Jimmy doubted
he would be full even then. Exhaustion blanketed him.

"I just ain't up to it," Jimmy said.

J.T. tugged at his pants waist and sucked at his
teeth. "Fine. Then give me your damn car keys and I'll
do for myself."

Jimmy started to refuse, then tossed the keys to
J.T., who bobbled them, dropped them, and snatched
them up off the floor. "You best decide why you came
here," J.T. said, and stalked out, leaving Jimmy puzzled
as to why J.T. would say such a thing. Jimmy heard
his tires screech above the hum of the air-conditioner.
He winced, then scooted up onto J.T.'s bed. The pillow
smelled sour, but it bolstered his neck, sore from two

nights in a chair. He regretted not going with J.T., but his arms and legs were as heavy as wet corn. Surely J.T. would lose whatever he had, Jimmy just hoped he wouldn't get drunk and kill himself in a wreck too. He flinched. The dingy ceiling wavered. Chemical stench, like burnt metal, mixed with the bug killer to lace the air. His head crackled and distorted. The pouch in his pocket bulged like a rock, so he removed it and set it on the bed stand. He thought of the menace of the trio outside then of Sandra's silence. He belched, then shut his eyes and licked his lips for the remnant of her lipstick.

Jimmy sat up in the dark, pasted with sweat. A siren howled somewhere. A dim square of light floated on the spot where his penis pressed hard against his jeans. He didn't know where he was until he sorted out J.T.'s scent on the pillow, then his hand touched the bulge in his pants. *Sandra*, he'd been dreaming about her. What exactly he didn't remember, but it had been good. He considered lying back to try and relocate the dream, but the heat and the quiet AC caused him to drop his feet to the floor. The air-conditioner had blown a fuse or J.T. hadn't paid the bill, he guessed, then it came to him that someone might have cut the electricity to rob him. Didn't figure, he thought. He hoisted himself and squeezed his temples as whiteness built before his eyes like static. He smacked his parched mouth, touched his empty belly and waited until his vision cleared, then opened the door into the hall. The wet heat lurked there like a giant membrane scented with refinery odor. Street light dusted in through windows, and Jimmy peered into the shadowed corners. Here and there on the pale walls, splotches he knew were roaches paused to see what this intruder did. He tried to recall a fuse box, took out his lighter and headed into the kitchen. He opened the cabinets and examined the walls, glanced in the bathroom and the front room before returning to the bedroom. He was hoping there might be a circuit breaker, even though he knew how small that possibility was, but when he parted J.T.'s clothes in the bedroom closet, he discovered an old box with a single glass fuse. Between J.T.'s hanging shirts, the heat itched Jimmy into the

thought of holding his lighter to the clothes, walking out
and never looking back. He wondered what time it was.
If he was lucky, Elma would have an extra.

Chemical stench gagged him when he stepped
outside. On the horizon, towering flames tore loose from
flare stacks. He glanced both directions and walked
toward the blue TV light playing against Elma's curtains.
He hesitated before knocking, then rapped twice.

"It's Jimmy, Miz Elma, from next door. I'm sorry to
trouble you, but my lights went out."

Jimmy heard the slide of a deadbolt and a chain,
then Elma appeared in a green robe with cauliflower
ruffles. Jimmy was certain Elma was older than J.T., but
she looked more energized. He wondered what his mother
would look like, how old she would be.

"Your fuse blow?" Elma asked.

"That's what I figure. I'm sorry it's so late."

"It ain't but a little after ten. Come on in." An
oscillating fan stirred the soggy air of her living room. "I
got to be careful what all I run at once and my son did
some wiring on mine. Electricity's terrible. Wait and I'll
get you my extra."

Jimmy studied the small room, its creased curtains,
framed photos, sway-backed couch and comfortable,
frayed recliner. A poor person's house, not nearly as
nice even as his and Floyd's cheap place in Houston, yet
something about it was nicer than he'd ever had. The
aroma of fried pork chops rumbled his stomach.

"Here it is," Elma said, and handed him the glass
cylinder.

"I sure appreciate it, ma'am."

"Ain't no bother. It's good to have unexpected
company sometime. My son came over earlier, but he had
to get on to work after he ate. Just hired on as a security
man. Didn't think he'd get it after he'd been in jail, even
though that was about fifteen years ago. His other job laid
him off after the place shut down."

"Well, I best go on and let you get your rest."

"Your daddy took your car again?"

"Yes, ma'am."

"You ate anything? I got some leftovers. Chops and
greens."

"I couldn't put you out."

"You ain't putting me out. I don't need all this food. Come on in here."

Jimmy followed her into the kitchen, where dirty plates, silverware, a pot and a greasy frying pan sat in the sink.

"I seen you talking to them boys this afternoon," Elma said as she brought two bowls out of her rust-speckled refrigerator. She set the bowls on the table and motioned for Jimmy to sit. "They're just testing you. They ain't bad boys. One had some run-in with the police, that oldest one, about some fighting, but I don't think it's too serious. Don't want you worrying they gone take your car or hurt your daddy cause they ain't that type."

"Anything ever get by you in this neighborhood?"

"Not if I can help it." She placed a pork chop and a heap of greens on his plate and poured him a glass of tea. "Go on," she said. Jimmy cut a piece of pork and felt its taste spread through him like a balm. "Sorry my kitchen's a mess. I wait till it's cool morning to clean." She eased into the chair across from Jimmy, her knees cracking. She grunted and rubbed them. "Damn arthritis. You mind if I smoke a cigarette?"

"No, ma'am." He thumped one out for her and lit it. She blew smoke toward the ceiling and slitted her eyes.

"Liked to killed me when Roland went to jail," she said. "Police caught him and some others up in somebody's house taking they stereo. It wasn't the first time. He just got caught up with the wrong boys, and I wasn't doing what I was sposed to. I try to talk to some of these around here but most don't wanta listen. They out for getting what they can. I can't blame 'em too much since that's what they see on TV."

Jimmy washed down a bite of greens with a gulp of sweet tea. Somewhere J.T. was losing money and doing who-knew-what with Jimmy's car, while a woman Jimmy didn't even know fed him and calmed him. He thought maybe he should help Elma move and tell J.T. to fend for himself. "J.T. said he wanted me to go out with him, and I wouldn't, so I know he's off gambling."

"He bad to gamble?"

"Real bad."

Elma nodded. "I figured it was something like that for him to come on in this neighborhood. I can't speak against him, though. I like to play bingo myself."

"Miz Elma, you mind me asking why you live here?"

She laughed and took another drag. "Can't afford to live nowhere else. Too tired and worn out to work anymore. Cleaned people's houses till I couldn't squat down and get up again."

"Your son can't help you?"

"Roland always says, 'Momma, I'm gone buy you a car and a big house some day,' but he and his wife struggle to make it themselves with three younguns. I'm an old woman anyway. Just turned sixty-three. Long as I have my air-conditioner at night and my shows in the afternoon, I'm fine." Elma lifted her chin and paused mid-drag. "Your daddy's home," she said.

"Ma'am?"

"Just pulled up."

Jimmy took a last bite of pork chop, surveyed what he was leaving and pushed away from the table. "I better go see."

"Might be good to let him stumble in the dark a while." Jimmy laughed, took out his cigarettes and offered them to Elma. She snagged two.

When Jimmy stepped onto the stoop, J.T. was getting out of the car, which was angled into the yard. He looked at Jimmy, glanced at his own house and scratched his head. "Had to borrow a fuse," Jimmy said, walking toward the front door.

"Shit. Thought I'd forgot where I lived." J.T. caught Jimmy at the door and slapped him on the back. "You a good man, Jimmy. Always taking care of things." His voice sounded thick but not drunk. Jimmy went straight to the fuse box, J.T. close behind him even when Jimmy entered the closet. "Yeah," J.T. said, "some folks don't take care of their own, but that ain't you, son. I can see that." Jimmy screwed the new fuse in, kicking on the lights and the air-conditioner simultaneously. He paused in anticipation that this fuse might blow too. J.T. grinned. "That's great!" he said. "Just great."

"Pardon," Jimmy said, and edged past him out of the closet.

"I understand if you're sore, son, I do. That's why I came back right quick even though I was up. I was on a blue damn streak, but I saw it was getting on past ten o'clock and I thought you might want the car to see that girl, so I collected and came on home."

"I ain't really sore," Jimmy said, standing between J.T. and the hall. He dreaded going out in the stew of the rest of the house, considered getting in the car himself and going . . . where?

J.T. pulled a small wad of bills from his pocket. "Won forty-six dollars, and it wasn't even a high-stakes game. I'm telling you, since you been here, everything's gone right and I'm gonna make it all up to you." J.T. counted out twenty-one dollars and handed it to Jimmy, then he kicked off his shoes, unbuttoned his shirt and spread his arms in front of the air-conditioner. "That shyster Charley was in the game, and I took some of his money too. Send his goddamn goon over to rob from my boy. I showed him."

J.T. turned toward Jimmy. He took off his outer shirt, exposing his thin shoulders, and tugged at his pants waist. The walls and the light seemed overpoweringly yellow, and J.T.'s tan slacks and jaundiced complexion almost camouflaged him. He stroked at his cheeks and chin as if clearing a spider web. "I know I ain't been the best father. I should of come found you a long time ago, but that's all behind us now. Me and you, we're a team. I decided I'd go with you to look for a place," he raised a finger, "*if* you'll go see that lawyer with me." Jimmy clenched and unclenched his fists. A small wheel of vertigo spun in Jimmy, then he nodded. "Damn straight!" J.T. said. He came over and shook Jimmy's hand with both of his, slapped him on the shoulder and flopped onto the edge of the bed. He stared toward the wall. "I ain't a loser, son. I've had some bad runs lately, but I ain't a loser. I'm gonna do right by you. You'll see."

The tastes of Elma's food seeped into Jimmy's mouth. Beyond J.T., cracked paint and brown stains uglied the wall. Jimmy longed to return to Elma's kitchen and finish his meal, longed to settle onto her couch and sleep. Pain stabbed at his temple and traced like fire down his neck. He'd become more afraid and ashamed as a man than he'd ever been as a boy, and he couldn't even say why. He walked close to the bed. "I want to know about my mother," he said.

J.T. lay flat on his back, his expression nearly stricken. "After the lawyer's. I promise."

Jimmy's hands ached to shake J.T. for information, but he stretched his fingers and sat on the floor.

WHAT J.T. COULD REMEMBER IF HE
WOULD REMEMBER: 1958

Four-hundred fifty-three dollars of blackjack money bulged in J.T.'s pocket when she walked into Chief's. Her posture had the slight tentativeness of a bender, but her dark beauty in the room, her mocha skin, her black curly tumbling hair, her lean legs strutting out from her gray skirt held sober grace. She seemed a little too dark-skinned even for Chief's, where the rules bent a lot more than across the river in Baton Rouge, but her features didn't seem too colored, so maybe she was Spanish or Italian or Creole, although J.T. was never sure exactly what Creole meant. Not that he cared. Rules didn't snare him anyway, and tonight he was King J.T., all the luck in the world sprinkled on him like magic dust.

She took a table by herself in the corner and peered out at the unbroken partying, dancing, loud-talking honky-tonking, a rowdy Thursday night. He touched his pocket, strode over to her and extended a hand. "J.T. Strawhorn. Can I buy you a drink?" Her almond eyes glinted deep down, as if there were a smolder a thousand feet below the surface. She reached into her purse and withdrew a twenty. "You can get us both one," she said. "Bourbon." Her forwardness set him back but also made him smile. J.T. took the money from her, even though he planned to give it back, sauntered to the bar and finger-curled the bartender in. While he waited for the drinks, he watched her from the corner of his eye, distrusting his own sight. Pretty girls came here, but none in her league, in any of her leagues. Exotic, cultured-looking, expensively dressed, gorgeous. He'd had a bit to drink since he cashed out of the game, but no amount of drink could cause an apparition as lovely as her. He straightened himself to his full, carried the glasses to the table and placed the twenty down with her drink. "My round," he said. "I'm on a streak." She raised her glass and sipped. "Never seen you in here before," he said. "What's your name?"

"Morita," she said, her voice sultry with cigarettes or fatigue and barely audible above the music.

"Morita. That's nice. You wanta dance, Morita?"

"I want to drink. If you want to drink, you're free to join me."

J.T. lifted a toast to which she did not respond, although she looked full-on at him for the first time. She appeared significantly younger than his thirty-one years, but maybe even tireder and tipsier than he'd originally thought. Maybe slightly darker and even more beautiful too. From a small purse she took out a pack of cigarettes and put one in her mouth. J.T. had a match lit before she could reach back in. Her fingers were elegant, slender with deep red manicured nails. She took the smoke in like it was her lover and let it slowly escape from her full lips. She was from money and class, a woman J.T. normally wouldn't consider approachable, but tonight he was flying high and she seemed low enough that their orbits had intersected.

She finished her drink before he did his, and when he turned his up to match her, she pushed the twenty to him again. "I insist," she said. By the end of her second drink, her shoulders sagged, although J.T. figured only he could tell. Despite the weight in her eyelids, she looked alert, though focused on something beyond this room. A couple of J.T.'s acquaintances had come sniffing around, one shyly, like a supplicant to her good looks and J.T.'s winning streak, the other with a raised eyebrow. She had responded so politely yet cooly that she constructed a force field that prevented them from trying to sit. J.T. grinned inside. This night he had been given a special realm, and his confidence rose in direct proportion to every minute he stayed near Morita, and to every drink they downed.

"You hungry?" he asked her near the end of her third, the only thing he'd said in an hour. She studied him as if decoding his words, then plucked at a lash.

"I suppose I should eat."

"I know some place we can get eggs."

"Ugh."

"Or a burger. French toast. Something to take the edge off."

"Do you know a place I can get a bottle?"

He nodded. She pulled out more bills, but he held up his palm.

Outside, a cool damp breeze pasted her skirt to her thighs, and she paused a second and teetered. Then she handed him her keys, a move that unnerved even him with its recklessness. "That's mine," she said, and pointed to a powder-blue, T-Bird convertible. She waited for him to open her door and slid into the passenger seat. He lingered a second, touched the roof of her car to make sure it was solid, then strutted to the driver's side as if he'd done this every day of his life. At the truck stop diner, he shielded her some from the stares and ushered her to a corner booth. Any woman this beautiful was certain to attract attention, and he wanted to keep intrusions to a minimum. She slumped a little in the booth, smoked and really took him in for the first time it seemed, her demeanor loose enough to finally show her young age— early twenties?—but still bolstered by a sort of royal bearing.

"Perfect cards all night," he said. "Took every dime they put down. Nineteen, twenty, twenty-one. I couldn't drop below seventeen."

"Blackjack?"

"That's my game. You play?"

"I have for fun. My daddy plays." She sucked her cigarette and blew out as if there were suddenly a bad taste. "I haven't been in a place like that bar since I was a little girl."

"Ain't much of a little-girl place. Ain't a place that sees women as fine as you either."

She gazed flatly at him.

"Thank you," she finally said, and shifted her eyes out the window.

"Where you from, Morita? You don't strike me as Port Allen."

She flicked her smoke. "Washington D.C." He waited for more, but it didn't come.

"I'm from Baton Rouge. Been on a down streak, so I crossed the river to change my luck. It evidently worked." She nodded and stubbed out her smoke.

They didn't talk as they ate, even though J.T. was bursting to recount every hand of the evening. Morita nibbled at her french toast, drank coffee and a glass of milk, then excused herself. He relived his evening, re-enacting the laying down of cards and his multiple declarations of Blackjack, until Morita's skin occupied his mind again. Ten minutes later, J.T. worried that somebody might have bothered her, worried that she might have passed out. He could see her car through the plate glass, had the keys in his pocket, so he knew she hadn't left. Just as he was gearing up to check on her, she came back around the corner, make-up freshly applied, the rims of her eyes red, her complexion paler, and sat. "I paid," she said. "You ready to go?"

"Sure," he said, but she didn't move. "Where to?"

"I need to sleep. I was thinking about that motel we saw a little way back. You can join me if you want, but just to drink and sleep. I mean it."

He scratched the side of his head. "My house is just across the river. Fifteen, twenty minutes."

"I'm not going that far."

Morita sat in the single straight-backed desk chair, sipping whiskey from a squat glass. J.T.'s food had landed atop his booze like a soporific, but he was too jazzed with good fortune and the oddness of this situation to sleep yet. He surveyed his surroundings, everything worn to a dull shade approaching brown, then let his gaze settle on Morita again, the sight of her stockinged feet nearly closing his throat with possibility. "I seen The Shady Inn a hundred times, but I never thought I'd be doing time here."

"If you want to sleep, I'll keep count of the bed bugs."

A joke! He perked up. "That's charitable of you. You can join me if you like."

A quick shadow passed over her and she twitched. "I wasn't kidding."

"I hear you. Then I'll take the floor. You look like you could stand some sleep."

"I'll be fine right here. More whiskey?"

"Hell no. I'll be hungover a week like it is." He slipped off his shoes and rubbed the arches of his feet, the aged springs of the bed creaking with each slight movement. "I have to admit, I can't exactly place what the hell's going on with you." Her expression gave nothing as she poured a bit more in her glass. "You always drink like this?" he asked.

"When I'm thirsty. You always come to motel rooms with women when you're only getting conversation."

"If you're paying. Why you even want me here?"

"Company. You seem nice and harmless enough." Her description was like a thump to his nose. He snorted. She drummed her fingers on her purse, and he wondered if she had a tiny pistol in there and planned to rob him. Both instability and assuredeness roiled off her like a complicated by-product of her exoticism and drunkenness, and that by-product somehow relaxed him with its shattering of the typical rules and pressures. He reclined on the bed and stared at the ceiling, drifted and jolted up after dozing for a second, he thought, except that his back was aching, drool was soaking his cheek and sunlight was slicing through the crack in the curtains. Morita still sat in her chair, unmoved it appeared, an inch of booze still in her glass, her eyes lifeless. She stood, tottered to the bathroom and closed the door behind her. He heard running water, then vomiting, a pause, more retching, then splashes. J.T. tried to stand, but the full impact of his hangover and lingering drunk slammed him. He moved beneath the covers and dropped his head on the pillow.

* * *

That afternoon they headed west in Morita's T-Bird per her instructions. J.T. worried about his car in Chief's parking lot, but ten miles on the road, top down, the wind lashing Morita's thick hair behind her reclining scarved head, he let the worry go. The T-Bird sailed beneath him like a dream rocket. The fall sun was warm, and Highway 1 lay flat and straight through the Atchafalaya Basin. Beside him sat the finest woman he'd ever spoken to and ahead lay the full-bore juke joints of Cajun country, so who cared if his gills were as green as the foliage zipping past. He had cash and boundless potential for fun, gambling, and maybe even sex with a goddess. He checked out Morita's profile, eyes shut behind her sunglasses, a slight snore rattling from her. As far as he could tell, she hadn't slept all night, but when he awoke a second time, she was showered, made-up and dressed in turquoise pedal pushers, a yellow blouse and light jacket, her suitcase and make-up bag closed and standing near the door. As she examined him from her chair, J.T. felt briefly exposed for being where he didn't belong. Then she had said, "Let's drive to Lafayette," skittering warmth across him.

They ate and bet some ponies late afternoon at Evangeline Downs, Morita telling him her father used to bet horses at The Fairgrounds as she started on bourbon again. J.T. won enough to cover the meal and drinks, and after a ride in the country they went to supper at a fish house, Morita wearing a scarf tied firmly around her head and face. She laughed at a story he told—the first laughter he'd heard from her—ate her entire meal, then fell into a funk. As soon as they entered the motel room, which he'd rented while she slouched in the car, she passed out fully clothed on top of the bedspread. Somehow it didn't bother him. He sat and watched her sleep, her lips slightly parted, her features softer in relaxation than he'd seen them, even when she mumbled and tossed from a dream. He briefly considered going through her purse to see if there was a pistol there, but that seemed like risking the roll, so he counted his money and sacked out next to her without a touch.

The next morning she was up, clean and drinking when he awoke. He rubbed his face and smiled at her. She simply muttered, "Hi," without smiling, which irked him. When he came out of the bathroom, showered and shaved with the razor and cream she'd left on the sink, the curtains were opened to bright sun. "You always sleep so late?" she asked, and even though her voice wasn't sharp, the words slid up his spine. "You always drink breakfast?" he asked. She didn't answer. After lunch they went to the track once more, Morita seemingly uninterested in any of it except the liquor, although she kept scanning the other bettors. J.T. distractedly watched her from the corner of his eye as if she might vanish or take up with somebody else and leave him stranded. When he lost fifty dollars and threw his ticket to the ground, she suggested they go. "Like where?" he asked.

"Anywhere away from here. I don't like these people," she said.

"These people? You mean people like me?"

"No. People who might know my daddy."

"Your daddy? Ain't he in D.C.?" She walked away.

They drove the rest of the afternoon, breaking a couple of times for tense walks, but saying nothing besides basic terse communications. She bought a pint and drank it with Coke and ice, then drank more at supper. By the time they reached their motel room, he had even less idea of who she was than when they'd started. She went straight to the bathroom, vomited, and stayed for a while, J.T. stewing more when he couldn't see her. Her steps were stiff and wobbly when she came out, but she poured another drink that irritated him as if she were pouring it over his head. "What's going on here, Morita? Why you traveling with me if you don't like me?"

She didn't look at him. "Who said I didn't like you?"

"You ain't said two words since we left the track, and you been knocking 'em back like I'm something you want to forget."

"It has nothing to do with you."

"Oh, so I'm just your chauffeur."

She looked up, her eyelids fluttering to focus. "I know it's killing you to drive that car."

"That's mean." He paced to the window and parted the curtain. "Why you afraid folks might know your daddy?" She didn't answer. "I've never done nothing like this before, pick up and go with a woman I don't even know and just watch her drink and drink. I don't know what to make of it."

"I haven't asked you for anything."

"You ain't gave much either."

She sneered, lit a cigarette and crossed her legs. "I'll buy you a bus ticket and take you to the station if you're ready to go." She blew a stream of smoke at the ceiling.

J.T.'s mouth filled with saliva. He cleared his throat, blinked at the hot wire glowing behind his forehead. "I figured the spoiled rich girl would come out when you got your fill of me."

"Fuck you," she said, her words slurry for the first time. "You mad you haven't gotten any pussy yet? Is that you want, some pussy, or else you're going to show me something? Well, fuck you, you're not getting any."

J.T. almost staggered back. He'd only heard women use those words a few times, had never had one say them to him in those ways. For her to say it—this woman more marvelous and cultured than any woman he'd ever met—was like a punch to the chest. He scanned the room as if he might have a bag to take, but all he had was the shirt he'd worn when he met her, which was in the car with his dirty drawers, and the shirt she'd bought him yesterday, which he was wearing. In a way it seemed like all he had anywhere. He dug her car keys out of his pocket and tossed them on the table.

"Been real damn great getting to know you. Have another drink."

She threw the glass, which missed and thumped off the door. She screamed and bent at the waist, shoving her face into her hands and still screaming. J.T. went out the door, her rising wail like a spear through his back. When he shut the door behind him, his knees quivered so badly he almost went down, but he caught himself and marched fast, every step a loss of the J.T. who'd begun to grow so large every second he was with Morita. He stopped. He had no idea where the bus station was. He knew he should go back to Check-In and use their phone, rather than walk these strange streets with his pocket still chock-full of cash. Then he was drooping and shaking, J.T. before the roll, before coronation, but more than that, J.T. knowing Morita was breaking down. He rubbed his face, turned and shuffled back. Outside the door, he pressed his ear to the wood. She was still crying and also talking, her voice unintelligible but younger than he'd heard it, afraid. He didn't want that, any of it, the crying or the talking or the afraidness, but his fist rose and he knocked anyway. She went quiet. "Morita. Let me in."

"Just go on," she said, but her voice wasn't harsh.

"I wanta talk." There was no sound and he drifted, not knowing that his cheek and temple still rested on the door until it opened and he jerked upright. She looked at him startled, black streaks tracing down from smeared-mascara eyes, her whole face sunken. She narrowed her eyes, more to see, he thought, than out of emotion. "I was thinking about the roll," he said. "I was scared I'd lose it. I shouldn't of said all what I said."

She opened the door wider, and he stepped inside. She shoved the door shut, then grabbed him hard, pressed her head into his neck and wept. "Don't go," she said. He wrapped his arms around her and she dug her fingers into him. He didn't know what to do, her body limber with booze, then her mouth moved to his neck and bit him lightly. He moved back an inch, but she pulled him to her, her liquored mouth hot on his, her breathing still mixed with crying, her cheeks wet with tears. "You want me," she said, and it sounded like a threat. He kissed her harder.

The next morning he wasn't clear exactly how they'd gotten into bed, clear only that he'd been aware of her complexion, that he'd hesitated because he didn't have protection, and that she told him it was all right because she knew her rhythm. "Made love" were the words that came into his mind—even though love had been the last thing in what they'd done—and the words terrified him before he drove them out. He hadn't done more in six months than make-out with a woman by a pinball machine, but he and Morita had had sex loudly, vigorously, angrily, tenderly until J.T. fell dead away. He woke up exhausted, his dick sore, his heart a sponge steeped in rich wine, woke up horny, woke up by himself. He sat up, his lack of sleep countered by his saturation with her, a fatigued joy. Then he heard her sobbing in the bathroom. He grimaced and held his head. He had been here before. Drunken sex with conviction followed by hungover regret and recrimination. The door offered itself as escape, but he was sodden with emotions that were slowing him.

He swung out of bed, crossed the small room and tapped on the bathroom, resenting his second timid tapping in less than twenty-four hours. He heard her suck her tears back in. "I'm busy," she said. He thought to say something to comfort her, then he retrieved his strewn clothes and dressed, examining his own body as if its connection to her body had made it more valuable. The bathroom door flew open, and she emerged in a bath robe and plopped onto the bed, her hair stringy wet. J.T. yearned for a simple glance of her body and his yearning heightened his resentment.

"You leaving?" she asked.

"You want me to?"

She pulled the robe more tightly around her hunched shoulders. J.T. wanted to sit and hug her to him, but he had no idea how she would react. He knew she was sick from the booze, but he also believed she was sick from him, as if he were some toxic injection. He wished there were a way to spread his ribs and show how she'd gotten inside him, then he hunched at the thought of what she might do with what he showed.

"Quit staring," she said.

"You're sick from that drinking."

"No joke." She shook her head at the floor. "Where the hell am I?" She went to her purse and took out a cigarette, her hands shaking so badly that she threw it all down. "It's all wrecked. I can't go back. I don't even know who you are. It's shit, all shit." She burst into tears and closed herself in the bathroom again. An emotion swooped toward him like the emotion he'd had the day each of his parents died. He sat on the floor. The day was bright and clear through the crack in the curtains, a beautiful day before the winter days of rain and chill. He had both those kinds of days inside him right now.

The drive back to Chief's was the longest of his life. He wanted to kiss her, slap her, console her, scold her, fuck her, hold her, make love to her, hear her voice. She said nothing. She drove, top still on, and Highway 1 slanted precipitously downward, the T-Bird's wings tucked into a dive. At Chief's she put the car in Park and turned it off. J.T.'s car waited unchanged except for what looked like a beer poured on its hood. The last several days seemed delusions. He touched his reduced money roll and wished he'd been cruel to her, wished he'd told her all he'd wanted was a piece of ass, but then he didn't wish it. Everything quavered as if he'd been walking a long plank and all that remained was the final step off the shaky end. "Guess I'll be heading home," he said, the shirt she'd bought him itching like burlap, even though it was the nicest shirt he'd ever owned. Morita slouched, smaller than he'd seen her, her fingers hooked loosely on the lowest arc of the steering wheel, the fingers that had held him and stroked him. "Go on then," she said.

"Where you gonna go?"

"What's it to you? You'll find something else."

J.T. flinched. His car and his unbound life waited ten steps away, but when he looked at Morita, he remembered the sounds she'd made and the love words she'd said. She breathed as if she were going to cry again, and a mix of compassion and revulsion boiled in him until he reached and touched her hair, a gesture he was certain would be like acid to her. She fell sideways, not so much a movement toward him as a crumpling against him. He embraced her just the same.

J.T. always disliked the bridge's skinny lanes, but now the claustrophobic orange girders narrowed like a chute. There was no room for error, no margin of escape if someone veered or a tire blew, only the crash through railing and the drop to the brown Mississippi below.

He checked to see if Morita's T-Bird still followed in his rearview mirror—as if she could have turned around on this bridge—then focused forward again. Ahead on the river's bank, the aluminum plant chuffed white smoke. Already the bauxite burn-off stung his eyes, and he pictured Morita recoiling at it and continuing south to escape the industry that lined the road to J.T.'s house. Then he pictured the house, boxy and white, an inheritance from his father who'd died in a fire at nearby Standard Oil. He cringed at how Morita would see it as poor and cramped, then kept watch on her as they descended the bridge and turned onto Scenic Highway. He expected her to keep going straight when he turned, but she followed.

Next to the road the tangle of pipes and stands of flare stacks grew thick. He had grown up with this as his natural surrounding, but the blight of it was obvious in the heightened coloration Morita gave his sight. He considered driving past his neighborhood and on to the Garden District, where he would pull up in front of some lovely house and step out, except he saw the short life of that plan, no more than five seconds of fantasy before Morita closed the distance between their cars and the truth slugged him. He turned onto his street, the ridiculousness of what he'd just considered following him like a rancorous fart. The houses along the road squatted pitifully among towering oaks that some plantation owner had seeded here long ago. In his mirror, Morita still spitefully followed, diminishing his life, tainting his childhood, reducing him with shame. He crept into his driveway like a kicked dog dragging home, but when Morita stepped from her car, the vision of her lifted him above everything meager and tattered, if only for an instant. "Welcome to the palace," he said, and she took in the white box with a single glance before looking toward the refinery fence a hundred yards away. "I grew up here," he added, as if the words carried some sentiment that would alter the puny reality. "Me and my folks in that house."

"You sure you want me here?" she asked.

"I asked you," he answered, although he had never been more simultaneously certain and doubtful of anything. He opened the front door, and she crossed the threshold and sneezed. The house was stuffy and laced with the odor of crude oil and methane, smells he barely noticed. The front room was furnished with the same modest worn couch, two chairs, and coffee table his parents had bought. On the wall hung a photo of the three of them when he was a boy, and the recognition of this as the place he'd spent his entire life and from which his parents were gone forever tugged at him with longing and nostalgia. He took her on a tour of the kitchen and the two bedrooms down the hall. She stopped board stiff in the doorway to J.T.'s bedroom and tapped her fingertips together. She blinked when he flicked on the light, and he saw her in his house, her wondrous skin high with natural blush, her brown eyes moist and soft with an intelligence and a seeing he knew penetrated differently from his own. He'd had women here before, but never one like her, luminous with youth and beauty. These were qualities he'd known himself to resent, especially when combined with wealth, although he had screwed a well-off college girl for a brief period and a rich lady twice. No resentment visited him now. He was imbued with emotions at which he normally scoffed—charity, tenderness, pride.

He flicked on the attic fan, the thump of the louvered vent and upward suction startling Morita. "Make yourself at home," he said. "You can shower or bathe or rest or we can go get a bite to eat."

"I think I'll lie down a while. To sleep," she added levelly.

J.T. nodded. He considered lying down with her to at least soak in the proximity of her body, maybe to see if anything developed, but her resolve was as evident as the tired residue of their trip. He swiped the moisture from his sideburns, though it wasn't even hot, as if Morita's sensitive skin had become his own, then raised the window, the fan's pull billowing the heavy curtains inward. "Sorry for the warm," he said, although why he was sorry for the climate in which he thrived he couldn't say.

Morita appeared not to hear him, her posture unchanged but visibly weary, as though J.T. could see her skeleton bowing under extreme gravity. "I'll be fine," she said, but it sounded like rote. J.T. re-joined her at the doorway, his body alive with the memory of her touch. He thought to kiss her, then he flattened himself and eased past.

In the front room he spread his money on the coffee table, separated it into piles of ones, fives, tens and twenties and summed the total, well below his initial winnings but still enough to keep him from calling Kirbye for construction work even if he didn't win anything for a couple of weeks. Except that there was Morita. The extra cost of and the unknown length of her stay. It was true she'd had money on their lark and had insisted on paying at every stop, but he knew it was his job to pay. Who knew how much she really had anyway? And besides, he didn't actually want her paying, despite the drain on his winnings. He closed his eyes and let himself re-experience how she had shared the exquisite softness of her flesh and the transcendent intensity of her kisses. He touched himself, half hard, opened his eyes and scooted straighter in his chair.

J.T. carried a bucket of chicken and the two Jax from his fridge down the hall, stopped and peered around the door frame, expecting Morita to either be curled on her side or somehow gone. He found her in profile, sitting on the bed with her knees pulled to her chest, the orange light of refinery flares throbbing over her. "You live a block from hell," she said.

"It ain't bad."

"It smells like a gas station burning."

J.T. came and sat next to her, handed her one of the beers. "Guess I'm used to it. My daddy worked at that refinery till it killed him."

"I wish something would kill mine."

"You ain't serious?"

"Sometimes I am." The shadows and light played across her like something living. She tipped up her beer and he watched her throat move as she swallowed. She took a cigarette from the pack on the bed stand and lit it. He noticed she'd retrieved an ashtray from the living room. He imagined himself as the smoke curling over her lips, sweeping into her lungs and resting there content in her blood. She exhaled. "Thank you."

"For what?"

"For letting me come here. I'd already been driving around for two days. I don't know where I would've gone."

"You're welcome." He pulled the top from the bucket. "I hope you like chicken."

She dragged on the cigarette, the cinder lighting her brighter than the plant light, then blew out through her nose. It struck him as odd how a woman so young and good-looking did things like a man, and a tough man at that. "I've been thinking," she said. "Because you brought me to your house, you have a right to know some things." Her voice was different than it had been, and he'd heard her talk with several voices. "I've never told a man any of this and I'm only going to say it once. Never ask me about it again, you hear?"

He bit a drumstick, chewed and washed the bite down with a swig of beer. He'd done his best not to wander too deeply into sticky places he couldn't step back out of, and she was clearly about to take him to such a place. But she was already in his room. How much stickier could it get? "If you wanta tell me."

She took another long drag and blew it at the ceiling. "I'm from New Orleans. I took off two days before I met you, just driving around, drinking and sleeping when I could, trying to decide where I was going to go. I considered taking off for New York or Los Angeles, but those places seemed like too much too soon. All I know is I can't go back to New Orleans, and I can't go back to D.C. I was in school there, and I can't go to any of my friends where my daddy knows I might go. If he found me here, he'd do awful things to us."

J.T. stroked his cheeks and chewed the last bite of his drumstick. The fires at the plant were tall tonight, flames firing hundreds of feet from their stacks and backlighting the storage tanks in the foreground. "Is that it?"

"No. He wants to keep me."

"What's that mean?"

"I went away to college for a year, and I had to beg

him two years after high school to get that, and there he had somebody keeping an eye on me. He found out I had boyfriends and he called me home, told me I was going to live in his house until he decided who I was going to marry, but I'm sure he doesn't want me to get married." She stubbed out her cigarette and lit another one. "Do you get what I'm saying?"

"I ain't sure, Morita."

She clicked her teeth together. "Christ. Oh, well, you've seen everything about me already anyway." She frowned and looked out the window again. "He used to be normal I guess. Then my mother was sick with cancer a long time. She died when I was eleven, and that changed him. He was already well-off and powerful, maybe a little ruthless, I don't know, but after she was gone he was furious all the time, drank too much and stayed out late. The men he brought to the house were loud and so were the women. The friends they'd had when Momma was alive stopped coming around, and I heard talk about hurting people and taking advantage of business situations and paying politicians. He started looking at me differently."

She scratched at the label on her beer, balled it and rolled it between her fingers. "I think he was mostly lonesome, and he didn't know how to replace her. He didn't want anybody else except her. He said I reminded him of her. When I was around twelve, he stopped letting me go anyplace except to school and church or places with him. No friends could come to my house. I could see that other people were afraid of him when he talked to them." She drained her beer and dropped the cigarette into the bottle. She held the bottle toward the window as the smoke curled inside and wavered through the neck. "He married a bitch who didn't like me and divorced her after less than a year and remarried and that lasted a little longer, but even when they were there he didn't stop thinking the way he did about me. And I'm sure those women knew. I was actually glad they knew, and were jealous, and I rubbed their faces in it."

Morita tapped the empty beer bottle with a steady clink. J.T. was still, studying her fierce profile, her eyes glistening and almost standing beyond her face with their intensity. Her jaw muscle pulsed, and he realized that his own hands were about to cramp from holding his beer so tightly. "You ain't got to tell more," he said. She turned to him as if her mind were returning from another state. He'd never had a woman look at him the way she looked at him now.

"A week ago I told him it wouldn't be like that anymore, and he showed me it would. So that night I took the fancy new car he'd bought me for coming home and some money from his safe and I took off. He'll have people out looking for me. Even police. He owns some police."

J.T. swallowed down against the beer and chicken rising into his throat. He blew out through his lips and shoved his hair back off his forehead, looking for words he couldn't find.

She said, "I understand if you want me to go."

He shook his head. "He ain't gonna find you here."

"Don't count on that." Morita let go of her legs, stretched them off the bed and stood. "I think I'll get what's left of that bottle from the car."

"You oughta eat."

As she passed him, he had the urge to grab her arm and pull her back to him, but his limbs wouldn't move. He watched her swaying behind and felt nausea that threatened to surge his chicken and beer again. He grunted, surprised, and saw her father, a colored, faceless villain, hated him and then Morita, unfamiliar rage pushing through him. His pristine treasure was damaged goods and somehow she was also to blame, no matter how unreasonable. He touched the spot where she'd been sitting, the bedspread warm, and sniffed the air for her perfume. Last night he'd kissed along the arc of her rib cage so slowly that he'd lost himself in the sound and vibration from her chest. He licked his lips.

Before him the stacks woofed with the intake of air and spit of flame. He watched them as closely as he had when his mother told him as a child that the fire was good dragons going home. He was a fool to have Morita here, but having her here still didn't feel foolish. No thug from New Orleans would look here, not for a woman like Morita, and even if he did look, J.T. believed that he could protect her. How, he didn't know, but just being with Morita made it plausible.

DAY SIX

The sun played its brutal tune on Jimmy's scalp as he crossed the asphalt parking lot. He'd had to force himself not to be waiting on the sidewalk when Sandra showed up for work, so he joined Elma for coffee, then endured his morning constitutional in J.T.'s sweatbox bathroom, a few roach bodies his unwanted company. He showered, too, but by the time he was back in the air-conditioned room drying himself, he was already covered in a sheen of perspiration.

It hadn't surprised Jimmy that J.T. was gone when he woke up. What surprised him was that the car was still there and that J.T. had managed to sneak past his bedroll on the floor without his stirring. But then Jimmy had been so whipped that he had fallen asleep in the midst of J.T.'s yammering, doubted J.T. had actually slept he'd been so wired recounting the night's game and the gratitude he had for Jimmy's arrival, not to mention the big plans he had for their life of leisure when the win streak continued—Las Vegas vacation, fancy car, crawfish bisque at Antoine's.

Jimmy paused outside the drugstore door. He didn't know what the fallout from yesterday's kiss and ensuing quietness would be, or if there would be any fallout at all. He did know that his shoulder was kinked like cheap hose and that he wanted to kiss Sandra again. Or at least see her smile and hear her laugh.

Sandra barely raised her eyes from behind the counter when he clanged inside and grabbed the cowbell behind him. She looked different, dressed in a brown sleeveless dress, her hair tied back, her lips white with lipstick, but his heart bumped up anyway. He coughed and moved over to her, his feet barely in contact with the floor. "Howdy," he said, and she glanced at him, then down again to a paper she was writing on. "You look pretty," he said.

"No, I don't," she said. "I couldn't sleep till four and I woke up too late to get ready." She touched her hair, which was pulled taut above her ears, then bit her fingernail for an instant before jerking it to the counter. "I didn't think I'd sleep good, but J.T. talked me out." Jimmy willed himself to say more. "I couldn't hardly wait to talk to you." Sandra laid her hand on the back of her neck and tilted her head both ways, a crack sounding each time. "Damn," Jimmy said, "you keeping a pistol in there?"

"You don't like it, you don't have to listen."

"That ain't what I meant."

Sandra snatched the paper off the counter and stuck it underneath. "I'm going outside a minute!" she called. A man's and a woman's voices answered Okay from the pharmacy in the rear. She marched to the end of the counter and around, then whisked past Jimmy with a "Let's step out." She paced a distance down the sidewalk, her white legs flashing below her knee-length skirt, her calf muscles knotting and stretching. "This won't work," she said, and spun on him.

Jimmy pulled up short and staggered back. "What?"

"This. It won't work. It's going too fast. All last night I kept chasing after it and it just won't work."

Jimmy blinked. "What're you talking about?"

"You know. I don't know you, you don't know me, we don't know each other. I like you and I liked," her hand fluttered, "whatever it was we did yesterday, but I just can't go there yet. You understand?" Jimmy pinched a cigarette from his pocket and placed it in his mouth. "I wish you wouldn't do that," she said. "I don't like that."

"You bothered by my smoking too?"

"I'm not *bothered*, I don't like it. I don't like what it does to you, even though I don't even know why I care. Like I said, you'll probably up and go back to Texas any minute."

Sandra hugged herself. Jimmy took the cigarette from his mouth, coughed and returned it to his pocket. "I ain't give you reason to think that," he said.

"*Ain't give me reason.* What's reason? What if I believe that and then one day I'm waiting for you and you never show? What then?"

"You getting out ahead, ain't you? Didn't I say yesterday I wouldn't do that."

"You wouldn't? Did you know you would come to meet your father? Did you know you would meet me? Did I know? No. We don't really know anything, Jimmy, not anything."

"I know I liked yesterday."

"But not right now you don't. And what about fifteen minutes from now? What about when you go off and think how after only a couple of days how unpredictable and needy I am or how irritating I am or how I told you not to smoke, how about then? You don't know how you'll feel."

Sunlight exploded off the several cars by the grocery store. Jimmy squinted. "There ain't no call for this," he said. "All I did was come see you."

Her eyes teared. She balled her fists. "Damn, damn, damn, damn."

"I can go if you want."

"No! Shit. I don't know. I don't know what I know."

Jimmy scuffed his boot on the concrete. He gazed past the flat roof of the mall at the blasted sky above J.T.'s house, saw J.T. laying down the last of his winnings and it not yet ten o'clock. Jimmy's insides coiled, then numbness traveled through him as if his organs and veins had brassed over. It struck him again how much of his life he'd been paralyzed by fear, each time a little worse. What did he want? To know how to read. Yes. Sandra? Yes. But then maybe not. Here they were doing the same old frustrating maneuvering, the unknown waiting like a pit in the dark. He coiled more tightly; his shoulder locked.

"This ain't right," he said. Jimmy wiped the mist from his forehead and stood straight. Sandra rubbed her forearms.

"You ever had anybody up and leave you?" she asked, a ferocity in her voice. "Somebody you think you know and, poof, they're gone? I don't mean just physically either, I mean gone in every way."

His mind flashed to Pepper and J.T. He shoved his fingers into his back pockets, touched his wallet in one and nothing in the other. *Nothing.* Panic lit his skull. He patted his pocket as if the pouch might have shrunk, then remembered setting the money beside J.T.'s bed. He had an instant of relief followed by a sheer drop. The string in his legs loosened.

"You okay?" Sandra asked.

"I ain't sure."

"Is it me?" She stepped forward and wrapped his wrist with her fingers.

"It's something over to the house. I need to see something."

"Can you come by later?" She stepped toward him.

"Yeah. I got to go, though." He was loping toward the house before he even knew he had moved. His boots clopped along the sidewalk, then on the asphalt in the rear of the mall, then on the street to the house. He told himself the money would be there, that J.T. wouldn't take it, told himself that borrowing the car yesterday was just borrowing and that J.T. had repaid part of the money Jimmy had given Squint. He broke into a sprint.

He hopped to the top of the stoop, threw open the door and halted. He coughed until he caught his breath, sweat breaking on him, and moved inside. J.T.'s bedroom waited like a trap. Even if the money was there, something was changed, the suspicion that J.T. might have taken it proof of what little was really between them. Pain fired from his shoulder through his head. The room swayed. Jimmy's arm trembled as he turned the door knob and stepped in. The bedstand was vacant. He moved across the room, knelt to check the floor and patted beneath the bed. He stayed on his hands and knees. The money might be somewhere else, maybe part of a misunderstanding, but he knew his own rationalizations before they were fully formed.

He shot up from the floor, threw the egg-crate bed stand and kicked the partially-open door, splintering the frame. Several roaches hustled from the cracked space and he crushed them with his shoe. He paced the short length to the kitchen and looked out the back at the trashy overgrown yard. Sandra was near, she would talk to him, but they had just now barely navigated some slim, crooked path, and he had no idea how'd she be if she saw him like this, had no idea how he'd be if he saw her. His savings were gone, everything gone except the money in his wallet. It was possible J.T. would win and come home with something, maybe at least a portion of what he'd taken, but that didn't really matter. Everything that mattered was gone—the money Jimmy had earned with humiliation; the plan to get J.T. a better place; the illusion of a father. Jimmy's body hollowed and refilled with venom.

He spun and strode into the living room, the heat smothering, lifted J.T.'s chair and flung it against the wall. The ancient sheetrock collapsed in jagged fragments and dust. Jimmy spat at the hole and gritted his teeth. He was certain if J.T. cruised in right now, he'd hurl him after the chair. He had never badly hurt anybody, just busted a nose and blackened an eye on a couple of no-good transient hands on the ranch, but he itched to do to J.T. what he'd steered Squint from doing, itched to sling him across gravel and stomp his ribs. Hot tears filled Jimmy's eyes. A burning wire traced a line between his shoulders. He marched out of the house.

His tires left smoke behind him, the street narrowed to a tunnel before him, but he was already slowing by the time he reached the first stop sign. He wrenched his palms on the steering wheel. Where was Charley's? He slapped the dash and gripped his face. He pressed the gas and moved, turned onto the road he had careened off of the day he arrived. Traffic hurried along, people going to jobs, to friends, to somewhere, a stream of cars with destinations. He thought for a moment to stay with the stream, keep going until he ran out of gas. Would Sandra care? Would she even notice? He wiped his mouth, dry summer dirt, plugged in a cigarette and kept going. He was after J.T., but he himself was already tracked by what he'd never had to do, look for a job without help. Sparks had set him up at Home Depot, no questions asked, no forms to fill. But the future was in his head like a movie lit with fire, the application forms like ice picks between the eyes, the looks from bosses at garages, construction sites, junk yards, people not half as smart as he was yet holding the power to make him a dumb boy. Jimmy shook so hard the cigarette tumbled from his mouth and onto the dash, surprising him that he was draped over the wheel as if riding hard. He scrambled to pinch the cigarette, found his fingers too trembly, opened the window and swept the smoke and cinders into the wind.

Twenty minutes later the yellow machinery next to Charley's appeared. Jimmy banked in front of oncoming cars and slid into the gravel. Squint's car sat next to a purple Cadillac that Jimmy suspected belonged to Charley. He trudged as if going uphill, kicked rocks at the Caddy, threw open the door to the bar and stepped in. Darkness closed behind him. His ears hummed, the room pitched like a ship's deck. As his vision cleared, he saw several men sitting at the bar, Squint's massive form among them. "Morning," he said. "Pull up a stool."

Jimmy scanned the small room—several tables, a quiet jukebox and two more doors at the rear. "Where's J.T.?" he said without moving.

"He's not here," Squint said, and gestured to the room.

Jimmy spun and moved toward one of the doors, but Squint was off his stool and in Jimmy's way much faster than Jimmy thought the large man could move. "Hold on, ace," Squint said, a meaty hand held inches from Jimmy's chest. "Don't mean to be rude, but that's Mr. Charley's office."

"I'm here to do some card playing. I know they doing it in there."

"Jimmy—that's it ain't it—*Jimmy?*—why don't you let me buy you a beer and I'll get Mr. Charley. You can talk to him." Squint touched Jimmy's shoulder and made to turn him, but Jimmy shook him off. "Whoa," Squint said, "don't get touchy. I don't like touchy."

"I wanta see J.T. It ain't nothing with you and your boss, just I need to see J.T."

"I said he's not here."

"Then I'll have to look for myself."

Squint tugged at the skin just below his chin. "That wouldn't work."

To Jimmy's side the other door opened, light slashing across the floor as a tall pale man in jeans, a bolo tie, and white shirt came out. "Mr. Charley," Squint said, "this is J.T.'s son that paid up his tab." Charley nodded and held out an arm to shake. When Jimmy didn't respond, Charley looked at Squint.

"What's going on?"

"He wants to see J.T."

Charley hmm-ed at Jimmy and scratched at his chin. "Why don't you let me buy you a drink."

"I know J.T.'s right there in that room, losing the money he took from me this morning."

Charley glanced at Squint, sniffed and pinched at his nose. "I can't let you go in there, so you either let me buy you a drink or I'm going to have to ask you to leave."

Jimmy crouched and spun, lifted on his toes and shoved Squint under the chin with both palms. The huge man reeled backwards, but Jimmy realized he was going with him, Squint's mitts clenched on Jimmy's wrists as tables and chairs bounced out of their way. Jimmy felt Squint regain his footing, then felt himself flying, swung like a child. He braced just before he crashed into the wall, saw bright light, was lifted by his collar and belt. Cursing floated to him as his vision began to return, then sunshine and heat greeted him just before he flew again. He extended his arms to break his fall, and gravel bit into his palms before he rolled and skidded to a stop. He scuttled, expecting a kick or a stomp, but when he focused, he was by himself.

He shook his head, pushed himself up and brushed the rocks from his skin. Blood dotted the pads of his hands. He studied the door, then headed around the corner of the building. Below a blackened window, he spat against the wall, pounded on it, yelling for J.T. to

come out, kicked it until the siding tiles cracked. Squint
rounded the corner at a run. "Quit it!" he said. Jimmy
froze for a second. Squint charged like a rhino. Jimmy
held his ground until Squint was close, then hopped to
the side and raked at Squint's face. His glasses spun into
the grass, stunning Squint, his eyes wide like a startled
child's. "That's it, mother fucker!" he yelled. He lunged,
and Jimmy landed one on Squint's nose before Squint
tackled him flat to the ground. He gripped Jimmy's
throat, shut off his windpipe, released, shut it off again
and said, "Find 'em." Without thinking, Jimmy slapped
both hands flat against Squint's ears, slapped again and
again, one of Pepper's long-ago lessons. Squint shrieked,
toppled and rolled on the ground. Jimmy scrambled to
his feet and sprinted for the entrance again. Near the
door his feet slid in the gravel, but he caught himself
and reached for the knob. The door opened inward. The
large hole of a pistol barrel greeted him.
     "That's enough," Charley said. "Simmer down and
go." Something pushed Jimmy to jump toward the pistol.
     "You sonofabitch," Jimmy said.
     "You go, you crazy bastard."
     Squint staggered around the edge of the building,
feeling his way along the wall. He looked more groggy
than anything. "I can't find my glasses," he said.
     "You should wear that strap I gave you," Charley
said. He waved the pistol at Jimmy. "Now get. You're
bad for business."
     "That's your ass," Squint said.
     "We'll see," Jimmy said.
     "Squint," Charley said. "That's enough."
     Squint pulled up. He rubbed his eyes, slitted yet
blazing, and looked in Jimmy's direction. "I'll give that
sorry daddy of yours a special hey."
     Jimmy glared a moment more, stalked to his car
and ducked in. He cranked his motor. For a split second
he considered flooring it straight through the wall of the
club. Instead, he turned around, checked his rearview
mirror to make sure Squint's car was right behind his
wheels and floored it, shooting a spray of rocks and dirt.
He fishtailed out into traffic, the bright day a blur, and
tried to breathe. Where the hell did he have to go? Not

back to J.T.'s shit hole. He pressed the accelerator to the floor.

J.T. was down, way down. And the muffled commotion in the next room wasn't helping either, although nobody else seemed bothered by it, except maybe Bean, who'd dealt him pocket 10s, and then placed a sawed-off pool cue on the table when he heard a crash outside. But then the other players were all high rollers, fellows for whom losing the kind of money J.T. was losing didn't mean what it meant to him. Or so he thought. He couldn't be sure because nobody else was losing the kind of money he was losing, and nobody else had borrowed extra money from Charley on top of what they'd brought. Plus, none of them had to suspect that the ruckus outside might be their long-lost son come to find his thieving father. What was worst, though, was that the crash of tables outside had distracted J.T. so much that he'd thrown in twenty dollars more on a hand he'd considered folding and now eighty of his, or Jimmy's, or Charley's, depending on how you cut it, lay in the pile on the table.

The other men in the game looked deadly, out of his league, and this psych-out was something he'd never anticipated this morning when he'd awakened to the pinwheel in his chest, the feeling that always told him he was going to rack up, told him that luck was coming in like spring time after gray winter. And that's why he'd lifted Jimmy's money, a sure thing, a no-lose way to get all of Jimmy's money back with cash to spare, to make Jimmy proud and show that J.T. could take care of him. But Jimmy had been a distraction even before he showed up outside (if that *was* Jimmy outside), because J.T. worried that Jimmy would go ballistic as soon as he found the money missing and worry hurt the pinwheel. And if that *was* Jimmy making the racket, he'd really become a distraction. Not that J.T. could blame him, unless, of course, the worry had seeped into the cards and spoiled them, because all J.T. had been getting served was rotten fruit. Or maybe the bad luck was just draw poker, not J.T.'s number one game. And maybe it was just this particular Hold 'em game at Charley's, an eccentric, early-morning game J.T. had always known about but never had the money to play until today when he had enough to sit at the 25/50 blinds and ten-dollar antes. At least he had the money earlier, until everything went sour and he borrowed five-hundred more dollars from Charley, Charley lording over him, shaking his head and clucking. When Charley left the room, J.T. had stuffed two-fifty in his pocket, something to give Jimmy just in case, but also another bad lack of faith in himself. He doubted he'd ever hear the pinwheel sing again.

"You still in?" Bean asked, and J.T. snapped to, the whole table watching him, he and two others of the six the only ones left. He was almost out of table money as it was and he licked his lips as he stared at the scatter of bills in the center of the table. If he folded or lost he was out, gone, dead.

Yelling penetrated the building from outside, then booming as if someone was kicking the wall. Then J.T.'s name, Jimmy's voice. The blood left J.T. like someone had pulled his plug. "What the hell?" Bean said, and gave J.T. a puzzled look. "Is that nut calling you?"

"I'm in," J.T. said, not even knowing what he said, and tossed in much of what he had left. Jimmy's voice fell in volume and was joined by another voice. The voices blended in J.T.'s mind to the whistle of an arrow hurtling toward his ear. His mouth went drier than he believed it could and still be called a mouth. He imagined Charley's enforcer pummeling Jimmy outside. His arm shot out, he clutched the money he'd just put in and stood. "Wait, I fold, I'm out."

"Whoa!" said the next man at the table, a fellow who called himself Kingfish and wore a red beret. He grabbed J.T.'s wrist. "You're in once you laid the money down, slick." J.T. considered taking a swing at the goateed man, but he glanced at Bean and the pool cue in front of him, then at the other hostile expressions around the table. He plopped back into his chair. Kingfish smiled and stroked his cards. "I raise to one-hundred."

"I'm in," said the only other man still holding, a beefy fellow with egret-white hair and pink cheeks. "And I raise ten."

J.T. felt the money clawing like an armadillo to escape his sock. These bastards had been bluffing and beating him on bad cards all day, so maybe his pair of tens had as good a chance as any cards he'd yet laid down. The pot called to him like salvation. He pictured himself stuffing the money into Jimmy's hand and saying, "From your old man," but a yelp pierced and deflated the image. He gritted his teeth, squeezed the money needed to stay in, heard nothing more from outside and went stiff. He dropped his cards and stood again. "I fold," he said, and stepped to the door before remembering the deadbolt the dealer had the key to. "Let me out."

"Sit the hell down, J.T.," Bean said, upright in his chair. "Nobody leaves in the middle of a hand."

"But I got t—"

"Sit down! And you interrupt this round again you gonna lose more than you have already."

J.T. shifted between his feet, considered for a split second leaping across the table to grab the stick and wrestle the key from Bean, then saw in the hard gaze and sinewy forearms of the man a sure ass-beating. He shuffled to his seat and sat. "I'm still in then."

"Tough tits," Bean said. "You done folded."

"That's bullshit," J.T. said. "You know me, Bean." Bean cracked his knuckles and looked hard at J.T.

"You have something to do with that ruckus outside?" Kingfish asked.

"Mind your own business," J.T. said, crossed his arms and slumped. He roved the table, meeting the gaze of everyone there until the dealer hmphed and asked the Kingfish what he wanted to do. J.T. strained to hear anything outside, but the tussle sounded like it was over or at least to a point where somebody had been taken down. He suddenly hated the men at the table, hated Charley and the mountain who worked for him, then recalled his own quiet footsteps that morning, recalled his quick pilfering of Jimmy's satchel, the pinwheel singing like a turbine behind his ribs. He inhaled, the pinwheel exhausted and smoldering like heartburn.

"Call," Kingfish said, and showed his cards, two nines.

The other man shook his head, sneered and showed

two sevens. Kingfish gave a loud Ha and scooped the money in. "Every man a king, but only one the Kingfish."

"Shit!" J.T. said, and sagged. "Open the damn door."

"It's been a pleasure," said Kingfish. "Hope we see you again real soon."

J.T. stared at Kingfish as Bean turned the bolt, then he pivoted and left. He braced, expecting to see Jimmy sprawled on the floor. Instead, Squint hunkered at a table, clutching the sides of his head as the bartender and the three other patrons crowded around Charley at the bar. Charley rubbed his knuckles on his chin. "That was your son just left," he said.

"He did that to your boy?" J.T. said, and smiled.

Charley frowned, pushed off the bar and pointed at J.T.

"You're a low snake, J.T.," Charley said. "Stealing from your own son. You lost it all, too, didn't you? You stole, you borrowed and you came out an even bigger loser. Well, that's it, J.T. I used to think you were all right. A bad card player but not a snake." Charley wiped the back of his hand across his lips and came so close that J.T. smelled Charley's cologne. He pulled a pack of Rolaids from his pocket, popped several into his mouth and chewed. "So this is how it's going to be, J.T. Tomorrow Squint's going to come by your house at noon and you're gonna give him a hundred dollars or you're gonna have to figure out a new way to hitchhike. Then, the next day, a hundred or a new way to wear rings. And so on. If you pay all those days, you get the sixth day off, but on the seventh day you better have the five-hundred dollars principle or you won't be walking around this town. That clear?" J.T. wanted to say something about Charley thinking he was so cute with all his ways of saying threats, except he'd never heard Charley making these kinds of threats, never seen him so angry. He studied the bar, considered getting a shot and a beer before he set out into the sun but simply straightened his collar and strolled to the door.

"Fuck y'all all high and mighty," J.T. said.

Squint stood, but Charley raised his arm. J.T. pushed out into the blazing sunlight. The heat almost took his knees from under him, but he thought of Jimmy slapping Squint down, rolled his shoulders and chuckled.

Then the ton of money he'd abandoned bullied him toward the road. A half mile down Airline Highway, his energy evaporated as quickly as his stake. The heavy traffic intensified the heat, and J.T.'s nice clothes stuck to him as if they'd been painted on. He tried to work saliva into his mouth. The sun beat on him like a hot iron mallet. It had been years since he worked outside, years since he'd been that kind of chump, breaking dirt on a chemical plant construction site, throwing pipe on a drilling rig, sweating his ass off for some rich bastard he didn't even know. One summer evening he had decided to leave the sun forever and head inside and he did, not that the shit jobs didn't exist there too. Shoe salesman, dry-wall hanger, stock clerk, insurance salesman. That last had been the worst, *insurance,* the door-to-door con to convince people to buy something he wouldn't even have himself. He smiled his way into their chump houses, lounged on their chump furniture and drank their chump coffee as he listened to their pathetic helpless chump stories about crummy chump jobs and too many chump kids and not enough money, nodded understandingly as they shared their chump woe about illness and bad health coverage and general chump unhappiness, all the while angling in his head how he was going to pitch so they'd take a swing, so they'd buy the safety net for when the head chump checked out. It made him sick. He *was* the man when he was selling that malarky to poor saps who could barely pay their grocery bills. Insurance in this life was about as much protection as a slingshot on a beach head. So one day he'd done all his clients a favor, torn up their premium cards, tossed them in the air and got drunk on the cash in his pocket, a lesson on how much protection a policy gave you.

An eighteen-wheeler zoomed past, kicking up gravel and blasting him with a diesel breeze. He careened and almost tumbled into the ditch by the road. The setting around him was bleak, warehouses and failing or failed businesses, power lines dividing the sky at crazy angles. For a moment confusion spun him, making him unsure exactly how to get back to his apartment, unsure for a moment exactly where his apartment was. Then, when his address clicked in, that bit of revelation pained him even more. Why would he want to go there? The only reason he'd gone in the first place was to get away from that asshole Charley, and if he went back there now, Squint would surely find him. J.T. had two-hundred fifty dollars in his sock, twenty-six in his pocket. Options: He could hail a cab to the bus station, catch a ride the hell out of town to New Orleans or even Atlanta, enough money left to find a game of blackjack; or he could go home and wait for Jimmy. He wiped the sweat from his forehead and tried to focus. He wasn't running. He knew it. Not this time. This time it didn't matter how far he ran, the real problem would track him—a different kind of debt collector.

He tried to picture the best way to get back to his apartment. Several blocks ahead was Evangeline Street which, if he could hitch a ride, would take him in the direction of Plank Road, although that direction was mostly black, making him wonder if he got a ride whether he'd still have Jimmy's money by the end of it. That was his only real choice, though, besides using just enough of the money to catch a cab. It wouldn't be that much, but anymore spent seemed significant now. He had to give Jimmy as much as he could in order to say he'd tried at least this much, quit out of concern with at least this much left. Surely that would mean something.

J.T. shook his head like a dog drying himself and pushed his feet along the shoulder again. Up ahead a McDonald's quavered like a hallucination. He smacked his lips. His stomach growled. He had to get out of this sun, maybe spend just a smidgen to eat. When he entered the McDonald's, nausea hit him with the cool air. He forced himself to the counter, the bright yellows and greasy odors reeling him, propped himself there and tried to read the menu. A pretty young black woman, skin the color of Morita's, stepped up and asked him what he'd like, and for a moment he was lost, swirling backward in time. He squeezed the counter and tried to tug himself back to now, until finally he saw the girl looking at him strangely. "Sir?" she asked.

"Cheeseburger, fries and Coke," he said, going on auto pilot, and she spun away. The bustle of cooking and ordering pin-balled around him, and he kept hold of the counter. Morita tried to step into his mind again, but he pushed her out. The pair of tens replaced her, floating between him and the milkshake machine like a taunt. He almost tried to catch them, but his hands were locked on metal, his knees shaky, sweat saturating him even more now that he had stopped walking. The tens darted closer then drifted arrogantly away. All that money in Kingfish's possession, another undeserving jerk, this one without even the cleverness or slick charm or outward advantage that most of the luck usually gravitated toward. Maybe J.T. deserved something ill, but not this humiliation. After all, he'd folded to help his son, to keep the remaining money and to save Jimmy from a beating, and this is what he got, another cruel tease from the universe.

"Here's your order," the black girl said, and he dared not look at her. He passed her a five, plucked the lid from the Coke and drained half of it, the cold sugary thickness landing in his stomach with the grace of moonshine. He belched and swallowed down the acid. The girl placed his change on the counter. He picked it up without counting, was struck by panic because he hadn't checked if the change was odd or even, then turned and walked to a corner table. He nibbled at a fry. Would Jimmy come back? He'd half expected him to be lurking near Charley's, expected him to skid up next to J.T. on the highway and order him in, a gruff savior. He hadn't fully considered that Jimmy might be badly hurt, since it was Charley's boy who'd been hunched and tending his ears. Now J.T. wasn't absolutely sure. Had somebody whacked Jimmy with a bat and somebody else driven him off? No, he remembered Charley threatening Jimmy too, a sign of Jimmy's health, which meant Jimmy was probably off seeing that girl at the drugstore. At least J.T. hoped he was and not headed back to Texas. Or to the cops.

J.T. popped a fry in his mouth, opened a packet of ketchup, squirted it on the fries and popped two more. The salt tasted good and so did the sweet ketchup. Maybe these good tastes were the beginning of another good thing. He'd eat, hitch a ride, find Jimmy and give him the money. Jimmy would think of a way to protect him. He and his son would think of a way.

*   *   *

Sandra tried to concentrate on stocking the shelves, but Jimmy's anger and expression before he ran wouldn't leave her. That morning she'd come to work with something like resolve to break it off. Now her mind was chasing its own tail. She had said Yes, then No, then Yes, and he'd taken off running. Sure, he said it wasn't her, and that at least was different from Hilly, she supposed, although she couldn't really know. Didn't really know Jimmy enough to know anything except she liked him. And why? Because he was as lost as she was? Because he'd been even more parentless than she was and understood what that was like? That, yes, but mostly the palpable vibration from her navel up and down, not like the simple *attractions* she'd felt for some of the men who'd come in the store, but more like the impulse she'd had with Hilly, to charge headlong into passion and loss of control. And where had that led? To days of love-making that passed like dreams free of loneliness after the loneliness of flings with men she liked and who liked her, but with whom she had nothing beyond.

She reached to place a can of shaving cream on the top shelf, bobbled and dropped the can with a clang that shot up her spine, followed by a metallic roll that made her cover her face. "You juggling them cans, Sandra?" came Mrs. Rideaux's voice from the rear of the store. "No, ma'am, just fumble fingers." She listened to her own voice, almost certain it sounded normal. But then, what did she know about normal? She'd barely interacted with anyone outside the store in half a year and for months even before that, cloistered and depressed in her apartment up north. Had she ever even wanted to be normal anyway? She doubted it. Not even when she thought it might bring her mother back to her.

She snatched the can from the floor and set it on the shelf, closed her eyes and focused on breathing. She needed to get back inside herself, create some space and stop floundering in her scramble of thoughts. *Breathe.* So what if Jimmy didn't come back. That had happened before, and much worse, and she'd survived that. *Breathe.* Except she thought she'd learned enough not to get back in this spot. *Breathe.* "Shit," she muttered, slammed the last can on the metal shelf and headed to the front, trembling all the way. The hell with her if a stranger gave her such grief.

Closer to the door, Mr. Rideaux was taking the week's money from the small safe, tallying it and placing it in a canvas bag on a table behind the counter, the ritual he'd been following for twenty-seven years, he'd told her, and which irked her with its risk. She'd finally asked him why he didn't at least lock the door, to which he replied that the day he didn't feel safe loading up money in broad daylight was the day he'd know he stopped trusting people and he might as well be dead. She understood this, but she also felt like what he was doing was stubborn and foolhardy, a temptation to some of the desperate people around her, and she'd seen some eye the bag. The only cautious thing was he switched the days and times. Still, it was just reckless and stupid. She knew reckless and stupid.

She began shuffling items behind the counter, barely aware of what they were, a flush of agitation sheening up her chest. The clang of the cow bell shot along her spine. She dug her nails into some papers and almost screamed before she saw it was Jimmy. She nearly levitated with relief at the same moment irritation and doubt crested in her. Then she really saw him, his complexion high pink, his eyes scowling incandescent. She could see his aura, a line of coal inside of which burned confused reds, oranges, and yellows. She inhaled as Jimmy paused and studied the store. His eyes moved over her, but they showed no sign of recognition, showed no sign that they *saw* anything until he locked onto Mr. Rideaux filling the bag. He blinked, his mouth open almost dumbly, raised his hands, extended his fingers and pushed together all ten fingertips until his middle joints seemed to bend backwards. Sandra meant to say his name, to do anything to make him look at her, show him she was with him, but she had seen people she loved look at her as if she'd morphed into something less than they previously believed, and now fright shot through her as if she were seeing someone possessed.

Jimmy took three quick steps, braced his palm on the counter and cleared it like a low fence. Mr. Rideaux yelped and stumbled away. Jimmy grabbed the money bag, launched back over the counter and loped toward the door, his movements almost as mechanical as they had been swift and smooth seconds before. She called his name without thinking to, and then she was after him, her consciousness left behind for an instant like an after-image. Her hands hit the door just as it clanged shut behind him. The outside heat swatted her. He was running along the covered sidewalk, his stride stiff, not quite running. She went after him, both of them in a swampy dream, her mind not yet closing on it all. When he passed through the narrow exit to the back lot, sunlight exploded on him like a spotlight and she yelled, her legs finding their sprint. He pulled up as if lassoed and turned, the ugly aura disintegrated by sunshine, Jimmy himself again, though dazed. Sandra glanced over her shoulder to Mr. Rideaux, just staggering out, stretched her arms and grabbed Jimmy's wrists at full stride. She twirled him behind a building out of Rideaux's sight and tugged the money bag, Jimmy's expression only half-registering.

"Let go!" she said, and he did. "Go!" she said, and pointed to his car. "Run!" she said, and shoved him. He started as if waking, stumbled once, his mouth opening, hands gesturing as if to explain. "Meet me at my house," she said. "You remember how to get there?" He nodded, his Jimmyness fully returning, his expression signaling recognition and shock. "Go!" she said. "Now! I'll meet you." She wheeled and dashed toward the walkway, heard the car start and tear away as she closed on Mr. Rideaux, who was reeling up the sidewalk. Mrs. Rideaux exited the store a few paces behind him, and she and Sandra caught him and each other simultaneously.

"You all right?" they all said. "I'm fine," she said. "Let's get inside."

"We have to call the police," he stammered.

"Inside," she said, and turned him, Mrs. Rideaux taking his other arm.

Once through the door, he shook them off and stood straight. "I have to lock the door. One of you call." He took the keys from his pocket, fumbled them, dropped them. Sandra grabbed them up, found the right one and turned the bolt.

"Don't call!" she yelled to Mrs. Rideaux. "He didn't know what he was doing. He's not right."

"You know him?" Mrs. Rideaux asked.

"He's been coming in. I've been trying to help him." The Rideauxs looked at each other. "It would be bad for him to be arrested. He's not dangerous."

Mr. Rideaux pointed at the bag. "How did you get it back?"

"I just asked him."

"We should still call the police," Mrs. Rideaux said.

"Please," Sandra said. "There's no need for that."

"He robbed us," Mr. Rideaux said.

"He didn't know what he was doing." She paused and glanced at both of them. "He's retarded."

The Rideauxs looked at each other. Then, without more words, the three of them gathered at the counter. Mr. Rideaux ran his fingers threw his pomp of thinning, black hair. "Thank you," he said. "But don't do it if it ever happens again."

"We'll lock the door from now on," Sandra said. "Take better precautions."

"I told you, Tony," Mrs. Rideaux said, "but you're so stubborn. *Long as I do it at different times*, you said. We hire somebody to come from now on." He nodded.

"He won't come back," Sandra said. "I'll put the closed sign up and stay here in case somebody needs their medicine. Why don't y'all go to the back?"

The Rideauxs exchanged looks that seemed to Sandra a silent communication, a glance that made her look away lest she break down. They turned in unison and headed back toward the pharmacy.

Sandra watched them, still unsure whether they would call the police. Somehow she didn't care because she'd make it not matter. She realized the money bag was still in her hand and dropped it on the counter. The thrum from her navel was going in every direction, her body humming as if wires had been implanted beneath her skin. She ran her hands over her stomach, along her hips, let them rest on her thighs and breathed. Breathed again and again. Heavy anxiety and worry were ahead, she knew, but for right now she loved that she was this alive.

PEPPER

Jimmy and Pepper lived thirty miles from Sparks' main property and an hour by truck from the ranch house itself. It took them fifteen minutes to reach paved road, then forty-five minutes more to reach the nearest town. Pepper acted like that was too close, although he stuck to their routine to visit town once a month until Jimmy was nine, even when Pepper was deep in his cups or just down. They would leave the ranch after morning chores, Pepper closely shaven, his good boots polished, jeans creased, best hat brushed, his shiny black go-to-town eye patch applied. On the road, Jimmy would watch through the rear window as their ranch house and the large mesa beyond the house disappeared in a plume of dust, then he would settle in for the ride, sometimes nauseous with excitement. Pepper stayed quiet on the dirt road, cursing at new washes and peering off to spot cattle in the distance, but when they hit the main road, he turned the radio to a country or rock n roll station. He couldn't sing worth a damn, but once in a while, when he was feeling good, he'd prompt Jimmy to sing along to a tune—Buddy Holly or Johnny Cash or Hank Williams, all of whom Pepper had records of—tempering Jimmy's anxiety about town and saving him from the silence that could turn the trip into suffering.

The town of Eden seemed like a metropolis to Jimmy. First stop was always the library, where Pepper talked to Mrs. Schmidt, a tall, big-boned woman who gave Pepper the records (and later cassette tapes) he'd ordered from Reading for the Blind (even one eye lost in the war qualified him) and suggested titles he might want to consider for next time. She always had a glossy picture book—dinosaurs, ships, animals, planets—for Jimmy to examine while she talked to Pepper, always including how Jimmy should go to school. Pepper listened without speaking, then they'd go.

Second stop was the supply store, where they'd stock up on feed and other things they couldn't provide themselves at the ranch. If Pepper was in a good mood, the third stop was the record store for a new music album, the store's owner, Chub Wells, always ready with some free candy for Jimmy since Chub had a sweet tooth. Next stop was the diner. Jimmy liked a thick cheeseburger with lettuce and tomato, a glass of sweet tea, and a slice of apple pie with chocolate ice cream. The waitresses there talked to Jimmy but little to Pepper, who barely looked at them, even when he ordered. After lunch they'd stroll the short downtown, Pepper smoking a cigar and making quiet comments about the men even though he didn't know them: "That one there's mighty proud of himself," or "He don't know which end of a horse the shit comes outten, but I guarantee it's the same end he come out." About the women he muttered, and Jimmy, sensing Pepper's stewing, didn't ask what the words were. Then they would go to the tiny movie house, where Jimmy would take in the matinee. Pepper seldom joined him and when he did he fell asleep and snored so loudly that Jimmy would move to another row. Other times Pepper would leave and be waiting for Jimmy after, smelling of whiskey and sour smoke. With or without Pepper, Jimmy loved the movies, the huge lighted action onscreen driving away any sleepiness lunch might have caused. There were days when Jimmy wished he could live in town, or at least go there more often, but after a few days back on the ranch, Pepper grousing about people or sliding into quietness, Jimmy figured if that was the effect towns had on people, he was better off out here.

* * *

Over the years, the two Peppers grew more exaggerated: one, the talker who shared stories, records, and what he knew of the world; the other, the angry, bitter drinker who shut off during the maddening wind of plain's winter and caught brain fever during the pummeling heat of summer. Jimmy had come to the small ranch—a two-bedroom homestead and seldom-used two-man bunkhouse—at the age of five. He had no memory of parents or of the orphanages that Mr. Sparks told him he'd lived in before becoming Sparks's ward, knew only that Mr. Sparks told him that a woman who worked for the state had called asking if he might be interested in taking in an orphan boy and he'd thought it'd be good to have a young hand grow up on the ranch. Not long after Jimmy arrived, Pepper convinced Sparks to let him take Jimmy over to the smaller spread for company and then just kept him there.

At night Pepper slid discs of fat vinyl from their sleeves and placed them on the record-player spindle. Pepper would press a button, a record would splat down onto the circling turntable, and the needle would lower to the edge with a pop. Pepper sank into his rocker. Often music would rise, but just as often a woman's voice reading from a book would crackle out. The topics ranged from physics to novels, but Pepper's favorites were geology, geography, and history. Pepper stared, sometimes in Jimmy's direction, sometimes nodding and uh-huhing at a spot on the ceiling, asking Jimmy if he heard that, or lifting the stylus and placing it to replay something of particular interest. When inspiration swept Pepper, he stopped the record player and told a story of his own travels in the Navy during World War II, the stories making Pepper's eye shine with intensity, yet always ending with how it was best to stay here away from betraying women and the unfairness of the world.

Pepper had grown up the son of a sharecropper who grew cotton, corn, and watermelons and raised chickens and hogs outside Eutaw, Alabama, and who thought school so frivolous that Pepper never went. When the letter arrived calling Pepper to boot camp, he mourned leaving the girl he'd already asked to marry him, even though he'd only kissed her twice. He traveled on a train across half the United States, crossed the Pacific as part of a great fleet and met men from all over the country, heard stories of places that seemed like made-up places— New York, the painted desert, Chicago, North Dakota, the Sierra Nevadas—but the more he saw dead people and destroyed places, the more he just wanted to return to his girl and the red clay of home.

When Pepper was depressed and drinking, he would remove his eye patch and reveal the mottle of cloudy white and green. "Never seen a second of combat, just the after-combat when the Marines and Japs was dead, but I still got got. One second I's tugging on a damn rope line, the next second I's trying to figure how lightning come to strike on a clear day. Never seen a second of action and there I was with my eye took. Not that I'd of cottoned to killing folks, but there I was young and strong in the middle of the biggest thing that ever happened, and a goddamn lashing rope takes my sight away forever."

For a long while, he stopped there, but one night when Jimmy was nine, Pepper kept going. "They sent me on home and I got hitched to this woman I'd asked before the war, even though she hadn't wrote me but one letter, I guessed cause she knew I couldn't read 'em. They wasn't no other boys back from the war yet 'cept another that'd got hurt, and she was still living with her mean daddy, so I reckon that's why she married me. She didn't talk too much, but that was fine with me. She just left me to my work mostly, so I thought she was fine. I knew her and me both wanted younguns and for some reason we wasn't having none, and I'd took to having bad headaches around her. Other fellas started coming back from the war and one day when I come back early from picking up some things in town and bringing her a new dress, I caught her there taking up with an old boy I knowed she had seen before he went off to the army. They didn't hear me come in, but I heard them and my head just started to split and I was whupping on the both of them with a heavy chair I'd snatched up before I knew it. Liked to killed 'em both I reckon. Might should have. I can't say I'm really sorry for it. I just lit out, swore that's the last time I'd have to do with women." Pepper wiped the cottony spittle forming at the edges of his mouth, pinched at his nose and killed the whiskey in his cup. Jimmy braced, lightness swirling through his head. Pepper sneezed violently ten or fifteen times, brushed the tears from his eyes and shook his head before slipping his patch back on and gathering breath.

"I stayed on the road working, till one day I was hitching and Sparks picked me up and told me I could help with a round-up on his ranch if I had a mind. I took a liking to being out where nobody bothered you, and when he bought this little spread, I asked him if I could come run it and bring you along. He barely paid you a mind, so he didn't have no problem with that."

Pepper heaved out of his rocker and headed outside. In a little while, Jimmy heard galloping hooves. He waited until he woke up on the floor, checked Pepper's empty bed and went to his own room. The next morning Jimmy was finishing up his early chores when Pepper returned, dusty and tired-looking, and dragged inside without a word.

The winter of Jimmy's tenth year, the wind screamed in from the northwest for months. Cattle died, and Pepper's horse Captain broke his leg, forcing Pepper to shoot him. Pepper took to whiskey more, stayed nearly silent for days on end, and then went into rants, often at the mesa a third of a mile from the ranch house. The March morning they were supposed to head into town, Jimmy awoke to find Pepper pouring whiskey into his coffee, his bad eye unpatched, his good eye both agleam and sunken, as he stared toward the mesa through the kitchen window. "Damn thing just lording over us. Don't even look like it's supposed to be there." He lit the cigarette he'd rolled and sucked furiously on it, slugged back his coffee and grunted at the evident burn. He pointed his hand at Jimmy, his good eye glaring. "You know what's best for you, you won't go out there, boy. All's it is is cheatin' and lies." He took another slug of coffee, topped it off with a little more whiskey and went to his rocker. Jimmy considered asking him if they were still going in, but Pepper had slapped him the previous day when he asked a question. Instead, he went out to feed the animals. When he came back in, Pepper had combed his hair and put his patch on, but he hadn't shaved his gray-frosted stubble or put on his best clothes. "Well get on it, son," Pepper said as if Jimmy had been dawdling.

When they pulled up in front of the library, Pepper turned off the engine but didn't move. They had barely listened to the new-fangled cassette tapes Pepper had gotten the past two months or watched the television Sparks had bought them for Christmas, and Jimmy could almost hear Pepper's thoughts that picking up a new tape would be a waste of time. Jimmy wished he could say something to make Pepper feel better, but he said nothing, afraid to set him off. Pepper peered at the library as if a man with a pistol were waiting for him inside. "I hope that bitch don't give me no noise today," he finally said, and threw open his door. "And don't you repeat what I said," he added.

Jimmy could tell from Mrs. Schmidt's expression that she read Pepper's state, but rather than softening, she grew taller and set her own face. Without the usual pat she gave Jimmy's arm, she handed him a book about sea creatures, and he marched to his familiar table. The cover had a color picture of what he knew to be an octopus, and his fingers tingled to open it, but he sat with the book closed. "You had a strong breakfast again," she said to Pepper as she went around behind her desk.

"You a expert on that now too?" Mrs. Schmidt's mouth tightened, then she took a seat and gestured for Pepper to do the same in the chair opposite her. He examined the hard seat as if it might have a turd on it and remained standing.

"How old is Jimmy?" she asked, her voice not lowered as it normally was when she took this tone. "Isn't he ten this year?" Pepper crossed his arms. Mrs. Schmidt leaned forward. "It's time to think about getting him some schooling. In fact, it's long past time."

"He's getting schooling. He can near bout run the ranch his self now."

"Is he learning to read?"

Pepper's tongue bulged in his cheek. He pinched
at his nose and snorted. "He listens to them records and
tapes with me. We talk about matters."

"But he can't read. He's ten and he can't read."

"It ain't hurt me none."

"How do you know? I'm not saying it has, but it
might have. It will hurt him. What if he doesn't want to
stay on the ranch?"

Pepper sneezed, but only once, took out a red
kerchief and wiped his nose. "I can't see that."

"It's not for you to see. I know folks who are
schooling out that way, and people who can come out
once in a while. I just want you to consider it. I think
it's really time to consider it." Mrs. Schmidt stood and
straightened her skirt. She came toward Jimmy, her
back stiff, and glanced at the book still closed in front
of him. A prickly brush swiped his scalp. "You haven't
opened your book," she said.

"No, ma'am."

"Wouldn't you like to be able to open that book and
understand the words?" Mrs. Schmidt had stationed
herself to block his view of Pepper. "Wouldn't you like to
go to school and be able to do what other children can do?"

"I reckon, ma'am." Pepper's sneeze sounded like a
wet rag splatting against the wall. Jimmy flinched. "We
listen to them tapes," he said, even though they hadn't
in a while. "Me and Pepper talk over things. Last month
I learned all about the Roman Umpire and such."

"Achoo!"

Mrs. Schmidt shifted her feet and looked, not
behind her, but simply to the side. "That's very good,
but I would like to see you in a classroom with some
other children, or have someone come out to teach you
to sound out your letters."

"Achoo, achoo, achoo, achoo!!!"

Mrs. Schmidt pivoted. "Are you coming down with
something?"

"Ma'am," Jimmy said as Pepper sneezed again.
"That's why he's called Pepper. He sneezes when he's
riled."

Pepper's steps sounded on the wooden floor.
"ACHOO!" He appeared behind Mrs. Schmidt, his eyes

watery from his attack. "Let's go, boy," he said. Jimmy sprang to his feet, leaving the book on the table. "Thank you kindly, ma'am," Pepper said. He pointed a finger at the door without raising his arm.

"Pepper, please, I'm only trying to help." Her voice had changed, and it tugged at Jimmy to go back and retrieve his book. "Your tape, Jimmy's book."

"Tell Mizzuz Schmidt thank you, boy."

"Thank you," Jimmy said, and then they were outside, the bright sun striking Jimmy like a shove to the forehead. He staggered for a couple of steps, then the chuffing of Pepper's sneezes cut through to him. Jimmy spread his feet to catch his balance, tried to focus on Pepper, who was bent at the waist, sneezing and coughing. "Get in the truck," he said between spasms. Jimmy took a step toward him, afraid Pepper might collapse. "I said *git!*" Jimmy went to the passenger door, hesitated, then got in when Pepper recovered enough to walk toward the truck. He was muttering, *Busy body* and *Bitch thinking we ain't good enough,* then he stopped and kicked the truck, slapped it too before he hopped behind the wheel. "We ain't ate yet," Jimmy said, wondering if food might help Pepper. Pepper's hand shot out and stung Jimmy's cheek. "I don't want no lip." Jimmy's fist balled, then he looked out the window, eyes watering.

Pepper drove faster than ever before, and when they arrived home, he took his bottle and locked himself in his bedroom, where cursing and crashing came through the door. Jimmy thought to knock, touched the place he still stung, then went outside and brushed his horse Sandy until his arm grew weak. That evening Pepper didn't join him for supper and Jimmy fell asleep in front of the snowy TV. In the middle of the night, a fading gallop awakened him. He went to the porch and called out, even though he knew Pepper couldn't hear him. Next morning he found Pepper on the porch, sitting in a chilly wind and staring at the mesa. "That goddamn thing just waitin'," he said. Jimmy looked out at the mesa's long side. "Wind working and working on it, whittling it down and down and it not giving a thing. Where the hell'd it come from out here. It don't belong. Don't give a goddamn thing."

Jimmy studied it, its level rocky top and sloping ends. He and Pepper rode near it all the time, its height dizzying with nearness. Pepper had said they'd climb it one day, but lately he hadn't said it. Lately Pepper had been more spooked by it and today Jimmy was spooked too. He wished Pepper would stop looking at it, stop talking about it, wondered if it had cast some spell on Pepper.

"Why you scared of that thing?" Jimmy asked. Pepper's expression shifted to something Jimmy had never seen before. He'd heard Sparks talk to Pepper about the early days when Pepper was wild and mean, and now he understood the wildness and meanness in Pepper's look. "We need to patch that roof," Jimmy said, hoping to distract him. Pepper stood.

"Step off the porch, boy," he said. "I'm gone teach you a patching lesson." Pepper glanced at the mesa once more as he stood, then he had Jimmy's collar and was walking him onto the dirt. He shoved Jimmy and told him to put up his fists. "You gone mouth off, you need to know how to back it up. Know how to hurt the other fella 'fore he hurts you." Pepper jabbed Jimmy in the chest, and Jimmy flailed backward into the dust. "Get up quick," Pepper said, and Jimmy scrambled, his feet overcoming the surprise. Pepper slapped him down on the shoulder, and again when Jimmy stood, kept on until Jimmy rushed him, his ears filled with noise like he'd never heard, angry tears burning, his body hardening for the next blow. Jimmy forgot where he was, who Pepper was, until finally Pepper bear-hugged him and kept holding until Jimmy grew too tired to struggle. "Fine," Pepper said, and let him go. "You mad enough to take care now. Next time I'll show you some tricks to get a man offen you if he gets you on the ground."

Pepper turned and ambled away into the barn, leaving Jimmy with skin that stung as if buffed with rough leather. Jimmy's brain throbbed, and when his sight landed on the mesa, his balance rippled, then dropped him to the ground.

* * *

Pepper threw himself into chicken-raising, persuading Sparks to provide materials and chickens even though he told Pepper west Texas was too hot and dry to raise chickens and it was bound to lose money. Sparks also gave this advice: "Make sure you build it east of the house. Downwind." Jimmy hated the chickens. The smell, the noise, the die-offs, the gathering for shipping to be slaughtered. But Pepper stayed after it, the chickens' plight a reflection to Jimmy, even so young, of Pepper's own.

First time back in town, Mrs. Schmidt asked where Pepper was and looked sad when Jimmy told her he was waiting in the truck. She gazed toward the door as if she could see through it to him. Shelves of books towered around Jimmy, and he could have sworn they were leaning. "Here," Mrs. Schmidt said, and gave Jimmy some cassettes for Pepper whose titles she said she'd chosen on her own. "Tell Mr. Pepper I missed visiting with him." At the pick-up, Jimmy repeated the words exactly, but Pepper harumphed and shifted into gear. That afternoon, when they reached the dirt turn-off from the highway, Pepper stopped the truck and came around to Jimmy's side. "Scoot over behind the wheel. Your legs can reach to work the gas." Jimmy hesitated. "Git," Pepper said, and Jimmy slid over. Following Pepper's instructions, Jimmy shifted and wrestled the clutch until finally the truck lurched into motion. Jimmy laughed, but Pepper didn't join him. "Never can tell when you might need to get by on your own," Pepper said. Jimmy wasn't sure what this meant, but he was sure he didn't like it.

On Jimmy's fifth trip into the library alone, Mrs. Schmidt sat across from him at a table. The book stacks behind her looked restless and ready to topple, but he focused hard on her green eyes. "I want you to take these books," she said, and gestured to a stack of several the size of the picture books she usually had him look over in the library. On the cover of the top one were flying machines and a man with wings strapped to his back. A rubber band held a cassette tape to the book. "The flight book is the first on the tape, and the tape is so you can read along. It'll tell you when to turn the page. That's your name spelled out on the label of the tape." Jimmy's fingers vibrated to reach out, but the thought of Pepper's disapproval gave the books a menace like a diamondback just out of striking range. "And this tape," she handed it to him, "has a message for Pepper from me. Will you tell him when you give it to him?" Jimmy said, "Yes, ma'am." "And one other thing." Mrs. Schmidt laid hands on both of Jimmy's forearm, her touch firing through him, then settling to soothe him so thoroughly that he wanted to rest his head. "It's very important that you learn to read, and I want us all to think of a way we can make that happen." She smiled, but Jimmy saw Pepper glowering, sneezes wracking him. He nodded even though he knew it was a betrayal of Pepper.

In the truck Jimmy didn't tell Pepper about the message from Mrs. Schmidt, and Pepper didn't say anything about the books and tapes Jimmy carried. When they were finished with their errands and headed back home, Pepper stopped on the highway a few miles from their turn and put Jimmy behind the wheel again. "Time for some main road driving," he said, then let Jimmy struggle with the details.

That evening they sat quietly for an hour until Jimmy slipped in Mrs. Schmidt's tape and pushed PLAY. The chickens had irritated Pepper all day, and Jimmy hoped Mrs. Schmidt's message could be a salve to Pepper like her touch had been to him. More than that he hoped that the message would bring Pepper back to the library and town like the old days. "Pepper," came her voice from the tape, "I want to say I'm sorry." Pepper almost lunged for the player, punched it off and removed the tape. "Did you listen to this?" he asked, a strange question since Jimmy had been on the range with him ever since they returned from town. "No, sir." Pepper snapped the tape in half, dropped it on the floor and marched toward the stable.

Jimmy fought the urge to go after him, knew that Pepper would just swat him away if he tried to stop him, so he sat rigidly until he heard Pepper's horse ride off. He stroked his forearms where Mrs. Schmidt had touched him and ogled the stack of books that he'd been surprised Pepper did not toss into the yard. Finally, he slid the tape from beneath the rubber band, the writing on it supposedly his name, plugged the tape in and opened the flight book. Mrs. Schmidt spoke again. "Jimmy, this book is called *The History of Flight.* Open the book to the page where I put the piece of paper." She paused. Jimmy almost hit the OFF button, his palms clammy, then he opened the book to the piece of paper with a flower drawn on it. He rubbed the paper between his fingertips, then looked at the book, where there was a picture of a man with large wings strapped to him. "Page one. 'Man has always wanted to fly. The Greeks tell the story of Icarus. He had wings with straps made of wax.' Page two. 'But Icarus flew too close to the sun, and the sun was so hot that it melted the straps. Icarus fell into the sea.'"

Mrs. Schmidt's voice continued, but Jimmy was transfixed by the man plummeting toward the water. "Page three," he half heard, but he couldn't take his eyes off the man, experienced himself levitating and gripped the arms of his chair. He held tight, the high mesa coming to mind, felt his stomach drop. "Page six," he heard and forced his attention down to the words beneath the falling man. He scanned them. They seemed not just indecipherable but alive, squirming and crawling and drifting. He touched them to reassure himself that they weren't somehow actually moving, then he raised his eyes to the wall, saw Pepper cursing both the mesa and Mrs. Schmidt. The book slipped from his hands and fell to the floor. The wall did a slow spin, and he gripped the chair more tightly, Mrs. Schmidt's voice unintelligible as the room continued to spin. He wanted the room to be still, wanted Pepper home, thought of trying to stand, to go to the stable and saddle Sandy to follow Pepper. But he imagined the wide darkness and the mesa rising and Pepper's displeasure and shut his eyes against the vertigo threatening to throw him down.

The old Pepper faded like daylight shrinking toward winter. He exploded often when Jimmy or a visiting hand did or said something that rubbed him wrong, then one day punched a young wrangler from the main ranch, starting a fight that lasted until Jimmy threw himself at the wrangler and he stopped hitting Pepper. The young man looked at Jimmy as if ashamed and stalked away. When Pepper staggered to his feet, he popped Jimmy upside the head and told him never interfere, he could take care of himself. That night Sparks called Pepper on their new telephone and talked a long time. After the call, Pepper cursed and slammed around before heading toward the front door. Jimmy stood in his way, but Pepper slung him aside and didn't come home for two days. He trudged past Jimmy on the porch, trailing a cloud of whiskey, and collapsed on his bed until Jimmy found him bathed and drinking coffee the next morning. Pepper didn't speak or react at all when Jimmy took a spot close to him without sitting.

"Four of them pullets died while you was gone," Jimmy said.

"They'll do that."

"I think they were too hot. I think a bunch more of 'em liked to died."

"Let the stinking things die."

"It was your idea to raise 'em."

"You ain't got to tell me that."

"Then you oughta help tend to 'em."

Pepper sipped from his cup. "You old enough to tend to things. You old enough to go to town and fetch your own books."

"You oughta go. You oughta do something besides what you do." Jimmy had never spoken to Pepper like this, but Pepper said nothing. The bruises on Pepper's face brought back the fight, the cracks and grunts of fists landing, Jimmy's attempt to help, Pepper's tossing him out of the way after. "You shouldn't of fought him," he said. "You shouldn't oughta ride off all the time neither. Mr. Sparks don't know you going off, does he?"

Pepper touched his lip with the tip of his tongue. "That's enough," he said.

Jimmy's breathing was shallow. He wanted to be big enough to reach across and slap Pepper. "We needed that fella cause you ain't done your chores and now you done run him off. Where you go anyhow?"

Pepper stood, drained his coffee and left through the front door, his boot steps echoing from the porch. Jimmy shattered Pepper's mug against the wall, but Pepper didn't come back in.

After three years Jimmy was illegally driving into town alone, and Mrs. Schmidt was giving him tapes that Pepper didn't listen to and books with no pictures that Jimmy still couldn't read. Jimmy knew Mrs. Schmidt wanted him to say he had learned to read, but he had given up on looking at words. Every time he tried to follow them, to take the initial step toward deciphering them, the symbols on the page rioted, rearranging and blurring as if Pepper were stirring them, until Jimmy's pulse fluttered at just the thought of reading. Instead, he listened to Pepper's tapes, women's voices teaching him, keeping him company when Pepper was gone or sleeping it off. At times a voice even attached itself to a notion of who his mother might be, the notion coming as faintly as a desert flower's long-traveled scent on the wind.

In Jimmy's thirteenth summer, two weeks of heat killed all of the chickens while Pepper festered drunk and Jimmy fought to save them. Jimmy's dizziness grew worse, until sometimes it spiraled him so hard it seemed he would be tossed from his own skin. And it wasn't simply dizziness, but rather his entire surroundings tossing and whirling so that more than once Jimmy believed that the earth was actually moving beneath him. Pepper didn't seem to notice any of it.

One day near dusk, Jimmy came from the barn toward Pepper sitting rigidly on the porch, gaze fixed on the mesa, whiskey glass in lap, his complexion so possum gray that Jimmy's spine tingled. Jimmy had mended fence all day in the sun, and although the evening breeze was blowing cool, the heat seemed locked inside him. He stepped up on the porch, and the whiskey's odor reached him. He glanced at Pepper's caved cheeks, then at the mesa. A chill crept through him, as if Pepper's fear of the thing had finally been transferred fully from Pepper to him. Jimmy stepped in front of Pepper. "I want you to stop drinking that shit," Jimmy said.

Pepper rocked, his lanky legs extended, his fingers clasped on the arm of his chair. "You hear that? That sumbitch whispering. It's been staring us down ever since we come here." Pepper pulled his legs in and sat straight.

Jimmy widened his stance. "I'm sick of you drunk and going off, leaving me to run this place." Pepper took a sip. "You ain't going off no more at night. And you gone work full days too."

Pepper narrowed his look at Jimmy. "You ain't too old for me to step out in that dirt with you."

"You ain't going out at night no more and sleeping up in the house all day. All them chickens died cause you was laid up drunk."

"The hell with them chickens."

Jimmy had piled the stinking birds away from their pitiful house, doused them with gasoline and set them ablaze, the stench of their burning so pungent he smelled it even now.

"It ain't right what you doing. What's wrong with you? Where you go anyhow?"

"Ain't none of your business."

"It is my business. Things need fixing and no hands wanta come over here."

Pepper eyed him for a long time, the glow that signaled a slap or some loud craziness brightening around his pupils. He drained off his glass and tapped it on his thigh. "I'm tired of it. I go off by myself just to get to where there ain't nothing I have to tend to and that goddamn thing ain't watching down on me."

The skin on Jimmy's back itched. He wanted to scoff at the mesa, but he could almost swear it was inching toward them. "It ain't nothing but rocks, Pepper."

"You don't know what it is. That thing was a mountain and now it's all whittled down. You think you know what goes on? What's out there? What folks can do? What can get after you? You don't know nothing."

Jimmy touched his forehead. He was certain Pepper was crazy, and that made the sense that Jimmy heard in Pepper's words all the more frightening. "We gone climb it," Jimmy said. He pictured Pepper struggling, pictured himself carrying Pepper if necessary. "Tomorrow. You used to say we was, so now we are."

Pepper's cheeks and nose twitched, his eyes watered, but he didn't sneeze. "I ain't doing nothing but what I want."

"You just scared."

"Shut the hell up."

"We gone climb it."

Pepper's features adjusted as if he could see through Jimmy. Jimmy wobbled. He tightened to keep from turning to make sure the mesa wasn't slouching toward them. Pepper pushed himself up from his seat, wavered and gave a haunted look over Jimmy's shoulder before he banged through the door.

Jimmy expected him to grab his bottle and leave, and he resolved to fight him, but first he would turn and look at the mesa, douse the dread of it that Pepper had put into him, see it for what it was. He turned. It lay black against the molten puddle of the setting sun, its symmetry unnatural, its long top a crouching predator's outline. Its base was shrouded, yet connected to everything beyond it, bigger than anything he could comprehend and only the start of all that he didn't know. The blackness of the backlit mesa cart-wheeled. He stepped backward and held a chair. The door exploded open, a rifle barrel appeared, and gunshots blasted near his ear. Jimmy fell to the wooden porch. Pepper kept firing toward the mesa. Jimmy covered his head, straining to level himself and stop the world's spinning. He knew he had to stand and grab Pepper, knew he could will himself if he had the strength, but the spinning worsened. Pepper cursed the mesa, dropped the rifle to the porch and strode toward the barn. Jimmy was steadying, felt his legs coming back, but he lay there, vision blurring, and watched without moving as Pepper fetched his horse and rode away.

Jimmy lay on the porch until the moon rose. He peered in the direction Pepper had gone, expecting to miraculously see Pepper's moonlit silhouette atop the plateau, until finally he stood and weaved inside. He flopped into a kitchen chair, one second disgusted and remorseful that he hadn't forced himself to stand and tackle Pepper, the next second furious that Pepper had left him again. Later, he trudged to the barn, his eyes on the ground, and saddled his horse, thinking he would track Pepper. But as he readied to mount, his mind traveled outside to the darkness and the murky distance. He thought of Pepper riding away from him and his scalp burned. He undid the saddle, slung it against the stable wall and rawed his throat screaming. He marched back inside, where Pepper's empty chair watched him like a specter. He smashed the dusty album on the turntable, smashed another and another until black shards littered the floor. Finally he retrieved from his drawer tape "1." He plugged it into the player, started it and settled into Pepper's chair. Mrs. Schmidt's voice warped and shifted in pitch from the worn tape, her spoken words nearly as unintelligible as the written ones. He found himself thinking what it would be like to have a mother's voice. Then he was missing Pepper, not from tonight but from all the years. He shut his eyes, wondered what he'd done to cause Pepper to start leaving, wondered what he could've done to keep him here, knew there was something he hadn't been able to read in Pepper, something he hadn't understood but should have. He drifted.

He snapped to, the chair pitching and bucking. The room began a revolution so powerful that he clutched the chair arms for fear that he would be launched against the wall. He clenched and concentrated on a pine knot in the opposite wall, trying to slow himself, but he did not slow. Mrs. Schmidt's voice had gone and there was a roar in his ears louder than the twister that had once passed close, louder than the rifle shots near his head, somehow the noise of everything beyond the house. He grabbed the knees of his jeans and jerked forward to his feet but collapsed onto the floor. There he curled until the movement stopped and the noise quieted.

Late the next morning, when Pepper's horse returned alone, Jimmy saddled up and cantered out, looking away from the mesa and the complex pattern of vultures wheeling above the plain. He'd been telling himself it was a cow, but now he tried not to think of what he knew was ahead. The sun pointed straight down, fiercely, the kind of heat that maddened Pepper. Jimmy tried not to think of that either. His legs were weak against the horse's sides, his stomach unsettled, but at least he knew that Pepper couldn't stop him from bringing him home.

DAY SIX, AFTERNOON

Jimmy figured it had been an hour since he watched Sandra leave the bus and almost jog to her apartment, yet he still couldn't approach her place. From behind the trees lining the capitol grounds, he scanned the cramped street of two-story stucco apartment houses for lurking cops. He cleared his throat, impossibly thirsty, thought maybe he should just head for Texas, maybe even turn himself in, but he emerged from the trees and strolled down her street. He stepped up to her place, the array of unreadable doorbell labels prickling his gut as if he'd swallowed cactus, before the door opened and a hand pulled him inside. The suddenness and surprise almost caused him to shove, but Sandra's arms wrapped him and her soft cheek pressed his. Her aroma, peaches mixed with a drugstore's antiseptic, ballooned in his nostrils. She tugged him up the stairs and into her apartment, seated him in a chair, took his face in her hands and kissed him close-mouthed on the lips. She leaned back a few inches. "You found me," she said, her features large in their nearness.

His cheeks melted into the touch of her smooth palms and long fingers, but he fought the urge to draw her fully to him, his legs tingling to flee. "I'm parched," he said. She spun to the sink, her kitchen nearly a part of her living room. Everywhere bright colors—a red tea kettle, deep blue dish cloths, a cartoon poster of a small-bodied woman with a short dress, short black hair, giant eyes, and a large head. Betty? Jimmy squeezed shut his eyes, then reopened them to Sandra's white-lipsticked smile a notch too wide. He took the cool glass of tap water and downed it, asked for more and two glasses later placed the glass on the tiny, yellow, circular table.

"I was worried you wouldn't remember how to get here," she said.

"I waited behind them bushes to make sure nobody followed you."

"Nobody did."

"Them folks call the cops?"

Sandra blinked and touched her lips. "They don't know anything except you'd been in to talk to me." She plucked Jimmy's empty glass from the table and rinsed it. "I didn't tell anybody anything."

"I wouldn't of blamed you if you had." Jimmy massaged his own shoulder. He wanted to hole up here and never leave, then he glanced around, noticed the stacks of paperbacks and inhaled against a sudden tightness. He popped his shoulder, an internal crack that took him back to Charley's and then to the blur of clearing the counter.

Sandra placed the glass in the drainer and turned to him, drying her hands. "I want to get out of here, just in case they're checking. I have it all planned." She stepped next to him and turned her back. "Unzip me," she said, and he did, his fingers all nerves as he exposed the strap of her bra and the white of her shoulders and waist. She hustled past him into a closet-sized bedroom and with her back to him dropped her plain brown dress, revealing the wide curves of her hips, her dark bikini, the length of her back. Jimmy turned toward the window and braced against the table, the tall capitol in full view, thought he heard a mesa-like whisper and looked at the floor. He had no idea why she trusted him, why he trusted her, barely had an idea of what had happened, the drive to the drug store a haze of rage, the money bag a mirage of justice and revenge. He had flown over the counter and out the door before he had a thought, his legs ahead of his brain until Sandra's voice lit inside him. If she hadn't called out, he had no idea what he would have done, and what he had done repulsed him, made him no better than J.T. She bustled into the kitchen dressed in a flowery dress and began to stuff a red vinyl bag with items from the cabinets and fridge. Beautiful, he thought, but he pushed that down and was once more drawn to look out to the capitol, gray against the deepening sky. Earlier he'd followed the thirty-four-story spire toward Sandra's place and parked in its lot. When he stepped out, it loomed above him like a gray rocket. He'd swallowed, then craned to see the building towering above the flatness. Its solemn face gave nothing. He held onto the door handle of his car to steady himself. He'd needed water, so he forced his fingers to open and waded through the humidity and up the impossibly-wide concrete terrace of steps to the capitol's entrance. He glared at the letters carved into each step, his legs heavier and heavier, until his palm hit the brass cross bar and he pushed his way inside. A cavern of darkness expanded around him, then the door crashed shut behind him, jolting him forward, the sound bouncing into corners he hadn't yet adjusted enough to clearly see. His heart thudded against every point in his body as his eyesight began to seep back in. Flags hung from the wall before him, marble statues stood frozen, voices echoed off the marble walls. Cave air enveloped him, then he saw two guards watching. An old vertigo fluttered through his forehead. The elevator opened across the lobby. A force like a vacuum sucked at him, then his consciousness traveled without his body into the elevator and up, higher and higher, zooming, until he exploded into light and space and his body scattered. He stumbled backward, caught the guards' looks, wheeled and was out the door, descending, the vacuum reaching after him like a tentacle.

"You ready?" she asked, startling him as if she had materialized from nowhere. She was brighter than the bright room as she stood erect, the vinyl bag before her as if they were going on a picnic.

"You ought not get mixed up in this anymore," he said.

"That's for me to say." She smiled, obviously crazy, just like he'd been. He lifted from the chair, his body soggy, and she took his hand, stinging with gravel cuts from Charley's lot. At the bottom of the stairs, she paused, cracked the door and peeked outside. "Where'd you park?"

"Up by the capitol," he said. Simply saying its name cast dread over him. She tugged him along behind her into twilight, the air rich with a scent of bloom and rot. Jimmy kept his sight downward as they hit the tree-lined sidewalk and ascended the slope toward the parking lot. The capitol was a monstrous presence in his mind, its beckon to him mixed with the sound of Pepper's sneezing.

"You're hurting my hand," Sandra said, and he released his grip, looked up enough to spot his car and point. He went to his side, got in and unlocked her door from there. Sweat broke hard on him, and when the seat tremored with her sitting, he sweated even harder. "It's not far where we're going," she said. "We could really almost walk, but it's safer this way." He lifted his gaze ever so slightly to pull out, saw the building's tremendous steps with their incomprehensible writing and felt pressure, like a stone shoved against his brow.

She directed him several blocks through the mostly-deserted downtown to park on a high street overlooking the levee, beyond which he knew lay the dark expanse of the Mississippi. She came around to his side, and he grunted to raise himself. "There," she said, and pointed toward an old-style, white-brick high-rise. She hooked her arm in his and they paced toward a long, blue, cloth awning beneath which light spilled onto the sidewalk. They turned into a recessed foyer and entered a maroon-carpeted lobby lit by a grand but dim chandelier, everything headed toward shabby. Behind a tall counter, a young black man perked up with a puzzled expression and laid down a book.

"We'd like a room," Sandra said, sitting her purse on the counter and removing cash.

"We got plenty," the young man said.

"Are there any upstairs?"

"We're open to the fifth floor on this side of the building."

"We'd like a fifth floor room then."

Jimmy's gut tightened.

"I gotta warn you, that floor isn't very cool," the clerk said. "AC hasn't been on. I probably shouldn't say, but that floor is haunted too. And I wouldn't open my door unless you know who it is. Lately most of the folks come here seem to be prostitu . . . . " He paused and ran his eyes over Sandra's bright clothes and make-up and Jimmy again. "I wouldn't open my door. Security guard gets here in a few minutes."

"I think this place is beautiful," Sandra said. "I've seen it from the bus.

"Honestly, this place is about to go under. Any day in fact. They thought if they opened it back up, people'd be having parties and such and legislators'd want to stay up in here, but everybody's still staying down at those new joints."

"We're on our honeymoon," Sandra said. Jimmy's startled look met the young man's surprise as he scanned Jimmy's haggard appearance. Jimmy unhooked his arm from Sandra's.

"Well, happy honeymoon," the young man said. "Staff's already gone, but the room should have soap and towels in it. The AC in the room should cool it off in a few minutes." He handed back her change. "Elevator's over there. It's slow."

"Thank you," Sandra said.

A tingle traveled through Jimmy, but before he could consider anything more, Sandra had hooked her arm through his again and they were on their way to the elevator. Jimmy's feet resisted as if trudging through fresh cement. He didn't know why he didn't just leave, except his legs were as tired as if he'd been running since Houston. It looked like he was going to get what he wanted, get Sandra, except that her voice was so high and trilling, her actions so pitched, that he was less sure now than ever what he was actually getting. Every second called into question the little he knew. Hell, he'd never even stayed in a hotel before. He would've collapsed to the floor laughing or crying if he didn't think he'd shatter from even that small impact.

The elevator door closed. Jimmy shut his eyes.

"Nobody'll look for you here," Sandra said. The elevator creaked into motion, and he strained to hold himself together against the pull he'd felt in the lobby of the capitol. He needed grounding, but he imagined the elevator cables dry-rotted and frayed, saw them snap and coil to a heap at the bottom of the shaft, the elevator dropping hard. He braced, then the doors slid open and Sandra guided him into the hall. He peered into the dim corridor, certain some specter would step out, accusatory replicas of the pharmacist and his wife or maybe Pepper himself. Shame filled the hall like plasma, then Sandra said, "Come on," and gestured for him to enter the room she'd already unlocked.

As soon as he was shut in, Jimmy had the urge to scream. The air was as hot and stuffy as a wood shed, the must and mildew a physical presence. Sandra sneezed and flicked on the AC floor unit but not the lights. "This will get rid of some of the closeness," she said, and headed into the bathroom. The sink faucet sounded, followed by sloshing, then Sandra stepped back into the room. "You wanta take a cool bath or shower? You could probably use it."

"Uh uh," he said. The air-conditioner spewed a stale, cool breeze across him. He rubbed his shoulders.

Sandra reached into her bag and brought out a banana, a thermos, bread, and a wedge of cheese.

"You need to eat." She unscrewed the thermos. "Drink this, it's herbal tea."

"*Ur*-bull?" Jimmy asked, then wished he hadn't.

Sandra bit her bottom lip. "It's good, just drink it."

Jimmy sipped the icy beverage, its taste hidden behind the cold, then nausea churned in him, faintness misted his forehead. Sandra tried to hand him a peeled banana, but a twinge shot across his gut and he shook his head. "You'll feel better," she said, and he met her look, the dip of her brow a kind of concern he couldn't remember ever being focused on him. He shivered and walked away from her toward the other side of the small room.

"Why'd you come after me?" he asked.

"The Rideauxs are good people. They don't deserve to have anymore taken from them."

"I didn't mean to take it."

"I figured you'd regret it if I didn't stop you. I knew the way you left earlier that something was going on."

"Something was going on with you too."

"I know. I wouldn't be here if I didn't." Sandra stood straight, put her feet together and pressed her hands palm to palm. "I think all this was meant to happen. Mr. Rideaux never fills that bag at the same time. What are the odds you'd show up at just that moment and be moved to do that?" Sandra reached into the bag, removed a small envelope, came over to him and put her mouth to his. Her lips were cushiony and warm. Heat surged through Jimmy, though he didn't return the kiss. When she took her lips away, his breath went with her. "Here," she said. She handed him the mauve paper square, went to the bathroom and shut the door.

Jimmy stared at the envelope, the room cranking in closer. He slid a finger in and broke the seal, removed a card with a sunflower on it and opened it. There was writing, her writing. Five words. None of them his name. He tried to think of what it might say, what she might say, but there was nothing. His vision began to pale, a humming whiteness bleeding into static. He slipped the card into his pocket and waited, his heartbeat full in his ears and temples. The card smoldered like a coal against his chest, the envelope became lead in his hand. He crumpled it.

The number and weight of things he'd never thought hard enough about swarmed him—Pepper's abandonment, his mother, his cowardly fears. Only an idiot would never consider those things. Or was it the other way? Only an idiot would. Forever he'd closed off, and now that he'd opened up to J.T., those things and more had bashed him. J.T. with tricks; Squint and Charley with violence; Sandra with . . . What? He'd pushed himself these several long days to allow himself to want her, but just this morning she'd seemed to push him away. When she came through that door, what would she want and what could he give? How long till anything they created flew apart?

Needles pricked his arms and legs as if they were coming awake, and when he shook them the pricking only increased. He tried to breathe deeply, but a fit of coughing hit him. Too little air, too little space, too many cigarettes, although he yearned for one right then. The room shifted and slowly spun like a carnival ride creaking into motion. He turned to the window and threw the curtain aside. Blank windows stared back from the facing building. He turned the lock and raised the window, a gout of sodden air meeting him. Like an old enemy—or was it friend?— the vertigo embraced him. The twister inside him uncoiled, funneling up and outside of him, on through the window. He braced himself against the waist-high sill, as something of him dispersed into the air. He looked down, the rectangular awning directly below, then shut his eyes. His mind zoomed back across the river bridge, over the highway, to Houston, Sparks' ranch, his and Pepper's spread and on across the endless sky. He opened his eyes and dropped the crumpled envelope, the paper ball zig-zagging to the dark square of cloth, where it landed and rolled off and down to the pavement. He heard the door behind him open. His legs swung over the sill and he fell.

The sun was setting purple, orange and pink beyond the chemical plants when J.T.'s ride pulled up in front of his shack. "Can I give you a couple dollars for gas?" J.T. asked the driver, a young black man who'd been J.T.'s third ride. The driver stared past J.T. at his ramshackle apartment, then shifted his gaze to him with what looked like pity. "Nah, my pleasure," the man said. He wore a shop uniform and had said he lived nearby in the shadow of Exxon, where J.T. had once lived and where Jimmy had been born, facts J.T. hadn't thought of in years and which constricted his chest.

"Thanks," he croaked.

"Yeah. You pass along a favor some time." J.T.'s eyebrows rose without his thinking, and he stepped out of the car's AC into the still ugly heat. He surveyed the mangy lot absent of Jimmy's car and almost flopped down in the yard. "He tore out this morning and ain't been back," came the woman next door's voice. He blinked as if he had imagined it, then looked over at her. "Left a big smokin' cloud with his tires."

"That right." The last thing J.T. wanted was to engage an old busybody, but he imagined the stuffy oven-heated bleakness of his apartment and shuffled over to the woman's yard. "Guess he had some place to go," J.T. said.

"He was going there mighty fast. Seemed mad to me. I don't think he somebody gets mad easy."

"You don't. You know him, do you?"

"I talked to him. He come had a smoke with me and set a spell. Ate some of my cooking."

"Huh."

"My name's Elma. I'm your neighbor in case you didn't know."

J.T. didn't need this shit, an oblique scolding from this stranger, but the thought of moving his legs made him want to collapse. "J.T.," he said.

"I know."

"You know everything goes on around here?"

"I keep an eye on things. Ain't got much else to do. You ain't carrying a cigarette, are you?"

"Nope."

"Well, you look like you could stand to sit and have some tea, so come on up if you want."

Elma grunted out of her chair, motioned to the lawn chair propped against the house, then went inside. The stoop was only two steps high, but J.T. had the disconcerting feeling that the walk-up was the stairs to a gallows. He climbed, unfolded the chair and settled in, his body nearly sighing with relief. Indignity. Humiliation. He'd fallen asleep in the McDonald's, been awakened by a kid who worked there and asked to purchase more or move on. After a long break in the men's room, he set out again, the sidewalk a griddle, the passing cars stirrers of a humid wind. He humped it a half-mile or so before he started hitching, managed to get two short rides, the first from a wild-eyed white kid who asked if he wanted to buy some weed and dropped him a block down when he didn't, the second from a black preacher who started talking immediately about eternal salvation. He dropped J.T. upon request. He'd sat to rest under a tree next to an apartment complex, dozed again, then awoke to find several young girls staring at him. He started and struggled to his feet. The girls screamed and ran. All in all an unpleasant afternoon.

Elma handed him a tall glass beaded with droplets and clinking with ice cubes. He drained half of it, the coldness shooting into his sinuses, groaned at the pain but held the chilly glass to his cheek anyway. "Drank it too fast," Elma said, settling into her chair and smirking.

"Thanks for pointing that out."

"You ain't much for pleasantry, are you?"

J.T. examined her expression, more playful than judgmental, and sheathed the dagger shaping itself on his tongue. "It's been a long day, lady."

"Call me Elma."

The icy core of pain in J.T.'s forehead began to reheat enough that he drained off the rest of his tea and stood. "Thanks for the hospitality, Elma," he said, and held out the empty glass.

"They's more in the kitchen if you want it."

"I appreciate it, but I got things to tend to."

"You right about that."

"What's that supposed to mean?"

"You know better than I do."

J.T. had the urge to tell the bitch to piss up a rope, then a wave of faintness wavered through him. He sat down.

"You fixing to swoon?" Elma asked.

"I'll give you warning if I am."

"Don't make any difference to me. I seen it all." J.T. blinked against the white dots playing like gnats in front of him. He wasn't sure that passing flat out wouldn't be better than enduring more of Elma's home-spun patter, but he doubted he had the energy to even get to his feet. "You wanta talk about what you did to make Jimmy so mad?" she asked.

"How you so sure I did something?"

"I heard all kinda bashing around fore he took out."

"I don't know nothing about that."

"Cause you were gone."

"And now I'm back and *he*'s gone."

"That appear to be the size of it." She sipped her tea with the daintiness of a queen, lowered the glass to her lap and gazed off at the darkening horizon. It was this kind of superior attitude that had put him off women long ago, that and their craziness and neediness and demanding nature. Here he was waiting for a blind giant to come by and snap his digits, and this woman was working to dredge up guilt.

J.T. smacked his lips. "Shit," he said, "a cigarette would be good."

Elma reached into the loose pocket of her dress, produced two cigarettes and a book of matches. "Here." J.T. cocked an eyebrow, then took one, struck a match, lit hers and his. She took a deep drag and blew out through her nose, slipped off her shoes and crossed her feet. "Jimmy left me them," she said. The taste went sour in J.T.'s mouth. "He seems like a good boy to me, J.T. Maybe it ain't my business, but what you doing to mess it up after you finally got a son?"

A tickle played in J.T.'s throat for a second. The sweaty lump of bills in his sock weighted him like a tumor. He pulled on the cigarette and let the smoke fester in his lungs.

"You're right," he said, "it ain't your business."

WHAT J.T. COULD REMEMBER IF HE
WOULD REMEMBER: 1958

Over the next month, Morita spruced the place with new towels, sheets, china and couch pillows, while J.T. kept his mouth shut about both her presumption and his appreciation. She cooked for him but ate little herself. A few times they went out at night, but she insisted they go back across the river, because, he convinced himself, she thought someone who knew her father would be less likely to spot her. Whatever her reason, he was glad that she was drinking and smoking less. Neither of them mentioned how long she might stay, which alternately relieved and disturbed J.T.

Their love-making was as irregular as the lead-up to it, a dance determined by moods and circumstances which J.T. sensed more than understood. Each rejected the other and each made advances. Sometimes the sex was tender, sometimes rough and punctuated with dirty talk. Some mornings they passed in bed with lazy foreplay and lovemaking, and on those days J.T. thought how great it was to lounge unemployed in Baton Rouge. When the sex was its best, J.T. also thought of other women, thought that a roll was a roll whatever the form, but he didn't go looking. On the days they didn't have sex, he had to contend with silence and the unknowable, with Morita reading books or staring off. Hours at a time she didn't speak—brooding, thinking, sulking, building to anger, he couldn't tell, except that he fretted she was bored, a privileged woman cooped up near a stinking refinery and severed from her friends. He strained to penetrate her thoughts and emotions without asking anything directly, and when the strain grew too much he sniped her into fighting, a miserable place but a place where he knew she was at least passionately engaged with him. On these days he was tempted to ask her to leave since he was sure she was going to anyway.

A week before Christmas, he persuaded her to go out with him to his favorite plate lunch place. She'd been sick all morning, sick off-and-on for two weeks, and hadn't eaten much in that time, so he convinced her it would be good for her to breathe some outside air and eat some home-style cooking. When she agreed he figured it was because she was too weak to argue anymore, but he still thought it was the best thing. She even agreed to their taking the T-Bird, which she didn't like to be seen in during the day.

They arrived after the lunch rush and took a booth against the wall of the old cinder-block room beneath a sign that said "Peace on Earth," the cashier and co-owner, Roxanne, not saying anything as she glanced back and forth between them, then not leading them to their table but simply pointing when they entered. "She's in a mood," J.T. said about Roxanne, but her mood barely mattered, the aroma of chicken-fried steak and collards touching him like an ace and a king. Morita hardly looked at the menu, her expression pinched. J.T. reached across the table to touch her, but she didn't lift a hand to meet him. He scanned the restaurant—only two other tables with patrons— and met the gaze of the couple at one of them. He smiled and nodded, but they continued to look sternly back. The waitress went in and out of the kitchen several times without even bringing water until J.T. called her name and told her they were starving. "Debra's usually setting water on the table before you settled in your seat," he said to Morita.

"Why'd you bring me here?" she answered. "I shouldn't have let you."

"Some food'll make you feel better, sugar," he said, and he didn't regret that he'd said "sugar."

Debra slapped two glasses of water on the table and asked what they wanted without a hello. "Y'all had a busy lunch?" J.T. asked. "Everbody seems touchy."

"We're about out of everything and trying to close a little early, so what y'all want?"

J.T. gave his order, and when he raised his glance he saw Debra looking sideways at Morita, Debra's cheeks lifted and her eyes squinted. "And you, missy?" Debra said to Morita. Morita glared back at her, then shut her menu.

"Nothing."

"You oughta eat," J.T. said, but Debra had already spun and strutted off.

"I really don't feel good. I need to go to the rest room."

"It's over in the corner."

Morita slid out of her seat and stood, but Roxanne intercepted her only a few steps from their booth. "Bathroom's out of order," she said to Morita.

"I'll take my chances," Morita answered, and moved past her.

Roxanne watched her back, then turned to J.T. and gave him a look he'd never seen from her. "What do you think you're doing?" she asked him. "What kind of place do you think this is?"

"A damn slow, rude place today. What the heck is going on in here?"

Roxanne shook her head. "We're serving y'all today, but that's it."

She marched off, her wake itching over J.T. like a rash. He was trying hard to think that the women in here were somehow jealous of Morita, but he was trying harder to keep down what was percolating beneath that thought. When Morita re-entered the room, her bearing was so regal that J.T. puffed up. She fixed the look of the woman in the couple who'd been ogling them, and when the woman looked down, Morita fixed on the man. He shook his head just as Roxanne had done, muttered something and looked across at Roxanne. J.T. stood without thinking, Roxanne coming toward him again, but Morita reached the booth first. "I'm not staying here, J.T. I told you I didn't want to come."

Roxanne came up close behind Morita, and when Morita turned, Roxanne was blocking her path. "Don't wanta see you in here again," Roxanne said to J.T.

"Excuse me," Morita said, "but we don't want to eat your pig slop anyway."

Roxanne jerked back as if slapped, then glared at J.T., whose feet hadn't yet reacted to follow Morita toward the door. "Jerry!" Roxanne called out toward the kitchen, and J.T. noticed that the men from the other two tables were also coming his way.

"Y'all gone crazy?" J.T. said. He scanned their faces, every one of them behind a wall he hadn't seen before. "Don't worry about me coming back to this, y'all acting so ugly." Jerry came out of the swinging door to the kitchen, wiping his forearm with a rag, but J.T. was already heading out the door. Morita waited at the car. A chilly rain had started and the wind let go a burst that hunched J.T. He scampered over and opened Morita's door, saw everyone from the restaurant peering through the plate glass as he rounded the front of the T-Bird toward the driver's side. Morita opened his door, and he dropped into his seat. "Jesus Christ," he said. "They acted like we had the nunonic plague."

"Bubonic," Morita said.

"Bluebonic?" Morita lay her head back and breathed, hugging herself.

"You should've known not to take me there."

"What do you mean, honey?"

She looked at him like he was ignorant. "Let's just go." He started the engine and accelerated onto the road. Morita's complexion was as pale as he'd yet seen it.

"You need me to pull over just say. I know you feeling terrible, but we still need to get you a bite to eat."

"I'm pregnant," she said, as if she were saying 'Turn at the next light.' The road blurred and writhed before coming into focus again. J.T. kept driving, Morita's words clacking through him.

"Say again."

"I'm going to have a baby."

"You sure?"

"Damnit, J.T., I've been sick every morning. Can't you see it's not just the fumes?"

He gripped the wheel so hard a tinge of pain shot through his knuckles. "Shit," he said quietly, a spill of emotion going warm then hot through him. "You said you knew your rhythm."

"Well I was wrong, wasn't I. Put me out if you want. I missed my period."

He stewed. Tricked. A girl on the run looking for some place to land, some sucker to pay. A vision of his life catastrophically altered fired through him—freedom taken, hard labor imposed, joy destroyed. He'd heard of people who could fix these things, dangerous yes, but not too dangerous he supposed, not so early. He didn't know these people, of course, but he figured he could find out. Then there was the money for it, who knew how much.

They arrived at the house in silence, and Morita rushed to the bathroom, where he heard her retching. He stood in the middle of the living room, part of him wanting to go to her and hold her head, the other part of him weakened and tense. When she came out of the toilet and turned toward the bedroom, he followed her, found her sitting on the foot of the bed. He moved around and sat on the side with his back to her. She sighed. "I can pack and go," she said.

"Go where?"

"I can find somewhere."

"I didn't say anything about going."

"You didn't say anything about staying either."

J.T. wiped at his mouth. The bedroom held a complex blend of smells—crude oil, perfume, sweat, cigarettes—but all these aromas were secondary to the aroma of Morita, her smell apart both primal and soothing. He couldn't recall his place without it. Then the worst possibility of whose baby it might be plunged into him like a broken bottle.

"You're pregnant with my baby?"

"Goddamnit, J.T., how can you ask that?" Her face distorted, and he realized it was her recognition of his terrible thought about who else the father might be.

"Well I never made anybody pregnant."

"And I've never been pregnant." She took a cigarette from her purse and lit it. Her foot worked madly. "I didn't mean to get pregnant."

"I didn't say you did." J.T. popped to his feet and paced, scratching his chest. He had the distinct impression of being pulled down by an undertow and of being slightly happy about it. He was two pieces that didn't fit. His feet stopped, his feeling for her suddenly incandescent with love.

He stroked her hair and broke into a smile. "Them girls at the lunch place was so jealous, they didn't know what to do," he said.

Morita rolled her cigarette between her thumb and index finger, studying it like tea leaves. "You really believe that?"

"You're the most beautiful woman I've ever seen."

She ground out her smoke and took his hand. "You're the father of *my* baby, J.T. *My* baby."

He grinned. "Ain't that something."

DAY SEVEN

Jimmy's eyes popped open to a wall radiant with sunshine. He blinked, fought the urge to collapse back into sleep and stared. His body felt covered with sandbags, his head filled with sorghum. Cool air blanketed him. A cheap air-conditioner rattled somewhere. He squinted. Whose ceiling was it? He knew he knew. Knew someone was in bed next to him, could sense it, knew far back in his brain that he knew who it was without looking. Also knew that he knew how he'd come to be wherever he was, yet he kept his gaze fixed on the ceiling, figuring it best to sort out a little before he took in a lot.

His shoulder and hip complained with throbs. Taking inventory, he stretched his fingers, twiddled them, made a fist and released. Okay. He lifted his left arm. Zap! A white hot brand dug into his shoulder. He gripped against it to keep from flinching. No pain was coming from his other shoulder, so he reached over with that arm and touched the sore spot, winced at the tenderness there. Enough inventory for the moment. Slowly he turned his head toward his side, his neck stiff and creaky, saw intense sunlight blasting beneath an undrawn shutter, saw a painting of a sunflower, moved down, saw paperback books stacked on a tiny bookshelf, and remembered Sandra before he actually saw her.

She lay fully clothed on her stomach atop the brightly polka-dotted quilt, her arms at her sides as if she'd been knocked unconscious from behind. Her pale face was so close that he felt her breath, smelled the faint sourness of morning as she exhaled with almost a snore. Her wispy hair fell over her cheek and across her nose, strands quivering with each breath. His hand actually trembled with the urge to touch her. He remembered.

He'd fallen bottom first, weightless for an instant, then his weight multiplying. He'd glanced to his side at the windows rushing past and flattened out, back down. The black sky expanded above him and he was flying, unbound, almost unbodied. Impact, a flash as if slapped by a giant paddle, then flailing off the awning, spinning in the air, falling again, then *thud,* sprawled in the street. The concrete pressed warm against his ear and jaw and he peered down the grainy alley of the street all the way to the capitol. He saw it with a clarity almost telescopic, a clarity unlike any he'd seen with before. He half expected blood to trickle from his mouth and head, but somehow he was sure even if that did happen he was all right. In fact, the blood was flowing through him, no, raging through him, and the rush of it tingled his fingers, aroused his hair, tickled his groin. He relaxed.

Footsteps clapped toward him, stopped, the feet only feet away. One pair of polished black walking shoes, the other a pair of ratty loafers with pennies in their slots.

"What the hell?" he heard the clerk's voice say.

"He must've bounced off that awning," the other voice said. "It's bent."

"Is he dead?"

"I can't believe it held. He must've jumped."

"He's not bleeding."

"Uh uh. He's smiling."

Jimmy shifted his glance upward to the men. A white man in a security guard uniform stood with the clerk. They took a step back. The hotel door crashed open and Sandra's feet slapped toward him. "Jimmy," she said, and knelt.

"Sandra," he said.

"Don't move." She looked at the men. "Call an ambulance."

"Nuh uh," Jimmy said. "I'm just scuffed." He pushed himself up, white heat firing through his left shoulder, and sat. Sandra hugged him lightly, supported him, her blue eyes alight. His head felt as though the barnacles of a lifetime had been knocked away. He wanted to touch her flushed cheeks, wrap her up and take her back to the warm pavement with him. He winked.

"Did you fall out the window?" the clerk asked. Jimmy saw the lopsided awning and blinked several times.

"Stand me on my feet," he said.

"Help me," Sandra said, and the men cupped Jimmy under the armpits and hoisted him. Jimmy braced himself on Sandra's shoulders.

"You sure you don't need an ambulance?" the check-in man asked.

"Uh uh," Jimmy said.

"What the hell happened?" the security guard asked.

"He slipped," Sandra said.

"Slipped? Out a window?"

"He leaned out the window and slipped," Sandra blurted. "He bobbled something and tried to catch it. Didn't you, Jimmy."

The hotel men looked at each other, then back at Jimmy and Sandra. "Look," the security guard said, and pointed at Jimmy's crotch. An erection tented his jeans. "What is this? Y'all some kind of freaks?"

Jimmy lifted one foot then the other to check for feeling, the second lift sending a blade into his hip. He swallowed and gripped Sandra's hand. "Run!" he said. They dashed past the men. Jimmy's hip screamed, pain so intense his leg threatened to sheer away, but he clutched Sandra's hand and kept sprinting. The hard surface pounded up through him, yet his feet were light and Sandra flew beside him. He listened for the men's footsteps, but there was only the chop of his and Sandra's breathing and the hammer of their strides. When they reached the corner, he glanced back at the men still standing in the street and pulled Sandra toward his car. He guided them to the passenger side, pulled up short and swung her into his embrace. He kissed her full, whooped and unlocked her door. She ducked in as he hurried to his own side and dropped in.

Her hands clutched her small purse still strapped over her shoulder.

"Your bag," he said.

"Forget it. There's nothing in it."

He cranked the car and floored it, joined the squeal of the tires with a howl. The car pitched onto the downward slope toward the river, a roller coaster dip, then Jimmy fishtailed them next to the levee, heading a direction he'd never been. Twice today he'd fled, but he didn't care if he was a fugitive, didn't care if a cell was waiting for him, a man who'd half-robbed a store and fully jumped out a window. He was alive, sight clear, penis hard, the beautiful woman he wanted next to him. The hell with cops anyway. He was so alert he'd sense them before they neared, escape like a jackrabbit in brambles if they closed. He followed the levee, bumping over railroad tracks and a cobbled street, broke clear of downtown on a dark winding road. He laid his hand on Sandra's thigh, thought of her lips on his, her full breasts beneath his palms, her nipple in his mouth, things he'd barely dared to imagine. Suddenly all things were possible. Sure his shoulder and hip smarted like mad, but that was living too and there was no pain that the sweet press of Sandra's body couldn't soothe.

A mile or so down the road, Jimmy veered up the levee and slid to a stop on the crest. Dust billowed from his tires into the lights of the car, clouding the thick trees between them and the river. Jimmy laughed like he was purging. He flicked off his headlights, dropping the trees into darkness, and laughed at that too. Then he looked to Sandra's quiet, shadowed expression, sucked in air and quieted.

He wanted her. He scooted across the seat and raised his palm to her smooth cheek. His other arm he wrapped around her shoulders. She burst into crying. He held her more tightly, felt her sobs like tremors. She shrugged him off and doubled over. Tears caught glints of distant light. The sound of her was terrible, desperate for breath and wet with . . . He didn't know what. He'd never been around a woman crying like this, anybody crying like this. His urge was to pull away, but he let his hand rest on her back until the heaving died down. She sniffled and sat straight, wiped her eyes and nose with her fingers. Jimmy pulled a kerchief from his pocket and gave it to her, her body stiff to him.

"Why'd you do that?" she said. Her voice quavered so badly that his own throat moistened. He sat back, put his hands in his lap and peered through the windshield. The levee sloped away from them into darkness. Jimmy's mind traveled down it and through the trees and marsh to the wide brown water, waded in and pushed off into the current. He snapped back to the car, found Sandra studying him. "You tried to kill yourself and you're not dead."

"I wasn't trying anything," he said. "It just happened."

"Just happened?" He nodded. "Has it happened before?"

"Not like that."

"What do you mean 'not like that'?"

"I was just looking and I went."

"I thought I was the crazy one and there you go . . . . " She pressed the sides of her head. "I liked you, I really liked you, I really *like* you, and you come in the store and we go to the hotel and this." She dropped her hands, turned toward him in the seat and examined him. "How aren't you dead?"

"I bounced off that awning."

"Like a miracle."

"Or just a real good awning."

"I'm not joking. You scared me, Jimmy. I'm still scared."

He wrapped his arms around her and brought her to him, but her arms stayed at her sides. He held her more tightly, the rhythm of her breathing fast and yet deep.

"I think it was just the day," he said. "Everything going all to shit."

"You mean robbing the store?"

"Before that. My father lit out with all my money. I tracked him over to the place where he gambles and started a scrap. Some fella pulled a gun on me."

Sandra sat back. "That happened before the store?"

"I was coming to tell you, I reckon. I don't really know what I was doing. I can't recall. I spose I seen that money just sitting there and I went kinda loco."

Sandra raised her hand and inserted her fingers between her teeth. Jimmy thought she was about to cry, then she balled a fist and hit her thigh. "I thought you were dead. When you went out that window, I thought you were dead. I ran out in the hall and hit the elevator button and took off looking for the stairs. Then I saw you lying in that street . . . ." She widened her eyes and hissed through her teeth. "You came to the store and you were so polite and shy and funny. You took me around and treated me so sweet and here you were grabbing bags of money and jumping out windows. That's not right."

His hand ached to reach out to her, but his hand seemed suddenly a transmitter of more pain. "I'm sorry I got you into all this. I'll drop you home."

"No! Let's go home. We need sleep. We need to make sure you're okay." She lightly shoved him toward the steering wheel and scooted herself close to her window. He thought to say something more, to reach across, but he didn't. He'd simply taken them back to her place, where they'd both lain atop the bed in their clothes, he on his back, she with her back to him. He lay awake a long time, not sleeping, the air electric around him, her body electric beside him. The sensation of his fall played over and over, mysterious and wondrous, even as the aches began.

J.T. slouched in his chair, examining the damage to his wall, a dark maw around an ancient joist, sheetrock dust spread like powdered snow. He'd perched here all night, dozing and watching the wall as if seeing Jimmy's last act might call him back. Pain stabbed him dead center of his forehead, the money wad in his sock ached like a giant boil. Jimmy wasn't coming back. What stupidity to think anybody would after you'd called them in from another state and snaked their money. J.T. surely wouldn't, wouldn't respect anybody who did. Still, he'd thought deep down that Jimmy would and that made J.T. himself more of a fool. He could've run, at least hid out, still could in fact. They'd never track him out of town—Charley wasn't that type—and he'd be shed of all this, bad old memories and new. But he wouldn't run, he still knew that. If Jimmy didn't come back, then . . . .

J.T. hoisted himself out of the chair and tried to unstiffen. He lifted his leg and hopped to keep his balance as he extracted the money from his dirty sock. He studied the crinkly green and white paper. How pathetic he was. All this trouble for this. Sure, there were the other things attached like cars in a long train—the challenge of taking money from arrogant bastards, the sensation of winning, the faith in yourself that you couldn't lose, the freedom winning gave—but none of that could explain taking Jimmy's money. Jimmy had bailed him out, and J.T. had wanted to pay him back to show he could do things right. Too bad he'd allied himself with the pinwheel rather than good sense.

J.T. walked to the front door and looked out the window at the sun just starting to climb. He had no doubt that Squint would be coming early, and it was possible he could stave him off a day with this money, but the thought of that pinched J.T.'s guts. He needed a plan. Even if he was going to get slapped around, he needed to make sure Jimmy at least got this money, and even if Jimmy didn't get it, J.T. still wasn't giving it up. Maybe it didn't matter if Jimmy knew, *he* knew, and he wasn't handing this over after he'd saved it for his son in the first place. A small victory, maybe even a stupid one, but a victory anyway. But that still didn't solve how he would get it to him.

And then he remembered the drug store, the thought so obvious that he snorted in disgust at himself. So simple, he thought, to walk over and find the girl. Give her the money and tell her. Better yet, ask her where Jimmy was and see if she'd tell him. But he imagined Jimmy's face, glanced at the rage-destroyed wall and reconsidered. Best to tell her that he wanted to see Jimmy and let Jimmy decide. Maybe best, too, to keep the money here and let Jimmy come for it, that part of the plan self-serving but still a way to tell Jimmy he was sorry and explain just what had happened.

J.T. considered the different hiding places for the money, recognized all of them as obvious, then went to the kitchen. He put the money in one of the paper bags Jimmy had brought from the grocery, rolled it and tossed it in the cabinet beneath the sink. Squint wouldn't look there, even if he thought J.T. had any money, and J.T. doubted Squint would think he did. *Squint.* J.T. went cold and faint, then he was shaking, jarring waves of fright coming from his core, quaking his arms and legs, rolling his stomach and throwing sweat from him as if he'd sprung a leak. He thought for a moment he was having a heart attack, managed to grab hold of the rationalization that he might have a virus, was grabbed himself by the image of Squint taking hold of his arm, then a worse image of Jimmy banging on the wall of Charley's as J.T. lost his money. He plopped to the floor, shook harder, his teeth clacking, thought to call out but imagined the echo coming back from an empty house and curled on his side.

When the shakes finally subsided, he was soaking wet and as tired as he could ever remember. His cheek pressed flat against the ancient linoleum, the smells coming to him—grime, mildew, and rotted food. He lifted himself, his arms so weak that he slipped once trying to sit. His shirt stuck to his chest as if someone had thrown a bucket of water on him. The stuffy heat of the room crowded him, even though he was glad the chill was gone. He wiped his hand across his mouth and walked himself up with his back against the cabinet, wooziness rising with him, then braced on the sink. He spat, held his mouth beneath the faucet and drank the metallic water as long as he could.

Outside, the day was moving. He tested his legs with a step, wobbled, and took another one. He had to get to that drug store.

* * *

Sandra blinked awake to Jimmy staring at her. "Morning," he said. The previous day came to her as if dropped from above. She rolled from her stomach onto her side and sat up. He lay flat on his back just as he had on the street, and she leaned away, tightening.

"Do you hurt?" she asked.

"Stove up. Was trying not to wake you. Ain't tried to move much yet."

"You should probably get X-rays." She swung her legs off the bed and stood, not knowing where she was headed.

"Maybe I should vamoose," he said.

"No," she said. She spun to him. "No more vamoosing." She went to the window and flicked off the AC unit. "I can't afford to run this all day. It shouldn't get hot for a little while." She faced him again. "You need to eat. Just stay in bed and I'll run get us some breakfast."

"You ain't got—"

"Just stay in bed." She went to the kitchen table, snatched her purse and hustled down the stairs. Her body and mind were going as fast as they had been the moment she'd seen him jump, as fast as if she'd awakened and been metaphysically transported back to that second. The morning heat walloped her as she exited, but she strode as though she was being chased. Her mind swirled and her hands trembled, twin tributaries of fear and excitement flowing together to rage down her arms and through her fingertips. *Keep the energy moving. Make space for choices made and for choices to be made.* She tried to inhale deeply, but her breath caught. What a choice she'd made! A lost, possibly illiterate man who in rapid succession had robbed her place of employment, jumped out a hotel window and ended up fully clothed in her bed. How was any of this possible, even for her? Before her mother changed, she said, "Sandra, don't pick a rose that likes a field of stink weeds," meaning not to pick a man who'd keep her there in that town and expect her to be typical. Well, she certainly hadn't done that this time. In her months here, she'd avoided talking to men she was attracted to, not wanting to risk the connection and inevitable severing, until tall Jimmy clanged in with his thick red hair, charming country accent and deep vulnerable voice, his brown eyes uncertainly communicative, the whole of him an odd mix of calm, jitteriness, and politeness. His presence had reached out like two gentle palms, one against her cheek, one against her abdomen. She'd lit with something like hope and exactly like desire, let herself risk everything she'd vowed never to risk again.

She breathed, trying to make space for the tension in her chest, but the tension was too complicated to settle for space. Was Jimmy's leap the karmic wheel spinning off its hub and smacking her? Her mother had called her "wanton" before she packed her off to California, and ever since that day Sandra had wondered if the perverse universe was paying her back for her sexuality. Who knew if he'd jump again, a prospect that even now terrified and thrilled her. His survival was magic. Miraculous. But that didn't mean she liked it. When he'd gone out the window, her chest had blown open as if cannon shot. She wasn't sure what else she could survive.

She stopped at the corner, having twice rounded the block, and peered at the glare on her bedroom window. Was he asleep again? Showering? Staring back at her? At least the window was still *closed*. She sighed, then felt the dead drop of other possibilities—suicide, simple escape—and almost sprinted toward the apartment. But he was still up there, she believed that, had to believe, and that filled her with joy and a tendril of panic too. She remembered the envelope in his car, a letter from a lawyer. Maybe he had done horrible things. She believed not, but maybe it could tell her something, reveal another secret, perhaps a secret that could keep them together, that she could even tell him since she thought it likely he couldn't read. She eased to the passenger side of his car, took the letter from the floor, thought to open it, then reconsidered. No more duplicity. She'd take the letter from the car, but she'd only read it in front of him.

At the front door she paused, key pointed at the lock. The awful, thrilling moment came to her: Jimmy swinging his legs over the sill; Jimmy disappearing; the foreboding silence; the wait for a sound that had

no precedent; the huge twang, suspense, and "Ugh!"
She shuddered, breathed, rubbed the key between her
fingers like a lucky penny. What would he do if she told
him the police had never come because she said he was
retarded. How quickly would he leave when he found
he didn't need refuge? She stabbed the lock, turned the
key and climbed the stairs. At her apartment door, she
paused, folded the envelope and entered. Jimmy sat on
the edge of the bed, his hair tousled high on his head.

"We must be eating light," he said, and smirked.

She pressed the letter to her hip. "Sorry. I forgot.
I'll make us coffee."

"Why don't you come over first?"

She moved toward him but kept several feet
between them. Dark crescents lay beneath his eyes, but
his eyes gleamed.

"Have you gotten up?"

"Thought to, but my body didn't seem real eager."

"Your shoulder?"

"Mostly. Stiffened up on me."

"Take your shirt off."

"What?"

"Take your shirt off so I can see."

Jimmy held her gaze without moving. She
wondered what all he might be thinking; whether this
were the pause before the departure. He reached to
unbutton his shirt and winced.

"Here," she said, and began to undo them for him.
When she helped him slip it off, he grunted. A purplish-
black patch covered his upper arm. She sucked in air.

"Guess I oughta work on that landing," he said.

Impulses rushed through Sandra—to laugh, to
cry, to scream, to hold him—but she pushed them down,
reached out and laid her palm on his bruise. "We need to
ice that," she said. "Do you wanta take a shower or bath?"
He covered her hand with his own, and she lingered a
moment before sliding hers away and backing up a step.
"Don't ever do that again unless you tell me," she said,
the intensity in her voice surprising her.

"Sorry," he said, holding his palm out as if it was
guilty.

"I don't mean that, I mean jump. I mean jump out

a window or jump a counter and take a bag of money or jump out of a car or whatever. Don't do anything crazy without telling me. I'm not saying don't do it, I'm just saying tell me first."

"All right."

"And don't leave either."

"But I—"

"Without telling me."

"But I'm telling you I never—"

"I don't care what you've done. I mean I do care, I care, yes, but next time, talk to me. You promise?"

"I promise."

"Good." She stalked to the kitchen counter and prepared the coffee pot in fast motion. Sweat beaded on her forehead, and she spun again, strode past Jimmy to the AC and turned it on. She paused to examine him, remembered thinking in the hotel bathroom that she ought to undress before she came out, remembered thinking a second later that she ought to run, remembered thinking why not follow him when he disappeared into the air.

Behind her Jimmy grunted again, the bed creaked, and he came into the tiny kitchen area and stood behind her. His presence urged her to turn, but she didn't. "That's something," he said. "So tall. And right so close." Sandra looked out the window at the capitol building, gray against the blue sky. She cleared her throat, recalling the day she had arrived, stepped off the bus and ended up in the tower, gazing at the Mississippi's winding brown back, at the bristle of refinery stacks and round storage tanks, at the forested area of LSU, recalled the option the tower offered to her sadness. Jimmy stepped closer to her, curled his arms around her middle, and lightly kissed her on the neck. Her body almost went toward him, then she turned and put her palms flat against his chest. "I want to," she said, looking down from his eyes so close. "But not yet." He slid his arms from her, nodded and stepped back. "I hear you," he said. He sat at the kitchen table.

She turned back to the counter and braced against an image of herself in north Louisiana trudging like a zombie toward the bus station. She had to stop herself from going to him, had to suppress a fear that threatened to make her vanish.

"That smells good," Jimmy said.

"What?"

"That coffee."

She turned again. The bruise on his shoulder lay deeply purpled and splotched, something simultaneously nasty and beautiful, a strange map of the miraculous. "You should ice that," she said.

"After while," he said, the fiery aura of yesterday and the uncertainty of before replaced by a calmness, still heated, but cooler.

She touched her chin and lightly stroked it, flashed to mid-air, dropping, then the impact on the awning and the crash to the concrete. She huffed, her eyesight blurring. "I want to know what it was like," she blurted. "To jump. I need to know. Not now, but sometime. Okay?"

WHAT J.T. COULD REMEMBER IF HE WOULD REMEMBER: 1959

When Morita was very sick, J.T. put warm or cold cloths on her neck and forehead, held her shoulders and kept her hair back as she vomited. She lived in the bedroom when she was cranky or volatile and came out to cook or read on the couch when she was better. Their lovemaking became more tender. Sometimes, when J.T. didn't have to work, they spooned and napped away afternoons, went for drives and walks when the sun shined and the air was warm and dry. Morita stopped smoking and drank only a little, but the sickness kept on past morning and into months where it should not have been. J.T.'s lucky roll fell off but didn't end, so that he still managed to win enough here and there not to have to work more than odd jobs. Morita offered money, but J.T. wouldn't take it except in the groceries or furnishings she brought home. On good days she told him about her twelve years of Catholic school, growing up in New Orleans and going to school up east, while J.T. told her how he'd acquired a taste for blackjack during his two-year stint at Standard Oil after high school, told her how steady jobs were a chump's life and how he'd worked hard not to weigh himself down with a chump's responsibilities. Morita didn't say anything to that.

Then one night J.T. went into a game with
two-hundred thirty-one dollars and came out with
one-hundred sixty-three. The next night it dropped to
one-eleven. Two nights later to seventy-three. Back home
he fretted, Morita's silence about his gambling acting
as coal tossed into the furnace. Later, when she again
mentioned she had money left and could help out more,
could sell her car if need be, he told her she was further
jinxing him. To break the jinx, he paced backward,
laid out every combination of twenty-one he could find,
smashed a pair of dice with a hammer and tossed the bits
over his shoulder. He rehashed the losses and figured out
that he'd started every night with an odd number of cash,
so he counted to twenty-one then back to zero and back
up to twenty-one twenty one times. Morita watched him
for a while, then she shook her head and left the room.
He thought he heard muffled laughter from the back.

DAY SEVEN, STILL MORNING

Jimmy rested shirtless on the bed, a heap of bagged ice against his shoulder at Sandra's doing. He stared at the ceiling, fatigue and achiness damping but not killing his earlier elation. He considered the possibility of staying right here forever.

Sandra stood next to his side of the bed, tingling, unsure where Jimmy's mind was, where hers was, what she should do next. Bathe before work? Lie next to him? Already she was tired from the churn of questions. "Is the ice helping?" she asked.

"I reckon."

She moved to the other side of the bed, crawled on and sat cross-legged. The queen-sized mattress left by the previous tenant had been her one bit of extravagant luck in Baton Rouge. "What're you thinking about?" she asked.

"You."

"What else?"

"Why's there have to be something else?"

"Because there is."

Jimmy inhaled until his chest complained. He blinked several times and tightened his mouth. "I suppose J.T."

"You wondering if he lost all your money?"

"I know that. I was wondering if what made him take my money and lie . . . I'm wondering if that same thing is inside me."

"You're not like him."

"I ain't? I was willing to take from them folks yesterday. I'm here in your place when it might bring all kinds of trouble down on you."

"That's different."

"I ain't so sure."

"It is. You came all the way here to meet your father and he betrayed you."

He turned his head to her. "What exactly did the police say?"

"We can talk about that later."

"I need to know now."

"Well," she said, the lie she was about to tell bracing her, "they talked about attempted robbery and how that's serious, but how it's not nearly as serious as successful robbery."

"Say what? That mean they coming after me?"

"I didn't really listen closely to that. I was worried about you and Mr. and Mrs. Rideaux." A clog rose in her throat. "We'll just be careful a few days and it should blow over."

Jimmy shook his head. "Shit. I never broke a law in my life till yesterday. Probly against the law to jump out a window too. I sure went for some dillies right out the gate." He stretched his neck and winced.

"The ice isn't helping?" Sandra asked.

"Ice is fine. It's my other shoulder giving me trouble. Gets all locked up on me."

"You want a massage?" She said it quickly before she could think of the complications of touching him. "It wouldn't be a regular massage, it'd sort of be Shiatsu pressure point, so it might be different from other massages you've had."

"Can't be different. Never had one."

"Never? Not once?"

"Never not once," he said.

"Okay," she said, and inched over next to him. "Just close your eyes and try to be in your body."

"Don't know where else I'd be." He smiled at her and let his eyelids come down like metal shutters. He was definitely already in his body, his skin and joints tallying every one of the past days' injuries—sore back and shoulder from sleeping in J.T.'s chair, bumps and scrapes from Squint, bruises from his fall. His body was so heavy that he thought it might be melding with the mattress, even though he still felt moments of weightlessness being so near to her.

Sandra shut her eyes to try and focus her energy, but her energy was darting throughout her, into her fingertips, her toes, between her legs, a wild careening that shortened her breath and made her imagine her own body blending so completely with Jimmy's that her misery would go with him if he left her. "This is not a sexual thing," she said, "but I will be touching you, so let me know if you're not comfortable. I'm going to touch some points that will cause pain because your energy isn't flowing, so don't forget to breathe."

"I won't forget."

Sandra put her fingertip to the bony point of his unbruised shoulder and pressed. Jimmy drew sharp breath, startled at the fire shooting across his shoulder, up the side of his neck, through his jaw and into his temple and skull. "Breathe toward the pain," she said. "There's information in it. Listen to it." The information was that her fingertip was spiked with agony so intense his nerves were igniting. He had the urge to cry out, but just when he thought he couldn't stand it in silence, she shifted to his forearm, her thumb probing until she found a spot equally excruciating. He gasped. "There's a meridian that runs from your temple all the way to your hand. Your energy needs to flow along it, but yours is locked up and that's why your shoulder hurts." His entire arm and half of his head vibrated. He tried to focus on her touch, but her touch sent out ripples of fire.

Sandra felt his energy move through her thumb into her own arm and spread like caustic. She almost flinched, the energy so like the last times she'd had sex with Hilly, his body a battering ram, his orgasm an injection of contempt and belittlement. She tried to open her own energy to Jimmy, perhaps find some mystical element that had allowed him to survive his fall or been created by it, but the intense negativity she felt made her fear that she was projecting her own emotions rather than receiving. "Your cells have memories," she said. "All that's ever happened to you and every way you've been taught to feel or act is contained in those cells and needs to come out layer by layer."

Jimmy would have laughed at such bullshit were his cells not screaming. What else could make for a pain so continuous and widespread that the old mesa dizziness was spurting through him. Sandra's hand moved to his other forearm and pressed. His jaw released as if a deadbolt had been thrown. He heard a groan that he didn't immediately recognize as his own, then pain was taking over again, heating inside the shoulder that had hit the pavement. He braced against the bed.

"Breathe," she said, but she was talking to herself now, her eyes clasped shut. She had locked away so much since she'd come here, an attempt to contain the murderer who'd risen inside her, the murderer whose only target was herself. When Hilly had finally told her he wasn't coming back, she quit her job and collapsed into the terrible daily sleep that was good only when she didn't dream, yet always better than being awake. A memory was coming to her now, that cold bright day, when she finally awoke with energy. She hadn't been sure what time it was, sure only that her body crackled with determination to swallow everything in the medicine cabinet, turn on the oven, open its door and wait, knew it so thoroughly that she understood her body and mind had planned it during her week of hibernation. She went straight to her chest of drawers, stuffed everything she could into her travel bag, crammed into her purse the cash she had left and set out toward the bus station two miles from her apartment. Several times she stopped to rest, the energy left behind in the house, her body murmuring, *Go back and do it*, until she mustered her determination and shoved off again. It seemed like days before she reached the bus station. Everything there— the dirty walls, the poor travelers, the smoky air—told her to return home, but she forced herself to the counter and bought a ticket on the next bus. On her mother's answering machine, she left a message that said she missed her, their first communication since Sandra had left.

She opened her eyes. Jimmy's stomach was pale and flat, the skin lightly freckled and without hair, almost a boy's belly. She lifted her hand and let it hover above his solar plexus—his warmth radiating—then lowered her palm to him, her fingertips on one set of ribs, the pad of her hand on the other, the slight rise of his smooth stomach beneath her little finger.

"This is a heart protection point," she said.

His stomach muscles grabbed. Sandra's touch traveled through his chest and upward into his head. Faces rushed him—J.T., Pepper, Sparks, Squint. "Breathe," Sandra said, but he knocked her hand away and sprang from the bed. He yelled at the pain in his hip and staggered.

"Goddamnit!" He bent and grimaced, hand on his waist.

"It's okay," she said. "It's good to get it out."

He sucked in air. "Get what out?"

"The grief. You're in your death layer. You've got to move throu—"

"Death layer? That what you said? Death layer?"

"Yes." Her hands rose to her own shoulders. "A layer of sadness and terror over what's happened to you."

Jimmy laughed a terrible laugh. He wiped the back of his hand across his mouth. "The death layer. I might show J.T. and them fuckers the death layer." He glared at her. His guts and chest felt blown apart, everything except his rage thrown beyond his reach. He snatched his shirt from the floor and dug out the note she had written him. He shook it at her. "What's this say? This note you give me, what's it say?" Sandra said nothing. "Tell me."

"It says 'Destiny sent you to me'."

"*Destiny?*"

"I believe it. You know what destiny is?"

"Yeah I know. Why the hell'd you give it to me?"

"Because I wanted you to know."

"Know what? That I couldn't read it?"

"Oh no, Jimmy." She rose onto her knees on the mattress, but he stepped back.

"You knew, didn't you."

"I didn't know. I mean I figured maybe, but I didn't care. I just wanted to give it to you and I'd tell you if you couldn't read it."

He pushed his palm against the bridge of his nose and exhaled, his expression more pained than any she had seen from his injuries. He dropped his arm and paced around the tiny room.

"Why you keeping me around, Sandra? You got to hide me here as is." He motioned to her books and faced her. "You're gone have to hide me all the time."

"No, I like you."

"That ain't enough."

"It is."

"No it ain't. All of what I did. And I can't read." Jimmy looked at the note as if it were burning his hand. "Shit, Sandra, why'd you open me up like this?"

"The massage? I thought you needed it."

"Well I don't need it." He tossed the note onto the bed. He grimaced as he slipped on his shirt, breathed fast and shallow as he buttoned it. Sandra felt as though the bed and floor were dropping beneath her. She clenched her fists.

"You're not leaving."

He rubbed his hip. "I'm going out to smoke."

"You can smoke in here. There's a back yard too."

"I'm going out front. The hell with the damn police. The hell with all of 'em."

He limped toward the door, slammed it behind him. Sandra gripped the sheet, slowing the sensation of falling. The lies she'd told Jimmy and the Rideauxs heavied in her chest.

Sandra restocked toothpaste, anti-perspirant, aspirin and hair products, trying to imagine herself into Jimmy's body as he slipped out the window and into free fall. How thrilling it must have been to move toward something awful but to move so fast and unbound that you became freedom. She wondered if he'd calculated or even seen the awning before he dropped, the difference between faith and desperation, hoped that he had seen it, although she guessed there could be faith either way. Not that he could articulate these things even if he fully understood what he'd done, and the thought that there was a world Jimmy understood at his core but did not have the words to speak made her sad. He wasn't dumb, absolutely not that, just alien to a world that meant so much to her, a world shaped and altered by words and by the ways of seeing and understanding that words gave. A world of metaphor, and, jeez, she was definitely dealing in the world of metaphor now. It was all jumping. Or not. Right this very minute she stood on the precipice.

She lifted her basket, sauntered to the store front and began to stock a candy rack. "Kids'll have it picked clean by month's end," Mr. Rideaux said from behind the counter. "When I opened this store, I doubt anybody took anything once a month."

"It's not that bad," Sandra said. She returned to the chocolate bars, but an image of Jimmy snatching the money bag struck her. She fumbled a Snickers, bent to retrieve it and heard the cowbell clang. Footsteps clicked in and died behind her. When she turned, a man who could only be Jimmy's father stood unshaven and bleary-eyed and a bit too close. "Can I help you?" she said, unsure if her voice quavered or not. He blinked and contorted his face as he studied her.

"You know my son Jimmy. He said something about a pretty girl working at this store." Sandra glanced at Mr. Rideaux, who raised his eyebrows at her. He had seen Jimmy grab the money. Would he see the similarity between Jimmy and the exhausted older man before her now?

"Beg your pardon?" she said.

"I'm Jimmy's father. Did he talk to you? You know where he is?"

She swallowed. "I don't know a Jimmy."

"Did he tell you to say that? I don't blame him if he did. But I have to see him. I have his money. A man wants to take it from me, but I still have it. Will you tell him?"

She wanted to lead him outside, say, *Yes, yes, let's go to him now*, except she was sure that Jimmy wouldn't want to see him.

"Sir," Mr. Rideaux said, "we'll tell him if we see him. All right?"

"You know him?" J.T. said, glancing between them.

"No, we don't know him."

J.T. pointed at Sandra. "She knows him. I'm sure."

"She says she doesn't, sir. We don't want any trouble."

"I ain't trying to start trouble. I'm in trouble. Deep trouble." He looked at Sandra once more, his blue eyes watery. "You tell him for me. Tell him I'll be at the house with his money. Tell him I'm sorry what I did."

"I will," she said.

J.T. started to turn and stopped. "And tell him if he sees that lawyer, it'll help him." J.T. clanged outside.

"Crazy people coming in here," Mr. Rideaux said. "Makes you wonder."

Sandra watched J.T. mope across the parking lot. She struggled not to chase after him and pull him to a bus. Her bottom lip quivered and she bit it to stop it there.

"You all right, Sandra?" Mr. Rideaux asked.

"It's sad," she said. "There's so much sadness."

"You're probly still shook up from yesterday, honey." Sandra heard Mr. Rideaux patting on the counter, a sign he was processing information. "Did you think that man looked familiar?"

"No, sir. Just lost."

She placed the last few candy bars on the rack, set her basket behind the counter and looked out the window at the gray sky. The day was sinking fast, as if J.T. had broadsided it. She tried not to fight the sadness, tried to let it have its space in her, but she knew its space would be soaked with tears, and that kind of reaction might make connections for Mr. Rideaux she couldn't risk.

"Mr. Rideaux, do you mind if I take off early?"

"You not feeling good?" he asked, peeling off his reading glasses.

"I haven't been sleeping so well lately."

"Me and Mrs. Rideaux get that. You need something to help you sleep, you just snatch it off the shelf." A slight smile crept across Sandra's lips. He and his wife had saved her. Her first couple of weeks in town, she had caught different buses just to get out of her apartment and avoid being sucked under in the way she'd barely escaped up north. The rides were alternately thrilling, intimidating and surreal, trips to nowhere that she knew, trips without purpose or destination, Sandra the only white person most of the time. Then one day the bus closed in on her. She had been daydreaming, but suddenly her breath was gone. Dark spots circled her like crows. Her chest walls closed on her lungs. She was sure she was going to die. She rushed to the front and pleaded to be let off, stumbled out in front of a dilapidated mall. She hurried along the sidewalk until she collided with a black man coming out of the Rideauxs' store, bent to help him with his scattered items and broke down. Everything blurred, except the man ushering her in, the Rideauxs tending to her, the man saying it was all right. The Rideauxs took her to the back, Mrs. Rideaux patting her back, holding her as Sandra sobbed and apologized. When they figured out she didn't have a job, they offered her one, one she was sure they couldn't afford.

"Sandra?" Mr. Rideaux said. "You best hurry to catch your bus."

She quickly hugged him and stepped outside. The air was laden with the excess burn-off the plants released on overcast and rainy days, and Sandra sneezed as she hustled to the bus stop. Not that the bus would be on time, but she was already ten minutes past its scheduled arrival and the next bus wouldn't be by for at least another hour. She jogged. The bus groaned to a halt up ahead. As she stepped on, wet heat and the smell of bodies enveloped her. The windows were down and people fanned themselves, the air-conditioner evidently on the fritz. Sadness weighed on her again, and she kept her eyes forward so as not to meet anyone's eyes as she moved to the rear. She felt so fragile that any transmitted emotion, whether sympathy or resentment, might set her off. The bus jerked into motion while she was still in the aisle and she held onto a seat and swayed before she caught her balance enough to sit.

She let her awareness go to her center, then, after a moment, pulled the lawyer's letter from her purse. She still hadn't read it, and she held it as though it were an omen. J.T. had mentioned the lawyer in the store, and she had seen the date on the letter was before Jimmy arrived. The probability that it was the engine of all that had happened chilled and excited her. She knew she had to admit that she'd taken it, tell him, too, that his father needed him no matter what he'd done. But then, what if his father was acting? Why would Jimmy's father have anyone after him if he still had Jimmy's money? That didn't add up. And yet, she was sure J.T. was telling the truth. Desperation had billowed from him, and Sandra was an expert on desperation.

Rain drops pelted the top of the bus and sprayed through the open windows, setting off hoots and laughter and frantic window raising. The shower lasted only a hundred yards, then the humidity was worse, filling the bus like steam. They crawled along, stopping time and again, as she leaned her cheek against the greasy window. She hadn't even allowed herself to think the worst until now, that Jimmy might be gone when she arrived home. And if he was there, how long would he be after she told him everything.

Jimmy had only spoken to her, late for work, to say take his car, even though he didn't know if she could drive. She'd refused, then left the AC on, but he'd flicked it off and let the temperature rise to meet his mood. He'd been driven from the den area by the books hunched around him like little judges, had taken the stares of their spines for a while, staring back at them as he fought not to rip out their pages, hurl them and stomp them. Finally he moved to the kitchen table, where now he stared out the window at the capitol building. It seemed to puncture the sky.

His mind was a garden of spikes, each spike a remembered slight: the looks from customers or others who'd sussed out he couldn't read; the final words of women he'd liked; the lies, negligence and back-stabs from every man who'd pretended to act like a father. He flicked open his lighter and slapped it shut again and again. He was done being shit on, and every click of the Zippo was the sound of murderousness increasing inside him. The feeling wasn't pleasant or unpleasant. Not yet at least. It was simply powerful. Rage. Beyond anger and spite and vengefulness. The feeling blasted through his blood and out his eyes to scale the capitol again and again. He shoved the chair from the table, stood, gritted his teeth and accepted the pain from his body. Vertigo twisted in him and he went for the stairs. Outside, the air was fat with smells, the sweet decay of summer and the mud and fish of the river. The capitol grounds spread before him like a paradise of grass, cedar trees, and moss-draped oaks, but his mind didn't take it in. He marched onto the winding sidewalk, not looking at the capitol. The building impended like some giant waiting to snatch him up and hurl him.He knew that Pepper had felt this. Jimmy kept moving. He tripped on the first of the many steps, stumbling upward before catching his balance and trudging on. A giant statue of a man with a sword greeted him, then Jimmy moved through the heavy door into the echoing foyer, the dim cool air enveloping him. With a glance at the guards, he stalked on toward the elevator. Sweat hemorraghed off him, his heart banged like a cop on a door. He entered the elevator and pushed the UP arrow. The door slid closed behind him.

The elevator shot skyward, the force leadening his balls. He almost laughed, but his mouth wouldn't make that gesture. The lighted numbers clicked higher at a crazy speed. He wondered if somehow he'd be launched into space, dispersed into particles. The dizziness took him, and he grabbed the rail and held tight until the elevator slowed and dinged, opened to another hallway. He nearly screamed curses, then he stepped into a short hallway, saw another smaller elevator, entered it and pushed its button. It squeezed him more tightly as it clanked upward several more floors.

The elevator door opened. Beyond tall windows sky and space spread forever. An old voice said, *Settle it*, and Jimmy walked forward. He pushed onto the observation walk and kept going to the waist-high wall. His hands gripped the rough cement. He swallowed and looked down. Gravity pulled. His fall came to him again—the drop, the bounce, the thud, the erection. Alive. Yes, alive. With Sandra. Her touch. Then rage. Still alive. But being alive also had its price. Pepper knew that, and it had scared him to death.

Jimmy looked toward the hotel, saw it he thought, so small from here up high. He hadn't known he would jump, hadn't chosen to jump. He'd felt Sandra's touch, felt the separation when she moved away, every stitch of him straining after her, his brain struggling to know what she was thinking, the way it always was with women. Early kisses stampeding through, first touches strumming like a hundred guitars. Then the wondrous moment of skin touching skin, body joining to body, and orgasm, like the moment he'd taken flight, intensity leading to abandon, to tumbling both joyful and terrifying, until he hit the ground. But no, not like that.

He stepped back from the wall and shot air from his mouth. He thought of Sandra's kiss, his promise to tell her before he acted crazy. Calm settled in him. Fleeting he knew, but still.

From the front door came a leisurely knock. J.T. thought of retrieving his single steak knife from the kitchen, saw the futility in that, and briefly considered offering up the money stored beneath the cabinet. He said, "No," out loud to himself, then sponged the sweat from his brow with his handkerchief, straightened his collar and controlled his shaking legs enough to walk. As he moved, sorrow as old as Jimmy swept through him, memories worse even than the prospect of Squint. J.T. unlocked the door and turned the handle. The purple sports-coated man filled the entire frame, a close-lipped smile etched on his wide face. "Thought you'd stood me up," Squint said. "Came by a few minutes ago and you wasn't home. If you'd had sense, you wouldn't of come back. Then if you had sense, you wouldn't be in this shitted nest." Squint pulled open the screen door and strode into the middle of the room. He leaned forward and surveyed the damage Jimmy had left. "See you been doing a little decorating." J.T. had backed away from him without even knowing it and stood at the mouth of the short hall. He curled his fingers around his thumbs and pressed his fists to his sides, peering past Squint. He hoped Jimmy would still show, then thought how that would just make things worse. "Set down in that chair," Squint said. "I don't like a rat moving around."

"Let's talk about this whole thin—"

"Shut up and set. I got no desire or patience to hear your noise." The little smile had left Squint, replaced by an expression that made his face seemed sucked into its center. J.T. sat in the chair he'd earlier found puncturing his wall. Squint swung the door closed. "I seem to recall you lived in a pretty nice neighborhood over by the campus that day you lipped off. You didn't think I remembered that was you, did you? Hell, you didn't even think I knew it was you. Thought I was some blind idiot and you'd have a little fun wasting my time. Well, J.T., all bills come due."

"You ain't got to do this. I didn't run. I got a nice air-conditioner I could give you till I get the money."

Squint jerked his head back. "You run a air conditioner in here? I'd be scared the wiring'd set the place afire." Squint paced around behind J.T. J.T. cringed, expecting a blow to his neck. "Relax," Squint said. "I'll tell you when it's coming. I'll tell you all about it." He strolled over and peered out the window toward Elma's.

"You ain't asked about the money," J.T. said.

"Don't care much about it to tell you the truth. I figure you ain't holding it in the first place, and in the second place I don't think Mr. Charley even cares about the money."

"How's that?"

Squint scratched at his forearm. "You oughta know he doesn't expect you to pay. After all the trouble you caused us yesterday, he just sent me over here to give you a message." Squint leaned on the windowsill, removed a hard candy from his pocket and slowly unwrapped it. "But I want us to spend some time together before that."

J.T.'s body had never felt quite like this. The trembling had moved from his extremities all the way to his core. He'd been in rough spots before—a knife swipe during a card game, a cave-in on a ditch he was shoring, a fire in his unit at Standard Oil—but he'd never experienced this kind of fright. He couldn't even be sure what it was. He dreaded the pain, shrank at the thought that Squint might even kill him, but there was something more that hollowed him, a lack of resourcefulness and an emptiness like death already. No matter what he'd

done, he'd never been fully trapped. No boss, no rich
bastard, no cop, no bad bet, no nothing had ever caught
him completely. Only he himself. He shuddered, feeling
a breeze like a sheet being pulled across a grave.

Squint snapped his fingers. "Get up and go stand
in that corner." J.T. popped up, almost lost his balance,
then steadied. Squint laughed. "Kinda woozy? Don't
worry. It's gonna hurt you a lot worse than it is me."
He slipped out of his sports coat and hung it on a single
spire of the chair back. His shirt was bright gold and
short-sleeved, showing arms as thick as pythons. J.T.
backed away until the angle of the wall supported him.

"You know," Squint said, "my old man was a son-
of-a-bitch. He was big like me and when he was riled he
would hold me by the scruff of my neck and talk to me,
not hit me, not then, just grip me and talk to me like
a puppy. Oftentimes I didn't even know why he was
riled, but I could see when he took me by the neck it was
something important. It always turned out to be about
his rules. Some of 'em was crazy, like don't drink milk
with green beans, but some of 'em made sense. And his
main rule was you didn't steal or lie, cause stealing and
lying were the same thing and once you lied you didn't
know what you were anymore." Squint rolled the hard
candy in his mouth, bulges here and there like an eyeball
being sucked. J.T. tried to swallow, but his throat was
too tight. Squint sat on the chair, creaking the old wood.

"But one day I lied anyway and he found me out.
Wasn't much of a lie. I was eleven. I think I'd set off a
firecracker in the house and told him I didn't. He could've
hit me and that probably would've taught me a lesson,
but he didn't. He said he wanted me to think about my
lie and the best way to think about it was for me to do
something that would make me spend time by myself.
So he took me in the bedroom and he went in his closet,
took out a bunch of them wire coat hangers with clothes
hanging on 'em and had me take the clothes off and fold
'em up neat to lay on the bed. Then he took ever one
of them coat hangers, eight of 'em I remember, and he
untwisted 'em and bent 'em out straight, even the hook.
Wasn't much scared me, still ain't, but I was feeling
weak cause them hangers was long and sharp and I

thought he might be fixing to whip me or stick me with 'em. Instead, he handed 'em to me and told me to go in the closet and bend 'em all back perfect like they was before. Then he shut me in there in the dark and set right outside the door for what musta been six, seven hours, I don't know, while I bent them suckers and rebent 'em and twisted that stiff wire till my hands was cramping up and bleeding. When he finally let me out, I could hardly see for the light, but I knew none of the hangers were even close to being like they were. He held them up real close to me and said, 'You see, boy, you see these hangers how they ain't right? Well that's a lie. You bend something different and it ain't never straight again.'"

Squint stood and came close to J.T. His face was almost apple red, the vein in his throat the size of a rope, and J.T. believed for a moment that Squint was a troll there to swallow him.

"He was a mean bastard, J.T. There was many a time I would've killed him, but I'd have still took him over you, cause I know he loved me and he tried to teach me right." Squint's pupils tightened. He squeezed J.T.'s shoulder. "You're all twisted wrong, you sorry shit. You don't love your own son and you don't care how many folks you cause misery. So here I am." Squint spread his arms wide and laughed a laugh that shook through J.T. so hard that his legs disappeared. Still, he didn't slide down onto the floor, wouldn't give Squint that pleasure.

"You a fine one to judge me, you big bully," J.T. said, almost a croak. "Do what you got to do and get."

Squint's smile dropped away. "I'm fixing to, mother fucker." He snatched his coat from the back of the chair and shoved his arms into it. His mitts clamped onto J.T., twisted his arms behind him and lifted him over to his chair, where he plastered J.T. stomach down sideways across the seat. "I want you to know," Squint said, "that I ain't never hurt nobody for Mr. Charley like I'm gonna hurt you." Squint smacked his lips. "I want you to know, too, that I'm gonna bust up your son for being such an idiot after I warned him what scum you was. He needs that lesson, seeing how he ain't got a real father."

"He'll kill you."

"He won't kill nobody." Squint held both J.T.'s

wrists with one hand, took J.T.'s hair in his other. "Now. Here's what's gonna happen. I'm gonna take your right thumb, and I'm gonna put it over the back of this chair, and I'm gonna snap it like a little branch. And if I feel like it, I'm gonna snap the other one. Or I might wait till tomorrow to do that one."

J.T. yelled and tried to squirm free. Squint flipped him onto his back, sat on his chest and stretched J.T.'s thumb like a neck on a guillotine. J.T. punched and flailed, Squint's weight threatening to crush his ribs, then Squint said, "Here goes," and hammered down with his fist. The initial pain stultified J.T., then lava was raging through his thumb. He tried to buck Squint off, but Squint stayed on him like a boulder. J.T.'s vision bleared, he raked at Squint's shirt, then everything began to fade, the agony and constriction traveling to a distance, his consciousness dropping into the comforting well of shock, Squint shrinking in a pinhole of light. The sensation of floating took J.T. and he relaxed into it. Then he jerked, tried to move his nose from whatever was assailing it, came fully into awareness again, Squint holding a smelling-salts capsule, the pain fully reconnected. "Stay with me," Squint said. "In a minute I'm gonna show you my work. The bone ain't even showing."

Somehow J.T was on the floor. He tried to pass away again, but Squint was straddling his chest and gripping his jaws. Murder welled up in J.T., but a wave of pain washed it away. He howled, tears bursting from him. "Pathetic," Squint said, and stood. "I'll let you admire it on your own." J.T. rolled onto his side and curled. The weeping shook him, somehow lessening the searing pain. Squint's toe nudged him and he curled tighter. J.T. clasped the wrist of his injured hand like a tourniquet to try and shut off the pain. "See you tomorrow," he heard Squint say, heard the screen door squeak and the car pull away. He opened his blurry eyes. The worn floor stretched away from him. Beyond the rectangle of the door frame hung the gray sky. He sniffed and blinked, breathed heavily. He watched the incremental crawl of the overcast clouds across the door, listened to the swishing approach of cars and their whisking past a block away while he kept his vision from the thumb he knew was maimed. His good hand squeezed the wrist of his bad so hard that he imagined the hurt going away, the broken thumb going away, all of it going away. Then the pain slashed through him again. "J.T.," he heard, and curled more. "J.T.!" He opened his eyes. A backlit womanly shape appeared at the base of the stoop. A slender blade probed his thumb all the way to its root and on up to his elbow. Faintness teased him. The shape climbed the steps, a rifle across its body, a hit man or woman arrived early. J.T.'s blood chilled, then Elma said, "Sweet Jesus," and stepped in with a shotgun leveled. "You alive?" she asked. "I heard the screaming and called my son. He on the way now."

J.T. groaned so loudly it surprised him, then let his eyes flutter closed. Elma's image stayed with him, but the image was rapidly shrinking as he receded from consciousness. "J.T.!" came to him with vigorous shaking and, try as he might to avoid coming clear, Elma reeled him toward awareness. "They coming back?" Elma called, and J.T.'s eyes shot open with uncertainty over whether Elma's words were a question or not. She stood over him, her breasts somehow reassuring. "They messed you up," she said, and bent from the waist to lay a palm on his cheek. "You cold to the touch. They hurt you anyplace else besides your hand?"

"Uh uh," J.T. said, although after he said it he had no idea if that was true, no idea whether Squint had cracked a rib or given him some kidney kicks that he just hadn't sorted out yet.

"That big Lincoln took out. They's nobody else is they?"

"Uh uh."

"Let's sit you in that chair then," she said, and put the shotgun on the floor.

"I'm fine here," he said. He let his eyes play over the double-barrel twelve-gauge near his head, the question of whose it was forming in his head.

"Come on," she said, and kneeled. She clutched his shirt, supported his neck and lifted him to a sitting position, the shift fully reawakening the startling pain. J.T. retched the little on his stomach. He began to apologize, not knowing if he'd covered Elma, then heaved again. "That's all right," she said. "It's just nastiness." J.T. regained himself enough to look at her, her dark pretty face almost making him recoil, and saw that he had missed her. She lifted his chin. "Don't look at it till we get you sitting up," she said, and it took him a second to understand she was talking about his injury. Grunting, she moved around behind him, cupped him under his arms and hefted him into the chair. His head swam once more, but he focused on the sky outside to keep his wits. Elma hovered over him, breathing sharply as she supported herself on the back of the chair.

"You okay?" he asked her.

"You worrying about me? I didn't think you had it in you."

He braced and glanced down. His thumb had two new bends, one where it was snapped sideways above the middle joint, and another where it was obviously dislocated. For seconds his thumb seemed like somebody else's problem, an unreal thing that he was spectator to, then a flat rock landed in his gut. He opened his mouth to speak, but to whom or for what reason was unclear. Here was permanent damage. Something had been done to him that could not be fixed. And he had done things that could not be fixed. The wish came to him, as furious as a bullet, that he was dead.

"Momma, what the hell is going on?" A short, wide-shouldered man in a security guard's uniform rushed straight to Elma and put his arms around her. "You all right?"

"What took you so long?"

"I got here fast as I could. I just stepped out the shower when you called. My hair is still wet."

"I'm fine," she said, and shrugged him off. "This man needs help."

"What's your shotgun doing in here?" he asked. He examined J.T.'s face, then grimaced when he saw the thumb. "Shit! Unh unh." He rubbed his fingers on his mouth as if sanding his lips. "Collector done that?" J.T. nodded. "Momma, what you got to do with this?"

"This man's my neighbor. I heard him screaming and I come over."

"And you thinking about shooting somebody? This man have some problems he needs to work out on his own." Elma straightened, took a step toward her son and pointed her finger. "We gone help him."

The security guard scratched the razored part in his short hair. He gritted his teeth and sucked in. "That shit's broke and shit. I ain't never seen a thumb done like that."

"You gone take him to Earl K. Long."

The man signaled an incomplete pass. "No, no. You going home and call an ambulance and I'm going to work. This man done pissed somebody off and we ain't getting in the middle of it."

The conversation was going on at a distance from J.T. even though the participants were within three feet of him. He was experiencing an odd drifting, even the agony of his thumb partially detached, yet his body felt so firmly rooted that he believed he would never move again. "I'm fine," J.T. said, his own words sounding from a well. Elma and the man watched him, waiting for more. J.T. himself waited for more, but he had become so heavy that even words could not rise.

"J.T.," Elma said, and placed her palms on his cheeks, "this is my son, Roland. He gone drive you to the hospital."

"No hospital."

"See there, let's go," said Roland, grabbing up the shotgun, then tugging at Elma.

"You listen now," Elma said to J.T. "If you don't go to Earl K., you gone lose that thumb. You can't go without a thumb."

"He's coming back tomorrow," J.T. said.

"Who's coming back?" Roland asked.

J.T. raised his arm. Roland glanced over his shoulder and bent close to Elma's ear. He whispered, even though J.T. could hear every word. "I can't be mixed up in this, Momma. Folks at my job won't like trouble."

"Then I'll take your car."

"You can't drive."

"I used to drive."

"You ain't drove in ten years. I got to be at work anyway."

"Don't tell me what you got to be. Help me stand him up."

They grasped him on both sides and lifted him, the nausea ripping through him green and vengeful. He wanted to lie on the floor again, but they walked him toward the door. He muttered that he couldn't go, but he was whimpering and struggling to breathe so much that he doubted his words were intelligible. The sunset sky had turned the clouds orange and bloody purple in the brief time that had elapsed, and J.T. saw it as apocalyptic, revelatory and damning, a vision so intense that he balked, but so weakly that Elma and Roland ignored his effort. His feet continued to move, but his consciousness ebbed and flowed until they were lowering him into the passenger seat of Roland's car. A pungent cherryish aroma brought him into awareness again like the smelling salts.

"What's that smell?" he asked.

"You going to the hospital," Elma said.

"There's cops at the hospital," J.T. said.

"You in trouble with them too?" she asked.

"I don't like cops."

Elma closed him in the passenger seat. "You stay in this car." Roland took her arm and they ambled across both yards to her porch, where she sat down. Roland moved as if to put the shotgun in the house, but she wrenched it from him and shooed him. He scowled as he came toward J.T., then plopped into the driver's seat and cranked the engine.

"What the fuck you doing getting my momma all messed up in this? If something happens to her you gone wish you had just a fucked-up thumb."

"Make the block and drop me in back of the house," J.T. said as the car jerked into motion, swinging and stirring the tiny red tree suspended from the rearview mirror, the insult to his injury.

"You going to Charity Hospital, cause if you don't, my momma'll take my head off. How you get home is your problem." J.T. held tight to the dash with his good hand as Roland careened around the corner and floored it again in the straightaway. The wind blasted past J.T. and he put his nose to the open window. "Don't puke in my ride," Roland said.

"I ain't puking. I'm trying not to puke from that cherry shit. You think that smells good?"

"Smells better'n your old white ass. You getting a

ride, so shut the hell up." Roland gave a pained glance at J.T.'s thumb and looked away. "How much you owe?"

"Who knows? Son-of-a-bitch told me he don't even want the money."

"Shit. You pissed somebody off good."

The buildings stopped clipping past as Roland settled into normal speed on Plank Road. The sky's fiery orange dimmed as the purples deepened to black. J.T. examined the insane jut of his thumb. The swelling had already begun. If he died, how would Jimmy find out? Would he ever find out? Would he care? He touched his injured thumb to his thigh, jerked and cried out. The hurt rippled through him before he fell into a dull place again.

Roland laughed. "Damn. Living in that little house. Going to Charity hospital. Bet you never thought you's gone be treated like a black man."

J.T. met Roland's eyes. "You don't know nothing about what I thought."

WHAT J.T. COULD REMEMBER IF HE WOULD REMEMBER: EARLY 1959

"Thank you, J.T.," Morita said. She lay on her back, naked, refinery light playing across her slightly-swollen belly. J.T. tried not to look at it even though he had liked it against his own only minutes before.

"For what?" he said, ready to drift away after carrying lumber all afternoon.

"For loving me so well." J.T.'s skin tightened at her tone of voice. They sometimes talked sweetly to one another while having sex, but she'd never thanked him and used the word "loving," especially not when they were through. "Did you hear me?" she asked.

"I heard."

"You heard me thank you."

"Yep."

"And you don't even say you're welcome?"

"You're welcome."

"That sounded sincere."

J.T. crossed his arms over his chest, very aware that he had no clothes on. He wanted to leave the room before this conversation went somewhere he couldn't control, but he knew leaving now would only get it there faster. "You know I don't like talking that way," he said.

"What way?"

"The way you're talking. It's best some things don't get said."

"You say plenty of things when we're making love."

"There you go again."

"Go where?"

"Saying things. Besides, it's different talking when we're getting together. Talking is part of it."

She turned onto her side toward him. He avoided looking at her, because he knew it would confuse him. "It's part of it for you. It wasn't for me till I met you. I like it. I just want you to be able to say everything when we're not making love."

J.T. scooted to a sitting position. Morita had been unrestrained that first drunken night they made love, and he'd missed it when she became reluctant and aloof. Lately, though, she'd become bold and expressive and sometimes even wild. He reveled in it, though he often felt strange about her being both that way and pregnant. Now he thought of what her passion might say about her history. Not that he was the jealous sort. It was just that with Morita her history was so different. And he didn't like being pushed to be a way he didn't want to be.

"Don't get mad when I ask you this, all right?" he said. "It's just a question."

"Go ahead."

J.T. licked his lips and took a breath. "How many boyfriends you had? I mean, how many you did this with?"

"You mean made love with or fucked or talked to?" Her tone of voice scraped against his spine.

"You know what I mean."

Morita snatched a shirt from the floor and put it on, slipped into her underwear and shot up from the bed. She walked around to face him, her expression a gun barrel. "I tried to talk to you, and this is what you do? It's two boyfriends. And I mostly liked it. Is that what you want to know? Or something else?" She stormed out of the room. J.T. heard an ice tray crack open, heard cubes ring into a glass, a cabinet close, then the front door slam.

Reluctantly he dressed, still wet from her. He muttered some curses and headed down the hall. On the stoop, the sound of the T-Bird's engine reached him, and he saw her behind the wheel, a pang going through him as if she were driving away. He walked around to the passenger side and settled in beside her, the heater blowing. She held a glass of brown liquid and wore a short unbuttoned jacket, her brown legs stretching from her underwear. "You shouldn't oughta be out here half naked," he said. "It's cold and there's bad characters wander through here more and more."

"Don't worry. I won't take up with any of them."

J.T. snorted at the heavy burn-off stinging his nose and thought how he was more sensitive to it since Morita moved in. "I didn't have a right to ask all that," he said.

"It's not about right, it's about why. Did you find what you wanted?"

"I just didn't want to talk about that other stuff."

"You mean how I love you?"

Morita swigged her drink and went into a fit of coughing that wouldn't stop. She swung open the door and gagged, and J.T. reached and grabbed her waist, her muscles tensing as she threw up. Finally she spat, shoved his hands away and sat straight once more. "I can't goddamn breathe," she said. "How do people live here?" Behind her the plant flarestacks raged, lighting the entire horizon. J.T. thought to defend the place, then turned away.

"Let's go back in," he said.

"No."

"You want me to fix you another drink?"

"I'm sick of drinking." She wiped her mouth with the tail of her shirt, exposing her brown belly. The pooch that had bothered him earlier now called out to be touched, but Morita put her head on the steering wheel. "I can't take back anything that's happened and neither can you," she said. She stepped out of the car and padded across the small yard back into the house. He wasn't sure he knew what she wanted to take back. He tried to think of something to say or do when he joined her, wished he could take back his earlier questions and say Thank you back. Instead, he rested for a minute, the smell of the T-Bird a comfort to him.

* * *

Under the punitive, early spring sun, J.T. hammered nails with murderous intent. The construction work he had tried to avoid managed to sap his cranky humor and the camaraderie that would have made the labor more bearable. The end of each day was a tug-of-war to decide if he would go straight home or roost in a back room card game somewhere. Morita didn't demand that he come home, and although he was often too tired not to go home, he still resented having to even consider a choice. Why should a free man have to dread repercussions and guilt if he wanted to bet the money he'd sweated to make? Nonetheless, he usually headed home, his body gritty with sweat, dirt, and sawdust, his limbs and brain hard-baked and dull, his emotions swinging like a wrecking ball.

Morita often looked terrible from nausea and vomiting, long after that sort of thing was supposed to have stopped. A greenish pallor had crept into her, and at times she closed her eyes to him because, he could tell, he was moving as if on a swing. He wondered if maybe she was sick simply from being alone in a shut-up house. He knew she tried to be awake and to have supper ready, but even when she wasn't awake, even with her sickness, she still radiated energy, although a different kind than before. Before him was the ominous miracle of her transformation—her belly curving outward like a new planet, her breasts expanding to the secret message from their child, her entire self glowing as if the baby were a miniscule star inside her. On good days he hugged her, laid hands on her stomach, kissed her, even made love to her. On those days her body and her presence transformed him into a man beyond exhaustion and restriction, a man transcended into a connection that generated responsibility. For hours he could be that man, finding himself calm and clarified, able to stay in the present and to want the Morita before him. On most other days, he sulked as if the house contained a gas that made him sullen.

* * *

J.T. came home to no car in the driveway and a note that she'd gone to New Orleans to see a doctor she knew at Charity Hospital. Numbness, then twitching and sweating overtook him. Was she lying? Was she gone for good and trying to delay his searching? Had she gone back to her bastard daddy or down the road again? He tried fix himself a sandwich, tried to pace away his nervousness, but the house had an unbearable silence that he absorbed until he had to leave. He returned about ten to find her swollen-eyed and quiet in the hot living room. Exhiliration swept him then swept past. The baby was dead, he knew, and he knew he might die, too, if Morita left.

"I miss home," she said. "I miss my friends, everything. I have nothing."

The words poked at J.T., but he let go of them the best he could. "You saw the doctor?"

"I waited and waited with all those poor people until he could see me." She inhaled as if drawing breath took all her strength. "The baby's fine. The doctor gave me some pills to stop feeling so sick and said I have to eat more. He was shocked to see me. He used to come to our house. I told him he couldn't say anything to my daddy or anyone."

J.T.'s emotions traveled in several directions at once, but he latched onto the one most like support. "We'll get you some good food. Ice cream and whatever you like. We'll get you better."

She plucked at the end of the chair's arm rests, ends that had been frayed before he came home one day to find the chair re-upholstered. "I can't live like this," she said. "In this house. I'm sick from fumes all the time. It's so ugly outside and it's getting hotter."

"I'm gonna buy one of those air-conditioners for the bedroom."

"I can't stay here anymore. I'm selling my car so we can afford to move."

"No."

"It's that or I work or you find something better."

He surveyed his surroundings, saw how much

nicer she'd made them since she moved in and wondered why she couldn't be satisfied. The beers in him increased in volume to gallons. His slight buzz became a throb in his temple. He was prompted to tell her to move out if she was too good to stay, go back to New Orleans and see how that worked, but the earlier fear of her absence stopped his words. "All right," he said, and touched her hair, although he wasn't sure which part he was agreeing to.

Morita's search did not go well. She said she thought maybe landlords weren't willing to rent to an unmarried pregnant woman, and neither she nor J.T. mentioned that there might be another reason in the neighborhoods where she was looking. Eventually J.T. went with her on weekends, but when they arrived together, the realtors examined them and said the place had just been rented or quoted them a price much higher than before. At times they argued with these people, and when J.T. nearly came to blows with a man, Morita suggested that they might have to try different kinds of neighborhoods. She also asked how J.T. thought they would afford any of it if he wasn't willing to put his own house up for sale. J.T. suggested that he look alone, but she said she wasn't going to move some place and then be run off. After that, neither of them said anything.

By her final trimester, Morita's health improved, even though the plant fumes still nauseated her. J.T. began to stop at bars more often on the way home. One night he arrived after eleven to an empty driveway again, bolted into the house and found Morita asleep. His whole chest shook both with relief that she was there and outrage that the car wasn't. "You sold it?" he said.

"Yes," she said.

"I ain't moving then." She went back to sleep.

He headed across the river and mourned the T-Bird by blowing several days' pay, which he blamed on Morita. Her looks, her style, her car had made his life large, but now her actions were reducing him to a puny working stiff with bills to pay and a crummy ride.

That night he slept on the couch and woke up sweaty and late for work. The next week he bought them a window unit for their bedroom on credit.

The next afternoon Morita was sitting on the stoop when he pulled into the drive. Her beauty mowed down his resentment, but he gathered enough indifference to say only Excuse me as he edged past her. Just as his fingers touched the door knob, the refinery boomed, shaking the house and making him duck. He pictured noxious gases rolling toward Morita, grabbed her under her armpits and lifted her, but she pointed skyward at an object, a black dot, sailing very high and toward them. J.T. knew it was a pop-off valve no larger than two-feet in diameter, but he imagined it larger and crashing down to crush their house. He held her more tightly as it kept coming, flew above them and arced down behind trees a block away. Morita looked back toward the plant, detached J.T.'s hold and went inside. He heard sirens from the refinery, then from police cars and joined her. She sat in the chair he'd moved from the living room to the bedroom, watching the flare stacks through the window. He waited for her to speak, to ask or demand, to say, "See?" but she said nothing.

J.T. stayed home more, grieving for the T-Bird while he watched Morita fashion the place for the baby. She turned the second bedroom into a nursery, cleaned unkempt corners, read out loud, talked and sang to the baby inside her. It divided J.T. even more to respect her so much in her care for their child while that care put her in a world from which he felt excluded and ignorant. Plus, she seemed more comfortable with his silence. Sometimes he fled the house to avoid her lack of recognition. Other times, his attraction to her overwhelmed him, and he persuaded her to make love, her globular body atop or beneath him a thing that could either take him to new excitement or cause him to wither. Often he believed that what little he'd known of himself before, he knew less of now.

One night J.T. came to from dozing on the couch, aware that she had come out of the cool bedroom and

was watching him from the chair that had become hers.
He sat up, his blood pressure rising despite the lingering
sluggishness from the heat. "I know you're scared," she
said. "I know you don't want me here half the time. I
can see you don't understand things, but I still feel like
you want me, maybe even love me, even though I think
you don't want to love me and you've never said you do."
She spoke slowly and stiffly as if she hadn't spoken to
another person in years. "Neither one of us were ready
for this, and that's why I don't blame you for how you
act. But we're having a baby and you have to face it."

J.T.'s eyes flitted over her belly. "I'm facing it."

"You think you're trying as hard as you can, but
that's not enough. I think you want to love the baby, you
just don't know how. I think you will if we get married."

"Married," he said, as if it were a newly-coined
word. Marriage had never crossed J.T.'s mind, although
he realized now that he'd unconsciously dreaded and
prepared for this day.

"It might be a mistake," she said. "I might still be
here just because I have nowhere else to go." She paused.
"No, that's not true. I do love you. You try to take care of
me more than anybody ever has." He thought she might
cry, but then he saw that she might have learned how
not to cry ever again, saw her as both the person he knew
better than anyone in his life and as an exotic stranger
accidentally arrived. "So," she said, "you have to marry
me or I have to go someplace else."

His fingertips went cold. "There ain't no need to
say that."

"There is a need. It's my need. There's need for a lot
more too. You'll have to do better when the baby comes.
Find a better job and move us somewhere we can all
breathe better air. Maybe north. I mean it."

J.T. bristled momentarily, then the bristles lay
flat. She was right, he knew, and he allowed himself to
hear her. The bigness she had originally filled him with
came to him again and he glimpsed himself as a father
taking care of his wife and child.

"Come sit over here," he said.

"You have to answer me, J.T."

"I'll give better answers if you come over here."

Morita took a spot at the opposite end of the couch.

J.T. scooted toward her and stretched his arm, rested his palm on the tight skin of her stomach. Whoever was there answered with a kick. "That happen a lot?"

She snorted a laugh, removed his hand as if peeling away a sticker and placed it on the cushion. "What do you say?" she asked.

"Okay," he said.

"Get married you mean?"

"Yep."

"I think we'll have to go to New Orleans. A Justice of the Peace. It's a risk because we'll be in the records, but I think that's the easiest place to get it done."

"That's fine."

"And the other things I said."

"I'll do my best."

"No," she said. "You'll do it all. Better job, better house. Even leave the South. I'm sick of being trapped here."

J.T. tried to imagine an elsewhere and drew a blank. He'd only been to Texas, Mississippi, Alabama, and Arkansas. The amount of things he'd have to leave and that he'd have to learn fell through him like fractured rafters. "You sold the T-Bird," he said. He didn't know why he said that. Morita's stern expression didn't flinch.

"I hated that car. It was a leash my daddy tried to tie to me." Her cheeks blushed and her chin quivered, and before J.T. knew it he had wrapped an arm around her shoulder. She leaned, her nose and forehead ramming into his neck, and stayed. Her breath expanded and fell against his side and he slid his arm down until the fine ladder of her rib cage lay beneath his fingers.

DAY SEVEN, AFTERNOON

Jimmy's heart lifted as he walked toward where she sat
on the stoop. Sweaty strands of hair dangled in front of
her eyes. He thought she was home early, but he couldn't
be sure. "Hey," he said.

"Where the hell have you been?"

He stopped in front of her and hooked his thumbs
in his belt loops to keep himself from sweeping the hair
from her forehead. Her mood clouded around her darker
than the actual sky, heat lightning playing in her eyes,
but even so, seeing her calmed him.

"Out walking," he said.

"What if the police saw you? I'd be in it then." She
shot to her feet, slung open the front door and tromped
up the stairs. He watched her ascend before he followed
her. When he entered the apartment, she put her finger
close to his chest. "I thought something had happened to
you. I saw your car here and ran toward the hotel until
I thought how foolish that was and stopped halfway. I
almost broke down."

"Ain't you home early?"

"Yes I'm home early. I was scared. Jesus, Jimmy,
I don't know what you might do." Sweat beaded in her
eyebrows and traced her cheeks. He moved to hold her,

but she spun, went to the kitchen counter and stared out the window. He moved closer. He thought of telling her about going up in the capitol, considered it best to wait.

"I walked on down by the river and downtown too and had to stand in a doorway till that little storm went through. Sorry I worried you."

She slapped her palms on the formica and faced him. "Don't apologize," she said, her voice the sharpest yet. She flicked a dish towel from its holder, wiped her face and arms and tossed the rag onto the table. "I saw your father," she said.

"Do what?"

"Your father. He came to the store and told me to tell you he was in trouble. He said he needed you. I had to act like I didn't know you."

"You sure it was him?"

"Of course I'm sure. He looks just like you, or like an older worn-out you, except for his blue eyes." She touched the sides of her head. "He told me, too. Mr. Rideaux was there listening so I had to act like he was just some crazy person. He looked so sad, Jimmy." Sandra pulled a chair from the table and flopped into it. Jimmy felt gut- punched. It was hard to believe that only a couple of days ago he'd trusted J.T. enough to tell him about Sandra. And why had J.T. remembered? To catalog information and hope he could use it? Jimmy tensed. He knew that trick. Another similarity between them.

"You all right?" he asked.

"He was so pitiful. I know you don't want to hear it after all he's done, but he looked like the whole world was on him, and there I was having to deny him."

"Ain't nothing you could do for him, Sandra. He put himself where he is." Jimmy sat next to her. The image of Squint in J.T.'s ramshackle apartment covered Jimmy like an eclipse, then he let it go. "I done all I can do for him. I'm just glad you came home."

She bit her thumbnail, then jerked it down. "I've been lying," she said. "I lied in this talk we're having now."

"You didn't see J.T.?"

"No, I saw J.T. I lied that I came home only

because I was worried. I came home because I wanted to see you."

The corner of his mouth rose. "That ain't much of a lie."

"That's not all." She pulled an envelope from her pocket, the envelope from the lawyer he saw, dropped it on the table in front of him. "I took this from your car. I saw it was from a lawyer and I wanted to see if it was anything, I don't know, anything that said something about you I needed to know, like something you'd done. I snuck it from your car this morning."

Jimmy stared at the white rectangle, a canker that wouldn't heal. "You had a right after all I've done."

"There's more." Sandra tugged the edges of the envelope as if trying to widen it. Jimmy interlaced his fingers and gripped. Had she told J.T. where he was? So what if she had, she had done it because her heart was good, and even if J.T. came, Jimmy didn't have to see him. She shook her head. "The police never came. They were never after you. I told you they were so you'd stay with me." She stared at him. "I kept them away by telling the Rideauxs you were retarded. I told them you didn't know what you were doing because you were retarded."

Jimmy had the sensation of everything going to mud and sliding out from under him. Through the window, the sky itself looked smeared.

"I didn't mean it, Jimmy."

"I can see how you thought it."

"But I didn't. I would never think it. It's the last thing I would think."

"It was still what come to mind."

"I would've said anything to keep you safe." Sandra pressed her lips to thin lines. She reached over to Jimmy's locked fingers. "You're here with me, aren't you? I wanted you here and you're here, isn't that what counts?"

"It's tough to know what counts about this." He recalled the day he and Sandra met, his pitiful attempt to pretend he could read when he set J.T.'s directions in front of her. How many other hundreds of attempts had been as transparent as that one? Was that another ability of the ones who could read, the ability to spot those who couldn't as if they had a mark? "I might of thought it if I was you," he said. "I should of told you I couldn't read. That's like a lie."

"No it's not. It's not much at all."

"You don't believe that. Tell me what you really believe."

Sandra's thumb rose toward her mouth again, but she stopped it. "I don't think much about it." He stared at her. "Okay, I think it's a shame. I want you to read so you can have what I have, so we can share everything."

"You consider I am retarded? Elsewise why wouldn't I of just learned like everybody else?"

"You're not retarded."

"Well I'm something most folks ain't."

"Have you tried to learn?"

"A passle of times. The words just jumbled, and a sickness come over me, my legs and arms about dead and my belly filled up with cold eggs. That's what it's like for me to even try."

"I don't care," she said. "I mean, I care, but it doesn't put me off."

Tears coursed the sides of her face and she brushed them away. He saw her clearly, beautiful and smart but in a rough patch, and once that patch smoothed out, the world would be available to her.

"You say that, but you ain't sure you mean it. You don't know all what I can't do that I seen other people do. I can't read highway signs, I can't order from menus, I can't fix my own taxes, I can't go to the grocery store and tell the signs that say what aisle something or other is on, can't fill out a job application, can't work a job where they need reading and writing, can't read words on the TV—"

"Okay!"

"No, it ain't okay. That's a world you don't know nothin' about. You love your books and you been to school, and I don't know a thing about any of that. That the kind of man you can be proud of, that you won't be ashamed of? A man can't ever make a good living?"

Sandra grabbed his wrists and brought his hands to her lips, kissed his knuckles and held them to her cheek. "I can help you." She lowered his hand to the table, sniffed and cleared her crying. "I'll show you."

Jimmy bit the inside of his cheek. "I got something to tell you, too," he said. "I went up in the capitol today."

"To jump?"

"I just went. You told me to tell you if I did anything."

"Anything crazy."

"Well. I wanted to tell you cause I thought of you. Up there, I was thinking of you."

She kept her elbows on the table and studied him. He had no idea what she thought she saw. She scooted her chair back, came around behind him and laid her long-fingered hands on his shoulders. She let her fingers simply rest on him, leaned and kissed him on the cheek. She circled her arms lightly around his chest and pressed her cheek to his. The smell of her sweat and perfume mixed and traveled the length of him. "Tell me if I hurt anything," she said.

He reached back, guided her to his side and placed his hands on her hips. He looked at her soft eyes, her high rounded forehead and pale hair, brushed the back of his knuckles across her chin. "Does it scare you I went up?" he asked. She took him by the collars and raised him to his feet. She put her mouth gently to his, her lips even fuller and softer than he remembered, then she pulled him close, her breasts firm circles against his chest, and kissed him harder. Her hands slipped under his shirt and onto the flesh of his back. He spread his hands on her shoulder blades and across the firm canal of her spine. She pulled her head slightly away but held him even more tightly. "Stay," she said, and kissed him again.

"You might be lucky cause it's Tuesday," Roland said as they pulled up to the Emergency Room at Charity Hospital. Several cops and lots of black people smoking cigarettes crowded around the brightly-lit glass entrance. J.T. wondered how a day of the week could make a difference, wondered if he'd simply chosen a wrong day somewhere in the recent past. Roland jerked them to a stop, but J.T. didn't move. A ball peen hammer was working on his thumb clean up to his elbow, and the red haze distanced him from all else. Roland's door slammed and then J.T.'s opened. Roland took J.T.'s bicep and guided him out. His ears rang and everything brightened when he stood. He was vaguely aware of Roland's grip tightening. "Stay with me," came Roland's voice through a cloud, and J.T. breathed, his thumb surging into his consciousness again.

"Can't leave that car there," a white cop said, and took J.T.'s arm, chilling him. "I'll help him in while you park."

There seemed to be a stadium-full of faces watching J.T. as the cop led him through the cigarette smoke and the sliding doors, then he entered a hot hall clogged with the odors of ammonia and sweat. Black people lined the walls, men and women of all ages, kids, babies, some nursing bandaged body parts, some glaring, some hunched with an invisible misery. Their presence oppressed him with claustrophobia more intense than he'd ever experienced and he would have turned and left had the cop not been ushering him. At an open window the cop placed J.T. in a plastic chair and said, "That must hurt," before he went off down the hall.

Beyond the window a black woman and a white woman glanced at J.T., then continued talking about how somebody named Willie had threatened to sue his girlfriend for slander after he slashed her tires and she had him arrested. A shriek ripped through the hall nearly knocking J.T. from his chair and setting a baby to crying. J.T.'s ears sharpened, bringing to him a chorus of suffering—moans, yells, sobs, stern voices—seemingly coming from the recesses of a giant castle. Roland clapped him on the back, giving J.T.'s heart a bump. "They seen you yet?" Roland asked. J.T. shook his head. "Hey! Somebody wanta tend to this man?" The look the women returned reminded J.T. of the look Squint had given him just before he smashed down.

"Everybody here needs tending," the white woman said.

"Yeah? Well where they get it?"

The black woman licked her lips. "Has he been shot

or stabbed or something busted inside of him?" She was thin and had a puff of curly yellow hair.

"His thumb is broke out the socket."

The women dully examined J.T. as if he were a cow among a zoo of exotic animals. "I'll talk to you after while," said the white woman and sauntered to the window. She took her seat meticulously, shuffled through her desk a bit before she finally fixed on J.T.

"A lot of people die at your window?" Roland asked.

"Don't get smart or I'll call a real policeman in here. I'm fixing to help your grandpaw."

"I ain't his grandpaw," J.T. said. Roland and the woman laughed.

"What's your last name?" Roland asked him.

J.T. pressed his forehead. "Why you asking?"

"Cause I know my momma gone want me to fetch you when I get off work."

"Strawhorn. J.T. Strawhorn."

Roland looked at the woman. "You take it from here?"

"I'll manage somehow," she said.

Roland nodded. He leaned close to J.T. "Strawhorn, remember what I said about anything happening to my momma. That leg-breaker'll look like an angel compared to me." Roland straightened. "See you in the morning if you ain't home."

"Thanks," J.T. muttered. He slumped as the woman took his information, information so tentative and sketchy—address, occupation—that he felt it the rumor of a real life. At one time he would've taken pride in such light baggage, but tonight he seemed so light as to be in danger of a turned page whisking him away. That is, except for the injury, which anchored him like a torturer's shackle. The woman continued to type, each tap and snap of a key and letter arm a little thump to his temples. "Next of kin?" she asked.

"What?"

"Next of kin. Closest relative. Who we should contact in case of emergency."

J.T. twitched. A week ago he would have said Nobody without a blink, but now thoughts flooded his mind. To tell or not to tell, and if he told, would it put Jimmy in more danger, although he didn't see how that could happen since J.T. didn't know where Jimmy was. Still, if J.T. told and then died and they did find Jimmy, would Jimmy take revenge and end up hurt himself? J.T.'s head swam so badly that he covered his eyes. He believed that if he denied Jimmy again, he might die right here.

"Are you about to faint?" the woman asked.

"No. My next of kin is James Thomas Strawhorn, Junior. I don't know where he is and I don't want him contacted, but that's who he is." He uncovered his eyes to her befuddled expression. "How long you think it's gonna be?" She gave a puzzled look, typed a little more, ripped the paper from the carriage and held out a pen.

"Shouldn't be too long. We try to get to bad bone breaks quick, plus it's slow right now." J.T. waited to see if she was joking. When her expression didn't change, he took the pen in his left hand and printed his name. The woman took the paper and rang a counter bell.

A nurse appeared, a short squat black woman, and took the paper from the counter. "Let's see," she said, and gently lifted his arm. "Hm. We'll take you back now." She stepped down the hall, unfolded a wheel chair and returned to help him stand.

"Can y'all give me something for pain?" J.T. asked.

"Just swing over into this chair." J.T. pushed off and half stood. Sweat broke on him, but he made it to the chair. He belched, then saw the people along the hall watching him.

"Don't get a lot of white people here, huh?" J.T. asked.

"You're the first on this shift. No extra charge, though."

She wheeled him down the hall and into a large green room with curtained cubicles, some curtains drawn, some not. Fluorescent light struck him and he blinked several times before he could focus on the people he passed, a couple stroking the hair of a little girl who was still and quiet, an old woman in an oxygen mask, a man with a bloody bandage on his head humming a weird monotone. The noise he'd heard at a distance was much louder here: the previous shrieker protesting that whatever the doctor was doing was killing her; another person half-crying, half-groaning; staff and visitors chatting or busily conversing. The cubicles lined the perimeter of the huge ward and he wondered how they would ever be able to see him, much less all the people here and all the people outside and all the people yet to be hurt or struck ill. It was senseless that he was here anyway, considering there was worse to come, but he didn't have the strength to struggle or the means to get home.

An orderly fell in beside them. "We can put him in 17," the portly young black man said, and J.T.'s spirits fell more that he was in an odd number. The chair turned briskly into a cubicle and halted. The nurse and orderly cupped his armpits and helped him onto the bed, the business-like movement causing pain to charge anew into J.T.'s thumb. A thermometer was plugged into his mouth, a band wrapped around his arm and pressurized. J.T. rested his head on the pillow and kept his eyes closed to the tunnel-vision he knew was likely happening on the other side of his lids.

"Your blood pressure's up pretty high," the nurse said.

"I wonder why," J.T. answered without looking. She chuckled.

"Doctor'll be here soon," the nurse said. "You just lay here and don't move."

J.T. heard the metallic whisk of the curtain rings skimming across the rod, then footsteps receding. Light pierced his eyelids and the reek of alcohol and ammonia made him feel his skin was about to be stripped away. A small panic bloomed in him to be closed off and left alone. New screaming shattered the air and J.T. tried to find the cushion of distance he'd felt earlier, tried to focus on the sounds below the anguish. From the next cubicle he heard murmuring, one voice, no two, and almost told them to shut up until he realized they were praying. He listened hard, but the words were gibberish. Outside his curtain a voice asked what was wrong in seventeen and another voice said it looked like a broken and dislocated thumb. In eighteen there were complications from leukemia. The teenage car accident victim from earlier had died. The curtains shimmied open again and a black doctor who looked no older than Jimmy strolled in with the nurse. "Mr. Strawhorn, I'm Doctor Larosso."

"You're my doctor?"

The doctor glanced over his shoulders. "Looks like it."

"Never saw a black doctor."

"I'm the only one here, so it must be your lucky day." J.T. harumphed. The doctor cradled J.T.'s forearm and wrist to examine him, while J.T. watched the wall and braced for what he knew was coming. It came, the probing, and J.T. would have sworn the doctor was using a scalpel. The room began to throb as if J.T. were inside a giant bass drum. He heard his name spoken loudly, but through a tube, then smelling salts entered his nose again and he jerked, expecting Squint once more. "Hold on, hold on, you're okay," the doctor said, holding one arm while the nurse held the other. "You were going into shock."

"Just let me go."

"No, we're gonna get you set." The doctor patted his shoulder. "How'd you do this, Mr. Strawhorn?"

"That ain't none of your business."

"I guess that's true. If you did it hitchhiking, though, I'd say stand farther from the road."

"I hope you ain't charging for the comedy."

"We're not charging for anything." The doctor put a sling on his arm as J.T. clamped his teeth. "It's broken, but I don't think it's snapped. You're fortunate the joint gave way to save torque on the bone."

"Fortunate."

"Okay, maybe not fortunate, but your thumb could be worse off. We'll get you X-rayed, and I'll come back and give you a cast after while."

"How bout something for pain?"

"We'll give you ten Tylenol fours if you're not allergic to codeine."

"How bout a shot or some Percosets?"

"Tylenol fours." The doctor brushed through the curtains, leaving J.T. with a reinvigorated throb and the nurse who was writing on a chart. From another part of the ward exploded a fresh howl, this one from a woman. J.T. flinched.

"How you stand all this?" he asked the nurse.

"Oh, it's quiet. You want real fun, break something on the weekend." She held out two small tablets and a cup of water. J.T. pinched them from her palm, tossed the pills and the water back and swallowed. She waited, a kind smile on her lips.

"Would you tell me something?" he asked. "All those people out there, they all waiting to get emergency help?"

"No. Most of them are here just to see a doctor. No insurance."

The woman somewhere beyond his curtain howled again, then there were yells and sounds of a scuffle. J.T. shut his eyes as hard as they would shut, plugged one ear and hoped the pills would quickly go to work. Behind his eyelids his memory kicked into high, the instant Squint cracked down on him returning full blown. He bucked and groaned, then quieted himself, hoping no one had heard. Then she came to him, unbidden and unwanted, Morita, her image, still young, but also her self in dimensions he couldn't fully comprehend. Her passion, her ferocity, her love for him and Jimmy. He tried to shove her out of his brain, but he couldn't, so he cringed, wishing the people next door would pray again, and loudly.

WHAT J.T. COULD REMEMBER IF HE
WOULD REMEMBER:1959

For the next several weeks, J.T. fawned over Morita,
checked on jobs at a couple of plants, saved money and
put his imagination closer to himself as husband and
father. He went for his blood test and called the court
house; he tried to set a date with her; he asked if she
wanted to go to Biloxi for a honeymoon. And in exactly
the way he expected the universe to work, Morita
closed to him like a fern. Nonetheless, he bought a gold
engagement band on credit from a guy he knew. Morita
put it on the coffee table, fled to the bedroom and cried
until late that night. He slept on the couch, then asked
the next day if she was sick and if the baby was all right.
She told him she doubted that he really cared, then said
she needed time to think. He drank a six-pack, watching
the abandoned ring as if it might grow and encircle him,
and fell asleep in the living room, a blowing box fan
giving him dreams of a hurricane. She woke him in the
middle of the night with a kiss that he could sense as
sisterly even in his sleep, and said, "Let's do it tomorrow."
She slipped the ring on and went back to the bedroom.
    The next morning, when she stood before him in
a white dress, gloves and hat that he'd never seen, he

was stunned by a beauty that was not like the beauty he'd known, but a beauty like a priceless painting, magnificent and haunting, pristine and distant, untouchable and charged with darkness beneath the surface. Like so much, he didn't have the words to say these feelings, and that only added to his separateness. And to add to that separateness, he thought how odd for a pregnant bride to be wearing white.

He put on his only suit and tie, scruffy next to her, and without speaking they set off toward New Orleans on a road shimmering with heat. He had allowed himself to fantasize a grand wedding with hundreds of guests, a long-trained gown and a long-tailed tux, but his romanticism embarrassed him now. Maybe if she had let him put the ring on her, spoken to him once about her joy at being his wife, expressed pride that she was having his child, then his vision could have been, if not glorious, at least not shameful. Instead she'd said nothing to him except which way to go. What kind of wedding day was that? His tie pressed his adam's apple, flushing his neck, and he drove on, out of Baton Rouge and onto Highway 61, lined with mossy cypress and bayous. White egrets poised to spear crawfish and frogs, pirogues rested on the still water by makeshift fishing camps. He wondered if he would arrive to find her father ready to reclaim her at some predetermined point, another groom picked out, and loathed himself for thinking it. How many times had he rejected her? How many scars had he caused? He eyed her stomach, imagined its firm cafe-au-lait roundness as a magic globe and wished he could touch her.

"J.T.," she said, her quiet voice startling him like a shout, "I guess you know that my birth certificate says I'm a Negro."

He almost jerked the wheel to stop the car from swerving, then realized they were still traveling true down the endlessly straight road. "What?" he said.

"I'm tired of this game of not saying."

J.T. veered to the shoulder and coasted to a stop. He exited the car and marched toward the roadside bayou. A blue heron took slow flight from the marsh grass like his former life leaving for good; Spanish moss swayed in a slight breeze. J.T. stopped at the soggy edge of the water and pursed his lips. He heard the car door shut. Seconds later her white dress brightened his periphery.

"Don't act like you're surprised," she said, her voice flat.

"I thought you were Creole."

"I am Creole."

"You still should've said you were Negro."

"Please. You've always known. Should you have said you were white?"

"That's different."

"My daddy would think worse. He wouldn't have let anybody like you in the front door."

"What like me?"

"White. Especially without money or connections. He'd have worked you in the yard."

"Your daddy can rot in hell."

"I hope so. He'd still shoot you if he knew I was having your baby."

J.T. looked at her. "You'd probably like that."

She shrugged. "You want to shoot me right now." She smoothed her dress, its hem touching the grass. "I guess I still love you, J.T., but I can't stand you half the time. I know you feel the same about me." She turned and left. J.T. considered throwing himself into the murky water, pulled the hair on the sides of his head, then threw a chunk of log into the bayou instead. He followed her path and dropped behind the steering wheel. "There's more," she said, her voice zombie-like.

"What, you a communist too?"

"I don't think I can go to New Orleans. I thought getting our names on the record there would force you to move, but now I'm scared he'll already be looking because I went to the hospital."

"Does he know everybody?"

"I sold the T-Bird so he wouldn't find us. After those rednecks at the diner, I knew word might somehow get back to him that a mixed couple in a T-Bird was in Baton Rouge."

"You're kidding. He ain't gonna find you like that."

"You don't know his world, J.T. You can't imagine what all he can do. He can find us, and if he does, he'd kill you and lock me up to keep the baby a secret."

"If you that scared, why the hell didn't you go to Charity in Baton Rouge?"

"I wanted to see a doctor I at least knew. I wanted to see my best friend, too, but when I called her from New Orleans, she told me not to say where I was. She said he'd already sent somebody around asking and she was sure he had someone watching her."

J.T. knocked a knuckle on his arm rest. His car had no air-conditioning and it was rapidly steaming as he tried to figure out how much of what Morita was saying was paranoia, maybe downright insanity, before they drove on. Not that her voice didn't have the ring of truth and foreboding. And not that the story of her daddy didn't make perfect sense with the way she behaved. He just didn't know.

"What do you wanta do?" he asked.

"I thought I might still call my friend and ask her to be my maid of honor, but I don't think we should risk it. Maybe we should just go back to Baton Rouge."

J.T. loosened his tie. The only person who would marry them in Baton Rouge would be some Negro justice, and he had no way of finding one short of going to Scotlandville and asking. And who knew if a colored Justice would even do it for fear of reprisal by some mean boys or the Klan, not do it because of pure disgust. J.T. sure didn't know. He studied Morita's sad, drained profile and the endless almond of her eye. He knew that he had known, not that her features boldly said it, or even her color, lighter than some tanned whites he knew. Negro. Colored. He couldn't see how they applied here. Granted, he knew a nigra or a nigger when he encountered one, the former pure of color, the latter a sorry breed, but he didn't consider himself one of those that hated for color's sake. Morita wasn't a Negro, and their child certainly wouldn't be a Negro to anyone except the government, and the government was daft. Still, why hadn't he just told himself? Daftness, the government's and the world's, his, could grind anybody down worse than the biggest boss if it geared onto a bad idea.

J.T. started the car and turned a U back toward Baton Rouge. His clothes were adhering to him with sweat, but Morita looked as cool as if she were sitting in a spring breeze. He admired her there in her wedding clothes. How and when had she bought them? They had to be recent since they were pregnant clothes. Had she taken a taxi, a bus? She met him, her expression still without animation.

"I'm set on moving north so our baby can have a life," she said.

He waited a while, not answering, then he patted her on the arm. "I'll take care of it," he said. "Of y'all. Of you and the baby."

She nodded as if tranquillized. "I need to pee," she said.

DAY EIGHT

Her smooth hip touched Jimmy's as they stretched side by side, the morning brightening across the ceiling. He could still sense her lips on him, see her blonde hair curtaining his belly a few minutes before. He smiled at the night before, their awkward fumbling from the kitchen to her bed, her bringing out the condom she'd bought for the hotel, the amazing connection at last of their bodies. Then after, his chest against her back in the cramped tub, his hands soaping her long breasts and pebbly nipples, his fingers skating the length of her stomach, across her abdomen and down. Now he moved his fingertips to the soft cup at the juncture of her thigh and hip.

Sandra turned onto her side. "We should probably get up," she said.

"You're off work, ain't you?"

"You know that's not why." She stretched her arm across him, her flesh a miracle. "You have to do something."

"No I don't. Why you have to bring it up?"

"Cause he's your father."

"Well he ain't acted like it."

"They're going to hurt him, Jimmy."

"Then he oughta light out."

"I saw him. He's not leaving."

"Let him steal from somebody else then. I got nothing left." Jimmy scooted out from under her, his hip and shoulder complaining with morning stiffness, and dropped his legs off the bed. She touched his back. He rubbed his face as if it were frostbit. "I can't stop them bastards short of killing them. I ain't sure they're the ones I'd want to either."

"There's that lawyer."

"What about him?"

"There might be some money. Something. He might be able to help."

Sandra rose from the bed, pulled on a tee-shirt and slipped into her underwear, a small loss passing through Jimmy. She came to him and laid both palms on his cheeks. "You're the only one who'll help him. If you don't, you'll never forget it."

Jimmy stared at her long white feet, her toes splayed, her arches high. He ached to hold them and stroke them. He rubbed his impact shoulder, glanced at the purples and yellows blooming there, then plucked his drawers from the floor and pulled them on. He groaned to his feet, put his jeans on and sauntered the short distance to the kitchen table. The envelope still lay there. He pinched his lower lip, tender from kissing and raw in a way he'd like it raw every day the rest of his life. He picked up the envelope and extracted the letter. "Tell me what it means," he said.

"I haven't read it yet."

"Then read it and tell me. Don't read it aloud though. Just explain it."

She took the letter and silently moved her eyes. She looked up, surprised. "It says you're a plaintiff in a class action suit against Louisiana. That means a whole bunch of people are suing the state for the same thing."

"Suing. So J.T. did figure if he tracked me down he could make a buck."

"Probably. It could still be important for you, though. Especially after J.T. took your money."

"If it wasn't for this, he wouldn't have had a chance to take it."

She walked over to the window and peered, her hips and shoulders plain beneath the thin cloth of her tee. J.T.'s distracting Jimmy from this moment was yet another reason to do him harm. She turned to him. "You'll think I'm silly, but we have to respect this letter. It put him in touch with you and you in touch with me and we have to follow through. It's not coincidence."

Jimmy almost said that was nonsense, but who was he to say anymore what nonsense was. The bruises on him had remapped all that. He went to her and took her hands in his. "I didn't tell you. Yesterday I went by that hotel and took a look to see how it was real."

"Of course it was real."

"No. I had to see how it was real. The awning's still crooked, but I don't see how it coulda bounced me. I just know it did and things've been different since. If I hadn't of jumped, last night and this morning couldn't of happened. You know?"

Sadness swelled in her eyes, a surprise to him. "No. But I want to."

"They cut you?" Roland asked, turning onto Plank Road with the stream of commuter traffic.

"Might as well have," said J.T., the side of his head propped against the passenger window.

"Momma called me at work to make sure I come back for you. She's probably gone have a big old breakfast cooked for us, eggs and sausage and biscuits. She make the best buttermilk biscuits you ever gone have." J.T. didn't answer. "You just tired or they got you drugged?"

"Both."

It had rained during the night and the sun was pulverizing the moisture into smaze as thick as a membrane. J.T. shielded his eyes by making his hand a ledge on his brow as he fought to keep the rattle of Roland's car from stirring his stomach. He had slipped his arm from the sling and rested the cast on his thigh, but he was hardly aware of its weight, his whole being drenched in sludge. The rapidity and efficiency of his hospital visit had ended when they wheeled him down to X-ray, where a line of debilitated and irritable people

waited along a wall like condemned prisoners. Next
to J.T. an ancient woman in a wheelchair had dozed
and mumbled, laughed and cried as she dreamed, and
J.T. wished he could join her as more seriously injured
or ill people were brought to the front of the line. He
was horrified at the amount of pain around him until
his meds and fatigue kicked in. An uncanny euphoria
came over him. The misery and desperation around him
softened, receded into a sort of stage setting. He was
not a part of all this, simply a witness. In a sense, he
had won, he told himself. They'd inflicted a nightmare
on him, yet here he was, the money he'd sequestered
for his son safely hidden. Sure Squint would return
tomorrow to break or twist something else, but this
quiet oasis of the mind would still be here for J.T. Every
day Squint would come and do his worst, and every
day J.T. would become more placid, more impervious
to torture and grief until at last Squint would kill J.T.
or leave him alone. If the latter, then J.T. would find a
good lawyer, the best, and sue the shit out of Squint and
Charley, take Charley's club, his assets, maybe even his
lending business. J.T.'s would become a place for the
low-stakes bettor, and J.T., in his magnanimity, would
protect the chumps from themselves, never lending
money to those he knew would plunge in too deep,
taking money only from those he knew could afford it,
and who would gladly repay him. A sort of Robin Hood
Hunchback of Baton Rouge he'd be, disfigured and
crippled, but with style and wisdom. Most important,
he'd set Jimmy up, take care of him the way a daddy
should. He'd smiled, rested his head against the wall
and dozed.

But the drugs didn't last forever. The wall
hardened against his skull, and the X-ray tech was none
too gentle with his thumb. Hours later they brought
him back to the hall outside the emergency room, and
as the night deepened, the incoming patients increased.
People gunshot, maimed in wrecks and crimped in
agony rolled past and into the E.R. J.T. watched and
never considered trying to leave, something he thought
so strange about himself that he almost pronounced
himself already dead. When the doctor finally set his

thumb, wrapped plaster strips around his arm and sent him into the hall again, it was dawn.

Roland turned onto J.T.'s street, the run-down shacks like a greeting party befitting the day. Still, he straightened and looked ahead, hoping that Jimmy's car was at his house, hoping that not all, or anything, was forgiven, but only that Jimmy had returned. When he saw the shoulder of the street empty, he slumped again. Roland pulled into Elma's yard, stepped out and came around to J.T.'s side. He tapped on J.T.'s window, startling him as if somebody had thumped him on the nose. "We here," Roland said, and opened the door. The steamy air gushed over J.T., lightening his head, but he collected himself and dropped his feet out one at a time, didn't resist Roland's help to stand. J.T. stared at his apartment, his torture chamber, and his body balked.

"Y'all come on to breakfast," Elma said, but J.T. barely heard her, continued to ogle his house as if the awful reality he was in might be revealed a hoax.

"Let's walk," Roland said, and guided him toward Elma's.

A bolt of pain sliced across J.T.'s forehead and he sweated as if he was breaking hard dirt. He cuddled the cast and grunted as a snap of anticipation came from his other thumb.

"J.T., you best put that arm back in that sling," Elma said. She loomed above him on her stoop in her apron and house dress. Through the door behind her he smelled the good scents of eggs and bacon and biscuits, thought of his and Morita's house. His stomach clutched, and his knees tried to buckle. Roland grabbed him, steadied him and helped him up the steps and inside to Elma's tiny living room where he set J.T on the couch. "You're mighty pale," she said, and laid her warm palm against his forehead. "Roland, get him some water, please." She sat next to J.T. "They put medicine in you? Is that what's making you sick?"

"He ain't slept all night, Momma," Roland said from the kitchen. "You know what Charity's like."

"Yeah I know. I'm just talking to him."

"I need to head over to my place," J.T. said, but he

made no effort to move. Roland placed the glass of water in his hand and it stayed perched in his lap.

"You need to eat and sleep," Elma said. "You need to get some strength."

"Strength ain't gonna help," J.T. said. "Ain't nothing gonna help."

"What you mean?" she asked.

"I think he means whoever came yesterday is coming again today," Roland said.

"We gone call the police then," Elma said.

"No!" J.T. said. "No police. I hate police."

Elma touched her fingers to her cheek and lightly scratched. "So you just gone wait for that man to bust on you some more?" she asked.

"I can't stop him."

"Damn," Roland said. "I should of left him at the hospital. I work all night and come fetch him here so somebody can send him right back. I ain't hauling him tonight, Momma, and I want you staying out of it. I'm reminding you, too, Mister, about what I said."

"What'd you say?" Elma asked.

"Nothin," Roland said.

"You just said you said something."

"He said don't mix you up in it. He's right. Nobody oughta be mixed up in it 'cept me." J.T. lifted the water to his lips, took a sip, cool and delicious, but grimaced.

"Roland, go fetch my shotgun," she said.

"What?"

"Just go do it."

"Momma, you ain't getting in this. I ain't gone let you."

"Roland."

He exhaled through his nose, pivoted and went out of the room. J.T. made to stand, but Elma held him to the couch, her grip surprisingly strong. Somewhere he had an impulse to argue, then to explain something, but both impulses were vague and without force. He had never felt this way before, hollowed yet as heavy as a truckful of sand, aware yet resigned, as if the resignation had a will of its own. Even the dread of Squint's return was dulled by a recognition that more physical injury would be only temporary and would at least have definition, a beginning and end, unlike the bleak space in which he now resided. He had no fight left, because more fight would only take him to the self he had been for as long as he could remember. At this moment he feared that self more than a cemetary.

"It's loaded with buckshot," Roland said.

"I know that, I loaded it," Elma said.

"I wasn't telling you."

"J.T.," Elma said, and placed the gun on his lap, "you take this. When that man comes in your house, you point and pull this trigger. You ain't even got to have two hands. Just prop it in your lap and lay it across your cast."

J.T. examined the tarnished steel of the long double barrel. A flash of glee at the thought of splattering Squint passed through him, then he saw the emptiness beyond that too. Kill Squint. Kill Charley. Even if he could it wouldn't put things right with Jimmy. There was only one killing he could even consider, and he doubted he had the courage for that. He was a coward with one stand to make and that wouldn't even be a stand, but a secret, the money he wouldn't mention to anyone except a son he would likely never see again. "I can't do it."

"So you're gone sit there and let him do what he wants?"

"I got my reasons."

"Well, them reasons ain't good enough. If you trying to punish yourself that ain't your place. That's God's place. Your place is to take care of you and yours."

"That's what I aim to do."

Elma snorted and shook her head. "My goodness. Let's at least eat some breakfast then."

"You nervous?" Sandra asked as Jimmy shut off the engine.

Jimmy glanced at her. The question raised in him a complex formula. Nervous? Yes, nervous. But not just nervous with jittery anticipation, not even with intense anticipation like the time he mounted the wild bronc he'd let Sparks and some ranch hands talk him into riding. More nervous on the order of his quick decision to come to

Baton Rouge, yet nervous in a way even more complicated than that. He had never been in a lawyer's office, and this office was perhaps a vault that held answers to mysteries Jimmy wanted solved—why J.T. had contacted him; who his mother was; his entire history and part of his future. But also answers that might be the worst blows so far. Still, it was nervousness, not terror, not a boy's fear.

He touched Sandra's leg. Her hair was pulled back in a ponytail and tied with a crimson scarf, the long lines of her cheeks and jaws exposed. At least he knew that no matter what happened, afterward she and her apartment and her bed would still be where they left them. At least he thought he knew.

"Let's go see," he said.

It seemed like years ago J.T. had brought him here, but he remembered the office, a pretty little house with a porch and a green yard. He stepped out and Sandra took his hand and he was moving. The house expanded before him, its entrance enlarged with all that might lie beyond. He opened the door and let Sandra go in.

"I'm Jimmy Strawhorn," he said to the woman behind the desk. "We called a little while ago." She nodded, her expression unclear, then crossed the room, knocked on a door, spoke and turned back to them. "He'll see y'all now," the woman said. The door swung open and a short, stocky man with ruddy cheeks, night-black slick hair and a light gray suit gestured them in.

"Ray Bourgeouis," he said, and shook both their hands. His brow furrowed as he saw Jimmy. "You're James Thomas Strawhorn, born August 25th, 1959?" he asked, his eyebrows raised. Jimmy nodded. "Please make yourselves comfortable." He shut the door and moved behind his desk, a range of papers. Framed documents covered the wall. Jimmy smelled coffee and potpourri, then noticed Bourgeouis gesturing for him to sit in the leather chair next to the one that Sandra had already taken. Jimmy lowered into it, blinked at his feet and turned to the long framed photo of the snaky Mississippi taken from high above. "That's the course from Baton Rouge to New Orleans," Bourgeouis said. "Friend of mine at NASA sent me that." He sat. "Y'all like some coffee or water?"

"I'm fine," Jimmy said. "Sandra?" She shook her head. Jimmy pulled the letter from his pocket. "We're here about this," he said.

"I know," Bourgeouis said. "I'm glad we finally found you. A lot on the list we figure we'll never find."

"What list?"

Bourgeouis wrinkled his nose, exposing his front teeth, then reclined. "I have a complicated story to tell you, Mr. Strawhorn, and you may find out some things about yourself that are, well, quite surprising. I want to make sure you're ready to hear it and that you're okay with Miss . . ."

"Sandra," Jimmy said, realizing he didn't even know her last name.

". . . with Sandra here."

"Anything you need to say, she can hear."

"Fine. Just to warn you, I've told a lot of clients this story, so if I'm going too fast, just stop me." Bourgeouis paused and took a sip from a black mug with gold letters on it, then leaned back again. "Around three years ago, a woman we'll call Terry M. came to me. She's about your age and she'd grown up as a ward of the state of Texas, being bounced around and thinking both her parents were dead. Like anybody, she'd got to wondering about her real parents. The people who'd been her guardians couldn't tell her anything about her past and neither could the Texas Child Services, so she and her guardians started to do a little investigating and finally managed to find out that she had a sister who was also a ward. She searched out her sister, who was also in Texas, and together they started to contact folks to find out where they came from. Eventually they found out they were originally from Louisiana, but even then Texas couldn't tell them much about their parents or circumstances, except that in some sort of arrangement, Louisiana had sent them there in the sixties as orphans."

Bourgeouis shifted in his seat, sipped his coffee again and scratched at his ear lobe. To Jimmy he seemed as if he were both receding and coming closer like a man on a pendulum. Bourgeouis glanced back and forth between Jimmy and Sandra. "Any questions so far?"

"Keep going," Jimmy said.

"After that, somebody in Texas wrote to Louisiana's Child Services and after a good bit of wrangling discovered that Terry originally came from Baton Rouge and was put up for adoption by her mother, who Terry'd always been told died when Terry was a child. This obviously surprised her, and she came to Baton Rouge hoping she could get some more information. Unfortunately, she wasn't really prepared to deal with state government and didn't get very far. That's when somebody nice who works for the state gave her my name because she knows I do adoption cases." He turned his palms up. "When she came to see me, I didn't think there was going to be a whole lot I could do for her because of laws protecting parents who have given their children up for adoption, but I decided to go ahead and call some folks to find out what I could. Turns out the records from the early sixties were a mess and everybody there was too busy to give me much help, so I enlisted another lawyer who's familiar with those agencies and we began to run into a lot of strange cases in the records." Bourgeouis leaned forward and made a steeple under his chin with his fingers. "As it turns out, in the early sixties Louisiana sent hundreds of foster kids off to Texas, Georgia, and Mississippi, the majority of them classified as mentally deficient or orphaned, but all of them were sent out of the state illegally, without their relatives' knowledge."

Jimmy's head floated ever so slightly. He gripped the arms of his chair. "How come?" he asked.

Bourgeouis sat back again. "That's hard to know. We suppose that Louisiana didn't have the resources to deal with the kids and worked deals to pay these other states to take them, which would be cheaper for them in the long run. These were shady dealings, of course, like kickbacks to bureaucrats who engineered the deals on both ends, but the reason the kids got sent was because they were poor and sometimes unwanted and had nobody to stick up for them. Most of them ended up in orphanages or other institutions where the living conditions were substandard and where there was no real professional care for the problems they had. In almost all the cases, nobody kept good records of them, so they'd know where they came from or who and where their families were. Then we found out that some of these kids were placed in 'foster homes' with the purpose of making them workers on farms and ranches and factories, and that some of the guardians had paid to take them or been paid."

"They paid folks to take 'em and folks paid them to get 'em?"

"So it appears. Then the foster kids had to work. Does this describe your situation?"

"Near about."

Bourgeouis nodded slowly, collected his breath and cocked his head. "Anyway, when the magnitude of the case became clear, I contacted some other lawyers to help me and we started subpoenaing records from these states, and the more records we subpoeaned and the more folks we talked to who worked at the agencies in question during that time, the worse it smelled and the more children we found had been involved. Hundreds in fact. We decided to file a class action suit against the state of Louisiana. That was well over a year ago, and we've managed to search down a lot of them. But like I said, some I doubt we'll ever find." Bourgeouis pinched at his nose and adjusted his tie. "You're qualified to be part of this suit, but I have to tell you I was surprised when I saw you."

Jimmy dug his fingers into the leather. "Why's that?"

Bourgeouis licked his lips and moved his gaze to Sandra and back to Jimmy. "Because all of the plaintiffs in this suit are legally black."

Jimmy's vision drifted to the side of Bourgeouis and out a window to the sky. A giant cumulus hung like a mountain suspended in air. "What're you saying?"

"That our records indicate that you are black. I don't know your situation, but in Louisiana if one of your parents is black, then that's how you're classified. And you do seem to be the person in our records." Elma appeared in Jimmy's mind with the bizarre possibility that she could be his mother, a possibility almost calming. Then J.T. popped to mind. Jimmy held more tightly to the chair.

"What about my mother, Mr. Bourgeouis? You know if she's alive or her whereabouts?"

"I don't. That's not part of what we're handling."

"But she's black, that's what you're telling me?"

"Your records indicate that you're black." Bourgeouis glanced at Jimmy's file on his desk. "It says you were classified as an orphan and sent to a facility for black children, then shipped . . . I'm sorry, not shipp—"

"Shipped fits." Jimmy thought of his brown eyes and J.T.'s blue ones. The absence of his mother grew larger in him, a thing as unknowable but as real as the distance he'd seen from the top of Pepper's mesa. Jimmy tried to think of a path across that distance, thought that he wouldn't know how to find the path, much less travel it.

"Do you have any questions, Mr. Strawhorn? About the nature of the settlement, or anything pertaining to the case?"

Jimmy leaned forward. "Sir, I'm wondering why y'all got in touch with my father before letting me know."

"That was a mistake, and I apologize if it's caused you any inconvenience. The truth is we were grasping at anything we could to find all the plaintiffs. We sent word to a place in Texas we thought we might find you, and when we didn't hear back, we found your name in the phone book and sent word. That was evidently your father's number."

"Say you sent word to Texas?"

"Yes. I can check the name of the owner if you'd li—"

"Sparks is the name. Did y'all tell him about my father?"

"No. We simply sent Mr. Sparks a letter saying you should contact us."

Jimmy rubbed at the weave of his jeans. He knew already that J.T. and Sparks had spoken, but it stung him that Sparks hadn't . . . hadn't what? Tried to find out something, anything, before he gave J.T. Jimmy's address? Hadn't contacted Jimmy? But then why should he think somebody close to being family should have looked out for him.

"Jimmy," Sandra said, "I think we ought to find out what the settlement is."

"What's the settlement?" he asked.

"We've agreed that all plaintiffs will receive a cash settlement of five-thousand dollars. The more important part is you'll receive support for whatever education or job training you want within the state of Louisiana or the state where you were wrongly sent. Some will receive life-time assistance for board and medical care, depending on their circumstances, especially since many of the plaintiffs have mental disorders."

"You mean retarded."

"In some cases."

"Is that why you didn't just try to get us more money to deal with as we saw fit, because you thought we weren't able?"

Bourgeouis frowned. "I understand what you're saying, but the truth is we found that most of the plaintiffs have very little education. We just figured that helping them go to school or get job training and assistance was more important than a lump sum of cash. It doesn't seem like a lot of that applies in your case, but you have to realize that we were dealing with hundreds of people and we thought it best to set some general guidelines."

"You mind if I ask what's in all this for you and the other lawyers?"

"The state's going to pay us for the time we put in on the case, but we're not taking any damages for ourselves."

"And I spose you can't you tell me my mother's name?"

"All I can tell you is that you were put up for adoption. The law prevents me from giving you anymore than that."

"Is she still alive?"

"That I don't know."

Jimmy tried again to focus on the frames behind Bourgeouis's head. What were they? He knew the word for the documents, he was sure, but the presence of the document was scrambling him, print affecting him like senility, hiding the truth of itself. Was that the purpose of written words? Why lawyers and officials and fathers were able to use them like fog? Maybe meaning and communication weren't what words were for after all, not solid and real like a touch, but slippery and elusive like promises. Jimmy strained to remain focused, as if maybe this time he could see through the layer of what he didn't know and into some essence of printed word, but even as the object's name popped to mind, diploma, the ink bloated and smudged and sent him off kilter. He shoved himself out of his chair, nodded and thanked Bourgeouis.

"You'll have to sign some papers," Bourgeouis said, standing. "I'm terribly sorry about the mix-up with your father. Let me know if I can help with anything."

Jimmy was outside in the heat before he remembered Sandra. He pulled up short, meaning to get her, and she bumped into him, both of them stumbling before they caught themselves, her arms wrapped around him from behind. He hugged her arms to him, watched his sun-glinted car start to cartwheel, then broke from her and hurried to the driver's seat. He cranked down his window to release the heat, rubbed his lips and let his hand linger over his mouth.

"Jimmy?" came Sandra's voice from next to him. "I'm sorry," she said.

"About what?" he asked.

"Everything. The lies, your momma, J.T."

"J.T." He strained to remain anchored in his seat. He looked at Sandra. "Does it matter to you what the lawyer told us? About me being black?"

"Only if it matters to you. Does it matter?"

"It don't seem much compared to all else."

He took her wrist and lifted it to his lips. The slight aroma of powder and peaches touched him. He lowered her arm to the seat.

"I reckon I got to try and find some more answers."

WHAT J.T. IS BEGINNING TO REMEMBER: 1960

"What the hell is this?" J.T. asked, holding the heavy thirty-eight snub nose like a rock in his palm. Morita stood from the rocker in the corner of their bedroom, while Jimmy gurgled over a rattler in his playpen. The smell of baby hit J.T. with the ambivalent wave it always did, then the odor of whiskey laced the smell and he saw the glass of brown liquid by Morita's chair.

"What were you doing in my purse?" she asked, her flinty expression almost pushing J.T. from the room. The crescents beneath her eyes told him she hadn't really slept in days.

"It was on the commode tank."

"You stay out of my purse."

"It was on the commode tank." J.T. fiddled with the pistol until the chamber fell open, dumping the bullets onto the floor, thuds followed by rolling sounds like little bowling balls.

"Give me that." She came toward him. She'd taken to ranting and screaming and even throwing things when she was drinking, but he hadn't seen this potential lightning in her, hadn't seen the wild instability crackling off her quite like this. "Goddamn you," she said, reaching, and when he held the pistol away from her, she grabbed his arm and tugged it down, her strength surprising him. She pried open his fingers, and he tried to shove her back, but she took the pistol and gathered the bullets. The several beers he'd had on the way home made him feel porous, then sodden and lethargic, a slow spectator.

"It ain't right to have that in here, Morita," he said.

"What?" she said. She snagged the last bullet from under the bed and plopped it into its chamber. She came close to him. "You leave us here all day and half of every night without protection and you say what's right. He's going to find us and you won't even be here."

"He ain't gonna find us. He would've done did."

"You don't know anything."

"You don't need a gun in the house with a baby."

Her irises were lined with burning platinum, the pistol at her side. "The baby. I'm shocked you even know there is a baby."

"Cause I go out to pay the bills?"

"Because you act like we're not even here." She spun and returned to her chair, laid the pistol on its seat and picked up her drink. "I know you think I'm crazy. Well a man in a suit came to the door two days ago and I didn't answer. He came back yesterday, while you were barely here the last two nights."

J.T. searched for words, but his mind was a whir. He didn't know who the man was, wasn't certain there had actually been a man, but he was certain it wasn't somebody her father had sent. At least he thought he could be certain. He believed her father would do what she said he would. J.T. had asked Chief about him and found he'd heard of him and the reach he had. J.T. feared him, he just didn't believe they could be found. Nonetheless, J.T. had ignored Morita and the baby and he carried the guilt of that, even though Morita had also ignored him most of the time since their marriage, their couplings about as reliable as a yo-yo whose string lengthened and shortened without reason, her distance since the baby's arrival increasing more and more so that they hadn't touched in two months. Entering the house most days was entering indifference, or a wake for the death not only of whatever had been between them but also things in each of them J.T. couldn't begin to name. He wanted the old her now as much as he ever had—a wanting that scoured everything he'd been and left only discontent—but the old her had been replaced by someone too thin and too unstable and he knew the old her wasn't coming back.

Jimmy grasped the bars, pulled himself to his feet, and gave a goofy grin. J.T. watched, astonished and unsure if he'd seen Jimmy stand before. A pellet of joy passed through him, and he started to ask Morita how long the baby had been doing that. But when he looked at her, her head was cocked as if she could read the despicable uncertainty inside his mind. "I was looking for a smoke in your purse," he said.

"Liar. You're the only person I've known who would rather tell a lie when the truth will do."

"I found the purse on the commode, then I wanted a smoke. I could smell the drinking up in here."

"I wish that's all I'd smelled on you," she said.

"You ain't got a right to say that."

"Why, because it's true?"

J.T. caught a whiff of himself—the sweat, sawdust and beer—and hated her for knowing him. There *had* been other smells, and he *had* looked in her purse, but to see if she was hoarding grocery money and old money from the T-Bird. He knew she had money left, more than he gave her, money for the baby stuff she bought and her cigarettes and whiskey. That's what he was looking for when he found the gun. "Where'd you get that thing anyway?"

"From that pawn shop down the road. That redneck bastard said, 'You gonna use that to feed your baby, honey?' I wanted to shoot *him*."

In his playpen, Jimmy started to wind out like an air raid siren. He didn't always cry during their fights, but a certain pitch in Morita's or J.T.'s voice could trigger him.

"Now see what you did," J.T. said.

"Go to hell," she said. She lifted Jimmy and patted his back so that he quieted almost immediately.

"I'm sick of you talking to me like that. I pay your damn bills and you talk to me like that."

"Yeah, you pay bills enough to live in this shit hole and you gamble and drink away who knows how much. You think it's good for Jimmy to live here? This baby right here? You think that's good for him? He's had the croup twice. You remember those promises you made about a job and moving? You remember me and Jimmy? This is your son, J.T. When's the last time you held him?"

Jimmy screamed again as Morita yelled at J.T. The vein he used to love when she came rose on her forehead. He wanted to tell her he often thought of holding Jimmy, thought of his small noises and tiny body when he was pounding nails or lifting boards, wanted to tell her he thought of her skin so rich it seemed to blend with his, thought of it so intensely that it affected him the two times he'd gone with other women to spite her, except that now when he thought those things, the sense of loss that plowed into him was almost more than he could bear.

"I'm going out," he said.

"Good," she said. She put Jimmy down in his playpen and strode across the room. She shoved J.T. "Leave me in this little prison, you bastard. Maybe he'll come back and kill us and you'll be happy. Or maybe I'll just get on a bus. Maybe I'll go back to New Orleans and take it. It couldn't be worse than this." She shoved him again, so hard this time that he bumped into the wall. He glanced at Jimmy screaming and at the pistol, and his legs almost gave. She had been angry and loud, but she had never shoved him. Something in her had broken. He thought of grabbing his son and taking him, then he hustled down the hall and paused at the kitchen. He took out the nearly-full bottle of whiskey he'd told her was just for him, and which she'd not touched, poured two fingers and tossed it like lava down his throat. He almost gagged, clutched his burning chest a second and went out the front door.

The night was cool for early May, the air dry. Down the street, the refinery wasn't burning too much. In the driveway his car pouted. He walked away from the plant and into the neighborhood, figuring he'd eventually loop around to Scenic and land in one of the bars there. The asphalt beneath him sogged and mired his footsteps; his life was hands slipping from a rope hung high. He thought he still heard Jimmy crying and Morita cursing, but he knew they were left behind, like almost everything he'd carved from the world for himself before Morita. She'd changed it all, making his life more and his previous happiness less. He broke into a lope, hoping to pump blood where sludge was filling him. He loved his son, he did, loved Morita too, but they weren't his, not really, not in any sense he could understand. He ran, into the section where more and more Negroes were moving, ran, his shortness of wind and struggle to catch a breath no match for the thoughts pumping into his brain. Where had the collapse started? The moment they met? The moment they made love? The moment the baby formed inside her?

On their marriage day, they'd driven back to Baton Rouge and gone in search of a black Justice of the Peace. Morita never met J.T.'s eyes, never saw the love that elbowed aside his resentment and offered him up for a brief time to her. Home again, she cried and slept for days, wouldn't eat, sicked on herself and fell asleep again when she grew too weak or defeated to move from the bed. J.T. tended to her, afraid she was killing the baby, placed ice between her shriveled lips, finally forced her to drink water and then to eat sliced bananas until her will returned. But it was different, the place she'd gone to like a distant, shrouded continent. Her only connection was to the baby inside her, a baby who J.T. began to see at best as a rival and at worst as the enemy crouching in Morita in order to do him harm.

When her contractions began, she refused to go to Baton Rouge's Charity Hospital. J.T. sped her to New Orleans, terrified at her pain and at the prospect that a state cop might stop him and hassle them with no time to spare. In the waiting room, he'd breathed shallowly with his head down. Part of him had clenched, anticipating Morita's father bursting in and dragging him out, while other parts of him soared with eagerness, and floundered in shame. He was having a child, would be a father! Except his child would be a Negro born at the poor people's hospital. He loved Morita, yet loathed her for tricking him. He fantasized the distance between them closing, her arms opening to him again. The baby would bring them together, and she would offer J.T. love so powerful it would fill him with love for their child. Then he imagined her shrugging off his touch, and he pined as if she were already gone.

J.T. heavy-footed to a stop, his whiskey and earlier beers surging into his throat. He plopped onto the grass street side and fought to swallow air. A fresh sweat broke on him, mixing with his work-day sweat and unleashing the stench of the bar, but also releasing Morita's and Jimmy's smells so powerfully that he held his breath until he stood and forced himself to walk again. He turned a corner and headed down a narrow street back toward Scenic. The faint sound of radio music and a chipper woman's voice wafted to him through the open window of one of the houses close to the street.

J.T. trudged on toward Standard Oil, crossed Scenic Highway and curled his fingers through the chain-link fence between him and the metal structures hissing and spewing. He didn't know why he was here. He'd meant to go to the bar and throw back enough shots to loosen some of the tangle in him. But here he was staring at the place his father had worked and died, the place he himself had worked for seven months, the place Morita suggested he return to, a fiery dead place. He hated it all: the stench, the heat, the endless valves, the hard terrain of piping, steel, and concrete. When he quit, he swore he'd never go back to it or any job that put the clock in charge of his life. And mostly he hadn't until Morita. Then he thought of her curled against him, thought of her sturdy laugh and her proud walk, thought of how she'd loved him, not just sex but love, and how that love was why he'd been willing, almost, to commit himself to this place or something like it again.

A flash of her stuck in that house, alone except for the baby, for how long, eight, nine months?, lit so powerfully in him that he thought he might incinerate with shame. Her spiral came to him in snapshots— her haunted fear, her pleas to him, her attacks, her debilitating anticipation of her father's men. He shook the fence and howled. Dread surrounded him like a deadly gas. He was halfway home again before he even knew he was trotting, propelled by every conflicting thought he'd ever had, the world around him a smudge. He had no idea what he would do when he got there, but he ran on, across the yard and up to the door. He paused, heaving, his wind sucked away by exertion and alcohol and the vacuum closing in. He waited for his breathing to calm, then went inside and closed the door quietly behind him.

Her singing down the hall met him like mourning song. She often sang to Jimmy, but this song was unfamiliar, French maybe, her voice slow and high, a voice he'd never heard. He shivered. He padded to the kitchen, found the bottle, poured himself two fingers and gulped. All the windows were closed, the room hot and filled with the rattle of the ancient refrigerator and the hum of the circular fluorescent light. The room was clean, the counters scrubbed, the floor mopped, the dishes stowed. Even at her most disheveled, she kept the place this way. He moved to put the glass in the sink and bumped into a chair, knocking it over onto the scuffed linoleum. The singing stopped. Impossible she could've heard him, he thought, not with her voice and the air-conditioner on in their room, although he knew that lately she'd taken to turning the air-conditioner off so she could hear, no matter how hot it was. Carefully, he put the glass in the sink, but no sooner had his hand released it than he heard her footsteps coming stealthily toward him. He pressed his lower back to the counter and waited. Near the kitchen the footsteps stopped. "Morita," he said, his voice quavering, amazed it had come to this. He pictured a flaming barrel, lead tearing into him, his body slumping to the floor. She stepped around the corner, the humanity blunted from her face. He stepped back.

"You," she said. She wore her sheer summer night gown, her body an outline inside it. Her hair held a waiting energy like sleeping snakes. She was nothing but power, mad power that buffeted J.T. from clear across the room. The pistol dangled by her side. "I thought you were gone," she said, her voice a file.

"I came back," he said.

Her eyes pierced him, then went to the front door.

She disappeared into the living room. J.T. heard a click. She reappeared at the kitchen. "Don't unlock that!" she said, and went back toward their room. He heard their AC start up, the door shut, then her steps up the hall again until she reappeared, took a spot at the end of the couch, and placed her pistol and glass on the coffee table. A rush of whiskey dropped a soft curtain in front of J.T. He steadied himself, grabbed the bottle, retrieved the glass from the sink and poured two fingers more before he stepped into the living room. She didn't look at him, and he wavered, considered going to the bedroom, then thought of Jimmy.

"I'm taking him and leaving," she said.

The mix of nightmare and freedom in what she'd said ricocheted around his skull. He'd believed this was both inevitable and impossible. He went to his chair and downed the whiskey in his glass.

"That taste good?" she asked. "Better than with some bitch in a bar?"

"I been out walking."

"That what you call it?"

J.T. put the glass on the table. "You ought not drink anymore."

"The hell with you. We're going north tomorrow."

"Go then. After all I did."

Morita exploded into laughter that pushed J.T. farther into his chair. She raked her hair off her forehead and doubled over, shifted into heaving as if she was unable to catch her breath, her sounds almost orgasmic.

"Shut up," he said, and she did, her focus completely on him, her tears glistening.

"You worthless piece of trash," she said. She wiped a tear and studied him as if he were deformed. "Tell me why trash like you hate people like me."

"I don't hate you, you just come at me."

"No, I mean it. Don't you know you're trash?" She spoke with the tone of someone stating a fact.

"That's enough, Morita."

"You never knew you were trash. You suspected it, but you never really knew. You think you can go out and slut and come in here and ignore your child and still have me. That's what you think."

"I ain't had you since you tricked me into marrying you. You might of let me fuck you a coupla times, but the having was done."

Her mouth sagged. "The looks you give me and Jimmy. You don't love us. We're nothing but chores. You don't care that we choke here in this dump. Don't care what might happen, some man coming up in here for my daddy. You don't take care of us. And you think you're a man."

"I said that's enough."

"Trash. Slutty, worthless trash."

"Yeah? Well, you think you're a goddamn queen. You kick me out the bed and act like that nigger thing of yours is golden." J.T. went hot at his own words, then colder than he'd ever been. "I'm sorry. I shouldn't of—"

Tears crested in her eyes. She bared her teeth. "I hate you," she said. "I wish I'd never met you. I wish I'd never had your son. If he turns out like you . . ." She fixed her eyes on the table.

"Mor—"

"Don't talk to me, you ugly piece of shit. You're worse than my father." She looked through him, a snarl passing across her lips and nose. "You think I'm insane, but you don't know." An eerie, shaky smile trembled across her. "I never told you. He used to come to my room all the time, even when he was remarried. So I ran away. I ran away and hid in the Quarter, but some men he hired caught me and called him. My daddy didn't hit me. He just dragged me to his car and brought me back to my room. He took my throat and held me there all night. Said he'd find me wherever I went. He did that seven nights in a row." She blinked and focused on J.T. "But you're worse. I think at least he cared about me." She reached for the pistol, but J.T. slammed his hand down on hers. "Let go!" she screamed, and jerked the pistol away.

He shrank back into his chair. "You are insane," he said.

She clutched a handful of her hair and tugged. "I hope you die. I fucking hope it!" She snatched up her glass and weaved down the hall. J.T. sprang up and caught her before she could turn toward him. He wrapped his arms around her and grabbed the pistol, then crumpled to the floor with the gun curled into his gut. Morita fell on him, pounding his back and slamming fists against the side of his face, but J.T. curled in more tightly. Finally she dropped to the side, crying, Jimmy screaming again in the bedroom. J.T. didn't move. After a while she gathered herself enough to stand and went to join Jimmy.

J.T. sat against the wall for a long while before he rose to a knee, dizzied, collected himself and wavered to his feet. He was tipsy, but it didn't lessen the sting from where she'd hit him. Hand on the wall he moved back to his chair in the living room. He put the pistol on the table in front of him, her image hovering, cloaked in damage. He'd known what her daddy had done, but what she told him rippled his bones. She shouldn't have told him that. There were things people shouldn't say. It made them different.

A mountainous sadness humped up on him. He closed his eyes and dropped his head. Beneath him, the chair began to sink. Beige and red swirled behind his eyelids, and he stayed with them as he descended. Why open his eyes? He knew the empty room, and there was perverse comfort in letting the sinking that had begun long ago take him to the bottom, however close the bottom might already be. An image of Jimmy inside his kid's cage, helpless and ready to live, rushed J.T. A thunder burst of emotions shook him, emotions too big and unruly for expression, emotions which recreated both the helplessness and hopefulness of the baby's cries and small perfect body, emotions that he despised as weakness. The images kept rolling until they turned into memories. Sometimes, when Morita nursed Jimmy, J.T. posted himself nearly at attention and watched, his chest cracking, until Morita leveled her sullen gaze on him. He could remember nothing he'd ever wanted more than to cross the room to his wife and baby and embrace them so hard they might be crushed, but he never did that, never said that was what he wanted to do. Once in a while, early on, he'd held Jimmy, his arms nearly paralyzed, his own heart throbbing, the baby a conductor of love and vulnerability so intense that it almost stripped his flesh and threw him into the yard a pile of bones. His arms would tighten until Jimmy squirmed even more, then the baby would cry, and Morita would peel him away from J.T. Nothing had ever been more terrible than that peeling—not his parents' deaths, not the emptiness when Morita disappeared into indifference—the peeling like being gutted only seconds after discovering he had guts.

DAY EIGHT, STILL MORNING

Through the dingy kitchen window the brightness jabbed at J.T.'s eyes and head. Across from him hunkered the rear of Elma's house, then beyond that the other shacks like his. Still farther, the smokestacks of Exxon, his former neighbor, rose against the hazy blue sky. He pressed his temple. He had barely slept, and he was in the kitchen again for what must have been the twentieth time, the grainy texture of the grocery bag in his grip. Its smell wafted to him with the dankness of impending decay. He supported the bag in the curled fingers of his casted hand and unrolled it once more, saw the money nestled at the shadowy base of the bag, rerolled the bag and slid it beneath the pipes again. It was silly to check the money, he knew. Squint and Charley didn't really want it and Jimmy wasn't coming back. But still, the money mattered. All night, he'd sat on the hard chair that Jimmy had smashed into the wall, and where Squint had smashed him, and sworn that if he could keep the money for Jimmy, then it meant something. *What* he couldn't quite name. Restraint? A private pledge to his son? Defiance of not only the money-takers but his own weakness? Whatever. It mattered.

The throb in his thumb was growing again. He

picked up the bottle before him and examined the childproof cap. He tried to hold the bottle with his wriggly cast fingers while he opened it, fumbled, winced, tried again, then set the bottle on the counter and grasped it with his good hand. Why he'd closed it after he opened it the first time he didn't know. He pushed his cast down on the lid and twisted. The top popped up. He turned the bottle upside down and poured its contents next to the sink. Ten codeine tablets. He ran a glass of water, pinched up a pill and tossed it down. The water was warm but tasted as pure and refreshing as arctic ice. He scooted several of the pills with a fingertip as if they were chips at a roulette table. How many would it take to stem any pain Squint could offer? How many to put him beyond any hurt? He picked up a second pill, rolled it around like a jewel, then tossed the pill among the others.

He dragged through the living room and out to the front porch, where he reclined against the rusty screen door. Spangles of light played in the sky over the mall and he wondered if Jimmy's girl knew how the sunlight was dancing this very second above her work place. But then, maybe she wasn't even there, was off someplace with Jimmy, and this thought brought a momentary joy to him. He shifted his look to the incandescent white of his cast. It was working like a little oven and he was certain that if he tilted his arm sweat would pour out. He draped his good hand over the warm, rough plaster and squeezed it like a coconut, appreciating the solid architecture. Damaged though it was, his thumb was safe inside this hard cocoon, and he found himself examining his other thumb, naked and vulnerable. How strangely shaped, almost spoon-like, yet engineered to perform the most varied of tasks—shuffling cards, counting coins, brushing away a bit of food. He flexed it, gave himself a thumbs-up, bent it, then scraped its nail over the warty surface of the cast again. He loved his thumb and pitied its brother for the hardship visited upon it. How could he have allowed such injury to come to something so essential, allowed himself to be so reckless in the treatment of something so miraculous and fragile? Jimmy popped up in his mind like a carnival target. He thought of the pills again, then relaxed further into the screen, the rusted lattice creaking and cracking.

He sensed the low rumble of the engine before he actually heard it, a leviathan's shadow coasting into his subconscious. The actual engine sound rolled in and paused, stopped. Instinctively, J.T. closed his fingers over his good thumb and swallowed. He cringed, then released, almost levitating mentally until the shutting of the heavy car door jerked him upright and his eyes blinked open to the shape of Squint standing next to his Lincoln. J.T.'s mouth went dry, but he straightened and stuck his chest out.

"Morning, sunshine," Squint said, but he didn't move, his arms crossed. "Nice cast." He laughed. "I'm surprised you didn't hightail it. Since you didn't, I'll be extra gentle." Squint's size still mesmerized J.T. Surely a regular man couldn't be so large. He had to have been created symbolic, J.T.'s inexorable punishment, like a glacier grinding and squashing everything in its path.

Squint theatrically slid into his sports coat, tugged at his lapels and checked his cuffs. He took a candy from his pocket, held it close to his face, then slowly unwrapped it, the crinkling of the plastic wrapper like somebody crimping J.T.'s brain pan. "Mr. Charley wanted me to give you his sincere apology that he can't be here to share in all this pleasure. He says it's customers like you that make his business such a fine one." Squint laughed again. "He actually didn't say none of that. I told him how womanish you was yesterday and he just looked disgusted. He said to make that pipsqueak squeal like chiropracty. Think you got another squeal in you, J.T.?" Squint grinned and stepped forward.

Thunder boomed from the clear blue. J.T. thrashed, caught in a prickly web that bit with every move, until he realized he'd spun and launched his face through the screen. He wriggled out and saw Squint in profile, Elma coming across the yard with her shotgun trained on Squint.

"You got no idea who you're fucking with, lady," he said.

"The next one's gone be in your gut," Elma said

Squint spat the candy onto the ground. "This is

between me and him and my boss. Don't go dragging yourself in where you can't get out."

"He's my neighbor and you've already done him criminal harm. Now get on before something terrible happens."

Bright coronas laced Elma and Squint. The barrel of the shotgun flashed blue arcs. J.T. tapped his eardrum against the ringing there. In the street, the three teenagers J.T. had seen prowling the neighborhood jogged up. Elma glanced at them. "You boys see if he have a gun in the car." Squint made to move, but Elma uh-uhed him. One of the teens scooted inside, slid over to the glove box and emerged with a smile.

"His gun in there, but his bullets are right here," the kid said, and showed a fist. The trio cackled and high-fived. Squint nodded and faced J.T.

"I told myself I was gonna make it easy on you today, but now you gonna suffer. You and your nigger neighbors."

"Watch your mouth," Elma said. "I'm counting ten. One, two, three . . ."

"You boys have something to say?" Squint asked the teenagers, who laughed and bobbed.

"Yeah," one said. "Can we have your car?" They howled and shoved each other.

". . . seven, eight . . ."

"See you after while," Squint said to J.T. He adjusted his collars and dropped behind the wheel.

"Ten!" Elma said.

The teens yelled for him to get on. Squint pointed at everyone through his window. "I see four dead niggers and one dead trash." He slapped the door of his Lincoln. The car grumbled away.

"You should of took his piece," one of the kids said to the other.

"I don't like that stub-nose shit," he said. "I want me a TEC Nine."

"I got your TEC Nine." They laughed and sauntered away, dividing the bullets.

J.T.'s cheek stung. The day glowed exceptionally bright as if an aperture had further opened, glowed so bright that the glow ate away at the edges of the retreating teenagers. J.T. touched his face, saw spots of blood on his fingertips. Elma's labored breath came to him and he looked at her standing close to his porch, luminescence bleeding into her outline.

"What'd you do to yourself now?" she asked.

"You shouldn't of done that," J.T. said.

"You're welcome," she said.

"I'm serious."

"I can't stand by and watch him break you up."

"Then don't look. What you gonna do now?"

Elma set the shotgun butt on the ground and leaned against it. "Maybe you oughta be broke up. Making other folks watch it ain't right though. Putting it on everbody else ain't right." He dabbed at the sting on his temple. Elma held the shotgun out to him. "Take this here," she said.

"I don't want it."

"Goddamn you," she said. "That's why you ain't got nobody. Nobody wants a man so weak he can't even see outside his own self." Her skin seemed slightly ashen, but J.T. weirdly thought how pretty she was, how beautiful she once must have been.

"You need to sit down," he said.

"I'm not sitting with you," she said, and turned.

"Wait a minute," he said. The trip to the kitchen was kaleidoscopic. His mouth was so dry he felt as if he could be sucked into himself, but the sink faucet struck him as so unsavory that as he knelt he tried to work up saliva rather than drink. He grabbed the grocery bag and headed back to the front, wooziness teasing him. The ruptured screen looked like it had been burst by Elma's scowl. He creaked open the door and stepped outside. "Do this for me," he said, and held the bag out to Elma. "If you see Jimmy, give this to him. If you don't, keep it yourself."

She shook her head. "Whatever it is, you need to give it to him."

"You know I ain't gone see him."

"Not if you don't do for yourself."

"Please, Elma."

She shook her head and rested the shotgun against the stoop. "Here," she said. "Take care of what you need to." She turned and retreated, faster than he would have believed possible with her worn-out knees. J.T. peered at the shotgun resting against his steps. What all had she meant, "What you need to"?

Sandra dreaded this part of town, the curve away from the river that hooked the potholed road past the chemical plants and refineries and into neighborhoods of shotgun houses. It made her want to run, made her wish she'd kept Jimmy in her bed, made her wish she'd never told him she'd seen his father. She'd thought seeing the lawyer would cement something between them, make her feel—for some crazy reason—more secure. Instead, the old terror stirred in her with renewed vigor, the stench on the breeze and the blistering sun feeding it.

She plucked at the edge of the car seat as Jimmy lit a cigarette without asking and turned onto Scenic Highway. Her body could still feel their connection, but his expression gave her nothing she could absolutely discern. The energy coming off him was both calm and furious, a different energy than he'd brought to the hotel room, more resolute, but still elusive, maybe because of its power. Would this energy rocket him away from her just as it now rocketed him toward J.T.? Anxiety came to her as inevitable as night, made her want to press her mouth to his, take him home, even return with him to the hotel so he could show her how he'd gone past his fear. Sadness came to her with the rush of a virus, saturated her with the totality of her losses. Inside her, every cell compressed, shrinking her bones and organs so palpably that she feared she might collapse. Her legs tensed with an urge to spring onto the road.

"Maybe you were right," she blurted. "Maybe we should let him be."

"What?"

"They might hurt you. Maybe there's nothing you can do except get hurt."

His puzzlement was clear, then he nodded. "I understand you not wanting to bear anymore of this."

"That's not what I meant." She clutched his arm. Once more she saw him on the street, marvelously alive.

"I just . . . ." He glowered, filled with . . . what?, she wondered. Determination? Courage? Both? Here he was, screwed by family and state, blindsided by lineage, lied to and persuaded to rescue his Judas father by Sandra herself, yet taking it all on. She squeezed and released. "I'm going with you."

"I can drop you by the store."

"I'm going."

The street they turned onto was bleak. Sandra knew the people here as customers, hard workers, panhandlers, acquaintances, shoplifters, jokers, kind hearts, and strugglers, every bit of what she knew made more poignant by these ramshackle houses. How could anyone who lived here not be raw to the nerve with summer and uncertainty. She knew she'd never survive.

Jimmy angled his car into the yard of a shack with its door screen busted inward and front door open. "Shit," he muttered. He turned off the engine and stepped from the car, and Sandra followed him.

"You should of stayed away, son," said a woman from the stoop next door. Sandra recognized her from the store.

"You know if he's in there, Miz Elma?" Jimmy asked.

"You ain't gone like it."

"I figured."

He strode toward the house again. Sandra forced herself close behind him. He pulled open the screen door, entered and gave a sharp exhale. Sandra peered over his shoulder. J.T. perched on a chair in the center of the room, his legs splayed, complexion beyond pale, forehead propped against the barrel of a shotgun standing vertically between his knees. J.T. raised his brow from the gun and blinked. His face was scratched as if miniscule kittens had attacked him. "I knew you'd come back," he said. Jimmy pointed at the cast.

"Squint did that?"

"Squint. Me."

"Where'd you get that shotgun?"

J.T.'s gaze shifted to Sandra. "You the girl from the store said you didn't know him."

"I'm sorry," Sandra said.

"I don't blame you."

"J.T.," Jimmy said. "Squint sposed to come back?"

"I got something for you, son. I saved something."

"All right." Jimmy raised a finger to the rifle. "You mind?" J.T.'s fingers twiddled on it a second before they opened. Jimmy cracked the shotgun, pocketed the shell and sniffed the breech. "Elma run him off with it," J.T. said. "Shot in the air, and then bore down on him."

"Elma did?"

"When he came back. Maybe she shouldn't of."

Sandra's legs weakened. "Maybe we should get out of here."

"Let's move him out of this heat," Jimmy said. He set the gun on the ground, bent at the knees, slung J.T.'s arm over his shoulders and looped an arm around his waist. J.T.'s limbs appeared barely socketed to his torso. Jimmy lifted him and headed toward the bedroom.

"I'll get him some water," Sandra said.

"No!" J.T. said. "I want Jimmy to go in there and look under the sink. I want you to look in that grocery bag."

"In a minute," Jimmy said, glanced at Sandra and nodded.

Sandra eased toward the kitchen as if someone were hiding there. On the counter, lay white pills. She read the bottle, ten prescribed, and counted nine left. She swallowed, scooped them up and funneled them back into the bottle. She ran water into one of the two glasses in the cabinet, got the bag from under the sink and returned to the bedroom. J.T. was muttering from the mattress. "Get the shotgun and lock the front door," Jimmy said. She set the glass and the bag on the floor and went out. She had never touched a gun and she shrank at touching this one. Bracing, she lifted it, as heavy as she'd imagined, locked the front door, then saw for the first time the smashed wall. She hurried back and shut the door behind her to keep the struggling AC in.

"Bastard broke his thumb," Jimmy said low to her, his features set in metal. "I don't know what he did with his face." Sandra set the gun in the corner and stayed there.

"Open it," J.T. said, motioning to the bag. Jimmy frowned, then unrolled the sack and removed the money.

"This what's left?"

"That's what I saved. I didn't give it to him even when he was hurting me. I took a lot more, I know, but I didn't give him that."

"Were you at Charley's when I come looking?"

J.T. dropped back onto the pillow, stroked his mouth and chin, then looked at Jimmy again. "They wouldn't let me out, Jimmy. I could of won it all back with that, but I heard you and I folded. I swear."

Jimmy stared at the money, stuffed it in his pocket and trudged close to Sandra, his eyes on the rifle. J.T. raised himself onto his elbows. "Just take that money and go. They don't even want it. They just wanta make me suffer."

Sandra's fear stirred more, began somehow to strangle her from inside out. Jimmy took hold of the shotgun. She grabbed his arm.

"Maybe they'll take your car," she said. "Maybe that would settle it."

Jimmy tilted the gun and studied it. "All my money and my car." He rubbed his face hard and slow. He went near J.T. "Why'd you take it?" he asked.

"I had a feeling. I'm sorry."

"Sorry."

"Jimmy," Sandra said. "Let's call the police."

"No!" J.T. said, and sat fully up. "No police."

"You in trouble with them, too?" Jimmy asked.

"No. Charley's in tight with them. Most they'll do is roust that goon and he'll come back or Charley'll get somebody else. Y'all get on before he comes back with bullets. I'll use that shotgun if need be." He swung his legs off the bed and made to stand, but he tumbled forward. Jimmy caught him with one arm as he went down, Sandra lunging to help. They hoisted him onto the bed, his clothes so sweaty Sandra's palms came away wet. "I knew you'd come," J.T. said, eyes closed. "I'll deal." He went limp on the pillow.

"Let's put him in the car and go," Sandra said.

"So they can get Miz Elma? I've got to settle all

this. Besides, J.T.'s gone have to tell me some things."
He turned to the door still holding the shotgun.
"Please, Jimmy."
"I ain't leaving it here."
"Where are we going?"
"Next door."
They headed out into the bright, hot yard. Jimmy
ambled, but with intent, shoulders stooped, rifle loosely
held, head slightly hung so that he looked through the
tops of his eyes. Elma sternly watched them, fanning
herself.
"You were right," Jimmy said to her, "I didn't like
it."
Elma eyed Sandra. "How you mixed up in this?"
"I'm with him. How's your arthritis?"
Elma frowned. "I got a bigger pain now." She
strained to her feet. "Let's go inside and have some tea."
At the kitchen table, Elma pointed a fan that stirred
the humid soup around them. Jimmy set the shotgun
in the corner and parted the curtain to see the street.
Elma put iced teas in front of them and took a chair.
"Thank you for what you did," Jimmy said as he
sat. "He don't deserve it."
Elma pointed at the pack in his shirt pocket. He
took one out and lit it for her.
"I want you to listen, Jimmy," she said. "I dealt
with a lot of people, and I learned that after a place you
have to let 'em do what they gone do. You hear me?"
"Yes, ma'am."
"You ain't heard a word. You need to go on. Your
daddy dug his own hole and he has to live in it. Me, I'll
be fine."
Sandra watched Elma's expression, certain and
solid, the way her mother's had once been. Tears rose
into her throat. She dabbed the icy condensation from
her glass onto her neck.
"I can't do that," Jimmy said.
Elma laid her hand on his. "I'm telling you, even
if you set it right he's gone start up again. You need to
use some damn sense."
Sandra cleared her throat. "With due respect,
ma'am, that's his father."

"I know who he is. I saved him a little while ago."
Elma released Jimmy, leaned back and took a long drag.
Jimmy rapped lightly on the table.

"I'm going down there and offer 'em my car and the rest of my cash."

"You go in there and they don't settle, how you gone get out?" Elma asked.

"I'll take the shotgun."

"And just walk right in. How you think that's gone turn out?"

"This is my business."

"It's J.T.'s business. You're being foolish. If you got to, at least call the police."

"I need to handle this."

Elma and Jimmy both leaned their elbows on the table and watched the same spot as if there were some answer to be decrypted there. A trail of smoke drifted upward until the wind of the fan swept it away. The Terror rose in Sandra, slipped from her chest and stood near her. It was almost a character she recognized, partly her mother, partly Hilly, partly Sandra herself, but mostly the unknown faces who might harm Jimmy. The Terror stepped closer to her. "We could call the lawyer," she blurted. Jimmy and Elma raised their heads. "He said call if he could do anything."

"The damn lawyer again," Jimmy said.

"He owes you. We might be able to fix it with his help."

"You saying I can't without?"

"You know I'm not saying that. I'm saying we have to use everything we can. Except the shotgun."

Jimmy drummed his fingers on the table and stared at Sandra, his deep brown eyes picking up metallic reflections of light. He glanced at Elma, back to Sandra, and back to Elma again. "You mind if we use your phone?"

WHAT J.T. REMEMBERS

The wall and the dark window fluttered into view. J.T.'s forehead ached as if struck dead center with a hammer. He raised his head and his eyebrows, then leaned forward, the whiskey still pitching headlong enough to let him know he hadn't dozed more than a couple of hours. There before him on the coffee table sat the pistol. He'd never had a gun, had only held a few when card players he knew showed him theirs. He had seen people shot, though. A week-night gunfight outside Chief's near closing time, a by-standing woman punctured dead in the chest, the two shooters drunkenly dancing toward each other in the parking lot until both were hit, one mortally in the stomach, the other angrily in the hip. J.T. alone watched from under the car where he'd dived. When everyone was down, he crawled to his car and sped off. He didn't like guns.

Still, this one intrigued him. It was Morita's. He picked it up. Sniffed it. Gun oil, metal and her faint scent. He opened it and spilled the bullets into his lap, pretty brass cylinders heftier than quarters. With two fingertips he pinched one up and squinted at it, a lozenge, bright and lead-headed, touched it to his lips, then placed it in between his back teeth like a chaw of tobacco. When he bit down, it generated a slight charge, so he rolled it around his cheeks, then nestled it beneath his tongue where the bullet's cool smoothness soothed him. He cocked the hammer and pulled the trigger, the sharp click pleasurable to him. He fiddled with the pistol until its cylinder dropped open. He spat the bullet into his palm and placed it in a chamber, spun the cylinder and snapped it closed. Sighting down the barrel, he understood how it comforted Morita with its solidity and potential. The night came back to him. The crush of the mountain returned.

He exhaled as he lowered the gun to his lap, and after a long wait, fought to inhale. The knowledge of the single random bullet and its implications nudged a grunt from him. He settled the pistol like a prayer book in his palms and examined its clean lines, curving handle and careful tooling. He itched to know in which chamber the lone bullet waited. He'd known of people playing that game, men too desperate, drunk, jaded or rich to settle for simple money stakes anymore, but he'd never been around such a game. Nonetheless, it had a familiarity—his picking up Morita, her having his child, his fucking two other women, the constant threat of her daddy. Weren't all those roulettes of a kind? A lot of the blame for the death of his streak and the start of his slide had to go to Morita, but it also had to go to him. The universe gaveth and the universe taketh away, but some power rested with the gambler who believed in his own luck, had the faith to lay it all out there and know he could lose it, or win even larger. He'd ridden that faith into both the night he met Morita and the miraculous terrain of Morita herself.

His finger curled around the trigger. Did he have any luck left? Of course he did. The question was whether he had faith enough to find it, because without that faith he was dead anyway, sentenced to the hammer and shovel, doomed to be jostled and flattened by the need and greed of chumps and bosses. He extended his arm straight up and pointed the pistol at the ceiling, where his whiskey buzz cast a momentary pink blush. Five-to-one odds. One pull, one click, and it was either all over or all started over. He let his arm sweep slowly to his side like a clock hand from twelve to three, then curled his wrist back toward him. Unconsciously, his other hand cupped his crotch and his eyes drew shut. A cool breeze shushed through his head; he was atop the crushing mountain. He thought of Morita, their first kiss, thought of the nurse entering the waiting room to tell him he had a son. His finger tightened on the trigger, its delicate curl, its small resistance.

When the gun went off, J.T. rocketed to his feet. Pain shot through his knee ripping and red. He dropped the pistol, screamed and held his leg without thinking, then froze, realization turning him into a statue. He'd accidentally fired at himself and was alive. His ears rang. But had the bullet torn his knee? He trembled. Teeth clenched, he uncovered his knee like a card hand. No torn pants. No blood. Pain already diminishing. He kicked the pistol across the room. On the wall where the gun had pointed, he scanned until he saw a black hole and cracked plaster near the ceiling.

"Get down!" Morita hissed, peeking around the corner of the hall. Her gown was illuminated as if her flesh were a nuclear filament, her black hair a force of nature. She was beautiful like a tornado or lightning is beautiful and bristling with electricity. He would have gladly burnt himself up if that would let him be inside her again. "Get down!" She stumbled toward him and pulled him by his arm to the floor. She frantically scanned his hands. "Where is it?" He pointed automatically in the direction he'd kicked it, and she scurried to it, clutched it to her breast and pressed her back to the wall.

He held up his palms, then saw her face distorted so badly she appeared a stranger.

"I'm all right," he said.

"Where is he?"

"I missed," J.T. said.

"Did he get in? Is he outside?" She scrambled over and flicked off the light, disappearing herself for a moment. J.T. couldn't speak. His life was a tragedy and a joke, the woman he'd loved ravaged inside. He wished for an instant that he hadn't missed, then wished he'd drunk more.

"Ain't nobody here, Morita. I shot the gun. We're all by ourselves."

"What?" she asked from across the room. Jimmy was crying again, distantly.

"I shot it. I was messing with it and it went off."

Morita was in the dark, but the kitchen threw light that let J.T. see her mouth hanging open, her expression sliding toward blankness. She studied the pistol, then J.T. "You shot for nothing?"

"It was an accident."

She pushed herself upright against the wall and went rigid. She peeked through the curtains as if J.T. might be lying, flicked on the light, then glared at him. "With the baby in here," she seemed to say to herself. He shuddered. She came at him, the gun raised above her head. He tried to cover himself, but a bat of light struck his skull and dropped him. He resurfaced, balled up, to Morita's shrieking and cursing, her sounds more powerful than her blows. The blows stopped. "You fool," she said. He tensed, waiting to be shot even though he knew the gun had no bullets. He checked to see if her fingers were plucking strays from the floor, but her footsteps headed off in the direction of Jimmy's squalling.

J.T. waited a minute to uncurl, a ruckus of swearing, tossed items and Jimmy's crying filtering through the closed bedroom door. The crown of his head throbbed. He touched near his hairline and came back with thick blood on his fingers. He shoved himself to a sitting position. He was a little high, yes, but he was hurt too. He touched his head again, found it wetter, a bleeder, and climbed to his feet. He almost threw up, but somehow made it to the kitchen, opened the fridge and fumbled an ice tray that crashed to the floor. Tottering, he took a rag from the counter, knelt and gathered ice cubes into it, pressed it against his head. A crash came from the bedroom, and he expected her to barrel down the hall. Only Jimmy's screaming came his way. He managed to stand again, dropped his head over the sink and puked, the whiskey worse than the bile coming up. Forehead propped against the faucet, he cleared his stomach twice more, then waited for the sweats to stop and the spins to slow. When he regained himself, he checked the rag of ice and found a silver-dollar-sized spot soaked with blood. A phone rang insistently in his head, but he stood and slowly approached the bedroom, the hallway an amplifier of the turbulence on the other side of the door. A couple of feet away he stopped. Jimmy had settled into a steady saw of crying. Morita was still cursing, a stream of vileness about "he" and "him" without names. She sounded as if she was packing but flinging and kicking things too. He pictured her suitcase, then her carrying both it and Jimmy outside. A wedge of ice drove into his chest. She'd said she was going, but he hadn't believed her. He'd wished his house without a woman and a baby, but never imagined it without Morita and Jimmy. He dropped the ice rag on the floor and took the knob, tugged it and found it locked. He rapped against the thin wood. Her loud talking stopped. "Let me in, Morita," he said.

"Leave us be," she said.

"I'm gonna bust this door in." Only Jimmy's whimpering came to him. He cocked his ear and strained. "I'm serious." A trickle of blood streamed down his face, startling him, then he stepped back to kick. He thought he heard the snap of the gun cylinder, wondered if she had more bullets, saw her turn the pistol on herself and kicked it open. The pistol was leveled at him. In its chambers he saw the dull tips of thirty-eight cartridges.

"I'm done with it, J.T.," she said. She no longer wore her night gown but a green dress. "Go."

J.T. wanted to drop to his knees and beg her. He glanced at Jimmy, who gripped the play pen slats and panted. On the bed a suitcase was nearly filled. The woman with the gun was someone he no longer recognized. Heaviness draped him. He turned and walked. In the living room, the bullet hole caught his attention. Shaggy plaster surrounded the black entry wound. A clear picture of himself—neat hole in one temple, blasted skull on the other—came to him with a chill.

Outside, tires screeched to a stop. Car doors slammed. Footsteps slapped on the concrete apron at the front door, then pounding shook the door. "Police, open up!" a man yelled. J.T. did not move. The cop pounded again and yelled more loudly. J.T. glanced down the hallway. Morita came through the door, stricken-faced and holding the revolver.

"No, Morita," he said, and stepped toward her with long strides, his drunken feet in mud, the sound of the door banging open behind him. She pointed the pistol from her waist, and J.T. could already feel the burning tear of a bullet entering his guts as his pace quickened to a run, his palms held up. Morita's eyes stretched wider, seeing beyond J.T. as the cop yelled. J.T. slammed into her, expecting gunshots from front and rear. He and Morita flew into the bedroom and smashed onto the floor, Morita's breath going with an Oof. J.T. snatched the pistol and tossed it away. He held her as footsteps approached. Then one of the cops pulled him away while the other grabbed Morita, flipped her over and cuffed her. She and Jimmy wailed.

"It's okay," J.T. yelled. His cop held him on the floor and told him to shut up.

The other jerked Morita to her feet, shook her hard until she was quiet, then shoved her toward the door. "He'll find me, J.T.," she said. "Don't let them take me," but the cop roughed her into the hall and away. J.T.'s cop pulled him up by his cuffed hands, walked him to the living room and sat him on the couch.

"Got report of a shot," the cop said, standing above him. J.T. nodded. "You shot?"

"No."

"Your head's bleeding on your face."

"I got hit."

"She hit you on the head?"

"I think so."

"Think so? What the hell's she doing waving a gun in a room with a goddamn baby?"

"She's drunk."

"That fucking figures. Stay put." The cop went down the hall, where J.T. heard him shushing Jimmy. The other came back in from outside, a rangy man with thick forearms, and pointed at J.T. "What's your name?" J.T. told him. "She your wife?" J.T. nodded. "That baby y'all's?"

"His name's Jimmy."

The cop shook his head. "Even y'all's baby don't deserve that." He called to the back to ask if the baby was all right.

"Scared shitless," the other cop said.

"I don't want her to go to jail," J.T. said.

"That ain't up to you, boy. You should of thought 'fore you got mixed up in all this."

"I shot the gun," J.T. said.

"Don't lie. I seen her with it when we came in and she looked ready to use it."

"She's just scared of her daddy. She's sick."

"Her ass'll be sick in jail tonight. Yours too if I'm of a mind."

The other cop returned from the bedroom without Jimmy, whose crying had died down.

"You fit to take care of that baby tonight or you too drunk?" the rangy cop asked.

"I'm fit." He thought of asking them to take him to jail instead of her, but he knew he would return to an empty house. "Can't she just stay here?"

"We not leaving you two drunks in here to kill each other and that baby," the first cop said. "Everbody's gone get some time to cool down. She might get a lot of time for waving that pistol at us."

"Maybe you could just take her to the hospital?"

"Maybe you oughta just shut your mouth 'fore we run both of you in and give this baby to somebody can take care of him." The rangy cop went into the kitchen, came back and tossed a rag on J.T.'s lap. He undid J.T.'s cuffs. J.T. pressed the rag to his scalp. "Now tell us what happened."

J.T. calculated for a moment what would happen if he did tell the truth, how he might go to jail too, then thought how a lie that she'd shot might send her away for a long time. "I did shoot the gun," he said. Then he told the truth the best he could.

When the police finished taking his statement, they told him he could come see about her in the morning, told him they better never have to come back. He thought to move to the porch to see Morita, then simply listened to the car pull away. Jimmy made a sound, almost like a word. J.T. froze. Jimmy sounded again. J.T. checked his scalp. His fingers came back dry. He felt as though a powerful wind had blown through the house, and he sat for seconds more before shoving himself to his feet and starting down the hall. When he entered the bedroom, Jimmy was standing and holding the bars. "Hey, bub," J.T. said. Jimmy's eyes and face sagged, puffy and red. "You must be wore out." He shuffled to the playpen, where Jimmy stared up at him, both of them strangers to the other, J.T. thought. He grasped Jimmy under his armpits, slung him across his shoulder, where Jimmy bawled once more. J.T. gritted his teeth and shh-ed him.

He sat in the rocker Morita had purchased and had dragged from room to room to rock Jimmy, according to her mood. It had spooked J.T., waking at night to find her facing the window with her back to him, staring at flames, Jimmy in her arms. He thought about what might happen to her—fingerprinting, picture-taking, unkind words and rough handling, maybe even worse. And what would happen tomorrow? What charges? What lies would the cops have told? What would bail be? Would he even have the ten percent to post it? He imagined the expressions from the police and the judge. There would certainly be more shit muttered about his colored bride. Besides all that, if Morita came back, she wouldn't stay. And even if she did, would Jimmy be better off with her as wild as she'd gotten? He moved away from thinking about her father.

J.T. kept rocking. Jimmy quieted, became heavier in J.T.'s grasp and began a labored sleep-breathing. J.T. gingerly stood, fought the-whiskey-and-head-blow wooziness down the hall and laid Jimmy in his crib. In the bathroom, he washed his blood-matted hair and forehead and carefully combed back his hair, made the mistake of looking at himself in the mirror. How was he qualified to be a father? He hurried to the bedroom, dumped the contents of Morita's purse, found seven dollars and change, then started in on her suitcase. Her smell rose like a specter, and he found his eyes watering as he rummaged through her clothes and undergarments, found Jimmy's things in there too. Next he spilled the overnight bag. Among diapers and make-up, a tiny red purse dropped out. Inside it he found eighty-two dollars. He jammed it into his pocket. He glanced around the room, guessing where she could have stashed the rest of her money, saw the new drapes and the playpen and the crib and toys as if for the first time, even though he'd seen them appear month by month without his spending a dime. He stuffed Jimmy's things into the overnight bag, tossed Morita's belongings out of the suitcase and began to pack it with a few of his own clothes. He supposed Jimmy needed a diaper change, tried to remember how Morita did it and set aside a diaper and powder. Jimmy would need feeding, something to do with formula since Morita could no longer nurse him. He'd resented her for nursing, was jealous of Jimmy always at her nipple, puzzled at why she had to do what he heard almost nobody did anymore. Sometimes she leaked and complained that she was so full she ached and would bring out the pump to relieve the pressure, an act J.T. couldn't bear to watch. He wondered what she would do in jail. Tears flooded his eyes. He flung them away and went back to packing.

Two hours later they were far west of the Mississippi, Jimmy asleep in the passenger seat, cradled in blankets. J.T. had managed to concoct some formula, taste it himself, gag, then feed some to Jimmy. He'd changed a diaper as well, although the finished product looked like battlefield surgery with safety-pins. In the rearview mirror, the sky was paling with morning, filling J.T. with apprehension, his shoulders prickling as if in a rifle sight. The road ahead was worse. Every second took him further into his past with Morita, that initial glorious past of high passion and loose cash. J.T. had never had a time like that before and was certain he never would again. He pictured her in her cell, weeping and screaming and worn out, her lovely face even further transformed by misery. The roadside swamp, emerging with morning, brought back their wedding day. A blot like death lurked in his peripheral vision.

J.T. started to sweat. He glanced at Jimmy, expecting something to be horribly wrong. He looked fine, still sleeping, his small cheeks flushed from exertion, his tiny mouth open and twitching, sprigs of red hair standing. J.T. reached to touch him without thinking, then drew his hand back. Where was he going? What would he do when Jimmy woke up? He passed the welcome sign for Lafayette, an ominous marker. He and Morita had nearly killed each other with love here. Hadn't they been killing each other somehow every day since? His heart went wild, as if it might explode. His windpipe shrank to the size of a straw. He clutched at his chest. He tried to slow his ragged breath, wondered if he was actually dying and his death would send the car careening off the road. At the next service station, he pulled in and hopped out of the car, his head spinning.

"Where's the hospital?" he asked the attendant as he strolled up.

"About a mile up the road. You having trouble, mister?" The attendant's face told J.T. that he was.

"The baby's sick. There's a sick baby in the car."

The attendant looked through the window. "Huh. I can call you an ambulance."

"No, no, just fill 'er up."

"You sure?"

"It's almost empty." J.T. looked in at Jimmy once more. His pulse kicked higher. He staggered to the bathroom, vomited, and splashed his face without glancing at the mirror. He pissed hard, then leaned against the wall, hands trembling. He was terribly thirsty and suddenly hung over. The tile bathroom walls cranked in on him. He pushed outside, where the attendant stood waiting.

"You sure you gonna make it?"

"Yeah, yeah. I took my pill." J.T. stared at the older man's long nose and rheumy eyes. "Hey, you got a pencil and paper I can have?"

"Say what?"

"I need something for when I get to the hospital. Can you help me out?"

"Come on in the office."

J.T. paid, then took the yellow sheet of paper the man offered. J.T.'s heart began to slow, the blood to return to his face, the sweat dry. His hand still shook, but he wrote, "James Thomas Strawhorn, born August

25th, 1959." He thanked the man and strode to the car. He folded the paper and tucked it in the front of Jimmy's diaper. J.T. wondered why he hadn't put Jimmy in the carrier, which he'd placed in the back seat.

Back on the road, he locked his vision forward and concentrated on breathing. He didn't deserve this, he told himself. None of it. He hadn't asked for it. Plus, his luck was back, the errant bullet proved that. Maybe some of it would rub off on Jimmy. Anything would be luckier than staying with J.T., though, of that he was sure. And beside, they'd make Morita better and by the time she was better, they would've tracked down that Jimmy was her son.

J.T. pulled up in front of the hospital, leaned out the door of his car and gagged. He steadied himself on the car as he moved around to the passenger's side. He opened the back door, took out the baby carrier and set it on the ground. Then he opened the front door and lifted Jimmy. His eyes popped open to J.T., startled, but he didn't cry. His sweet baby smell entered J.T. and J.T.'s chest clamped again, more than before. J.T. opened the back door, carefully placed Jimmy in the carrier and headed toward the emergency room door fifty feet away.

"You need a hand?" he heard, and saw a guard. J.T. went cold. He knew the booze was still on his breath.

"I found this baby."

"You found him?" The guard pressed the tip of his index finger to his chin.

"At a rest stop back on the highway."

The guard jerked his head back. "I'll be."

"Right in the bathroom. Thought I oughta bring him here to make sure he ain't sick."

The guard let Jimmy grasp his finger. "Hey, little fella," he said.

"Hey, sir," J.T. said. "Would you mind holding him while I get my car out of the way?"

"It's not too bad in the way."

"I'd still be obliged if I could move it." J.T. put the carrier in the guard's arms.

The guard shook his head. "What kinda person would leave a baby at a rest stop?"

Everything J.T. had ever felt dropped through

him to the ground. He braced not to follow. His throat quavered. "I can't imagine," he said.

DAY EIGHT, LATE AFTERNOON

Snoring awakened J.T. and it wasn't his snoring. He hopped out of bed, tweaking his back, and crouched, unsure of what new menace he faced. On the other half of the bed reclined a black woman, vaguely familiar, who'd evidently produced the snore. The room was strange, cool, lit by a small frilly lamp in the corner and cluttered with womanly stuff. His mind careened to the past, sketched a fictional domestic history, then locked into the present with such regret that he experienced an interior whiplash. He sighed, caught himself midway and straightened.

"Settle down," the woman said, still on her back, hands linked on her stomach.

"How the hell . . . ." The fog of his first sound sleep in days parted enough to recognize Elma and note the slice of sunlight eking to the floor beneath the curtains.

"Jimmy brought you over before him and that girl went to tend to your mess."

The shotgun that had been between them on the bed came clear, then images were rolling in: Jimmy's putting J.T. into his own bed, rousing him, walking J.T. across the super bright yard and putting him into another bed. He noticed his cast and the dull throb in his thumb.

"Say what?"

"Him and Sandra headed to work out your bill."

"They went to Charley's! Holy Jesus, I got to—"

"Simmer down. It's too late. You'll only make it worse."

J.T. ogled the shotgun, considered a call for a cab, a rush to Charley's, a heroic burst inside, then . . . disaster. He bore a small wave of disgust at himself. "Why can't they stay put?"

"Just shut your mouth. Go get a cold biscuit and sausage off the stove or something. You could stand a shower too. It smells like an old dog crawled in my bed."

"You mighty damn spry."

"I don't get many cool naps." She smiled. "Jimmy give me fifty dollars to run my AC. Said it come from you." She laughed too loudly for his taste. "Bring me some ice water too."

"Yes, ma'am."

The heat slugged J.T. as he stepped into the hall, a turned-around replica of his house, except furnished and intact. He peered around the living room and down the hall, then peeked into the kitchen before entering. He filled a glass, drained it, refilled the glass and drank half of it. On the stove sat a cellophaned plate of biscuits and sausage. He balked a moment at eating her food, then lifted the plate and sniffed. He salivated at the aroma of buttermilk, flour, and pork, peeled the wrapping away and breathed more deeply. Queasiness teased his stomach, but he broke open a biscuit, laid a sausage between the halves and bit in anyway. The taste expanded in his mouth, richer and more complex than anything he had ever experienced. He chewed ravenously several times, slowed and let the biscuit melt over his teeth and into the pockets of his jaws. The second bite he chewed slowly all the way, washed it down with more water, finished the biscuit, fixed a second one and ate it all too. He belched, refilled his glass, then deliberated how he was going to crack a tray to make ice water for Elma. "Let me fetch for you, madam," he said beneath his breath, opened the fridge and found a pitcher full.

He paused just inside Elma's door to let his

eyesight adjust. She was sitting up in bed, her toes wiggling, her dress hiked to expose calves that J.T. ran his eyes along before snapping to. When he looked up, she was smirking. He handed her the water and took the chair across the room.

"How is it you so young and retired?" he asked.

"Me?" She laughed. "My knees wore out with arthritis from scrubbing and lifting. I get a disability check and some help from my son to allow me to live so high." She waved her arm to display her surroundings. "What's your excuse?"

"I ain't retired. You got to have a chump job before you can retire from it."

"Uh uh." She took a long drink and licked her lips. "That son of yours is something. I told him you weren't worth anymore trouble, but he went on anyhow."

"Thanks."

"My pleasure. But how you gone feel if he don't make it back?"

"He shouldn't of gone," J.T. said, flaring. "Shouldn't of even gone to that bar in the first place. Hell, he shouldn't of come here at all." His irritation dropped through him like an anchor. He lowered his face into his good hand.

"I wish he'd stayed away too," Elma said. "Tell you the truth, I wish I would of shot that big redneck that hurt you. 'Nigger this, nigger that.' Some buckshot'd cure his ass."

J.T. looked sideways at her. "You'd of really shot him?"

"Damn right I would. It'd be worth it to do away with something as mean as him. I ain't sure it'd even be a sin."

"I don't think I could of shot him."

"Cause you're a coward and a pitiful daddy."

"Hell, woman, why didn't you just shoot me?"

"It crossed my mind."

J.T. sneered. He scanned the room, the dresser, the photos of Elma and her son, her frilly pillows piled on a chest at the foot of the bed. Female bullshit, he thought to himself, but he felt a loss, doubted he'd ever have comfort again. "Let me ask you something," he said. "If you're such a prize, what're you doing all by yourself?"

"I got tired of men like you. Couldn't put up with all the nonsense." She chuckled. "Granted, they couldn't put up with me neither." She drained her water and leaned forward to rub her knees. "If it makes you feel better, I wasn't so good with my son either. I seen the trouble me and my brothers and sisters gave my mother, so I made my mind up not to have kids. Got pregnant late by accident, but I still wasn't grown up. I kept on catting around when I should of been raising him, and my poor momma took him for a spell. I took him back off and on, but he wasn't mine by the time he turned a teenager and I'd grown up enough to have some sense. By then he was already on the way to jail."

"The one took me to Earl K. Long was in jail? He's a security guard."

"I guess they figure he knows how to watch for crime." She smiled.

J.T.'s thumb was beginning to act up again. He recalled the pills on his kitchen counter and recoiled at ever entering that place again. "How long they been gone?"

"Long enough. They either be back soon or they ain't coming back."

"Don't say that," J.T. said.

"It's the truth."

"That don't mean you have to say it."

"I figure you to say that."

He gazed at the corner of the ceiling and shivered at the thought of Squint doing to Jimmy what he'd done to him. He looked at Elma watching him. "They'll come back," he said. "I'm willing to bet."

"I don't doubt that."

Jimmy's impulse was to ram Charley and Squint's big rides, but he eased to the end of the line of eight or so vehicles, shifted to Park and shut off the engine. In his head he could still see Sandra in his rearview mirror, her arms crossed as he pulled away from the McDonald's. She'd pleaded with him to let her come, just as she'd pleaded with him to let the lawyer call instead of Jimmy doing it this way. Maybe the second he should have done. But he hadn't. He had to do this part.

He stepped out, reached back through the window and laid on the horn. Not long passed before Charley and Squint popped out of the bar and came at him, Charley waving his arms and scowling. Jimmy let off and stood with his arms at his sides.

"Goddamnit, boy," Charley said. "You're pushing it like your old man."

"Wanted to make sure y'all knew I was here."

"Yeah. Well you and J.T. ain't out the woods yet." Charley held out his hand. "Keys. Let's get this sorry mess over with."

"In the ignition," Jimmy said. Squint smiled behind Charley. Spit filled Jimmy's mouth.

Charley slid in, cranked the car and revved the engine. Jimmy recalled the day Sparks had given him the then four-year-old Fairlane, five-hundred dollars, and a handshake as payment for running the spread and as a going-away gift. Jimmy's body had stiffened and numbed. He'd never been anywhere in his life, had harbored Pepper's paranoia of the world. For a second he thought of giving Sparks back the keys and returning to the small ranch, safe but lonely and bored, afraid even to try and connect with people in town who'd be different, schooled, experienced. Then his eyes had blurred, Pepper's body coming to him with a sense of loss and failure. He took the directions to Houston and tore out.

Charley stepped out with the motor still running and started his inspection around the car. Squint sidled up next to Jimmy like a building suddenly erected. "Don't think there ain't more payback," he whispered.

Jimmy's fists closed. He looked up at Squint. "I'm done listening to you, pardner." He walked toward Charley at the rear of the car.

"This thing's got some wear on it, but you've kept it in good shape. You got the title?"

"In the glove box."

"And the thousand?" Jimmy waited, staring into Charley's bloodshot, hazel eyes. He hadn't even sorted through how many ways this could still go wrong. Jimmy reached for his shirt pocket. Charley held up his palm. "Not out here, boy. I'm just asking. I don't do business on the street."

Jimmy eyed the bar. "How I know I go in there, I'm coming out?"

"You don't know. But it's either come in there, or deal with my man here later. You lucky you ain't dealing with him right now."

Jimmy gazed back in Sandra's direction. He knew she was waiting by the pay phone, dime at the ready, and out of her mind as the clock ticked. Maybe he should've done it like she wanted, just to spare her.

Squint nudged him to follow Charley. They entered the cool, smoky darkness, a few men at the bar glancing at them, and kept on going until they were in Charley's office. Squint shut the door behind them. Jimmy took in the small room, an institutional gray desk with two folding chairs in front of it, walls adorned with posters of women in bathing suits, beer boxes stacked behind Charley's chair. Jimmy thought to say something smartass about how nice it was, but Charley pointed to one of the folding chairs, went around to his chair, dropped the car title on the desk and sat. He pulled a pack of stomach mints from a drawer, broke off half the roll and tossed them into his mouth. "Your fucking old man," he said, and paused to crunch. "He used to be good for some laughs. Last couple of years he's just a loser, and now he brings you in. I've known him twenty years and he never mentioned no son." Charley swallowed. "And don't even tell me where y'all got a grand from."

Jimmy's jaw tightened all the way to his scalp. "I'm tired of y'all talking," Jimmy said. "Preaching after you broke a old man's han—"

Lightning struck both of Jimmy's ears. He bent and nearly went out, blinked his eyes, forced himself to stay conscious, the ringing in his ears like a steam whistle two inches away. He sat back up, the pain prodding outward against his eyeballs, and saw Squint smiling. "I owed you that," Squint said.

Jimmy wiped the water from his eyes. "You just a sorry-ass bully," he said. Squint's smile fell.

"That's enough," Charley said. "Just give me the goddamn cash."

Jimmy shifted to Charley. He wished for a moment that he had brought the shotgun. He licked his lips, the sweet taste of Sandra's lipstick still somehow there, if only in his mind. He inhaled. His hand went to his pocket, removed a flat envelope and tossed it on Charley's desk.

"What the hell?" Charley said. "This better have a thousand-dollar bill in it."

"Read it," Jimmy said.

"Read it?"

"That's what I said."

"Son, you, your old man, and that nigger woman are about to be fucked."

"Maybe so. But you best read it before the cops show."

"Cops?" Squint said, and laughed. "You want cops, just wait a hour or so and you'll see plenty of 'em right out there."

"The Chief of Police too? And the Mayor?" Jimmy pointed at the envelope. "I don't think y'all are the killing-and-going-to-prison types. Read it." Squint and Charley traded a look. Squint moved next to Jimmy, his crotch at head level. Jimmy looked sideways at him and raised the edge of his mouth, despite the ongoing ringing and the possibility of worse.

Charley roughly removed the letter from the envelope. He began reading, his face reddening with every movement of his eyeballs. Jimmy sat back. This must be what it was like to have a powerful hand, the feeling that J.T. chased after again and again. He snorted. He thought back two hours ago to Bourgeouis's office, the lawyer dictating to his secretary that Bourgeouis, the Mayor and the Chief of Police were good friends; that Jimmy was a high-profile protectee of the state; that Charley and Squint were liable for criminal charges for injury done to J.T. Strawhorn; that a civil suit could be aimed at all of Charley's holdings; and that the police would arrive if Bourgeouis hadn't heard from his client by five p.m. Jimmy remembered all of it. Not the exact words, but the meaning.

Charley looked up and thrust the letter toward Jimmy. "You cocksucker. You think this scares me?"

"What?" said Squint.

Jimmy looked squarely at him. "The what is y'all are fucked if anything more happens to J.T. or Elma or me. Ain't that right, Charley?"

"I oughta kill you."

"I guess that evens us up. Now give me my keys and title."

Charley breathed as though the air in the room were disappearing. He crumpled the letter and made a fist at Jimmy. "You really think you and J.T. can cheat me and get away with it?"

"Cheat?" Jimmy said. "You two break a man's hand and talk about cheat?"

"He owed me money. There never was a thousand either, was there?"

"You tell me. You sposed to be the smart one."

Charley bounced the letter off Jimmy's chest. Squint moved forward, but Charley stayed him with a finger point. "Shit," he said, took the keys from his pocket and tossed them on the desk. Jimmy pinched up the keys and the title. He stood, took out a cigarette and lit it.

"You acting mighty big now, you pissant," Squint said, his eyes strangely widening. "That letter's your death warrant." He cleared his chest and spat on Jimmy's chest.

Rage came up bloody and powerful in Jimmy. He believed he could kill them, Squint and Charley, right there, with just his hands. Knew he could. The ringing in his head increased. His body made to move. He stopped it. Then he felt himself rise, the sensation of flight, and Sandra was in it.

Jimmy put his smoke in his mouth, folded the title and shoved it in his back pocket. He picked up a clean bar rag from a stack of them, wiped his shirt and tossed the rag on his chair. He took a long drag, blew out and stubbed the cigarette in the ashtray on Charley's desk. Charley and Squint's voices erupted, but Jimmy barely heard them as he went toward the door.

*   *   *

She stood at the edge of the parking lot where she could see down the road toward Charley's a half mile away. It was all she could do not to run toward the bar, and her restraint caused her insides to grip all the way into her throat. Ten minutes left, she thought, and every second would be like another torturing water drop. She paced, the pads of her thumb and forefinger worrying the dime there. The rush hour traffic blew past, but she noticed it only as a noisy, incessant, glinting stream in her periphery. The smothering heat pasted her hair to her forehead, but she couldn't force herself to go inside or even into the building's shade.

She sucked exhaust-laden air, trying to control her breathing, the same frantic breathing as when she had rushed down the hotel stairs and sprinted through the lobby, the unknown awaiting. She stopped pacing and strained to stay still. She believed that somewhere in her was a strength and calm she'd never had if she could simply let it come to her. What came instead was a riot from inside, and with it an even stronger impulse to set out along the asphalt. Still, she didn't move, sensing that if she moved with this chaos she might finally and fully lose herself. She had to let herself expand, let the energy move while containing it. But only the riot expanded, hurling her history, fright, and despair against her skin and bones. The expansion pressed outward, threatening to take her beyond where she could hold on to herself, threatening to disintegrate her. The thought came to her: Was this what Jimmy had felt just before the jump, the space outside dismantling him molecule by molecule like a black hole's gravity, ravaging him until it dragged what solid self was left through the window, unwilled? Or was jumping his only solution, a plunge the only way to survive fragmentation, to challenge the stripping force? She rubbed the slippery dime between her fingers. Yes, one, or even both, of those. But there was no jump for her right now.

Her watch said five minutes. She strode toward the pay phone, whether to call Bourgeouis or call the cops herself she didn't yet know. The Terror from Elma's table joined her stride for stride, its presence reminding her that Jimmy might already be dead, that Jimmy might have given them the letter and headed back to Texas. She clutched the sides of her head until she reached the phone and pressed her forehead against the warm metal. The sound of car engines and footsteps passed by as she tried to gather herself, ignore the Terror until it at least stepped away for a moment. The terrible expansion continued. She focused on the seconds ticking.

"Hey," she heard. Jimmy's voice or self-deception. She zoomed outward for several seconds before she was able to turn to him still behind the wheel. He blanched at her face and stepped from the car. He hugged her. "You want me to call?" he asked. She tried to speak but couldn't, couldn't even raise her arms. He led her around to the passenger side, sat her in the car and took the dime. Jimmy. She knew she should feel relief, even joy, but she doubled over and hugged herself. It seemed all she could do to keep from flying apart.

The driver's side door opened and shut. A hand spread on her back. "Are you all right?" she heard. She sat up, blinked to try and solidify him, his face flushed, his expression tired.

"Oh, Jimmy." She put her hands to his cheeks, his skin a brief tether, then kissed him. She gathered herself as much as she could, like pulling a hundred strings attached to a hundred birds, until he moved away and studied her.

"You're sweating like crazy," he said. "You should of waited inside."

"I couldn't. I almost came down there."

"I figured."

"Did they hurt you?"

"Nah. Squint got a lick in, but that was all." He shifted into Drive and headed out of the lot in the direction of J.T.'s, a fifteen-minute ride to a place that seemed another world away. Jimmy's shoulders slumped as he drove. She knew he was angry and exhausted. She wanted to go with him to J.T.'s, be there if he needed her, but how could she be there like this? Be anywhere like this? Her eyes moved to the road again.

More words were coming up out of her, but she held

them, afraid what they would say. It was happening, almost everything she wanted, and it settled nothing. More trouble waited at J.T.'s and more trouble beyond that. She'd written that destiny had sent Jimmy, a word she'd never used before that night, a word she'd felt more than believed. But destiny seemed like a silly lie in the midst of the roil in her. The expansion inside her continued, and she knew she had to follow it or be scattered to nothing.

"Jimmy," she said. "I have to ask you to do something."

"Come on in, we in the bedroom," Elma said, as she opened the front door. Jimmy's eyebrows went up, then he followed Elma in. He stopped just inside the bedroom door. J.T. stood from a chair, an uncertain smile skittering over him.

"You're okay," he said, but nothing in Jimmy moved toward him.

"It worked out," Jimmy said. "I think we're shed of 'em so long as you stay straight."

"No problem with that," J.T. said. "Elma told me what y'all did. I appreciate it." J.T. shifted his feet and cleared his throat several times, neither a gesture that reassured Jimmy. "Hey, where's your girl?"

"She had some business at the store. She took your pills, but I brought 'em back."

Jimmy gave the bottle to J.T. He examined it, his tongue darting in and out, until he pushed it into his pocket and went almost to attention like a man awaiting sentence.

"Why don't I let y'all talk," Elma said.

"You can stay, Elma," J.T. said. He looked at Jimmy and waited. "Never mind," he finally said.

"You able to walk back to your place?" Jimmy asked.

J.T. exhaled and led the way. His pathetic shuffle made Jimmy's palm sting to cuff him hard just once, but he let it go. A sense of great height returned to him, his blood sharpening, yet there was no vertigo. He walked a kind of tightrope, but the rope was steady. At his house, J.T. glanced over his shoulder, his face droopy, and went inside. "The bedroom," Jimmy said, grabbed the chair that had been both bed and projectile and took it into the cool of the still-running AC. "Which?" Jimmy asked. J.T. gingerly sat on the mattress. Jimmy took the chair.

"I'm sorry, son," J.T. said.

"I wanta know everything," Jimmy said.

"I can't remember everything."

"Then tell me what you can. Start with my mother."

J.T.'s eyes reddened. "Don't make me do that."

"You owe me."

J.T.'s shoulders spasmed down his arms. He worked his fingers as if he might be having a seizure. "She's dead," he said, his voice quiet and different from what Jimmy had heard before.

Jimmy swayed. He gripped the back of his neck. He hadn't known until that moment that he believed she was still alive, and her loss, the loss of someone he'd never even had, bludgeoned him more than the force of everyone and everything he had ever lost.

"Keep going," he said.

"I heard it was suicide, that she shot herself. That was twenty years ago. Could've been her daddy killed her, too, from what I know."

"From what you know?"

"A fella name of Chief told me. He knew what went on in New Orleans and he showed me the newspaper article. She was shot at her daddy's house, but I don't know if she'd of gone there on her own."

"You never checked?"

"On whether she did it or her daddy it?" J.T. shook his head. "I was scared to check. I wouldn't of found out no how. Her daddy was a bad man. I was afraid he'd kill me if he found out about me cause I was white and had a baby with her." He licked his lips. "She wasn't white."

"I know."

"You know?"

"That lawyer told me."

"You went back to se . . ."

Jimmy glared until J.T. put his hand to his forehead and focused on the floor.

"What else, J.T.? What happened with me?"

J.T. squeezed and released his cast as if trying to pump life into it. His head lolled in time with his grip. "It wasn't good with me and her. I wasn't good. I didn't take good care of y'all. I think I made her crazy. One night I got spooked and took you, but soon as we were gone, I knew I couldn't take care of you, much less raise you. I put your name on a paper and dropped you at a hospital. That's the last I saw of you. That's the last I saw of either of you."

"And you never thought of me again till you thought you might make some money."

"That's about the size of it. I tried hard not to think about any of it."

Jimmy knew he could hurt J.T. then, knew he could throw him to the ground and kick him until his ribs gave way, but knowing that was useless. J.T. was already suffering and his suffering brought no pleasure. He was a small injured man who had been broken for a long time. A version of Pepper. A partial version of Jimmy himself.

"How come you think she didn't try and find me?"

J.T. exhaled through his nose. "I don't know if she could. Her daddy was sort of a gangster from what I heard. That last night there was police involved and they took her to jail. I don't know when she got out or if her daddy knew somebody that called him before she got out. Even if she could've looked, I don't know how she would. I know if there was any way she could, she tried."

Jimmy's stomach turned. His brain connected the dots that maybe his mother's attempt to find him had allowed her father to find her, or caused her to go to him for help.

"What was her name?"

"Morita. Morita Malveaux Strawhorn."

The ghost of a smile crossed J.T.'s face. "She loved you," he said. "She took real good care of you. I guess you were really all she had." J.T. focused on a middle distance, tapping each fingertip from his cast against a fingertip on the other hand. "She was something," he said. "The night I met her was the best night I ever had. I just felt like I'd never lose again." J.T. met Jimmy's eyes again. "I don't expect you to believe me, son, but that's the feeling I had when I took your money."

Jimmy rose, walked to the AC and let cold air wash over his chest. He remembered how happy he'd been to buy the AC for J.T., even though by then J.T. was already a pain in the ass. He turned to J.T.'s profile, almost his own profile except older and tireder.

"Does it hurt?" Jimmy asked.

J.T. studied his cast. "Not so much. I'll take another pill if it starts up." J.T.'s features tried to lift into the con man's smile, but they didn't quite make it. His face settled into sadness. "You think you gone stay on?" he asked.

"I ain't heading out right away. Got some things to tend to."

"Like that lawyer? I mean for yourself."

Jimmy walked over in front of him. He thought there should be more words, more information, and maybe later there would be. "You oughta get some rest," he said.

"I'll be all right."

"Then I'll see you after while." Jimmy turned to leave.

"Hey," J.T. said. "I'm serious. I really didn't think I could lose with you here."

The day's light and heat swarmed Jimmy as he stepped outside, but he took them and the firm ground as gifts. He thought how the past several days were almost unreal, thought how there was still more to go. At the top of Elma's steps, he gazed in the direction of downtown. Pepper used to talk about the things beyond, talk about cities and people and say there was nothing more to have than where they were. Now Jimmy's sight climbed past the low line of house roofs and over the trees reaching skyward. He wondered how much he could see with Sandra by his side, then knocked lightly on Elma's door. "Ain't locked," she said, and he entered. She sat on the couch, a magazine spread on her lap. "Decided I'd get out of bed," she said. "I might change the covers your daddy was on before I get back in."

Jimmy snorted. "Feels like a little of that cool reached in here."

"Brought it under a hundred, I'll bet. You wanta sit?"

"Not now. I just wanted to tell you I really think they're done with y'all. Wanted to thank you and your son again."

"You gone keep looking after him, ain't you," she said.

"One second I am, another I think I ain't."

"I know about that."

Jimmy riveted his eyesight to the floor. He half expected the wood to go translucent and reveal a mysterious depth that contained his mother. He raised his eyes to Elma. "I aim to keep visiting if that's all right."

"Any time. I'll make supper."

Jimmy took out his pack of smokes, walked over and handed it to her. "I'm gone try and quit. Sandra wants me to."

"Guess I will too. After these."

The sun's last rays glinted off her sunglasses as she turned. She moved toward him, her posture speaking heaviness even though she broke into a smile and her shoulders moved loosely. Each of her steps landed in his throat and twined around his lungs. She stopped and touched his arm as gently as a moth's wing.

"You came!" she said. "I didn't know if you would."

"How come you'd think that?" He raised her sunglasses to blue eyes charged like sunbursts. "Now why don't we just head out."

She removed her glasses and shook her head. "What did J.T. tell you?"

"That he give me away when I was a baby. That my mother is dead."

Sandra's eyes teared. She took his hand in both of hers. "I'm so sorry, Jimmy."

"What happened with you?"

She tightened her grip. "I told the Rideauxs everything. I think it liked to have killed them, but they said I still have a place there."

"You did the right thing."

"I did? For you? For them? I can't quite tell." Her shoulders rose from a long inhale. She stepped to his side. "You sure?" she asked.

"Are you?"

She nodded. They walked hand in hand toward the door beside the crooked awning, pushed into the lobby and headed toward the desk.

"Whoa!" The same young man as before popped up

and waved his arms. He came running toward them. "Uh uh!" he said. "Y'all have to go." Sandra took cash from her pocket book. "I don't care," he said. "I'm calling the cops."

"Hold your horses," Jimmy said. He reached into his jeans pocket and pulled out the wad of bills from J.T. "How bout two hundred?" Jimmy asked.

"That'll buy a lot of school books," Sandra said.

"What good's that if y'all kill yourselves?"

"We're not interested in killing ourselves," Sandra said. "Nobody's dead from last time."

"I still don't want to be responsible for people jumping out of windows. Y'all aren't planning to jump again, are you?"

"Nobody's planning anything," Sandra said.

"Why don't y'all just go to a better hotel like everybody else? I was about to lock the doors. The security man quit."

"Then you can pocket it all," Jimmy said.

The young man shifted his mouth so far to the side that it threatened to go beneath his ear. He crossed his arms, ogled the bills and shook his head. "Rooms haven't been cleaned since y'all came. Only the first floor's open now."

"We want the same room," Sandra said.

"No way."

"You give us the key and we give you the money," Sandra said. "If anybody knocks on the door, we both jump." She hooked her arm through Jimmy's.

"Shit." He went back around the counter, wringing his hands. Sandra and Jimmy spread the cash in front of him. "I must be as crazy as y'all." He retrieved the key and eyed the money as though it might bite. He blew out through his teeth and put the bills in his pocket. "Honeymoon, huh?" He locked on Jimmy. "Did you know that awning would break your fall?"

"I didn't think about it."

The man snapped his fingers. "I knew you didn't. The other dude said you did, but I knew you didn't. You just got lucky."

"I'd say so."

The young man handed Sandra the key. Sandra and Jimmy turned, but the man said, "Hold on," and brought

Sandra's bag from beneath the counter. "Nothing left in it, but the bag's still good."

Sandra linked her arm with Jimmy's all the way into the elevator. When the door hissed shut, the mildew stench and stuffiness crowded him. He'd been calm in the lobby, but when the elevator lifted, he stiffened against the drop of his stomach. The possibility of Sandra doing what he had done bubbled in his gut. She tugged him closer, the softness of her breast against his bicep. The elevator squeaked to a halt. The door opened. Jimmy put his mouth to hers and held her hard. He leaned back. "We could still just go to your place."

She touched his cheek. "I have to be here." She moved into the unlit hall before he could answer. He followed. She inserted the key, turned the knob and pushed open the door. The dimly-lit square of curtain met him. Blood whooshed into his scalp the same as the instant he'd dropped. He rubbed at his arm.

"You feel it, don't you?" she said.

"I feel something."

"Close the door." He did. He reached for the light switch. "Leave it off," she said.

"Sandra. Why are we here?"

"Because we have to be, just like you had to be. We just didn't know it then." Her body threw sparks in the near darkness. He wanted to take her to bed, hold her, fall into sleep until morning. But he knew that wouldn't change what was stirring in her, what had stirred in him, pushed him up the mesa and then out this window. He couldn't change that for her, even if he tried.

Sandra moved across the room, her steps without the mechanics of movement, like a magical act. She opened the curtain, turned the same latch he had turned and opened the window. A breeze ruffled her hair. She spread her arms as if the wind were cool and refreshing and not thick with downtown summer. Jimmy tensed to lunge toward her, but he didn't move. She turned to face him, her body a silhouette. "Tell me what it was like."

The window widened behind her, its width implying a vacuum that Jimmy no longer felt. He walked toward her, her features growing more distinct—the fine ends of her hair, the fullness of her lips, the bold features of her face—until he stopped a foot away. Something outside tweaked him, but its call wasn't the same.

"Tell me," she said. "It made you different."

He wanted to deny it, to take away any reason she might have to do the same, but he had felt the difference every second since. He closed his eyes. Her image that day flew to him.

"You were so beautiful. So beautiful when you came back in the room. I didn't know what you wanted, nor what I could give. It was all scrambled up."

"I understand." He opened his eyes to hers. He remembered their pull the day they'd met, saw how deep they still were. "Tell me what it was like," she said.

He stepped beside her to the window and felt her face it with him. Across the street other windows floated, and he let himself go toward them, gliding, his breath the breath of all that was out there. "It was something calling," he said. "I'd heard it since I was a kid, but when I come here, I was spooked at what I'd done and at what J.T.'d done to me. I guess part of me wanted you and the other part just wanted clear. You know what I mean?"

"I think so. Tell me."

The memory rushed through his body, the sudden weightlessness and sudden weight, a strange silence from the urgent pass of air. He'd gone still while the world hurried upward, everything released and taken on as gravity all at once. He struck the awning and the road: the cloth somehow harder than the street; the street strangely less brutal than the cloth. Both had taken him in their way. Then Sandra came wearing fright from a world gone by.

"I just swung over and dropped. I didn't know I did it. I fell and I was free and away from everything. Then I hit the awning and the street and I opened my eyes. After a minute I saw you."

He turned to her. She slipped her arms around him and pulled him close. When she let go, her separation was a loss he couldn't quite calculate, even among the losses he'd come to know these last few days. She peered outside and down. He wanted to wrap her up, whisk her to bed, undo her buttons one by one. He wanted her smart words and good laugh, wanted to press his lips to her throat, wanted to have her open a book and say its words. Wanted to love her tonight and the next and the next, and he knew that meant he had to love her right now. He let his arms hang.

Sandra pressed her hands to the sill. "I understand," she said, the meager light collecting to make her luminous. "I do."